The Covenant of Shadows

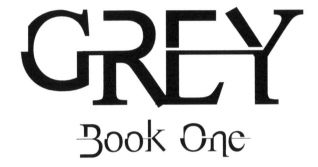

Kade Cook

Copyright © 2016 Kade Cook

Logo design by Jenna McLean/Adam Barry

Cover by Jenna McLean

Edits by Kayla Krantz/Proofreading by Michelle King

E-Book ISBN: 978-0-9948678-1-0
Paperback ISBN: 978-0-9948678-0-3

Third Edition November 2017

Theo & Quinn Creative Works
Shediac River, New Brunswick, E4R 6A7, Canada

www.kadecookbooks.wordpress.com
email: kadecook.author@gmail.com

For Jenna, James, Kaidyn, Liam, Meagan
And my little Channy man.

May they know
That I love them dearly.
In this world
And
In all those that follow.

Acknowledgements

First and foremost to you, the courageous readers that took the chance to pick up GREY.

Thank you from the bottom of my heart.

To my incredibly talented graphic artist, Jenna McLean, my wonderful editor, Kayla Krantz, and my very special proof reader, Michelle King, my biggest hugs and thanks for all their hard work.

And last but not least, to all the amazing minds that beta read GREY. Our many talks about imaginary people and your belief in me were what kept me going. Big hugs to Carrie T., Jenna M., Shanda C., Denise C., Brenda C., Doris M., Rachel O., Paula L., Marc D., Dawn D and Tammy C.

Long live the Coven-Nerds.

All things,

No matter how different they may seem,

Come from a common beginning

*

Beneath the sky and clouds,
beyond the reach of the whispering winds,
and far below the field of wild flowers that grow on the
precipice of Shadow's edge,
buried deep within walls of stone,
it begins.

Prologue

Buried Within

ALL THE TRUTHS spoken here today were born from the promise of a lie—a lie that could change everything.

Along the edges of the rugged Maine coastline, the morning mist slowly creeps forward and encompasses the walls of the weather-worn Centurion lighthouse. Standing strong for more than a century, it refuses to falter from duty.

Below its ever-seeing eye, the icy Atlantic air begins to shift and bend. From its midst emerges a tall, fair-haired figure; a woman yet merely the essence of one. She bursts forth with conviction to her mission, followed by her raven guide who shrieks loudly in announcement of their arrival.

Taking assessment of her surroundings, she glides quickly across the weathered field on weightless feet and halts just before a wooden gate, grown over by a large firethorn bush. Her form melds from air to flesh in order to access the tender surface of her skin. Pressing her finger firmly against a pointed barb that is ejected from the bush, a crimson dot appears, then grows vigorously downward across her index finger until it releases onto the ground below.

"Wendas." With a whispered word, her flesh is gone, her

form once again as translucent as a dream and the evidence of puncture, no more.

The watchful bird circles from above, keeping its sights on her. She glances upward at his ebony silhouette against the sky with a hopeful gleam in her eye, pleased at his unrelenting devotion.

There is a sudden rustling from behind the firethorn bush as an ominous figure appears from within its shadows. Instinctively, her senses flare out on high alert in debate of her flight-or-fight response. But catching a familiar scent of summer wafting in the arctic air, she exhales slowly, watching the figure step out into the light.

It's a Guardian—one of the keepers of the gate. Although she should be completely at ease with his presence, her pupils widen and the blood running through her veins quickens just the same.

"Welcome, Lady of Zephyr." The Guardian's sandy voice smoothens over the high-pitched screech of rusted metal hinges scraping against each other as he pulls the gate open for her. The raven gives her a soft gurgling coo to signify its satisfaction with her safety then takes flight to the north.

"Botah," Vaeda whispers. An illuminate shimmer washes over her body as it alters into its flesh form once again, radiating with her natural goddess features. "Always the gentleman, Tynan?" she toys as she walks through the opening, raising her eyebrows in an impish manner.

"Not always, my lady. There have been times that have called for less of one," Tynan responds, softly closing the gate behind her—his darkened olive-coloured skin reveals a slight shade of rose growing just under his flesh. "The House awaits your arrival," he quickly adds, changing the subject.

"Yes, I suppose I mustn't make them wait any longer." She exhales and turns to soak in every ounce of her time with him. Tynan extends his arm and holds out his hand awaiting hers.

She reaches out her doll-like hand and gently lays it in his. The warmth of his skin sets her flesh on fire, making her gasp slightly at the touch. He sweetly smiles down at her and the innocence in his eyes intoxicates her, making Vaeda want to follow him anywhere.

4

"Shall we then?"

Lost in his eyes, Tynan's words echo hollowly around her. Receiving no response, he inquires again. "Lady Vaeda, are you ready?"

This time the words stick. Realizing she has practically covered his feet in drool, the elating buzz of desire that had swept throughout her body is abruptly replaced with the sting of embarrassment.

"Yes, of course, Tynan." Red-faced by her obvious obsession, she smiles meekly and nods her head, readying herself.

Tynan clasps tightly onto her hand, securing his hold, and pulls at the fringe of Shadows, wrapping its magic around them.

And then there is darkness.

For a few moments, they are lost in the Veil of shadows, but just as quickly as they enter into it, they are expelled in the same measure of time elsewhere. Vaeda squints her eyes, adjusting to the light of the dimly-lit corridor she now stands in.

Tynan shifts his position slightly, catching in her peripheral vision, and Vaeda is reminded she is not alone.

"Thank you for your assistance, Tynan."

Her chaperone nods graciously and releases the impenetrable grip he has on her hand. "Always a pleasure, my lady. Shall I meet you here once you have decided to take your leave?"

Vaeda nods in agreement with one quick bow of her chin.

Tynan slowly slinks backwards and fades into the shadows once more.

Alone in the darkened hallway, Vaeda stands for a moment in thought. She searches within the Darkness of where Tynan had just stood moments ago, grasping at the edges of shadow, but finds nothing more than etched runes of spells embedded within the stone wall that stands in front of her.

She exhales slowly, the subtle frustration of her chaperone's noble stature as well as his flawless physique pulls upward at the edges of her delicate mouth in her wanton state.

"If only I could make you see me."

Staring at an empty wall and feeling sorry for herself gets her nowhere. She has an appointment to keep. Pirouetting gracefully on the spot, she starts her journey in the opposite direction toward the light. Low, incomprehensible murmurs interrupt her silent trek. She listens to the muffled voices as they echo like ghosts in the hall along the passage she follows.

And on this day, the voices have all come to discuss the matters concerning the keepings of the Silver Mage. They have come to discuss the child.

Hearing the decibels of the discussions raising, Vaeda hurries her pace to a swift canter and reaches the opening to the Great Hall in mere moments. She rushes out into the folds of Realmfolk scattered about, weaving her slender body in and out with exaggerated speed. She passes through them, practically unnoticed, as they move in lines like ants amongst the gargantuan marble pillars that climb endlessly upward.

Flailing hands and sudden outbursts of rehearsed verbatim at the high table stirs hesitation within Vaeda's stride, and she slows her pace to a mere crawl before coming into clear view. Leaning her weight against the darkened edge of the wall—just outside the opening of the Covenant's House table—Vaeda wields the cast of the pillar's shadow towering before her to sheath her presence. She remains in her anonymity for a moment behind the drawing crowd in observation of the accusations and tempers scratching their way to the surface.

"The child is showing behaviour of being more than just human. It is a bit late in her development to start displaying signs of being from the Realm, but it is not completely unheard of. Anyway, more importantly, if we allow her to remain without guidance, she may become dangerous." Ethan rubs the center of his temples, trying to make them see reason and knowing full well of the dangers they may be facing. He, being the Elder to the Borrower's Fellowship, can attest to the errors of slight oversights that have bled into heart-wrenching demise.

"That is true, we are not even sure what she will be," Cimmerian growls as he waves his hands around pointedly at no one in particular. "How could the Shadwells have been so negligent as to let this happen?"

"It was no fault of the Shadwells. They loved Cera, and only did as she had asked," Ariah chimes in, plainly irritated by Cimmerian's comments. Crimson grows more evident under her skin and begins to resemble the fiery colour of her hair.

"Ethan says that he can feel the girl's dreams—that she is

reaching out with her subconscious and has nearly found us," Caspyous shouts, smacking his flattened hand against the granite table in front of him, then sits back in his chair and folds his arms tightly over his chest. He glances around at the others in search of any hostility that his stirring of the pot may have intrigued.

"She is not dangerous, everyone. I have spent time with her, and I have every confidence that there are no signs of Darkness harboring within her." Orroryn clenches his fists beneath the cover of the table and away from the eyes of those who would test his calm demeanor as he pleads rationality to all who will listen.

"He was nothing like the evil that he became either, in the beginning," Ashen says then sucks in her breath and twists her head in Orroryn's direction with the realization she is just dousing fuel on the already fired up group.

"Maybe it is a sign of the Monster's return. The child was found a few days later near the barren ground that marks his demise," Arraumis adds, clasping and unclasping his hands together—his fingers whiten with every contraction while his eyes volley and bounce between the Elders in search of an answer.

"But Arraumis, he was bound to the Darkness. There is no possible way for him to break through. Cera saw to it. We all did," Kaleb interjects and calmly flattens his palms against the smooth surface of the granite slab before him.

"I agree with Kaleb," Orroryn says. His voice echoes around the edges of the room, aiding in his conviction that a reminder is necessary of the selfless sacrifice that was made many years ago. "She stripped him of his power and secured his crypt deep within the toxic depths of Erebus. The conviction she used to banish his existence here on Earth nearly vanquished her own. The child is an innocent and has nothing to do with any of it. She is merely a casualty of war and that is all."

A rustle of voices rush through the room on the tips of the people's tongues as the Fellowships whisper amongst themselves, discussing all the nightmarish visions they fathomed to be true. Hearing enough of this nonsense, Vaeda steps into the light and candidly thrusts herself toward them.

A hush comes over the multitude in discovery of her sudden appearance and they fumble backward, pushing against each other to make room as Vaeda cuts like a knife through the crowd of onlookers to approach the circle of Elders, taking her place at the high table. In Cera's absence, Vaeda and Orroryn hold the house.

"It is about time she showed up." A few voices grumble aloud within the masses.

"Nice of you to join us, Lady of Zephyr," Cimmerian says, rolling his eyes before he looks down the bridge of his nose at her.

Vaeda enters the circle with her honour intact and smiles sweetly, brushing off his discontent as if unnoticed. She is known for her civility and kindness, but her gentile ways can easily be set aside if need be. With one whispered word of Magik, she can bring down the wrath of oblivion for most of those seated before her. And they all know it.

"Oh please, Cimmerian, there is no need to be so formal. We are all friends here," she hums, and Cimmerian forces the edges of his mouth upward with tainted admiration as he readjusts his chair, looking away.

Feeling the weighted stares resting on her, she redirects her attention to the rest of the Elders and addresses the table.

"With all due respect to every Fellowship here today, we must not treat this matter of the child as a horrific or a tragic phenomenon but as a chance to groom a potential ally. I realize that we have all just recently discovered that the child Cera rescued is possibly a daughter of the Realm. I also realize that this causes you all reason for some concern. We don't know what she will become, that part is true. Would you rather we attempt to reach out to her, guide her, and teach her the ways of the realm or leave her to fend for herself where she may darken and become a threat? Are you all so confident in yourselves and your abilities that you are willing to take that risk?"

Vaeda looks to Orroryn. He gives her a subtle nod of approval with a glint of confidence in his eyes. She does not care how the vote goes. She has reserved her last breath to say what it is that she has come here to say—what needs to be heard.

"It is essential that we give this girl a chance. We owe Cera that much. She gave up everything to rid us of his Darkness and whether you agree or not, it is the least we can do!"

Chapter One

A Haunting Experience

THINGS FEEL DIFFERENT today. I feel different.

I am having one of those days that I am sure everyone has once in a while. Where you just cannot take another moment of listening to anyone else complain about their unfulfilling lives and petty problems that most people would just deal with. I would love to just lock the door, pull down the blinds, and pretend that I am somewhere so quiet and remote that I would have to drive a hundred miles to find another living soul.

Ironically, listening to the world's problems is my job. Though it may be hard on the head at times, and rips my heart out at others, being a psychologist has always been my passion. Since as long as I can remember, I have been fascinated by the human mind and how it works. My growing obsession to understand all of it led me to devour my way through my courses in a fraction of the time that it took everyone else—it became my disease.

I dreamed of practicing here in the city where there were so many people in need of someone to help get them out of the rut they dug themselves into and nudge—sometimes push—them in a more positive direction. It seemed like the perfect storm for me. So working with my father and taking over his practice after graduation was as natural as breathing. I was blessed with my uncanny knack of being able to guide my clients quite successfully, and I could never imagine wanting to do anything else or be anywhere else.

But lately, I cannot put my finger on it, something seems off.

I keep having these dreams of wide open spaces, green grass, and blue skies with clouds that float carelessly uninterrupted by buildings of concrete and steel. Last night, in my dream, I could smell the sweet scent of the meadow, bursting with life all around me. I heard the call of the ocean nearby. Then in the distance, I saw the silhouette of a woman with long, dark hair.

I would write it off as a midlife crisis, but I am barely in my twenties—okay, twenty-six, but still. I am in the prime of my life and doing well for myself. Why on Earth would I dream of stuff like that? I have not been to the country since I was a little girl, when my folks used to own a house in North East Harbor. I barely remember that. Why all of a sudden has my subconscious decided to go east and start vacationing in the country? And what is really strange about all this is that I can actually feel myself physically craving it. It seems quite out of the ordinary for me, to say the least.

Maybe my mind is hinting that I need a change of some kind, or maybe I am losing it. While some people are naturals at adapting to change, others like me seem to fight it all the way, even if it is a good thing.

A voice crackles through the intercom, quickly bursting Gabrian's tiny bubble of serenity with its sharp tinny sound as she scribbles her thoughts down within the pages of her personal journal.

"Dr. Shadwell, your first client is here to see you."

"Ah yes, thank you, Rachael," she says, pressing the intercom button then releases it. "Back to reality," Gabrian mumbles out loud, and her eyes drop to the pencil still firmly gripped in her fingers. She exhales as she slides it into the wire binding on her notepad then opens her bottom drawer and drops them in. "I suppose I can ponder my life dilemmas later."

A few moments later, she hears a light tapping at her door just before it swings open. Her assistant, friend, and volunteer sounding board, Rachael, escorts her first client of the day into her office from the waiting room. Gabrian swivels to the side in her chair and rises to greet them. As her eyes meet the stranger's stare, her whole world flares with the image of a large raven against a bright backdrop like a badly executed hologram—then is gone again as quickly as it had appeared.

Umm, what the heck was that? Gabrian thinks, forcing her face to hold its pleasantry. She tries to maintain her composure as best she can for her first-time client and continues on to politely introduce herself. Gabrian stretches out her hand to greet the woman and notices the wrinkled skin wrapped tightly around boney fingers even though the woman in front of her seems no more aged than she is. Gabrian's eyes shoot upward to analyze the face of her client once more. Their gaze locks awkwardly. Gabrian becomes transfixed with the way her eyes sparkle in the rarest shade of grey, that of polished silver.

How extraordinary! Gabrian thinks, captivated by an odd sensation that she has met this stranger before.

Her mind settles as her thoughts become foggy and deluged by sensory images that invoke comfort and warmth. Gabrian herself often induces these enhanced feelings of safety with her clients during a hypnotic session. But this mesmerized state is being brought on without the use of tools or words. She feels the manipulative pull on her emotions, gently drawing her in like the way the movement of the river calls to your soul and subliminally urges you to jump in without caution.

A moment of lucidness washes through her, and she shakes her head quickly in an attempt to break the mental embrace she has succumbed to. Her eyes dart around the room as she completely resurfaces then lands on Rachael who looks at her, open-jawed and wide-eyed, like she has lost her mind.

"Dr. Shadwell, is everything alright?" Rachael says, continuing to stare.

How much time was I absent? She realizes she must have looked like a crazed person to her new client by standing there in a stupefied haze. She apologizes quickly.

"I am so sorry. Mrs. Argryis, please excuse me. I was up late reading and clearly I did not get enough rest," she lies, hoping to sound believable. "Please, come and take a seat."

Rachael raises her eyebrows and tilts her head to the side, questioning her friend's odd behaviour. Gabrian cannot blame her. She is a bit perplexed about what just happened herself. Mrs. Argryis' face brightens with a slight smile, almost one of knowing as she turns toward the chaise situated by the large oak desk, showing no signs of concern to her doctor's oddity.

Pivoting left to follow her client, Gabrian glances back over her shoulder at Rachael who continues to stare at her. Her face twists with a raised brow, and she shrugs her shoulders while Rachael idles cautiously toward the exit and closes the door behind her.

Gabrian inhales deeply in an effort to gather her thoughts as best she can. *Get it together, Gabrian,* she scolds herself under her breath.

"Please sit, make yourself comfortable." Gabrian sweeps her arm toward the long oversize-lounge chaise to the right of them.

A strange wave of nausea washes over her, and she immediately rushes to her left, taking her assumed position within her trusty leather chair. Feeling its burly dark arms wrapped securely around her, she smells the Earthy scent of its smooth covering and nestles herself back against its strong familiar embrace, wanting desperately for this unsettling feeling in her innards to pass. She grips at both sides of the chair and rests all her faith in the fact her chair has been a trusted friend to her for as long as she has owned it and hopes it can make things right again. She has used its unyielding support through many sessions—some good and some, well...not so much.

Regaining some of her composure, she begins the session.

"Are you comfortable?"

"Yes, thank you."

"Wonderful...then shall we start?"

The woman nods as she removes her coat, revealing her slender frame beneath, and lays it down carefully between the two oversized pillows beside her. She is enchanting indeed. Gabrian watches her, in awe of her graceful and smooth mannerisms as she takes her seat. She is certain that she has never laid eyes on her before, but Gabrian's senses are cooing and whispering to her that there is something very familiar about her long black hair, her caramel-coloured skin, and her intoxicating silvery eyes. What is it about those eyes?

Gabrian plunges deep within her conscious mind, searching for the professionalism that exists within her, and tries to continue.

"So, Mrs. Argryis, how are you today?"

Her eyes shimmer as the soft edges of her mouth raise delightfully upward. "I am well, but more importantly, how are you my dear?"

A surge of electricity rushes across Gabrian's skin at the reversed and off-guard question. The tension in the air thickens as she begins to wonder who is actually in the client seat here. Her skin flushes—spreading a rose hue across her face and neck. She shifts in her chair and fidgets with a strand of hair that has come loose as the focus of the conversation tilts toward her.

"I am fine, despite the lack of sleep that I mentioned earlier."

"Yes, you did mention that." She chuckles and leans back against the pillows, resting her head on her hand.

"Shall we begin?"

"Of course, dear." Mrs. Argryis stares steadily at Gabrian then waves her fingers at her to continue.

"Since this is your first session with me, I thought that maybe we should discuss what it is that you would like to accomplish or touch upon in our time together."

Mrs. Argryis leans forward, shifting her body to mirror Gabrian's, and begins to speak. As the words musically roll off of her tongue, the woman's appearance alters. The alluring draw she has on Gabrian seems to try to reveal itself. Her skin takes on a more supple texture as its edges disappear and melds into the subtle glow that manifests like a halo all around her.

Gabrian wonders if this strange display is what some would consider to be an "aura." She has seen fragments of light emit off of people before, sometimes even in different colours, but always dismissed it as some sort of illusion of light. What she is witnessing now would definitely be hard to dismiss as just an illusion. Whatever transformation is taking place within Mrs. Argryis, it is pulling at Gabrian and oddly urging her to get closer, creating a yearning within her to be near the light.

"My dear Gabrian, you have grown up so quickly and into such a beautiful, intelligent woman. I have been keeping watch on you, and it seems that your essence is reaching out, breaking free, and the dissolution of the spell has sent for me."

Gabrian's face contorts against her will. "Excuse me? Sent for you? I don't even know you. Why would I, in any shape or form, be looking for you?" Gabrian voice squeaks, trying to maintain diplomacy. There has been many a nut job come through her doors in her few years, but today she is certain that the owner of the huge bag of marbles on her desk with "LOST" in bold letters printed across it has just been found.

Mrs. Argryis remains statuesque in her seat but raises her hand to tuck away her free flowing ebony locks behind her ear. Gabrian's mouth falls slightly ajar as she watches the faint glow follow the movements of her hand.

The woman's eyes dance around Gabrian's office, taking inventory of who she is, then jumps to rest upon Gabrian. Her head tilts slightly as if noticing some discomfort in Gabrian. "Please do not be upset. Your true self will be revealed in due time."

Gabrian can feel her heartrate jump through the roof.

What the...? My true self...am I missing something? I have to be misunderstanding something. Because the only alternative is that I have lost my mind. She inhales slowly, summoning her calmness in hopes of discovering some rational understanding of what her client is talking about.

I am the professional here, fully equipped to deal with situations like this. I have the paperwork to prove it, Gabrian continues her internal debate, eyeing the framed degree on the wall as she tries to convince herself.

"I am sorry, but I am not sure that I understand what is going on. Have we met before?" Gabrian lays out her dilemma politely. The remains of her confidence are holding steady, but for how long she is not sure as her sanity teeters on slight hysteria. And to make things worse, all she can think of is how she would love to have a drink to calm her nerves.

The delicate folds in the center of Mrs. Argryis's cheeks surface as her lips press impishly upward at the corners.

It is as if she had heard me. Gabrian takes note of her client's change in expression. *But that would be impossible...would it not?* Her uncertainties rush to her legs as they begin hammering against the bottom rung of her chair.

She wishes she could just flip a coin to make the judgement call—very professional, she knows. If it turned up heads, she would try to figure out whether or not there is any need to be worried that this woman might snap, taking down Gabrian along with her, or tails—she would just play this one out to see if there is any validation in her client's sociopathic yet confusing performance.

Ah, frig it. Here goes nothing. She holds her breath for a moment waiting for her near flawless intuition to kick in to help her decide.

Tails! Great!

For a crazy person, the woman seems extremely calm, so Gabrian resolves to play this one out. Her curiosity has many times outweighed her logic, and at this point, the scale had tipped heavily in its favour—which she knew it would anyway. It has always been Gabrian's Achilles heel.

Once Gabrian flips the mental switch to go forward with this conversation, her skin begins to tingle. The strange sensation that had consumed her moments ago seeps through her again. The steel grip she uses to rein over her emotions is lost and a forced calmness slithers its way through her veins. The pull on her is stronger than before, demanding every muscle in her body to refuse her commands. The logical being trapped inside of her useless form screams relentlessly as she tries to will her limbs to move, but she is prisoner within her own skin, unable to escape her invisible restraints.

A cold chill creeps up the back of her skull like someone has wrapped it in a towel of ice. Soft, incoherent words hum melodically around her and her fight-or-flight reflex submits to its suitor, accepting its reassurance that she is in no real danger.

Is it possible that this woman is doing this somehow? Logically, this cannot be happening. Can it? Gabrian claws desperately at her sanity.

Unable to do anything but breathe, her chest lifts and deflates in a slow rhythmic dance with the ticking of the clock on the wall. Gabrian's eyes reach for the woman as she begins to speak.

"You and I have met before, and so shall we meet again. Today is the day your essence awakens and you begin to see." She closes her eyes for a moment, searching for something within.

All colour drains from the woman's face as she glances into the distance like she suddenly has seen a ghost. A loud rapping at the window breaks her from her trance. On the other side, a large

Raven frantically tries to get some attention. Mrs. Argryis switches her focus to the bird momentarily and nods as if to appease its actions. Her eyes rush back to Gabrian, noticeably rattled.

"I cannot stay any longer, but I needed to see you. I needed you to know that even though your path has been chosen, how you walk upon it is still up to you. Be cautious of gifts and friends that feel like foe. Know that the shadows do not always mean Darkness and listen to the black feathers' warning as there is wisdom in their call. They will see when you cannot."

With her words at an end, the woman glides upward from the chaise and gathers her coat quickly. She turns to rest her gaze on Gabrian—her silvery eyes reach through with great intensity. Gabrian's heart flutters with the strange sensation that this woman is somehow speaking directly to her soul. Mrs. Argryis' face softens, and her eyes glisten, dampened with mixed emotions locked deep inside. It was a look of hope, yet it carried the weight of the world.

The woman's lips move with silent words and the vaporous chains that held Gabrian still are no more. Her muscles, still engaged in their strife, react with the sudden release of her binds and eject her from the chair, throwing her violently to the floor.

Now in control of her body once more, Gabrian looks away from the woman, still in shock of their bizarre encounter, but when she returns to look upon her again, she is gone. Not gone as in walked across the room, opened the door, and left, but gone...vanished into thin air.

"What the hell just happened?"

Chapter Two

Some Time to Ponder

GABRIAN JUMPS UP out of her chair and searches frantically around her office. The woman is gone, vanished without a trace. Scratching her head in disbelief, Gabrian starts toward the door, thinking maybe Rachael saw her leave.

Gabrian rushes across the floor and opens her office door. "Rachael, did you happen to see Mrs. Argryis leave? She exited rather quickly, and I did not have a chance to get all the information I need from her."

Her assistant, not sitting at her desk, stands in the waiting area engaged in conversation with a tall, dark-haired, man—Mr. Redmond, Gabrian's ten o'clock appointment. From what Gabrian has learned of him, he has spent most of his life working within the walls of a sunless office but somehow, his skin reminds her of the colour of soft toffee. Gabrian loves working with him, and his gentle demeanor, but she is not sure why he still comes to see her. Any time they have spent together, Gabrian would classify her findings as normal or without any major issues that could validate his need to see her. Still, he insists on returning bi-weekly.

Rachael smiles apologetically at Mr. Redmond and turns to rest her gaze on Gabrian. By the look on her face, Gabrian feels she must have morphed and grown two heads.

"Mrs. Who?" Rachael questions, obviously confused.

"Mrs. Argryis, the lady that just left my office," Gabrian's voice starts to shake, giving away the concern in clarifying her sanity. Rachael temporarily returns her attention to Mr. Redmond with a delicate smile and gestures for him to remain seated. "Will you excuse us for a moment? It will not be long."

Mr. Redmond agrees to wait. He glances over at Gabrian and nods in acknowledgement. She waves back and turns to meet Rachael who marches toward her. Rachael discreetly takes hold of Gabrian's arm and nudges her back in the direction of her office door.

She must think that I am losing it too and in dire need to have a talk in private, Gabrian tells herself. This is why Rachael is her assistant. She is good with the clientele and a wiz at keeping everything running smoothly even though she can clearly tell that Gabrian is distressed from her earlier answer—or rather, her question.

She enters her office casually with Rachael following behind. Slowly, Rachael turns to close the door behind them. Hesitating for just a moment with her back still turned to Gabrian, she turns around. "Are you feeling alright, Gabrian?" Her face flashes a look of concern.

"Yes, I am fine. I just need to know if you spoke with Mrs. Argryis before she left a few minutes ago," Gabrian says, taking a deep breath and trying to put things into perspective.

Rachael once again gives Gabrian an distressed look but remains silent, considering the correct means in addressing the subject.

"Mrs. Argryis? Gabrian, I have no idea who you are talking about. There has not been any one in to see you yet. Your nine o'clock appointment cancelled last minute. I did not have time to book anyone else into this morning's time slot," Rachael admitted.

"What do you mean no one was here to see me? I just had a session, a very strange session I might add..." Gabrian starts to mumble inaudibly and wanders around the room. "You escorted her in and introduced her to me in this very office about an hour ago! Long, black hair, silvery grey eyes...there is no way you could have forgotten her."

Rachael stands before Gabrian wearing a twisted brow and

pursed lips. She reaches out her hand and touches her shoulder in a comforting gesture, giving her a look like a mother would to a child who has just told her that they have seen a monster in the closet or under the bed. Gabrian stops her rant.

She lets out a loud sigh as she realizes Rachael believes her to be delusional.

"Gabrian, you have been alone in here since early morning. Are you sure you did not fall asleep in your chair again while preparing for your day and dream this Mrs. Argryis? You have been working a lot of extra hours lately trying to plan for the upcoming holidays." She tries to find a logical explanation as her instinct to protect Gabrian kicks in. "I have never heard that name before, and I am sure that I would remember scheduling it. It has quite an unusual sound to it—not your everyday Jane Doe kind of name."

"You have got to be joking...right? Listen, I just need you to book her for another session," Gabrian orders, hoping Rachael will relent and admit that this is one of her crazy pranks.

"Ah, sweetie, there was no woman. It was an empty session. You can check the books if you like."

Gabrian wipes the look of disappointment from her face and forces a smile. She is not going to get the answers she needs. She backs down and resists the urge to question her again.

It is like I am having a nightmare where I am screaming for someone to hear me, to help me, but everyone keeps walking by, going about their business like I am invisible, Gabrian thinks. *Is Rachael right? Did I fall asleep and dream this entire messed up thing? It would explain a lot of the oddities that took place. I would genuinely welcome the ability to dismiss all this and get back to a world where I am still in control.*

"Maybe you are right. It just seemed so real to me...huh!" Gabrian says, running her hands through her hair and scrunching it up in a knot. Turning abruptly, she saunters back to her desk and glances discreetly from the corner of her eye at the chaise. She swears she can still see white light faintly glowing where the imaginary Mrs. Argryis had sat. "Nah!" she grumbles under her breath, trying not to give life to the haunting just in case it might not have been so imaginary.

Gabrian sits down at her desk and tries to focus on something that might distract her. Rachael crosses the room and takes a seat in front of her. "Gabrian, when was the last time you took a vacation?"

"Just the other week, we took the Friday off right before Remembrance Day so that we could stretch out the weekend," she quickly answers, wearing a smug grin.

"No, that does not count. You spent most of your time off sitting in here by yourself, finishing up files," Rachael corrects her. "I mean a real vacation with time away from here, away from your clients, and anything else that might resemble your work."

Gabrian straightens her grin and places her left hand across her mouth in a thinking pose. "Never, okay. Are you happy now?!"

Rachael shakes her head at Gabrian's response. "Here is an idea. What would you say if I were to propose that we close the office for an extra week or so over the holidays and take some time to relax—for real this time. Maybe, I don't know...reboot your brain so to speak. What do you say?" Rachael leans in and rests her elbows on her knees then sets her chin within the palms of her hands and glares playfully at Gabrian. Gabrian is beginning to think that Rachael may need a bit of a break too. As much as she will never admit it, she is here almost as much as Gabrian is on her days off.

"How about we get through today, and we will go for a drink after work to discuss the details of this vacation thing you are talking about. Sound good?" Gabrian chuckles. Even though it is pretty early in the day to think about having alcohol, she is ready to get this day over with and have a sip of something to help smooth out the edges.

"Oh, now that sounds like a very solid plan. You have got yourself a date." Grinning from ear to ear, Rachael gets up from her chair and smooths out her skirt, then turns toward the door. "I better get back out there. Mr. Redmond is going to start thinking that we forgot all about him." Rachael giggles. "You know, it is too bad that we cannot date our clients! He is so nice...and really hot!" Rachael looks back at Gabrian and winks, quickly making her exit.

"Rachael, you wicked little thing!" Gabrian scolds her playfully. She is right though; he is pretty easy to look at—tall, dark wavy hair, an incredible smile...not to mention his eyes, like precious stones made of polished jade. *Oh, that girl! Now I am never going to be able to look at him again without noticing.*

Gabrian hears her addressing him on the other side of the door. It is time to get her game face back on. "Right this way, Mr. Redmond. Dr. Shadwell will see you now." Rachael opens the door and sees Mr. Redmond into the office. Gabrian leaves her chair and meets him midway across the room. Raising her hand to greet him as usual. Gabrian swears that she sees colours flicker ever so faintly around Rachael, mostly white light with iridescent specks. She looks toward Mr. Redmond, but there is nothing around him, at least nothing that she can see. Gabrian turns back to Rachael. Just as suddenly as the aura had appeared, it is gone.

Ah, what is going on with me today? Gabrian screams inside her head. Keeping her composure and trying to pretend like she did not see anything, she starts to chant silently. *Keep breathing. You are just tired. Act normal.*

"Mr. Redmond, nice to see you again. Won't you please come in and take your usual seat—feel free to make yourself comfortable. I will be with you in just a second." She waves her hand and gestures to the chaise then quickly reaches for Rachael. "When you get back to your desk, can you make reservations for us for dinner?"

"Sure, any place in particular?"

"No, you pick. Around six-thirty? I should be finished with everything by then."

"Are you sure you are okay?" Rachael tilts her head, and her eyes reveal a look of concern.

"Yes, I am good. I think maybe you might be right about me needing to take some time for myself." Gabrian's mouth pulls slightly upward at the edges as she gives Rachael a crooked grin. "Who knows, I might just enjoy it!"

Rachael laughs quietly and shakes her head, her red curls swing carelessly about her as she turns and closes the door behind her. Gabrian takes a deep breath, trying to refocus on her work and returns to her client who patiently waits for her. Mr. Redmond looks up from the pamphlet he was reading and gives her a wide, charismatic smile.

My goodness, he really is handsome, Gabrian realizes, seeing him in a different light. *Oh no! Damn that girl!*

Chapter Three

A Drink Anyone□

IT IS SEVEN-THIRTY. Rachael and Gabrian sit at the bar, waiting to be seated in the dining area of the restaurant where Rachael had made their dinner reservations. It is some new-age, trendy place called Beauty & Essex that serves the best organic foods, or so she heard. The place is busy and loud. Gabrian glances down briefly at her watch to check the time again and starts to think that this may be as close as she will get to knowing how good the food is here.

"I need to go to the washroom. I will check on the reservation again on the way back through." Rachael huffs as she gets up to leave.

Gabrian wishes her good luck. While Rachael is gone, Gabrian turns to see if she can catch the bartender's attention to order another couple of drinks.

Maybe it is the alcohol getting to her, but suddenly, she finds the young man behind the bar to be very attractive. Since she has nothing better to do, she watches him work, captivated by how he interacts with the people he serves. He is handsome, obviously, muscular and lean in a sporty kind of way, well-groomed, and now seems to have an orange hue drifting about him. When Gabrian looks directly at it, she experiences a calm, welcoming feeling. If it was not so interesting to watch, she would be freaking out again.

23

He notices her following his every move and starts toward her. "Hi again! Can I get you something else?" The words roll of his tongue sweetly and rehearsed.

"Oh, um..." Gabrian panics, trying to remember why she was staring at him in the first place. "Could I have two more drinks please? It does not look like we will be eating anytime soon."

He chuckles and nods his head in agreement. "Yeah, this place can get pretty crazy at times, especially on Friday nights. You wait until it hits nine and the band starts in the bar upstairs. The place gets so full, you can barely move."

Gabrian looks around and notices an incredible chandelier hanging from the middle of the staircase that must lead to the place upstairs that he spoke of. She was beginning to understand why Rachael liked this place. There is a fun, swanky charm about it that makes her feel like they are in a cover up for some gangster hideout from the fifties. The outside of the restaurant is actually a fully functioning pawn shop that they had to walk through in order to get to the door that led them inside. It is surreal.

"So what would you like to drink?"

Looking down and swirling around the remains of an ice cube in her empty glass, she begins to ponder. She always orders the same drink—Gin and Tonic with a slice of lime. It is safe, predictable, and reliable. Though after the day she just had, it does not seem to fit the occasion. Feeling a wave of recklessness hit her, she glances up at the bartender. "Surprise me!" she says.

Laughing at her answer—and looking completely delicious—he retorts playfully, "Are you sure? You are putting a lot of trust in me, and we have only just met."

She grins at his spirited banter, feeling her face heat up. He reciprocates the gesture then quickly turns to fetch the drinks. Out of the corner of her eye, Gabrian sees Rachael returning with a crinkle in her nose as she bites the tip of her thumb. It does not look promising.

"We have hit a bit of a glitch. The reservations are running behind schedule, and it might be a while before we can be seated," Rachael grumbles, taking a sip from the half-filled champagne glass she was served at the complimentary champagne bar just outside the bathroom. "I am so sorry for the mix-up. It must be because it is Friday night. I was here a few weeks ago, and it is to die for."

24

Well, all is not lost. The last couple of drinks they drank had pretty big limes in them—limes are considered a healthy food so Gabrian just counts that as supper. "Don't worry about it. It is not the end of the world. We will try to get a table some other time. Besides, I am really not that hungry anyway," Gabrian fibs to let her friend off the hook.

After a few more apologies from Rachael, she simmers down and starts to relax. Gabrian quite enjoys Rachael's company when she is happy. She is so full of life and in awe of everything that sometimes Gabrian envies her. Even still, she is grateful that Rachael is in her life. Having met in university, they have been through some pretty interesting times together. Rachael is the light-hearted yet level-headed one, and Gabrian is the clever but naive one. She is not sure why their friendship works so well, but she is just glad that it does.

"There you go, ladies!" the bartender says, wearing a seductive grin as he serves them their drinks. "It is called the Grinch. It is our specialty drink for the upcoming holidays. Enjoy!" he says, starting to move away then stops and leans back in closer to them, wearing an impish grin. "Oh, and by the way, the name is Thomas, so if you ladies need anything else, don't be shy. I am just a smile away," Thomas adds slyly as he rubs down the bar and moves on to the next customer, eyeing them over his shoulder.

"Yum!" Rachael purrs taking a sip from her drink then immediately looks over at him.

Gabrian chuckles out loud and wonders if she is talking about the drink or the bartender. Either way, she is correct.

Rachael and Gabrian manage to grab a small table upstairs on the other side of the bar to discuss the details of their possible vacation. Having stepped away from all the lights around the bar, Gabrian is suddenly aware of the fragments of colours around the room. They are not coming from lamps. They stream from the people sitting in the bar in front of her. The colours flicker gently, much like the flames of a candle, waving in different directions in the most delicate manner.

Most of the people exude a soft, opaque white, but there are also hues of red, green, even dark purple displayed beautifully in all different shades. Gabrian notices that she does not see any others that resemble Rachael's colours and that a few of them do not have any light at all. She wonders if she should mention any of this to Rachael but decides against it. Until she can figure out why she sees these things, it might be best to keep it under wraps for the moment, or else she might be the one sent to a shrink.

Gabrian takes a sip of her drink and turns to Rachael. "So, about this vacation thing you think I am so desperately in need of, when do you propose it happens?" Gabrian smirks.

"Yay, I am so happy to hear that you are considering it."

"Well, if I recall, you pretty much insisted that I take one. What was it you said? Ah yes, to reboot my brain. I like that one. It is a solid argument and so I concur." Gabrian takes another sip of her Grinch and watches her friend fight desperately to contain her excitement at her decision.

"Well, since Christmas is just around the corner, we should take the time. Most people are on holidays anyway, and your schedule is not that hectic as of right now. There is enough space in the next few weeks to reschedule everyone in, and bring over a few appointments from the first week in January, giving you at least a couple of weeks to take off. And you know, I am sure that your parents would love to see you," she reminds Gabrian.

"Yes, you are probably right. It has been a while since I have visited. They have asked me a few times about when I was going to come see them."

Gabrian wonders if maybe that is why she has been dreaming of the country lately. This past summer, her parents sold their house in the city and moved back into their cottage on the east coast. She figures that they had had their fill of concrete and steel and wanted to get back to their roots. She does not blame them really. When she was a kid, they used to go to Sand Beach almost every day in the summer. She remembers how intoxicating the majestic grace of the ocean could be. Maybe a few days away would not hurt. Besides, it is not like they are out in the wilderness or anything. There is a quaint little town about five minutes away from their home and the hub city is only about an hour's drive. It would not be the end of the world, and it might give her time to clear her head—maybe even get rid of all this 'aura' nonsense.

"I swear that you and my parents are in cahoots," Gabrian says, laughing.

Rachael picks up her drink and raises it toward her. So

Gabrian follows Rachael's lead, clinking the side of her glass against her friend's in a congratulatory salute.

"To vacation!" Rachael cheers then takes a big gulp from her drink.

"Ah, what the hell. To vacation!" Gabrian mutters, doing the same.

ACROSS THE BAR, a smoky coloured mist slithers its way through the room and stops directly in the entrance of the bar upstairs. Undetected by the human eye, it changes form and takes on the appearance of a handsome gentleman wearing a distinguished grey, tailored suit. He stands erect and searches the room, looking for something or someone. Finding what he came for, he makes his way back to the downstairs bar.

"Hey, bud, what can I get you?" Thomas addresses the gentleman.

With eyes the colour of hazel and sunflowers, the man looks at Thomas and points to the seat that Gabrian had sat in. "What is the name of the girl with the long dark hair that was just sitting in this seat a few moments ago?"

"Hm, I am not sure, bud, but I do know that she is sitting upstairs at the other bar." Thomas points over to the spiral staircase that leads upstairs.

"I know where she is. I just need to know her name," he articulates, clenching his vaporous fists.

"She is quite the looker isn't she," Thomas states. "No need to be shy, man, just go up there and ask her. She seems really nice."

His bodily facade starts to fade causing a glitch in his appearance. This triggers the well-dressed stranger to become agitated. He looks directly at Thomas, and his pupils expand briefly. Finding the link to Thomas's mind, Adrinn's irises darken to the colour of midnight as he connects to it.

"Go find the girl's name on her bill, and bring it to me now!" he commands, his voice authoritative and cruel.

"Her name is Gabrian Shadwell," Thomas reveals in a robotic tone. He had already memorized her name for his own benefit.

The fiend's mouth turns eerily upward at the edges. He has found her. "Send her and her friend a little gift for me, will you?

27

Make sure there is a mint leaf in it, a little something to give her instincts a boost," the man utters, sneering in delight. "Tell her that they are from Adrinn, and that he sends his love."

Thomas's thoughts are still buzzing from the mind compulsion. He does what he is told and soon the waitress is on her way to Gabrian's table with two more Grinches. Adrinn wants to ensure that the drinks reach their destination and follows the waitress along her trek. He observes the delivery—and satisfied with the service—Adrinn disappears, leaving only a murky grey resonance of his essence behind.

The drinks arrive and this time they are topped with actual mint leaves. The waitress sets them down on the table in front of Rachael and Gabrian. They both look at her, confused.

"Excuse me, miss, but we did not order these," Gabrian explains to the girl.

She smiles widely and points across the bar. "They are from that gentleman over there, the mysterious one wearing the dark grey suit."

Gabrian searches the crowd in the direction the waitress points but all she sees is the faint reminiscence of an aura—a dark aura that seems different from all the others she has seen tonight. It was lifeless, dull-looking, and resembled the colour of smoke.

How peculiar, Gabrian thinks. "I don't see anyone in a dark grey suit."

The waitress looks around, squints her dark brown eyes in the dim light in a quick glance over, then shrugs her shoulders, and whimsically smiles. "Well, he was there just a moment ago. He was very handsome too. He asked Thomas to give you these. So here you go, enjoy, ladies!" she pitches to them and starts to walk away. Then she stops after a couple steps and shouts back at them, "Oh, and Adrinn sends his love!" She twirls back around and continues on her way.

Well, that is definitely one for the books, she decides. Gabrian has never had that happen before.

Rachael looks at her slyly and smiles. "Miss Gabrian, holding out on me, are you?"

"I am in the dark just as much as you are about this mystery man so stop looking at me like that. Maybe this mystery man was interested in you!" Gabrian chirps back in her defense. Ignoring the smug grin on Rachael's face, Gabrian picks up her anonymous gift and sips it. She scans the crowd again nonchalantly in hopes to find the man responsible.

All Gabrian sees are the colourful auras as they illumine the darkness of the bar. Watching them float and intertwine with each other, she finds them to be quite intriguing and lovely. She breathes more deeply than normal, feeling more relaxed and rejuvenated with each intake of breath. She notices little white strands of light separating from the auras of the people next to her. They twist and turn in a delicate dance, coming toward her like she is orchestrating this whole thing.

It is beautiful, Gabrian thinks, getting lost in the illusion and inhales again.

This time, as she inhales, she breathes in some of the light fragments too. Intoxicating jolts of energy begin to flow through her entire body. It is like nothing she has ever felt before, and it envelopes her in a euphoria of sensations. A blur of colours, sounds, tastes, and smells ignite her hunger to taste more of it. She pulls the air in over and over again with more effort in each breath, exhaling out excess waves of pleasure. Gabrian feels alive and unguarded. Surging from all of the uncharted emotions flowing through her—feeling a strange rapture from this new energy that she draws in—she lets go of her self-restraint and allows it to overwhelm her to the point of collapse.

Where am I, and why is it so dark? I cannot see anything. Wait, I can hear something...birds, it sounds like Ravens." Lost in darkness, Gabrian's fingers begin to burn as panic sets in.

The cawing of the Ravens grows louder and louder. She screams at them, but her words are slow and jumble into an incoherent mess of sounds. She feels stuck in the dream again—the one where no one can hear her, where no one will help her. She catches the sound of footsteps coming toward her, but they do not stop—they just walk on by.

Gabrian hears someone laughing amongst the calls of the Ravens. It is getting closer and the ominous sound of it sends chills down her spine.

The Raven's cackles become deafening, but she swears that it sounds like they are saying something.

"He is coming, he is coming."

They shriek so loud that her eardrums feel as if they might explode. Her head aches from the bombardment of sounds battling for her attention. The pain slicing through her is too much for her to handle. She places her hands over her ears, trying to drown it all out, but they are inside her head, unrelenting and resolute.

A soft voice whispers above all the noise. "It is just a dream, Gabrian. Wake up, you must wake up."

She gathers every ounce of lucid control she can muster and screams until her throat aches with pain.

"Stop it! Just stop it, please!"

Chapter Four

A Raven and a Grinch

THERE IS ONLY the sound of silence, but the Darkness fades, and Gabrian sees fragments of light bleeding in slowly from all around her. She blinks and squints her eyes from the brightness of the sunlight that shines down on her face. She feels it embrace her body, filling it with warmth.

Surrounded by fields of green grasses and tall yellow timothy that dance and sway with the gentle ocean breeze, she sits up to look around. Perched on a rock beside her is a Raven. Quietly it sits, tilting is head from side to side and watches her as if it is concerned with her well-being. She searches for a clue as to where she might be and finds a tall lighthouse in the distance, worn by weather and time. Like a beacon of hope that shines through the night, it stands out against the sea of greens, yellows, and blue.

Standing between the lighthouse and the Raven, she notices a figure. Gabrian cannot quite make out who it is, but she knows it is a woman with long dark hair surrounded by soothing silver light. She looks familiar, but Gabrian cannot see her face clear enough to tell who she is. The woman raises her hand and waves at Gabrian. As she lifts her own hand to wave back, the sky begins to darken.

Clouds the colour of charcoal quickly cover the sun. The warmth she once felt has now been replaced with an icy breeze—

prickling her skin. The earth beneath Gabrian's feet rumbles and shakes. Crouching down and reaching toward the ground in hopes of stabilizing her footing, she looks over at the Raven, and it gives her a sympathetic look.

"Storm is coming!" it whispers to her then takes flight, flapping its large shadowy wings and disappears into a blur. Her eyelids droop, becoming heavy as the Darkness surrounds her again.

Gabrian fights to open her eyes. She reaches out with her hands to grab hold of something, anything, only to find a cool, smooth surface. The world has turned her upside down. She wakes to find herself lying on the floor of the bar where she was sitting only moments before, being gently shaken by Rachael. There are blurred faces all around her chattering, but she does not understand what they are saying; too many voices come at her all at once. Then she singles one out in particular:

"Gabrian, Gabrian can you hear me? Please say something," Rachael's voice echoes for a moment in her ears then clears as she continues to plead with Gabrian, gently stroking her hair. "Are you okay? Can you get up?"

From the expression on Rachael's face, Gabrian figures that she must have given her quite a start. She looks around and sees everyone staring at her. Some of them look at her, assuming she has had too much to drink, but others seem to have legitimate concern. She realizes she better become coherent quickly or the remainder of her night will be spent sitting in a hospital room. Regardless of the slight psychotic episode she has just endured, that is no way to start off the weekend.

"Yes, I can hear you. Yes, I am okay, and yes I can get up. Just give me a moment," Gabrian grumbles as she crawls her way back up into her chair. Readjusting herself, she overhears a conversation from the table in front of her—the origin of the light strands she had become so fixated with earlier. The two women speak as if they have had some kind of occurrence as well.

"I know just how that poor girl must be feeling. I kind of thought for moment that I was going to pass out and fall out of my chair, too. They must be making these drink specials extra strong tonight because my head feels like it is swimming." The blonde girl giggles.

32

"That is strange. I was feeling a bit peculiar myself. I hope she is okay though. It has to be the drinks." The girl chuckles then grins mischievously at her friend. "We should order another round." They both burst out laughing and agree.

"Do you need me to take you to the hospital?" Rachael interrupts Gabrian's eavesdropping and reaches for her arm.

"No, I am fine, Rach. A little exhausted from the day, I guess." Gabrian gives her a convincing smile. "I just need to go home and rest. I will be good as new in the morning."

"You are sure, Gabe?"

"Yes. I am fine."

Gabrian and Rachael gather their things from the backs of their chairs then head for the stairs. "I do have one request though."

"Sure, anything you want," Rachael promises.

"Next time we go out, maybe we should make sure we have something to eat before we let the Grinch out of the bottle. Agreed?"

Laughing out loud, Rachael hugs her friend tightly. "Agreed."

Chapter Five

Kettle and Smoke

IT IS SATURDAY morning and Gabrian's apartment is quiet. The streets below are even quieter. At five o'clock in the morning, life is yet to start pumping through the veins of the city.

"So why on Earth am I awake and so full of energy?" Gabrian wonders out loud.

After last night's fiasco, she thought she would be exhausted and sleep in until noon. But apparently that is not the case. There is no headache, no aches, pains, or any other signs that would suggest she took a tumble to the floor either. She feels great—like she is ready to take on the world. Well, maybe not the entire world, but a small manageable portion of it. She looks down at her hand where she had given herself a paper cut yesterday, but it was gone.

"Huh. That is odd. I could have sworn that the cut was pretty deep."

Gabrian jumps up out of bed and wanders around her apartment, trying to recall the events that had taken place the night before. What could have made her collapse like that? She had not felt tired or hungry—not really—not enough to make someone faint anyway.

"I need coffee. Coffee will help put things into perspective. It always does," she declares, absolute in the decision, and jogs into the kitchen. She pours some water into the kettle and turns it on then rounds two large tablespoons of coffee into her press, eagerly waiting for the water to boil.

"It is too quiet in here. I need some noise. I wonder who is up and wants to have coffee with me this morning." She reaches out her hand to turn the radio on, but before she touches the button, the vocal talent of David Levine bellows out of the speaker. "What the..." She jumps back. "That is freaky."

Gabrian scratches her head, trying to find a logical answer to this bazaar phenomenon. "Ah, I must have forgotten to shut off the alarm on the radio last night," she tries to convince herself, knowing full well that the alarm does not go off until six-thirty a.m. which is still over an hour away. Making it a point not to check the time on the alarm, she turns away and returns to stare at the kettle as it begins to whistle.

She pours the hot water into the coffee press and fills her cup. The steam rises slowly, and she closes her eyes as she inhales the incredible aroma of the brewed coffee as the room starts to shift and whirl quickly around her. Then it stops.

Gabrian opens her eyes and finds herself no longer standing in her own kitchen, but in a dark corner, back at the bar again. This time she is an onlooker of the events that had unfolded the night before.

She watches as her doppelganger stands mesmerized within a trance, inhaling multiple streams of light with every breath—light that is fragmenting off of the people beside her. Her mirror-self looks empowered by it as she devours every morsel, and her bodily form takes on the subtle glow of an aura that grows brighter all the while.

It is not like the other auras she has seen—it shimmers and sparkles like stardust. Suddenly, it turns to grey. Gabrian's mirrored-self wavers and becomes unbalanced. Just before she falls to the floor, her aura shifts colour again—turning dark and smoky—like the one she had seen hovering around the bar when she had searched for the mysterious man.

Gabrian hears laughter coming from somewhere behind her. She is certain that she has heard that laugh before...that ugly, cynical laugh. She searches around the bar to find its source, but she cannot see anything but grey smoke strangely slithering toward her mirrored-self. When it reaches her, the smoke hovers around the body, circling round and round as Gabrian's carbon copy falls slowly to the floor.

"That cannot be smoke," Gabrian whispers. "Smoke does not move like that! What the hell is that thing?" The smoke stops shifting as if it can hear her and turns, rushing toward her. "Holy crap, it is coming right at me!" Gabrian screams.

She turns around quickly to run but stops abruptly, realizing she is back in her kitchen, holding the kettle. "What the...?" she utters, bewildered. Gabrian covers her chest with her hand, feeling her heart beat like crazy beneath her skin. She glances back over her shoulder, looking for the smoke that had been heading straight for her a second ago.

She finds nothing, only the kitchen rooster staring back at her from the countertop and the microwave clock flashing seven o'clock over and over again. She slips backward, leaning against the fridge, and exhales a sigh of relief. Though still confused about what just happened, she is pleased to be back in her apartment and happy that that thing, the smoke or whatever it was, is gone.

"Wait a second! Seven o'clock? How did I lose almost two hours in the last few minutes?" She scratches the top of her head, trying to query the sudden absence of time. "That can't be right!"

Bang! Bang! Bang! Bang! A loud noise from across the room assaults her sense of hearing, thundering through her ears.

"Ah!" she shouts, jumping backward—almost out of her skin—as she drops the kettle on the floor.

Gabrian's eyes move toward the direction of the noise. There, on the other side of her living room window, sits a rather large Raven. It tilts its head from side to side then nudges the window gently with its beak. It looks directly at her. Now seemingly satisfied that she has given it her full attention, it flies away.

"Rotten bugger!" she yells at the bird then turns to look at the state of her poor kettle. Picking it up, she closes her eyes, hoping it is not damaged. "Oh, please don't be broken," she whispers, biting the tip of her thumb. Opening her eyes, she peeks at the kettle. "Aw no! That was a nice kettle too."

As she feared, the kettle has a large crack going up the side where it hit the floor. Gabrian reaches down and picks it up. Gently setting it on the counter, she moans with disappointment. "Mom gave me that kettle last Christmas. I guess it fits with the day that I am having."

She reaches out and traces the crack with her index finger. A warm sensation jolts through her fingertip, sending out a brief spark where she had touched the glass.

"Ouch!" she exclaims from the quick biting sensation on her finger, similar to a shock. Thinking that maybe she nicked her finger on the broken glass, Gabrian turns her hand over to examine it, but there is nothing. "Huh," she says.

Shaking her head in dismissal, Gabrian places the broken kettle on the countertop and picks up her coffee that is now ice-cold. She nukes it, determined not to let her rotten morning ruin the enjoyment of her first cup of the day, then heads straight for the shower. All the energy she had when she woke up this morning has now been almost depleted. Gabrian chugs down what remains of her drink and jumps into the shower, hoping the water will wash away this uneasy feeling running through her.

***

IN THE KITCHEN, the kettle's cracked glass begins to bubble and bend. Sparks flare and sputter along the fissure. The abnormal melding causes the glass to cast a brief red hue as it fuses back together. Any trace of it ever being broken disappears and the kettle stands as strong as the day it was created.

***

AFTER A TWENTY minute shower, Gabrian begins to feel better—almost human again, for the moment anyway. The occurrences of the last twenty-four hours begin creeping their way back into her mind, making her desperate for a distraction.

"I don't want to think about all this anymore!" she whines. "I need Mom."

As soon as the words escape her mouth, the phone rings, echoing through the bathroom and scaring the crap out of her in the process. "Bugger!" Gabrian curses.

Shaken, her hands tremble as she reaches out to pick up the

phone. "I am falling apart..." she mutters. "Hello?" Gabrian grumbles into the receiver, rubbing her damp hair with the towel.

"Hello, sweetie, how are you?"

"Hey, Mom, I was just thinking of you," she admits raising her eyebrows. *Literally, like two seconds ago.* A shiver tremors through her body but she shakes is off. *It is just a fluke.*

"Well, that is a fun coincidence." Gabrian's face softens and the edges of her mouth curl upward at the sound of her mother's voice on the other end of the phone.

"How are things with you?" Gabrian leans herself against the counter, preparing for a lengthy conversation.

"Oh fine, honey. You popped into my mind just now, so I decided to check in on you and see how things are going. We haven't talked in a while."

"I am doing all right. Sorry that I have not called lately. Work is keeping me quite busy," she says, staring up at the ceiling vent while she twirls a strand of her damp hair.

"Well, I hope you are not overdoing it. All work and no play will make you old before your time, young lady," she scolds Gabrian playfully.

"I know." Halting her hair twirling, she grabs a fist full of hair, and scrunches it at the top of her head, pacing the eight feet of space between the door and the toilet. "Say, what would you think about me coming out to visit you and Dad for the holidays, or do you guys have other plans?"

"Really? Oh, Gabe, that would be so wonderful. What day are you coming? How long can you stay?" Her mother's voice begins to squeak from obvious delight.

"Slow down, Mom, you are getting hysterical. You make it sound like I have not seen you in years," Gabrian teases, giggling at her mother's bombardment of questions.

"I am just so happy that you are coming. Your dad will be thrilled to hear it."

"I was thinking that I would try to finish up work by the twentieth of December and then see if I can fly out shortly after that." Gabrian halts her marching and stares down at her feet, wiggling her toes nervously. "And if it is okay with you guys, I might even stay for a while."

"Gabrian, that sounds great; stay as long as you like."

"Thanks, Mom, I can't wait to see you and Dad." Gabrian's voice begins to crack.

"You too honey...Gabe?'

"Yes, Mom?" Her words slip out across her lips in barely a whisper.

"Are you sure that you are alright?"

Gabrian wants to say, "No, Mom, I am not alright." And have a big heart-to-heart with her over the telephone, but she is not sure how to even begin to tell her mother about meetings with imaginary clients, about seeing people's auras, and the strange daydream she just had about smoke chasing her in her own apartment. How does one have a casual conversation over the phone about any of that without someone calling the men in white jackets to come take her away? She is supposed to be the one that people call to figure out what is going on in their heads, not the other way around.

Gabrian desperately wants to tell her mom how she is in need of counseling but has no idea who she would even talk to about these sorts of things. She hates the idea that her own logical mind cannot unravel her dilemma and that she may be in need of a witch doctor or something to that effect. And as luck would have it, she does not have one of those in her address book.

Gabrian resurfaces from her mental rant. She releases the knotted hold she has on her hair, letting it fall loosely around her shoulders then wipes the wetness welling up in her eyes and simply replies, "I am fine, Mom. I just need a little R&R." Her voice wavers, sounding defeated. "And Rachael made it a point to remind me that it might be a nice idea for me to go visit with you guys."

"Ah, Rachael. I always did like that girl. How is she doing anyway?"

"She is great, Mom, and I think quite eager to take her vacation as well."

"No doubt! You girls work too hard," her mother scolds. Gabrian hears some rustling in the background of her mom's phone. "Well, I have to go now, honey. There are some errands I need to tend to. I love you, and I will see you soon, okay?"

"Okay."

"Bye, honey. I love you."

"Love you too, Mom. See you soon. Bye." Gabrian sighs and

hangs up the phone.

There, done. She cannot back out now, especially after hearing how happy it made her mom. Gabrian grabs her empty coffee cup from the bathroom counter and heads back to the kitchen for a refill. Hopefully this time it might even be hot when she gets to drink it.

Gabrian reaches for her kettle then remembers it was cracked from the fall. She picks it up to examine it and notices that the crack is gone. It looks perfectly fine—no crack, no marks, no evidence that anything bad had ever happened to it. Scratching her chin with her hand and twisting her hair in a knot atop of her head again, she continues to stare at the kettle in disbelief of what she sees.

"Okay, this is messed up. I was sure that this was toast."

Standing in the kitchen with her empty coffee cup in one hand, and her perfectly fine kettle in the other, Gabrian wonders if she is actually awake or if she is asleep and dreaming all of this— the delusion of the smoke chasing her, the Raven banging at the window, and now the miracle kettle that fixes itself. She decides that the only way to tell is to give herself a good pinch. It always works in the movies so she figures why not give it a go.

Setting both the kettle and the cup down on the counter, she reaches over and touches her left arm with her right hand. "Please be a dream. Please be a dream. Please be a dream," she chants out loud.

The pinch comes.

"Ouchhhh! That smarts." She rubs her arm soothingly and groans. To her regret, Gabrian is now painfully aware that she is indeed awake.

Having only been up for about three hours, too many things have happened that she has no logical explanation for. Mentally exhausted and quite possibly suffering from a concussion due to last night's fall, Gabrian submits to the chaos, shakes her head, and admits defeat.

"It is too freakin' early for all this crap. I am going back to bed!"

Chapter Six

Storm Feathers

GABRIAN CLOSES HER eyes and tilts her head upward. The sun feels warm on her face as a gentle breeze blows through, rustling her hair. She does not remember ever feeling this free or unguarded in her life. The hypnotizing rhythm of the waves drowns out any chance the voices in her head have to disturb her in this place. Her eyes slowly open, and she delights with every colour that floods its way in. Everything is so peaceful and harmonious. It is like watching a symphony being played flawlessly. The waves sing an ancient song of change and renewal that makes her feel so small, yet empowered, and strong for knowing its existence.

She glances around, watching the long grasses sway to and fro as the wind dances through the meadow, flirting with each blade. Engrossed in the performance, Gabrian's attention is carried along with it, and she finds herself once more before a familiar old lighthouse standing resilient against the sea. Beside it, she sees the woman again, waving for her to follow. She steps out from the long grasses and starts toward her. The woman smiles sweetly, pleased that Gabrian has begun to follow her.

Looking down at the timothy and wild flowers all around, Gabrian runs her hands through them as she walks, feeling the tops of each plant tickle her fingertips. Gabrian glances behind at the woman, but she is no longer there so she returns her attention to her front. She sees a ragged set of steps that lead up to a stone path, their edges smoothened from wear. At the end of the path sits a small wooden house encircled by a cedar fence with a gated archway, guarded by a large Firethorn bush.

Something about this house calls to her. It is enchanting. Gabrian thinks it looks more like a cottage than a traditional-style house with its exposed wood and stones for siding, wild flowers, and green ivy growing freely all around it. It reminds her of a dwelling from a fairy tale that a hunted princess may have once lived in a long time ago. Gabrian gazes at it in admiration of its subtle beauty, then notices there are black-speckled things all around it.

Those cannot be stones, she thinks. *It does not look right*. She walks closer to the house to get a better look. The black spots begin to move.

Getting closer, she begins to realize that the spots are actually birds—black birds, Ravens in fact, and they are everywhere. *Odd,* Gabrian considers.

As she continues to watch the birds, she notices that they all seem to be focused on something. She turns her head, curious to see what has their attention. All she can see is fog rolling in off the water. But the more she looks at it, the more she notices that the fog has a strange colour. It is not white but grey, like the colour of smoke. One by one, the Ravens take flight and begin to circle the house; on and on their display continues until all of the birds are airborne. Gabrian is entranced by this bizarre phenomenon and is not sure what to do other than to stand motionless and watch. Suddenly, they change course and fly straight toward her!

They begin to circle her and, in disbelief, she succumbs to the paralyzing terror growing inside. Her limbs, completely useless, make any attempt to run away futile. There are so many Ravens around her that she can barely see the house or the gate through them. All she can see are spectrums of light fading in and out through the black wall of unkindness. Something gently brushes up against her, and she pushes it away quickly, startled by the touch. It is the woman from the meadow. The woman tilts her head and gives Gabrian a warm smile, causing the edges of her silvery eyes to crinkle. Gabrian realizes that this is the same woman from yesterday that supposedly does not exist.

"It is you. I know it is...Mrs. Argryis," Gabrian shouts in hysterics.

Now, beside her in the midst of the feathery whirlwind, stands a very vivid replica of her illusive imaginary client—disturbingly unconcerned with what is happening around them.

Gabrian feels her throat closing in as she begins to hyperventilate. Her mind screams at her to look for some way out. The birds draw closer than she can stand, and the terror building inside of her suffocates her ability to think logically.

"He is coming!" the unkindness screams.

With no other option, Gabrian warily reaches out to the woman standing at her side. "I am so confused. What am I supposed to do?"

"Do not be afraid," Mrs. Argryis calmly states. "They will not harm you. They are here to protect you."

"What are you talking about?" Gabrian shrieks as she folds her arms around her waist, resisting her immediate desire to swat at the encroaching birds. "I don't understand!"

"Listen for the storm feathers and heed their warnings as they will see when you do not."

"Storm feathers? Warnings...warnings for what?" Gabrian pleads with the woman for answers as she watches the birds, beginning to feel claustrophobic. "What will they see? Please, enough of these riddles. Just tell me what is going on." Gabrian places her head in her hands. Everything swims around her—the birds, the house...nothing is still.

She feels like she is caught in a whirlpool and is being sucked down deeper and deeper into an abyss with nothing to hold onto. Everything closes in all around her, suffocating her. She fights with all of her will to break free, but she cannot move, gasping for breath as she screams, "Please stop! Please make it stop!"

She swings her arms violently, clawing at everything and anything around her. Connecting with something pliable and soft, Gabrian fights harder now that she has found something tangible. She pulls and twists her way out of the confinements that have wound their way tightly around her body, partly covering her face.

Finally free from them, she sits up, looking around to try to register where she is. Disoriented from the vividness of the dream, she sits motionless for a few moments and stares at the pile of blankets on the floor that she has just defeated. Gabrian whimpers in a soft, saddened laugh and gathers the remainder of her wits. Her shoulders slump forward as she pulls her knees up against her chest and wraps her arms tightly around them. Leaning her head forward upon her folded limbs, her body begins to tremble— unable to hold back the chaos inside any longer. In a slow lulling rock, she closes her eyes as tears filled with uncertainty gently roll across her cheek.

"What is wrong with me? Why am I having all these messed up hallucinations and dreams?" she chokes out. "I just don't understand why this is happening to me."

Sitting in her room, alone in silence, Gabrian comes to the realization that if she does not pull it together that she may be in danger of losing it for real. And that she, the prodigy child of logic and psychology, may to have to find someone to help her cope— even if it is a witch doctor.

Chapter Seven

A Meeting of the Minds

ACROSS TOWN IN her apartment, Rachael reiterates yesterday's events at the office and of Gabrian's episode at the bar.

"I have no idea what happened in her office. I was not actually in the room with her," Rachael articulates out loud. "All I know is that she claims she had a meeting with Mrs. Argryis."

You are sure the name was Argryis? the first voice resonates within Rachael's mind as she uses her telepathy to communicate. Rachael's visitor's aura has joined in with hers as they continue to speak.

"Yes, I am sure, Elder Ariah." Rachael twirls her red curly hair as she responds to the white iridescent light that swirls about her. "There is no mistaking that name."

Did she happen to tell you anything that was said or what purpose Cera had to reveal herself like that? Vaeda's aura surrounds Rachael as she enters her mind.

"No, Lady of Zephyr, she did not," Rachael says to the other iridescent light. Feeling a strong presence enter into her living space, she glances over her shoulder to witness Orroryn appear from within the shadows cast over her kitchen door. He decides to join the meeting, hoping to help figure out why all of this is happening.

"Good Evening, Rachael of Vindere," Orroryn's warm voice fills the void of sound in the room as he addresses his host.

Rachael smiles sweetly at him as her body becomes well-aware of his immense presence. She gestures for him to take a seat, her face flushing from their close proximity.

"Good Evening, Orroryn, Elder of Schaeduwe," Rachael greets him, trying to contain a coy grin. "Welcome."

Orroryn, have you any news of where she might be? The Zephyr Elder asks, channeling through Rachael and using her voice to speak out loud so the Shadow Walker may hear the internal conversation.

"No, Vaeda. I have not found a trace of Cera. Not since she swore us all to secrecy before I helped her enter the Veil."

I am uncertain as to why she would risk surfacing while she is so weak. Ariah's aura shifts and swirls as she speaks. *She must be worried to allow herself to become that vulnerable.*

"Maybe it is time for us to take matters into our own hands and guide Gabrian without the council," Orroryn suggests, pushing his agile fingers through his messy curls. "Sarah Shadwell has been to see us. She thinks that when Gabrian goes home for a visit that it may be time."

"She had some kind of episode last night when we went to the bar for a drink," Rachael reveals to the elders.

The auras swirl and brighten around Rachael while Orroryn's haphazard gaze becomes more focused and intense.

"What do you mean 'an episode?'" The concern in his voice betrays his usual calm demeanor.

What happened? both Ariah and Vaeda voice simultaneously.

"She seemed to go into some kind of trance all of a sudden after taking a sip of a drink," Rachael explains. "It was like she was looking at things above the crowd. At first, I thought she was just looking for the guy who had bought us the drinks but..."

What kind of drink? Vaeda chirps, interrupting Rachael's story.

"It was a fruity drink with a Christmassy name...what was it again?" Rachael pinches her nose, trying to remember. Orroryn face's twitches in annoyance of her lack of memory and noticing his tell, she quickly recalls the name. "Oh, I remember. It was called

'The Grinch!'"

The iridescent lights swirl again, flaring as if they can almost spark.

No, no, youngling. What was in the drink? Were there any herbs in them? Vaeda asks her host again calmly.

"Now that you mention it, there was a mint leaf," Rachael announces. "I just thought it was supposed to be there."

A mint leaf; the Borrowers Fellowship often use mint leaves to stir the senses of their younglings while in training to spark their essences. It helps them to focus and see the energies more clearly," Vaeda expounds the significance of the herb to the others.

That cannot be a coincidence. Can it? Ariah questions the fluke.

"No, Ariah. I doubt it was a coincidence at all." Orroryn rises from his seat and strides over to the window to stare out into the night. His certainty is obvious as he voices his belief. "I have the distinct feeling that someone is very aware of what Gabrian is or what she may become."

But how? We were sworn to secrecy. No one else knows about her, Ariah discloses.

"Who did you say bought those drinks for you?" Orroryn turns to Rachael, and she catches her breath as she drowns in his deep-green eyes.

Rachael gazes, momentarily dazed in some other world, then catches herself and returns hastily with her answer, "The waitress said his name was Adrinn."

The iridescent lights surge with incredible brightness and become almost blinding as they swirl in a frenzy. Orroryn's motions completely stop, and his face turns pale for a few moments. His eyes, which were a second ago warm and welcoming, have lost their sparkle and are now dark jade, revealing the side of a darker spirit within.

Find her, keep an eye on her, Vaeda's voice stresses the urgency in her words to Rachael. *Speak to no one about this until I get back to you.*

Orroryn, I need you to go to her parents and tell them what is going on. They must be informed, Vaeda insists to her close and trusted companion.

Ariah, keep your connections open to everyone. Give no

indication to anyone that anything is wrong, but alert me if you feel any disruption in the energies, Vaeda requests from her dear friend then returns her focus on her host. *Rachael, allow no one but us three to see Gabrian or know of her location until I have said otherwise.*

Confused and concerned, Rachael agrees to Vaeda's wishes. Within moments, her connections to her Elders, Ariah and Vaeda, are gone leaving Orroryn as the only other one left in the room with her. The awkward silence becomes deafening, and she feels the weight of his eyes press against her. Her skin tingles, from his closeness, and her face flushes from the sudden rise in her body temperature. Rachael picks up a pen from the counter and fidgets with it, clicking it mindlessly in an effort of distraction. Slowly edging towards her, Orroryn clasps his large tanned hand around hers—ceasing the incessant clicking, then gently removes the noisy object from her hand and places it back where it came from. Rachael gasps at his touch and raises her chin, lifting her eyes to meet his gaze—once again the colour of a calm sea. Sharing a brief glance, she sees the clouds forming around him. His smile faintly covers the worry that his crooked brow cannot hide. He sighs and looks away, just for a moment, searching the shadows behind her, preparing to take his leave.

He reaches up and touches her arm gently. "Watch her closely but guard yourself as well. Something is triggering this, and unfortunately, once I figure out the answer to this riddle, I don't think I am going to like what I find." Orroryn looks down at Rachael, and she sees the angst in his eyes as he entrusts his fears to her. "I am going to the Covenant tonight, but if you need me, call out for me. I will be just beyond the shadows, and I will hear you."

Rachael nods and smiles at him wearily. "Who is Adrinn?" she asks Orroryn just as he turns to leave.

He stops and sighs then returns to her. Standing before her small fragile body, he raises his hand and gently slides the tips of his fingers along the bottom of her jaw. The warmth of his touch ignites a yearning within Rachael as her eyes raise to meet his intense gaze.

"Something you don't ever want to meet."

Orroryn's grim words leave the weight of heavy stone in her heart as he relinquishes his touch and steps back toward the shadows, vanishing within them.

Chapter Eight

A Hunger Within

AFTER SPENDING THE rest of Saturday in bed reading, watching TV, and doing just about everything Gabrian can possibly think of to distract herself from reality, the day is pretty much a write off.

Rachael had called her around supper time to see how she felt, but Gabrian is certain the real reason that Rachael called was to make sure she had not cracked up on her. After finally assuring her friend that she is fine, and feeling much better, Rachael lets her off the hook—sort of.

"How about I bring you over some takeout from the deli around the corner, and we can watch a movie?" Rachael presses.

"Thanks, Rach, but I am really not that hungry. I had a big lunch, and I don't think I could eat anyway," Gabrian lies.

She just did not want to sit through another Rachael lecture of how she needs to take care of herself better, how she needs to eat more, and then try to ignore Rachael as she gives her the pity stare all night. Sometimes, when she does that, Gabrian swears it is not Rachael looking at her but an entirely different person. It is so unsettling sometimes.

She knows that Rachael really cares about her, but today, she just does not have the patience for it. There is too much on her mind that she needs to figure out. Trying to concentrate all night on not telling Rachael anything about what has really been going on in her world the last twenty-four hours is just something she does not want to do or have the energy for.

"Are you sure? It is my treat!"

Gabrian becomes suspicious by her insistent need to check in on her. She is way too adamant. "Yes, I am sure, but thank you anyway. I really just want to go for a run to clear my head."

"All right, fine. I know when I am not wanted," Rachael snorts jokingly in defeat. "Oh, did you remember to call your folks yet to tell them the good news?"

"Yes, I did. So do not worry. I will not back out of taking some time off and closing the office," Gabrian assures her. "I think you need it just as badly as you think I do. "

"Ah, Gabe, you know how I love spending *all* my time with you. But I am really looking forward to hitting the slopes when I go home," Rachael admits. "I am going to call and make the reservations as soon as I let you go."

"Well, good for you. Just don't wrap yourself around a tree while you are gone. I can't run the office without you."

"Ha, you are so funny!" Rachael retorts sarcastically. "No worries about me. Just focus on having some fun yourself. You never know, you might get the hang of it!"

"I doubt it, but it is worth a try." Gabrian laughs and halfheartedly hopes that it would come true. "Anyway, I have got to go, Rach. I have some running shoes that I need to put to work before I change my mind."

"All right, have a good run, and I will see you on Monday morning!"

"I will—Monday morning, bright and early!"

"Oh and Gabrian..."

"Yeah?"

"Be careful, okay?"

"I will...Goodnight, Rach." Gabrian shakes her head, thinking that it is an odd request. But then again, the past twenty-four hours have not been exactly normal.

"Goodnight, Gabrian."

The phone goes quiet, and Gabrian hangs it up then turns to stare at the running shoes sitting by the door. She hesitates for a moment, giving them the stare down.

"Do I go, do I not go, or do I just crawl back into bed and see what tomorrow brings?" Gabrian riddles out loud. It has been a while since she has had on her runners and they look sad to her...if that is even possible. "Ah, fine. You win!" she yells at the sneakers as she turns toward her room to change her clothes.

***

IT IS A great night to go out for a run. The temperature is just above the freezing point. Cool crisp air fills Gabrian's lungs as she starts out on her journey to the park. She thought about running the streets, but it just did not give her the same experience. Continuously stopping and starting did not work for her. She needed the illusion of being secluded and surrounded by nature that the park provided while still knowing that whenever she has had enough trees and squirrels, she can return to city life in mere minutes.

Lucky for her, she only lives a few blocks from the park so it is only a few stop lights to go through before she reaches her destination. Entering the park gates, she notices it is quite busy. There seems to be a lot of people out tonight taking advantage of the mild weather. An abundance of couples sit close on the benches and drink warm beverages, engrossed in the moment.

Gabrian smiles at them as she passes by and wonders to herself if she will ever find someone. She never seems to have enough time to worry about it on most days, but lately, it seems to be on her mind more than not. An image of her client Mr. Redmond pops into her mind, and she thinks that maybe Rachael is right—he is rather dashing. Then another thought surfaces of the handsome bartender she had met last night.

"Ugh! I am pathetic!" she exclaims, shaking her head briefly to toss out the thoughts and all the nonsense that goes along with it. Blaming the holidays, she decides that it is the culprit playing on her emotions. This time of year really seems to wreak havoc on people. Most of her clientele tend to develop more issues or concerns the closer they get to the month of December.

As she continues to run the path that leads through the park, she begins to take notice of each person she passes. Now that she has developed this new gift of seeing people's energy fields, or auras, she starts to notice the colours. They seem quite different here. In the darkness of night, the colours take on more beautiful hues and displaying so many different shades of each aura. Gabrian also notices that not everyone seems to have one or at least one she can see.

As she relaxes, enjoying the light show, her breathing takes on its own rhythm as she runs, and she soon realizes that they have different levels of energy associated with them. Gabrian begins to feel the different strengths of the auras. Somehow, she feels an actual detectable vibration where some of the pulsations are stronger than others.

Taking in all this new information, Gabrian is mystified but still, she finds it strangely beautiful. If this new world of colours and lights is not strange enough, a new development arises—the colours are somehow making her feel hungry.

Not hungry in the sense that her stomach is growling, more like her body is responding to them, making her feel as if it needs to get closer, urging her to reach out for them.

Finding herself being drawn to the brightest and most fragmented strands of energy, she begins to get closer as she runs by these people—closer than she normally would just so she can feel it. Gabrian's breathing alters. She starts inhaling deeper when she nears the oblivious pedestrians.

I need to get closer, she hums almost out loud.

Suddenly, everything shifts. It is like every person around her has heard her thoughts and starts to move in slow motion. Gabrian continues at normal speed...or so it seems to her. She is able to get as close as she wants to the light without them even noticing. All those in her path stand motionless like a captive audience and unknowingly at her mercy. Gabrian becomes enthralled by this odd realization and draws in her breath deeply.

Small fragments of light particles dance and sway around the main auras and begin breaking off, slowly twisting and curling toward her, bringing with it an intoxicating aroma that makes her skin tingle. It fills her with warmth that spreads throughout her body.

"This is incredible," Gabrian drones unconsciously.

Once again, she is mesmerized by this strange happening and unsure of why it is occurring, but Gabrian has no interest in stopping. All she knows is that she is no longer tired nor is she worried about anything other than how she can absorb more light.

This sensation is euphoric beyond all measures of Gabrian's existence. The more she breathes in, the stronger and more elated she feels, but unbeknownst to Gabrian, she is also causing the humans around her to become disoriented. The more light she draws from them, the more drain she is putting on the life force that they survive on. Slowly losing consciousness, they begin to buckle at the knee, and one by one, they drop to the ground, falling helpless into a coma-like state, unable to fight the confusing symptoms entrancing them.

Without notice to Gabrian, there is now light blooming all around her, a shimmering light of hazy grey that reaches outward, engulfing everything around her. It takes on a life of its own and to Gabrian, it feels amazing.

She closes her eyes and breathes it in, embracing it. All the sensory nerves that circulate through her body feel like they are buzzing with electricity. She lets the tension in her arms go and tilts her head back, allowing her body and mind to be completely immersed, savoring every ounce of energy that she reaps. Her intoxication is so profound that the ground beneath her no longer carries her weight.

To Gabrian, nothing else exists but this.

***

RACHAEL ENTERS THE park, and the hair on her arms stands immediately. Sensing a massive energy source, she begins scanning the park, feeling it growing in intensity by the second. She gets a bad feeling that she knows who it has to do with and begins to jog briskly along the path. Up ahead, she sees Gabrian basically levitating off the ground, engulfed in light. Her aura has surfaced and revealed its colour, light grey, the colour of early morning mist but speckled in places with faint fragmented colours.

"She has an aura," Rachael gasps, open-jawed, the flawless curve of her brow now marred with worry lines from what she sees. "A Grey aura...wait a minute, she is a Boragen?" This revelation of Gabrian's essence is completely unexpected by her friend.

Rachael continues to run toward the surge of power which seems to emanate from Gabrian. The closer she gets to her, the more she feels the pull of time slowing her down. Irritated and unable to do much about it, Rachael pushes on. Getting closer to where Gabrian hovers, she sees a number of people lying on the ground in the distance, not moving.

"Oh, no!" Rachael cries out. Her eyes glaze over, and the colours begin to swirl within her irises. She centers her mind to reach out to her Elder.

Ariah, Lady of Vindere. I may need some assistance, please hear me. Rachael refocuses on her friend.

"Gabrian, what have you done?" she gasps then quiets. "What have they done?" she says more solemnly, upset at the Elders and the fact that they should never have left Gabrian in the dark about her heritage. Rachael feels a familiar presence stir within her mind—the connection to her Elder is successful.

I am here, Rachael. What is going on? Ariah's voice sings through Rachael's mind. *Have you found Gabrian?*

Yes, I have found her, but something very bad is happening. You might want to contact the Lady of Zephyr.

Ariah closes her eyes in order to make a solid connection with Rachael. Rachael allows Ariah to channel through her so that she can see what is happening for herself. Rachael's eyes begin to shift and turn from green to bright blue as Ariah's connection becomes transparent. Ariah's sight comes into focus and what she sees alarms her. Without hesitation, she withdraws from Rachael and reaches out for Lady of Zephyr at once. Within moments, Rachael feels another familiar presence seeking entry to her sight.

It is Vaeda.

Immediately, Rachael receives her, and her eyes once again become icy blue as Vaeda begins to see.

Oh dear! Vaeda exclaims. *It does seem that we have a situation.*

Rachael's eyes turn back to green, revealing that the Lady of Zephyr is gone, no longer looking through her.

Alone again with her thoughts, Rachael turns her attention back to Gabrian. She notices the air around her friend is beginning to metamorphose into ripples like a mirage on a hot sunny day. Then, from within the bends, the beautifully fierce-looking Lady of

Zephyr emerges with her Raven escort at her side.

The Raven immediately takes to the sky once they are through the portal and circles above Vaeda, giving a trifling squawk. Vaeda's long white-and-golden hair whips around her from the entry of the morph and reflects the light from the streetlamps hovering over her nearby, making her appear as an angelic vision. Not transforming into full-flesh form, Vaeda hurries to stand behind Gabrian's floating form.

Vaeda begins to chant. Closing her eyes, she raises her face slightly upward and opens her hands, turning her palms upwards toward the sky.

"*Momentumus Terminato, Encorpus Veilus!*
Momentumus Terminato, Encorpus Veilus!
Momentumus Terminato, Encorpus Veilus!
Decente Vapir, decente."

Though still embraced by the energy that she swims in, Gabrian begins to respond, becoming more lucid, and the sensation of falling rushes through her. She imagines the Earth rising up quickly to meet her, feeling her feet touch the ground once again. In the distance, she hears a voice yelling her name with concern.

"Gabrian! Gabrian!"

The light around her is being defused and withdrawn, but Gabrian still feels overwhelmingly alive. Her jaw relaxes and lowers, her full red lips parting as visible lines crinkle at the corners of her eyes in her delighted state. She runs her hands down the sides of her face then her body, feeling the skin tingle and burn as it vibrates on the surface—sensitive from the stolen life force still flowing wildly through her.

Vaeda opens her eyes but realizes that Gabrian is still engrossed in the energy. She uses one more cast. "*Awae cenan! Eode!*"

Gabrian is suddenly back—jarred from her delirium—and her legs give out from under her. Vaeda raises her hand, making a swiping gesture, and Gabrian is caught and gently lowered to the ground. Her eyes fly wide open, and she searches for familiarity, anything recognizable. Rachael runs as fast as she can to her friend's side and cradles her in her arms.

"Gabrian! Gabrian, are you okay? Gabrian, say something!" Rachael whimpers, holding Gabrian by the arms and looks at her through eyes that seem to shift colour every few seconds—blue then green then back to blue again—even her aura swirls different colours. Disoriented and confused, Gabrian thinks that Rachael is the most incredibly beautiful phenomenon she has ever seen.

Gabrian gawks around at her surroundings and notices people lying on the ground all around her. *Oh, my word, what is going on here?* she screams inside her head; unable to make a sound, her words choke her. Her lips continue to mouth out silent questions while her head pivots slowly, twisting from side to side abnormally far. Her eyes remain wide and unblinking—afraid to close, even briefly as her mind attempts to rationalize the calamity erupting around her.

Vaeda looks to Rachael and asks her to reach out to the Elders of Derkaz and Boragen to tell them they are summoned by the Lady of Zephyr who is need of their assistance. Quickly, the connections are made and the message is conveyed.

Rachael returns her focus to her friend and reaches out with her hand to take hold of Gabrian's chin, looking completely terrified. She gently turns Gabrian's face so that she can look her in the eye and make direct contact with her brain.

"Gabrian, are you okay?" she calmly whispers.

Gabrian nods up and down to signify that she is fine as her eyes go back to scanning all the people on the ground. Her heart races and her fingers feel like they are getting warm, really warm. She looks down to see faint sparks shoot from her fingertips. Her heart lurches in her chest and tremors begin to weave their way through her bottom lip. She bites down against the shaking flesh to make it still and curls her fingers under her sleeves as not to draw attention to herself any more than she already has.

What the hell is going on? her mind screams again. *Why are there people lying on the ground and sparks coming from my fingers?*

Rachael straightens Gabrian's face around with determination and looks her in the eye again. "Are you injured in any way?"

Gabrian shakes her head no.

"We need to go now. Everything will be taken care of," she informs evenly.

We are in the middle of the park with people lying

everywhere, possibly dead. Gabrian watches her friend's cool disposition and ponders, *How can she be so calm?*

"Taken care of?" Gabrian manages to gather enough sanity to speak. "What do you mean 'taken care of'? What about all these people? Why are they on the ground?"

As Gabrian expresses her concerns, Rachael listens to something inaudible to Gabrian then mouths words in reply that Gabrian cannot hear. Rachael's eyes and aura begin to shift colour, catching Gabrian's attention. Multiple auras surround her and swirl in chaotic rhythms. Rachael ends her private incantation, and her eyes regain focus on Gabrian.

"They will be fine, don't worry," Rachael assures as she looks over her shoulder in Vaeda's direction. "But we need to get you out of here before anyone finds you." She grabs Gabrian's arm with a bit more authority than normal and hurries her out of the park.

"Before who finds me, the police?" her voice squeaks.

Turning her head back around to look at the bodies again, Gabrian sees forms appearing out of a ripple in the air, and her heart rate surges. There are two of them—men. One is surrounded by a dark-violet aura with a blackish haze and the other wears an aura the colour of grey mist.

The man with the Grey aura pulls strands of the light from himself, wrapping the threads around the wrist of one of the people lying on the ground. Watching closely, Gabrian notices that the strand of light brightens briefly and then disappears. Repeating the process again and again, the man continues. The other summons what looks like spheres of blackened-violet light in both his hands then fires them at the ground surrounding the bodies, creating what looks like a barrier between them and the Earth that has grown oddly dark and murky.

"Gabrian, please, we have to go."

Chapter Nine

Confessions of Truth

SITTING ON THE corner of her couch in the fetal position, Gabrian rocks back and forth. In the kitchen, Rachael stands by the counter, preparing a large cup of coffee, hoping that it will help the situation somehow and uses this alone time to consult with the Elders.

Gabrian is struggling and in a state of shock, Rachael stresses to everyone. *To her, none of this makes any sense. Forgive me if I offend anyone, but I believe you are being cruel to keep her in the dark any longer.*

We understand your concern for your friend, Rachael, but we need to take into account whether or not she would be able to handle the knowledge that would be bestowed upon her, Ariah calmly vocalizes but hearing nothing more than excuses, Rachael clenches her small delicate fist around the metal teaspoon, turning her knuckles white as she tries to stay in control of her words.

"Handle it?" Rachael shrills outloud, her green eyes flare open as her hand slaps across her mouth. She rushes to the kitchen entry and peeks around the opening, hoping her sudden outburst in reaction to the elder's obvious hesitation has not drawn any unnecessary attention to the private meeting taking place. Taking a breath, she continues in a low forced whisper. "You are concerned if she can handle it or not?"

Rachael, please understand that this is not an easy decision and must be dealt with in the best interest of everyone involved, Ariah tries to reason.

Knowing that she is completely stepping above her station in Fellowship order—and most likely disrespecting the Elders by speaking up—Rachael cannot help it. She just cannot believe that the decision makers of her realm are not more concerned.

"Everyone involved?" Rachael quietly articulates, gritting her teeth and trying to gain some restraint on her emotions. "Elders, I know that you are all trying to figure this out diplomatically, but the reality is, Gabrian just took down three humans unknowingly and nearly left them for the Gargons to devour," Rachael says, stating the obvious. "If I had not found her when I did, those people would have been as good as gone."

Ariah, a bit taken aback by Rachael's boldness, makes it a point to remind her of her subordination. *Rachael, that is quite enough!*

Ariah, she is right, Vaeda intervenes. *If Rachael had not have been there, Gabrian may have stolen more of the human's life force than could have been restored. Cimmerian's and Ethan's quick entrance kept things from getting worse and by sealing the ground, Cimmerian was able to contain the Darkness, not allowing the Gargons to steal the remaining life energy. But now that of course opens a whole new situation that I must contend with, namely Cimmerian,* Vaeda admitted anxiously.

Orroryn, who has been quietly listening in from the shadows of the dimly-lit kitchen, speaks in a hushed tone as to not alert Gabrian of his presence. "Never mind Cimmerian, he is of no concern. Did the humans recover? That loss will cause more of a disruption than anything else."

Ethan was able to restore most of their energy, Vaeda informs him. *He took them aside and placed them on the benches nearby. He compelled them to believe that they were tired and in need of a rest thereafter eliminating the memory of seeing Gabrian or collapsing to the ground. Luckily, it was an isolated group of people, no witnesses.*

"We were lucky this time," Orroryn reminds them. "I think the youngling is right. It is time to bring Gabrian into the light and hopefully guide her into understanding. The alternative could be catastrophic," he says in a hushed tone, letting the words spill out across his folded hands as they press tightly against the straight drawn line of his lips. His sea-green eyes are attentive and still, like the calming before a storm.

Realizing that she is spending way too much time making the coffee, Rachael interrupts the conversation. "I have been gone too long. I need to get back to her before she gets suspicious of anything."

Rachael releases her grip on the spoon, dropping it on the counter. She grabs the mug from the cupboard and heads toward the living room where Gabrian is still seated. She reaches out and hands her the large cup of steaming coffee which she willingly accepts. Still half-frozen and soaking wet from the sudden shower of rain on the walk home, she welcomes the warmth, and wraps her hands carefully around it.

"How are you doing? Are you okay?"

Is she crazy asking me that? Gabrian thinks. After walking home in total silence with Rachael, she is not sure what to say or how even to begin a rational conversation without sounding completely insane.

"What do you think, Rach? No, I am not okay!" she snaps at Rachael and stares in disbelief of her indifference. "In what world would I even remotely be okay?"

Rachael seems so calm and reserved that she is making me a bit uneasy, Gabrian contemplates. *Why is she not freaking out like I am? Did she not see what I did?*

Rachael sits down beside her and places her hand on Gabrian's shoulder, giving her a look of sympathy.

"I do not want your sympathy, Rachael. I just want to know what the heck is going on."

Gabrian desperately tries to tell herself that she should not be so harsh with Rachael. She has been her best friend and sole confidant for a long time. She has always been there for her, never faltering. But this particular circumstance calls for a bit more bite than bark.

"I know things must be a bit confusing for you," Rachael says, her eyes shimmer from the tears welling up in them while her lips purse together—dipping in the corners as she mourns for her friend and watches her fumble helplessly—now drowning of ignorance in her own life.

"Do you think?" Gabrian squawks at her. "Nothing makes sense to me, Rach, and everything seems to be just a bit out of control." She stops rocking and gets up out of her fetal position then stares at Rachael with a pleading look. "I don't do out of control! So right now, I am really grasping for some kind of rationality here."

Rachael reaches out and touches Gabrian's hand, hoping to calm her down.

"What is the last thing you remember before you saw me?"

Taking a deep breath, and trying to compose herself so that she can attempt to recall her actions, Gabrian searches her memory but realizes she cannot actually recall much. At least nothing that can contribute to what took place in the park.

"I...I remember talking to you on the phone and telling you that I was going to go for a run," Gabrian starts and takes a moment to gather her scattered thoughts. "I remember entering the park and noticing all the people that were out tonight. I saw a couple sitting on a bench, and I remember wondering if I would ever find someone," Gabrian admits sadly. "Then I saw..." She stops quickly debating whether or not she is going to let Rachael in on the secret of her unusual gift of seeing lights around people. *She probably thinks I am insane now anyway, but I am not sure if I want to hand over the key to my white-padded room just yet.*

She considers her options.

"You see what?" Rachael pushes her question.

"Um...I see..." She stumbles for something to tell her friend but cannot. After that moment, everything becomes a blur of strange images that she cannot make heads or tale of. She decides to continue as best as she can.

"Well, I see you." Gabrian looks up at Rachael and confesses. "And I see people lying on the ground all around me." The vision of the lifeless people hammers her immediately with an unnerving feeling, making her feel nauseated. Her free hand rushes upward, covering her mouth. "Oh, my word, the people, what happened to those people...why did we walk away and leave them like that?" She begins to rock again, holding her head in her hands.

"You see me and the people...what is the next thing you can recall?" Rachael continues her inquiry without answering

66

Gabrian's concerns.

Gabrian stops rocking immediately. Her brow twists, wrinkling the edges of her eyes, and she whirls her head to the side, glancing over at Rachael. Confused as to why she is not addressing her questions, suddenly she recalls something else.

"Who was that tall woman in the park? The one that was shimmering and practically invisible?" She shakes her head in disbelief that those words actually came out of her mouth. "Was that real or are you about to tell me I am going crazy?"

Rachael pauses, gets up from the couch, and heads for the kitchen.

Gabrian has the sneaky suspicion that the reason she walked away is because she is doing that strange thing she did earlier—where she silently converses with the voices in her head.

Watching Rachael fiddle around in the kitchen while making more coffee, Gabrian notices the colour of her aura continuously changes and swirls, different from her normal iridescent colour.

"Because if I am going crazy..." Gabrian shouts out toward the kitchen where Rachael stands. "That would make my life a whole lot easier, and it would explain why I saw two men appear out of nowhere when you rushed me out of the park!"

Waiting for a reaction, Rachael's aurora borealis display of lights in the kitchen quickly stops shifting so violently. It becomes more stable, and Rachael turns around to face Gabrian.

"You do not remember anything else...anything unusual that you might have seen or felt?" she asks more insistent like she knows something, but she is waiting for Gabrian to say it first.

Is she kidding me? Gabrian scoffs in disbelief. "Anything else?" Everything in her body urges her to tell Rachael about the energies. It aches for her to let out some of the crazy and share it with someone, even if they do not understand, just so that she does not have to bear it all alone. *It is Rachael, she loves you,* her mind tells her. *She is your best friend. She will help you figure it out.*

Tell her! it screams.

"I saw lights," she exhales her words cautiously—unburdening herself from the crushing weight within them.

"You saw lights?" Rachael slowly approaches Gabrian as she speaks. "What kind of lights, Gabrian?"

"I saw lights around the people...I can see auras, okay? I saw them in the park. That is the last thing I remember before seeing you." Gabrian curls her head down in defeat and buries her face in her forearms, waiting for Rachael to start laughing at her and reach for the phone to call the looney bin. But Rachael does not.

"Gabrian, how long have you been seeing the auras?"

Slowly lifting her head, Gabrian looks up and stares at Rachael with wide red eyes—blurry and filled with wetness. Her bottom lip trembles as relief washes over her in violent tremors, registering the seriousness resonating in Rachael's low unruffled voice. *Does she actually believe me and wants to help?* Gabrian debates silently and sits back into the couch, relaxing just a bit.

Gabrian breathes out a slow, weighted breath filled with traces of her building courage, hoping that in these few moments of serenity that Rachael knows something about auras. Better yet, she hopes that she can explain why Gabrian is capable of seeing them.

Chapter Ten

Unexpected Guests

OVER THE NEXT couple hours, Gabrian tells Rachael about when she first started seeing the auras. Still guarded, she leaves out the incident in the kitchen with the demon smoke that came after her and the fact that the ends of her fingers like to periodically shoot out sparks unsure of how much more she can handle today.

While retelling her account of what happened in the park, she tries to explain to Rachael how she not only sees the different colours of the auras but that she can feel the diverse energy levels of them as well.

"It is like they all are different flavours of ice cream," Gabrian explains. "The more energy an aura has, the more colour it exhibits and the more appetizing it becomes to me." Gabrian's pupils begin to dilate at the thought of the colours, and she has to reign herself in from noticing Rachael's as she continues to explain. "It made me feel like I was starving and that I needed to get as close to those auras as I possibly could in order to stop the yearning."

She pauses for a moment and tries to recall what had happened next but nothing is clear. It all seems distorted and smeared like a chalk painting after the rain.

"Everything felt like it slowed down all around me and then

the auras changed," Gabrian reveals. "They began fragmenting, then breaking off from the humans, and coming toward me. I felt alive and elated. Then the next thing I knew, someone was calling my name. I came to, and then, well, you know the rest."

Gabrian gets up off the couch and walks over to the window. Staring out across the city lights, she notices the faded pink and blue hue on the horizon. It is dawn. A few blocks over, she can see the entrance to the park. Tired and unsettled, Gabrian's eyes well up at the memory of people lying lifeless on the ground because of her.

A slight movement in her peripheral vision catches her attention—something black. Looking closer, she realizes it is a bird, a Raven. Gabrian recalls the recent events and figures it must be the same bird that scared the crap out of her yesterday. It looks at her and hops closer from the balcony's edge. It tilts its head to the right and fluffs its feathers then tilts its head the other way as if it is trying to figure her out.

"Dumb bird!" Gabrian grumbles, still angry with it for startling her. She turns her back to the window and slowly lowers herself onto the floor, placing her head on her knees while gently hugging her legs.

Rachael watches Gabrian from across the room, still confused as to why she displays Borrower behaviours. Then Rachael realizes she has definitely been left out of the loop as to what her friend's true heritage is. Rachael decides it is time the Elders step in and help her explain to her best friend that she is not going crazy. The only trouble with this is that the revelation of who she truly is may indeed cause her logically-wired friend to lose her mind.

While Gabrian sits by the window, quietly lost in her thoughts for a few moments, Rachael takes advantage of the opportunity to speak with the Elders. She gets up from the couch and moves back into the kitchen, deciding to make some food for them while she reaches out to make contact again.

As her eyes begin to shift from green to varying shades of blue, she swims within the mental channels and reaches out to find Vaeda and Ariah.

I have been watching Gabrian for a while now, and she is displaying the aura of the Boragen. I realize that clearly I have not

70

been informed properly of what is going on with her, Rachael scolds. *The fact that she has an aura at all was a bit of a surprise, all things considered.*

We are sorry that you were not given all the details before embarking on this passage, Ariah apologizes to Rachael. *But we felt that it was a necessary precaution.*

We felt that the less that you knew, the less chance there was that you would display any energies that might trigger any suspicions in her, Vaeda explains, backing up Ariah's reasoning. *We needed her to completely accept you so that you could stay close to her.*

From the shadows harboring beside the refrigerator, Orroryn's voice gently breaks the silence. "Our actions were not intended to be malicious or cruel, youngling," his voice rumbles softly in Rachael's ears. "We only wanted to protect you both."

Although Rachael has always melted at the sound of Orroryn's voice, she raises her brow and shoots him an icy glare, perturbed about the lack of faith her Elders had in her and the fact Orroryn keeps calling her a 'youngling.' The people of the Vindere Fellowship may not continue as long physically as the other members of the Realm, but are equally aged with experience through numerous lives, and she is not nearly as young as he assumes.

"Fine! Whatever," Rachael snaps, twisting around to face Orroryn. Her eyes narrow and burn with irritation. Throwing her hands up in the air—flicking her wrists to the side—she declares her cease and desist of the matter. "This is way beyond my consolation abilities and what I can do for her. It is time for all of you to make your appearance, and I mean *now*. You need to try and straighten up this mess you made of her life."

Rachael goes back to cooking her toast before Gabrian decides to wander into the kitchen and witness her best friend talking to the shadows. She butters the toast, places it on the plates, and starts toward the living room, but stops quickly and makes one more request of the Elders.

"And can you please use the door when you arrive?" she quizzically insists. "I am not sure how stable Gabrian is right now. If strangers start popping out of portals and emerging out of the shadows from the dark corners of her apartment, I think it may

71

throw her over the edge."

Obliging, the Elders appear just outside Gabrian's doorway in the hall. Vaeda exits the portal last after setting her Raven guide loose just outside the building.

Rachael returns from the kitchen and serves the toast to the table. Gabrian raises her head and notices that Rachael's aura has stopped swirling. It now is her normal light, calm iridescent colour. The other brighter auras are gone, and her eyes are her normal colour of green. She also notices that Rachael seems irritated all of a sudden and hopes she is not to blame for her mental state. Gabrian's conscience has been constantly thinking about the people they left on the ground at the park and since Rachael already seems irritated anyway, she decides she might as well ask her about it again.

She gets up off the floor and ambles to the table. Gabrian pulls the chair out that is in front of one of the plates of toast and sits down, taking a bite. Swallowing it almost whole, she determines that she must be hungrier than she thought. Looking up periodically and gathering her nerve to speak, she stops eating and stares at Rachael who sips on her coffee—her eyes glancing over her shoulder at the door every few seconds.

"Did I kill those people?" Gabrian blurts out without warning.

Rachael jumps a bit at the sudden breach in silence and forcefully pushes down the coffee she has stored in her mouth. Quickly grabbing a napkin from the table, she wipes her lips and tries to register the question that has just been asked.

"What?" Rachael chokes out. "No!" she continues. "Not really."

"Not really?" Gabrian's voice strains as she tries to keep her emotions under control. She exhales a cackled breath as her head begins to bobble on her shoulders with confusion, and she leans back against the chair. Her hands quickly gather up her long dark hair and twists it chaotically into knots between her fingers at the back of her head. "How does someone not really kill someone? Either I did or I didn't."

"You didn't! Okay...you didn't," Rachael ensures her friend and begins to bite on her nails, eagerly awaiting her trio. "You might have though, if I had not found you in time, and if Vaeda had not stopped you."

"Who is Vaeda, and what exactly did she stop me from doing? I don't understand how I did any of this." Gabrian's questions trigger her emotions, and she feels the prickly nettles of hysteria biting at the surface of her skin again. The tips of her fingers tingle, warming around the edges. She pulls her knees up close to her chest and holds them tight in an effort to find a source of comfort. "How could I have hurt them? I don't remember even touching them."

There is a loud knock on the door.

It is about time! Rachael complains silently.

Mind your manners, youngling! Ariah reprimands her curtly in her mind's voice, correcting Rachael's attitude promptly.

I am sorry, Elder Ariah. Forgive me, Rachael retorts humbly as she gets up to answer the door.

"Gabrian, there are some people here I think you should meet," Rachael informs as she slowly opens the door, allowing entrance to the visitors on the other side.

Gabrian cringes and looks for a place to hide as the three majestic strangers promenade into her living space. *Wait a minute! That is Mr. Redmond from my office,* she thinks, recognizing Orroryn right away. *But what is he doing here? And who are those two women with him?* The whites of her eyes bulge uncomfortably in their sockets as her jaw drops, almost unhinged. Swinging her legs down and jumping to her feet—nearly stumbling over herself—Gabrian places the chair directly in front of her, creating a barrier between her and her guests. She digs her fingers into the cushioned backing on the chair in her attempt to stifle the feeling of being excruciatingly vulnerable as she tries to make sense of it all. Mr. Redmond is a lawyer, she remembers—a statistic which does not help her calm down. A lawyer making a house call on a weekend is never a good sign about anything. She panics as her mind races back to the people in the park.

Oh no, the women must be plain clothes officers here to arrest me. She grasps at reason, trying to decide whether or not to try to make a run for it. *What do I do? What do I do?*

"Rachael, can I speak to you for a minute?" she begs.

Rachael walks over to where Gabrian's feet are rooted, now biting the ends off of what is left of her fingernails.

"Why are these people here in my house?" she whispers in a shaky voice, fighting off hysteria.

Clearly seeing that her friend is terrified, Rachael gives Gabrian her best reassuring smile. Taking Gabrian gently by the arm, Rachael guides her to the living room and toward the couch to begin the introductions. All the while, Gabrian continues to look back over her shoulder at the unexpected company that seems to be staying for a bit.

She studies both of the women that follow behind her, oddly preoccupied by how incredibly beautiful they are, each in their own way. The short red-headed one looks a lot like Rachael, whom she has always thought to be flamboyantly gorgeous. And the tall blonde one seems to radiate with flawless beauty and charismatic ease. Gabrian becomes consciously envious of her confident yet humble demeanor.

Vaeda notices that Gabrian is watching and smiles at her sweetly, thinking that she resembles her mother greatly, and a pang of sorrow runs through her as the thought of her friend enters her mind.

A revelation strikes Gabrian as she sits twitching silently on her couch while Rachael seats everyone. She jumps up and in a very loud hysterical voice shouts, "It is her!" Gabrian's arm flies out, directly pointedly in Vaeda's direction. "It is you!" she continues, looking back and forth between Rachael and Vaeda.

She grabs Rachael by the arm and swiftly drags her away from the unwanted crowd, down the hallway, and into her bedroom. Slamming the door hard behind them, Gabrian exhales and leans against it.

"What the hell is going on here, Rach?" she demands, feeling her fingertips burn as they threaten to spark. "That is the woman I saw in the park—the tall blonde one out there."

"Calm down, Gabrian," Rachael says, trying to get her best friend to stop hyperventilating. "Take a deep breath and try to calm down."

"Calm down?" Gabrian jeers at Rachael. "Are you nuts? The last time I saw that woman out there, you know...the tall blonde stranger you just let enter my apartment without my consent, she was pretty much invisible with colours sparkling all around her." She has a flashback to the park and the strange voodoo Magik the two men performed.

"Holy crap!" Gabrian howls as she pulls her hands through her long dark hair and starts to pace. "This is messed up." She stops moving and turns quickly to face Rachael. She walks over to her and clasps her arms with her hands. "Rachael, what are these people doing in my house?" Gabrian glares at Rachael with eyes as wild as nature itself as she demands an explanation.

"Do you trust me?" Rachael hums, hoping she has built a strong enough bond with her that she will say yes. Gabrian squints and looks behind her at the closed door that stands between her and the living room, contemplating her options. Her fingers are still burning. Rachael tilts her head around so she can look Gabrian in the eye. "Do you trust me?"

"I...umm," Gabrian hesitates, unsure of anything right now then answers calmly, "Yes. Of course I do. You know that."

Breathing a sigh of relief, Rachael watches as the grey aura stops flaring so violently around Gabrian as she starts to unwind.

"Then you need to open that door and follow me back out there."

Rachael's words resonate through Gabrian's mind. She loosens the grip her hands have on Rachael, dropping her arms. She reaches for the doorknob and turns it, backing away. She pulls the door slightly ajar, allowing Rachael the choice to leave the room.

Rachael passes in front of her and starts through the open door then stops and looks back at her friend and smiles. "It's going to be okay. I promise."

Now, alone in her room, Gabrian feels completely helpless. With nowhere to run and nowhere to hide, she decides to leave her room and follow Rachael's lead, unknowingly taking the first steps towards a whole new world.

Chapter Eleven

Fight or Flight

THE TREK DOWN the hallway and into her living room is the longest, most difficult journey Gabrian has had to make in years. The closer she gets, the warmer her fingers burn. She is beginning to figure out that this will be the norm every time she gets upset or stressed out. Not knowing if she is the only one who can see it, she pulls her hands into her sleeves to hide them just in case.

By the time she reaches the end of the hall, her heart feels like it is going to explode. Like a nervous child, she stops just before the entrance to the living room and hides, peeking around the corner to try and assess the situation. Her timid eyes are caught by Vaeda.

She is seen and there is no going back now. She pushes her shoulders back and crosses her arms in front of her chest then sullenly walks into the room. All eyes are on her, and she hates it. She glances over at her friend who appears to be completely comfortable amongst these people. With her hand, Rachael pats the cushion beside her, gesturing for Gabrian to come sit on the couch.

Now seated across from her unwelcomed guests, Gabrian listens quietly as Rachael begins to introduce them one by one.

"Gabrian, I would like for you to meet Ariah, Elder to the

Fellowship of Vindere," Rachael says, pointing toward the smaller woman that holds resemblance to herself. "In common English, the Reincarnate Fellowship. This is the fellowship that I belong to."

Fellowship? Belong to? Is she in some kind of cult or strange group that I was unaware of? Gabrian ponders, silently deciding that she is going to make it a point to monitor her future employee's extracurricular activities a little more closely—not to mention screen her choice in friends.

"You already know Orroryn, or Mr. Redmond, as we call him." As she continues, Gabrian notices that Rachael's face flushes slightly as she speaks of Mr. Redmond. "He is the Elder to the Fellowship of Schaeduwe or the Shadows Fellowship better known as Shadow Walkers."

Ah, what did she just say? Shadow What? Gabrian's legs begin to tremble as she feels the angst building within. Her fingers have shifted from a warm tingling sensation to a full-blown burn. She hears Rachael still talking in the background, but Gabrian's mind focuses on trying to decipher what a Shadow Walker might be. All she catches is the word 'Air'.

"Excuse me, I didn't catch that last part." Gabrian giggles unwillingly. The comic book creations that her delusional best friend is trying to feed to her are a bit distracting. "All I heard was something about air." Gabrian closes her eyes and presses firmly against the bridge of her nose, reaching for reasoning while trying to sort through all the deranged details piling up inside of her mind. She hungers for some type of understanding of how any of this could make sense.

Vaeda interjects when it comes time for her portion of the introductions in a sultry voice. "I am Vaeda, the Elder to the Fellowship of Zephyr. We are the Air Fellowship as we are one with the wind."

Not knowing what to say to that, Gabrian just raises her eyebrows and nods her head slowly.

"Gabrian, we are friends of your parents, Sarapheane and Jarrison. Ariah, Vaeda, and I have known them all our lives for they too are people of the Realm from the Schaeduwe Fellowship like me. We have existed in each other's presence for eons, training in the ways of the Schaeduwe. Our ancestors are descendants of the ancients and act as the Guardians to the Covenant."

78

Gabrian freezes, the small rapport she had built with this man has now been obliterated by the words spewing out of his mouth. *He seemed so normal.* She shifts her view to Rachael. *She seemed so normal too.* She sits in a stupefied state, playing a tennis match with her eyes as she looks back and forth between them all, completely at a loss. She becomes brutally aware she is in a room surrounded by strangers who are absolutely, undeniably off their rockers.

Gabrian chews on her bottom lip as she contemplates how she ended up in this situation—youngest Valedictorian in her graduating class to date, undisputable ability to detect those in need of help in the reality department, and an obsessive need to be in control of all aspects in her life to a fault. How was Rachael able to fly under the radar and get close enough to her that she was able to put Gabrian in a situation this deranged—and possibly psychopathically dangerous?

Unsure of what else to do, Gabrian slowly stands up. Smiling her best I-need-to-get-me-the-Hell-out-of-here smile, she studies her route of escape and hopes to make it to the door of her apartment before any type of violent reaction breaks out with these people.

Rachael, having witnessed every altering mood-swing since the time she met Gabrian, senses her escalating anxiety. She takes note of how Gabrian's new, permanent grey aura, swirls and whips itself around her like a veil of protection and realizes what may come next—she is going to try and make a break for it.

"She is going to run!" Rachael yells just as Gabrian quickly darts toward the door.

Flying full speed across the room, she reaches for the doorknob and fumbles with it but manages to open it. With the door wide open, and the small glimpse of freedom in front of her, Gabrian bursts forward and tries to run through the open frame. In the same instant, Vaeda speaks in Zephyr tongue and curls her fingers gently inward.

"Claustra solidus," she whispers, and Gabrian slams into an invisible wall manifested by the will of Vaeda's words, knocking her backward onto the floor. Panicked and running on pure adrenaline, Gabrian picks herself back up for another try at escape.

"Silozan Dvarah!" Vaeda continues and the door of

Gabrian's apartment slams shut before she can reach it. As the door closes, Orroryn instinctively reaches for the hem of the shadow beside him and pulls it across his massive body. Almost instantaneously, he expels himself out of the darkened contour of the entry leading to the door. He thrusts his hand outward and twists the knob on the straight bolt before Gabrian can stand, halting her exit plans.

Holy crap! You are going to die! her mind screams, eliminating any chance of rational thought. Staring at the massive wall of man before her—and knowing the sparkly wicked witch of the west is behind her—Gabrian decides it is fight-or-flight time, and her survival instincts take over. Flashes of the bodies from the park swirl dizzily within her memory, blinding her sight with the visions of those left lying lifeless. She rushes into her mind and rips at the sensations that surround her, figuring it may be her only way out.

If she can take out three people without even trying, she can conjure up whatever is in her to slow down these crazies.

Concentrating feverishly, she feels the tip of the familiar hunger that consumed her in the midst of her delirium and grasps for it. Her eyes widen brightly and her pupils open with desire, dilating as before as she focuses on the taste of the auras she feels emanating in her home. She only senses three. There should be four, but Mr. Redmond has none, nor can she feel any kind of energy from him. None the less, she focuses on the three visible auras and inhales deeply. Immediately, she sees the colours begin to fracture and twirl. Delighted with her accomplishment, she draws in her breath again, tasting the energy as it arrives.

Realizing what is happening, and amazed at how powerful Gabrian has become so quickly, Orroryn swiftly moves into action. In an attempt to try and obstruct Gabrian's link to the auras, he grabs her and holds her tightly within his arms, hoping to alert Vaeda before it is too late.

Gabrian's sight blackens. Although she cannot see any longer, she can still taste the life in the room, and pushes her senses more desperately toward her intentions.

"Vaeda, she is draining your essence and quickly!" he yells at her. "We have to do something before she loses herself again!"

Now aware that she and her accomplices are in danger from

this wild youngling, she tries to reach Gabrian with her words.

"Gabrian, please stop. I know you are scared, but we are only here to help you." Any attempt to reach Gabrian is in vain, and Vaeda's pleas go unnoticed. Gabrian is not listening anymore; she is barely coherent. The amount of white energy she has already drawn in has sent her into a frenzied state of incoherence. Most Borrowers are taught to regulate themselves when they feed—which even for the experienced is a test in itself and difficult to control. The fact that Gabrian is green and has no knowledge of what she is doing makes her an extreme danger to them. If she is able to draw in too much of their essence, she can send them all into a comatose state where they would have to contend with the Gargons—not a battle Vaeda feels like fighting today.

"She is not responding to you, Vaeda," Ariah exclaims. "Take her out before it is too late." Rachael whips her head around, startled by her Elder's unexpectedly candid behaviour and grasps the scale of their ordeal.

Vaeda feels the effect of her depleting essence draining on her efforts and sighs, wishing she did not have go forth with what she must do. She had hoped for a more productive first meeting. Reluctantly, knowing this is her only option, she closes her eyes and points her index finger toward the youngling. She swirls her hand counterclockwise and lowly murmurs her command.

"Earem Silpnas," she breathes out her cryptic words laced with remorse. She had hoped it would not lead to this.

Gabrian feels the density of the air start to change around her, but she pushes it back and inhales with a vengeance. Her fingers flare with the mounting intensity of her frustrations as the Magik takes its effect, pulling her down from her enraptured state. She clings to the edges of light and forces her senses to wrap tightly around any and all tastes of energy.

Rachael's dwindling essence holds her captive to Gabrian's desire. She watches helplessly from the living room as her friend drains them all of their life and simultaneously duels it out against the Magik of the Elders. She stands wide-eyed and statuesque, pressing her delicate hands against her mouth—biting down hard upon her tongue in confliction of wanting to help her friend—but her need to survive keeps her silent. Watching the powerful gift of her young friend stand its ground against the practiced forces of

81

the Elders is quite intriguing and unsettling at the same time.

Impressed too by Gabrian's ability to resist her Magik, Vaeda speaks again, but her words carry more conviction this time.

"Retrahere Earem! Termanato Vapir, es Silpnas," she articulates. Her incantation bites its way through, and Gabrian senses something is different. In this distraction, her intense desire to pull on the essences starts to waver. The air around her tastes stale. The weight in her lungs becomes heavy, she cannot gather enough oxygen and begins to cough. Orroryn, still holding her, gets ready to brace her when she falls.

Still terrified of what her captors might do to her, she continues to fight, but her coughing is getting harder, casting spots against Darkness where light fragments used to be. Feeling helpless, weak, and barely able to hold onto her consciousness, her eyes search the room in hopes to find Rachael one last time. Finding only blackness, she releases her feeble grip of the auras and slips into the Darkness that surrounds her.

"Well, that did not go very well!" Rachael spits out, falling back into the chair behind her as she feels an instant release on her essence. Her heart aches with the bitter probability that she may have just driven away her best friend forever. Realizing she is still amongst her Elders, she quickly covers her mouth. Her curt comment should have remained silent and in her head.

Orroryn turns his head toward her, looking down the bridge of his nose. The emerald sheen in his eyes flares and the seriousness exuding from them catches on her conscience somewhere deep within. Rachael's face flushes at her inoperable shut up button and lack of discipline.

"Yesterday, I met with Sarapheane and Jarrison. They have been made aware of our suspicions, and I have been asked to bring her home to them if drastic measures were made necessary," Orroryn announces to his audience. "Depending on how she responds to her parents' intervention, Rachael, you may have to make the necessary adjustments to her professional schedule. There is no need to cause any unnecessary suspicions from her sudden and hopefully, temporary disappearance from her human life."

"Yes, I agree, Orroryn," Vaeda states, striding toward the couch where Orroryn has lain Gabrian's limp body. She reaches her hand out and strokes Gabrian's brow, gently removing the hair that has fallen onto her face during the struggle. Vaeda sighs in discontent then raises her weary eyes upward to her counterparts.

"The unfortunate occurrence here today will be kept from the other members of the Covenant. They are already in conflict about what actions should be taken due to Gabrian's recent ascension into the Realm. I see no need to cause any more unnecessary discontents until we can find a way to enlighten Gabrian about who she truly is and remove any fear of her new-found world."

All those who remained standing in Gabrian's apartment agreed in unison. Orroryn approaches the couch. Dipping down, he slides his hands beneath her helpless form and cradles her securely within his arms. He inches out with the tips of his fingers and touches the cusp of the Veil, tugging at its edges knowingly. With a heavy heart, he pulls its Magik effortlessly around himself and his precious cargo then vanishes into the shadows.

Chapter Twelve

A Measure of Silence

UPON A LARGE amethyst-speckled boulder, Cimmerian, the Elder of the Derkaz Fellowship, sits quietly, staring down at the darkened patch of ground beneath him—a section of barren Earth that still to this day holds no life-sustaining qualities; not even the sun bothers to shine there. Deep in thought, still grieving the loss of his only daughter all those years ago, he opens his moistened eyes and returns to the present.

"Lady of Zephyr," he solemnly announces—narrowing his eyes and gritting his teeth as he discretely wipes the dampness blurring his vision before turning around to face his peer on her arrival. With the Elder of the Boragen Fellowship, Ethan Borne, behind her and her Raven guide at her side, Vaeda steps out from the bending air. The Raven takes to the sky then perches itself in the nearest tree in order to keep everyone in its sights. The bird rumbles a throaty caw as it voices its evident irritation with Ethan's presence.

"Does he always have to act like that?" Ethan grumbles to Vaeda as he glares up at the Raven. She laughs at his annoyance with her friend then glances up at her guide, acknowledging his concern but silences him with a wave of her hand.

"You know what he is like when it comes to the Boragen—

always on duty. Always letting me know when you are near."

Shaking his head, Ethan rolls his eyes. "Maybe then he should learn how to tell the good from the bad." Ethan turns his attention elsewhere, closing his eyes to concentrate. His grey Borrower aura surfaces around him and flickers as he sends out his essence to seek out energies of any unwanted listeners.

Noticing Ethan's aura expanding around them, Cimmerian crosses his arms across his chest and watches him.

"What? You do not trust me, Ethan?" Cimmerian says with a sneer.

Ignoring Cimmerian's comment for the moment, he continues his search. Once satisfied they are alone, Ethan pulls his aura back into itself, and with a disarming smile, he looks back at Cimmerian. "Not everything is about you, Cimmerian. Vaeda requested that we speak in private, and that is what I am trying to ensure."

From within the Darkness of the encasing woods behind them, a loud snap silences their banter. Instinctively, Ethan's aura flares out to determine if this interruption is friend or foe; his muscles tense in anticipation of treachery. Unable to detect any signs of who or what lies in wait, the tension grows. Then, from the Shadowy Veil, emerges a familiar muscular silhouette—a Guardian.

Vaeda's face lights up at this unexpected arrival as she immediately recognizes his form. "Tynan, I did not know that you were going to be joining us." Her voice wavers as she tries to hide the wildness of her pulse so as to not give away the excitement of seeing him. But looking directly into his eyes, she gasps at his raw exotic beauty that has always made her breath quicken. Her efforts are useless. The Schaeduwe have a reputation throughout the Realm of stealing hearts with just a glance, and she did not want to allow anyone to know how true it was. "We were expecting Orroryn."

Stepping out of the shadows and into clear view, Tynan stands before them—larger than life, at attention, and as ever, on duty.

"Orroryn has asked me to step in on his behalf and to accompany you, Lady of Zephyr, as he is still otherwise engaged." His words are warm and soothing. "I hope that is not overstepping any bounds."

Vaeda shakes her head no, unable to catch her breath at the sight of him, and gleams in appreciation of his presence. She continues to gaze upon him in fear that he will disappear again if she dares look away.

Cimmerian clears his throat at the display.

"Would you two like to be alone?" he heckles the couple as he crosses his slender arms, tucking them tightly in front of his abdomen. He would much rather get on with the meeting and be rid of this unwanted exchange of words, not to mention the company.

Vaeda tears her eyes away from her muse, and her face grows with light traces of crimson just beneath her flesh. She quickly turns to face Cimmerian with an upheld commanding eye but a gentle grin, while Tynan stands with his shoulders back and chin held high, undaunted by the sarcastic remark. Ethan masks his amusement by covering his mouth with his hand, trying hard to hide his smirk.

"Of course not, do not be so snide," she replies, tucking her hair behind her ear as she returns her attention to the task at hand. She glides forward a few feet closer to Cimmerian.

"I have asked you all here today to discuss the assistance that I required yesterday in the park."

"You mean the cleanup job we had to do thanks to the wild Boragen youngling that is on the loose?" Cimmerian says in a haughty tone.

Ethan rolls his eyes at Cimmerian's lack of diplomacy and tries to address the subject in a statelier manner. "How did this go unnoticed, especially by her parents? They must have had some indication that she was more than human."

"We have kept an eye on her ever since she was brought to Sarapheane and Jarrison. Until recently, there was never any reason to believe otherwise," Vaeda tries to explain credibly, joining her hands together loosely in front of her. She levels the sound of her voice—maintaining direct eye contact—not wanting to reveal any cracks in her little white lie.

"She is a danger to all of us." Cimmerian huffs angrily. "She has displayed the characteristics of the Vampiric fever already. This must be dealt with immediately before she becomes a nightmare. I am quite certain that none of us here want to go down that road again."

"It will not come to that, Cimmerian, I assure you," Vaeda declares firmly. "We have made arrangements for her to stay with her parents. They can watch her and hopefully explain what may be happening to her in a more comfortable environment than we can provide for her." Vaeda grimaces, remembering their earlier failed attempt to enlighten the child.

"If I can assist in any way, let me know," Ethan interjects, stepping forward into the strained conversation. He brushes his hand lightly against her arm, extending his willingness to lend any invaluable experience that he has to offer. "The earlier they can reach her and help her to find control, the better. Ignorance of her powers can lead to a dark place very quickly, especially if she is a natural."

Vaeda knows that both Ethan's and Cimmerian's concerns are valid, but she needs just a little more time to give Gabrian the chance to find herself before the other Elders of the Covenant of Shadows find her first. She sighs despairingly, pitying the girl and the hard task that lies before her.

"I agree with both of you. Regardless of what has happened, I implore you both to keep this incident quiet until we can diffuse the situation and have a chance to speak with the girl in a more rational manner. Hopefully, we can bring her to an understanding and an acceptance of who she is without causing any more unnecessary adversity."

Ethan quickly agrees with Vaeda and gives her his word of silence while Cimmerian scornfully introduces Vaeda to the conditions of his agreement. "I will be silent for now but get her under control quickly or I will not hesitate to take this straight to the House and let them all know how much of a danger she is," Cimmerian's eyes narrow and his nostrils flare. His hand draws upward, pointing a long bony finger in her face, almost touching the end of her chin, as he growls out his warning. "I have no loyalties to the Boragen, especially one who is out of control."

Vaeda understands his concerns and is grateful for his collaboration, even with his unsympathetic stipulations. "I appreciate your cooperation," she says to Cimmerian, seeing the contempt in his eyes. "I will alert both of you if anything arises."

Turning back to her silent Guardian, she smiles and releases

Tynan of his duty, insisting that he return to his post at the Gate on the Shadow's Edge. "Thank you, Tynan, I shall take my leave now. Please inform Orroryn and the Shadwells that I will see them momentarily."

"Of course, my lady," Tynan hums sweetly; his eyes meet hers respectfully then he sidles back toward the dark side of the brush and slips back into the shadows.

Vaeda inhales deeply and pretends that his retreat does not affect her. She turns back to face Ethan. "Shall we?" she asks her escort, pressing her palms forward in front of where they stand, creating a gap a foot's width apart.

"Toran!" Vaeda whispers softly.

The air between her hands begins to twist and swirl, creating a whirlwind of energy from the air in front of her. The air begins to bend and bubble around itself, manifesting into a portal that will allow Ethan to return back to his private counsel office in town.

"After you," Ethan says politely, but she hesitates.

"You go ahead, Ethan. I will be right behind you."

Ethan nods then steps into the midst of the portal and disappears. Her Raven guide gurgles from above in appreciation of his departure. She turns to Cimmerian who wrinkles his nose at her.

"I know that you have much sorrow." She inches forward, encroaching on his space. "Your memories must burn like fire in your heart, and I am sorry for that, but I need you to find it within yourself to have some compassion for this child. We have failed her as a society. It is up to us to try and make it right."

Becoming agitated with Vaeda's sympathy for him, he glares at her with cold, black eyes. "I shall do as you request, but I will also do what I must if you cannot contain this wild youngling. I will not have innocent blood on my hands," he barks at Vaeda sternly, his eyes glistening with emotions refusing to be contained any longer. His hands rub at each other as if to cleanse themselves of their invisible stains. "Not again. Do you understand me?"

"Yes, of course," she says softly as sadness overcomes her, realizing how miserable Cimmerian must truly be. "Thank you, Cimmerian." She reaches out and touches him gently on the arm then rushes back toward the swirling vortex of air that awaits her and waves to her Raven guide. He promptly descends from the trees to rest at her side and together they melt into the portal.

Chapter Thirteen

Out from Beneath

ATOP THE BEGOTTEN lifeless Earth that rests mere inches behind Cimmerian, a blackened mist—darkened with thick and poisonous toxins pulled from the netherworld—begins to ooze from the midst of the desolate void. Climbing and twisting upward, it writhes slowly, taking a form resembling a human. The cynical sound of laughter jars Cimmerian from his present state of mind, and he realizes that he is no longer alone.

"Hello, dear Cimmerian," the creature hisses, its vaporous face sneering as Cimmerian revolves toward his unexpected company. "Long time no see!"

In disbelief, all Cimmerian can do is stare, his mouth gaped open. "Adrinn...but how could this be?" he stutters his words. Not because he speaks to an apparition but of whom it is. "You are supposed to be dead. She destroyed you, and we sent your body to rot in Erebus. This is not possible!"

Cimmerian's shock quickly fades. His pale white face alters into a crimson glow while his nostrils flare as emotions change into anger. He feels the blood in his veins begin to boil with hatred, remembering with clarity the night he stood in this very spot and watched this thing destroy his only daughter. Her naive and desperate effort to save this fiend, managed to pull her into the depths of Darkness with him.

"You murderer!" he shrieks at Adrinn, raising his hands to strike him down. Cimmerian's aura of deep violet begins to swirl and intensify as his pupils widen so large they swallow up all colour of his brown irises, becoming completely black. Great blackened spheres of energy emerge from the palms of his hands, and he immediately directs their focus toward the murky mirage of a man that stands before him. The energy orbs pass completely through Adrinn and sear the sides of the tree behind him. Cimmerian growls at his failed attempts and realizes that he must draw from deep within to conjure up the dark Magik needed to attack this monster.

Adrinn's face is wiped clean of its smugness for the moment. He knows that Cimmerian holds the advantage and can seal him back into the Darkness, delaying his efforts.

"Wait, Cimmerian!" Adrinn shouts.

Cimmerian's eyes blaze—filled with fire and lusting to destroy him once and for all.

"Wait for what, Vampire?" Cimmerian's breath heaves in his chest, but he forces it to steady—attempting to maintain control over his enraged fury. His vision reddens with hatred and the violet hue hovering over the center of his palms sizzles with desire for revenge—awaiting the moment of onslaught. "What could you possibly have to say to me that would make me not want to kill you?"

"She is not dead!" he yelps at his adversary, conjuring up his own Magik.

The deep violet hue hovering around Cimmerian sparks brightly at the words. He falters only briefly, but his stance remains rigid as his eyes bore into the devil in his sights.

"What did you just say?"

"She is not dead," Adrinn enunciates flatly as he wins the battle for Cimmerian's attention.

Cimmerian temporarily halts his attack but remains guarded. The orbs dissipate, but his hands still hold the spark—the necessary energy in order to thrust Adrinn back into the depths of Darkness from where he has ascended.

"I do not know how you have managed to avoid being devoured by the Gargons, or how you have pulled yourself out of the depths of Erebus, but let me make something very clear to you—I have no pity for you, so choose your words wisely as they may be your last."

Even with Cimmerian's threats, Adrinn knows he has a

slight upper hand. He tries to suppress his ever-growing delight of the situation, but as his sinister nature returns, so does his leery grin. He begins to chip away at Cimmerian's rage so that he will not be enticed to send him back—at least not until he gets what he has returned for.

"She is safe," Adrinn hums and tilts his hand from side to side, in resemblance to the balancing of a scale. "She is still surrounded by the wards you placed upon her right before she was dragged down into the Darkness."

Cimmerian's face twitches as he speaks which cues Adrinn to remember that he is still dealing with a ticking time bomb and he needs to be gentle with his words about her so called untimely demise.

"She is alive, but I fear very weak."

"If it were not for you, she would not have needed the wards," Cimmerian lashes out at Adrinn, his rage building again. "If it was not for you and your cunning ways, she would not have made herself so vulnerable to the Gargons' Darkness."

"She did that on her own accord, Cimmerian. I had nothing to do with that," Adrinn argues, trying to reason with him. He quickly realizes that this is probably a dangerous and moot point.

"She was young and impressionable; you should have left her alone," Cimmerian scolds Adrinn, pointing his finger at him. Feeling the pressure beneath his eyes building, he presses his fingers against the bridge of his nose and pinches it. Then lets his hand drop, sliding it down across the front of his face and rests it over his heart—clenching the cloth beneath at the pull of sadness creeping into his chest.

"We were both young, Cimmerian," Adrinn reminds him.

Beginning to pace and trying to regain his composure, Cimmerian realizes that this may all be a convoluted lie that Adrinn is feeding him. But what if it is not? He would never forgive himself if he had a chance to save his daughter and did not take it.

"How do I get her out?" Cimmerian's arms drop to his sides, hands trembling but no longer ignited.

A wide smile stretches boldly across Adrinn's face. He raises a blurry likeness of a hand and scolds Cimmerian with his index finger in a condescending wag.

"Ah, ah, ah!" he taunts. "Not so quick. Now it is my turn to ask a few questions."

Irritated by Adrinn's sudden change in attitude, Cimmerian's aura whips around him wildly, but he remains silent, gnawing the inside of his cheek.

"I overheard you conversing about a wild youngling earlier. Who is she?"

Cimmerian's brow furrows at the request but holding no loyalties to the youngling, he does not feel any need to protect her. However, disclosing information about a potential Vampire to an actual existing one does not really give him a warm and fuzzy feeling either. He had promised Vaeda he would not disclose any information about her to the Covenant of Shadows, but she said nothing about the undead. Balancing the weight of his accordance with Vaeda against the profound possibility that he may someday save his daughter—even if it means conceding to the requests of the monster that he helped destroy—seems a clear, obvious choice to him.

"The youngling we spoke of was an infant that had been rescued from the aftermath of the night of your demise," Cimmerian begins. "Thought to be human and orphaned, Cera gathered up the girl and gave her to Sarapheane and Jarrison Shadwell to care for. Up until recent events, she had shown no signs of being anything other than human."

"So Cera found her?" Adrinn mumbles to himself and slithers aimlessly around the barren Earth in thought. "Hm."

Cimmerian ceases with his reiteration of what he knows about the girl and begins to stare at the vaporish menace. He watches as the thing becomes oblivious to his presence—momentarily lost somewhere in thought—and wonders why in the realm this monster is so consumed with her story.

"What interest do you have in this girl?"

Adrinn halts his course and meets Cimmerian's curious stare.

"You mentioned that she is wild and untrained. Is that correct?"

"Yes, she was thought to be merely human, so she was never enlightened to the knowledge of the Realm," Cimmerian discloses.

Adrinn clasps his hands together in front of his face and

presses them tightly against his lips as his mouth draws up widely at the sides. He begins to circle Cimmerian's body like a shark that has just caught the scent of blood in the water.

"Well, my dear man, in order for me to rescue your beloved Symone, I will need energy—much more than I have now," Adrinn admits. "And since Cera was so kind as to have my gifts bound, restricting my ability to obtain my own energy, I am in need of a donor."

"So what does this have to do with the girl?"

"Considering that most Borrowers within the Realm are aware of the story of whom and what I am, it would be quite unlikely that one of them would be willing to have anything to do with me, let alone want to give me their essence. Most likely they would probably react with the same display that you did when we began this conversation."

Cimmerian nods his head in concurrence with Adrinn's reasoning, still unsure of his true intentions toward the girl.

"She is vulnerable and will be angry about her parent's deception. Chances are, she will rebel as most children do. If I can somehow manage to befriend her and earn her allegiance then maybe I can also sway her to lend me some energy. The necessary measures I need in order to enter the inner depths of Erebus and retrieve your precious Symone."

The edges of Cimmerian's eyes wrinkle as he furrows his brow. He flattens his hands and presses them tightly together— lifting his fingers to rest snug against his lips. His untrusting nature probes him to inquire more deeply into Adrinn's true motives. "All right, that I can comprehend but what are you truly after? What is in it for you, Adrinn? I have known you for years and in that last few, before you were bound, you proved yourself to be selfish and unkind. So far in your confession, I have only heard of you giving forth. What is it that you expect to gain in return?"

Laughing at Cimmerian's last few words, he twists his brow, amused by his perception then sighs. "Always the pragmatist, Cimmerian? You never could just accept a show of kindness when you saw one." He continues to laugh mockingly.

"Not when it comes from the likes of you," Cimmerian sneers, grinding his teeth and squeezing his hands into fists as he snaps back sternly. "So I will ask you again, what is in it for you?"

"Very well then, if you must know, I would like to someday leave this retched entrapment and be free of this binding, but as we both know, because a Silver Mage has cast it..."

"Only a Silver can dissolve it. Yes, I am well aware of the way things work," Cimmerian expels, understanding Adrinn's true intentions. "You want someone to find a Silver Mage to break the spell."

"Precisely!" he cheers mockingly and slides toward him, stopping mere inches from Cimmerian's face. "You are more clever than you look."

Cimmerian shoots him a poisonous glare and steps through his antagonistic irritant. He moves forward with both hands entangled neatly behind his back, scuffing his heels in the dirt with each step as he mulls over the proposed concept. Idling in thought for a moment, he stops abruptly to glare over his shoulder.

"Even if you could find a Silver Mage, which is a highly improbable feat I might add, how would you ever manage to coerce them into thinking that it might be a good idea to set you free?"

"Ah, baby steps, my good Mage, baby steps. First, we deal with the wild youngling and bringing your daughter back, then we find the Silver Mage." Adrinn's lips turn upward into a sinister looking curve—an attempt to assure his potential counterpart that his needs would be met forthright. "You would have me reveal the ending to the story before it has barely begun. Now I ask you old boy, where is the fun in that?"

Chapter Fourteen

Fable or Fact

GABRIAN GENTLY RUBS her eyes, trying to clear them of the haze that has clouded her sight. She watches as the light of day slowly breaks through the night's darkness and creeps its way through her window. The shadowy figures in the room that haunted her sleep through the night begin to shift and take shape. Subtle shades of sepia sharpen their contours and reveal them to be nothing more than lifeless furniture in the comforting light of dawn.

Her eyes sweep the room, taking inventory. She swiftly sits up in bed, astutely aware that she is not in her Manhattan apartment. There is nothing recognizable in the room. Her memory replays fragments of flashbacks of all the strange anomalies that have invaded her world in the past couple of days. The last thing she remembers is being trapped in her apartment—surrounded by what she would consider psychopaths—then losing consciousness. She hears the thundering of her pulse in her ears as her heart beats wildly beneath her chest at her sudden realization; she has been kidnapped.

A familiar voice breaks through the chaotic whirlwind of her panic attack.

"Did you sleep well?" the soothing words waft across the room.

Gabrian's eyes dart in the direction of the owner.

Leaning up against the side of the bedroom doorway, holding a steaming cup of coffee, Gabrian's heart begins to melt and tears blur her vision as she gazes upon her captor—the most caring and supportive person she has ever known. With her dark, chocolate-coloured hair tied up in a messy bun, and sporting a rustic pair of track pants with her favourite Eighties cutoff sweatshirt covered in paint, stands her mother. She is a sight for sore eyes.

Searching the space encompassing her mother, Gabrian finds no colour, no light, and no aura. She unclenches her muscles and sighs in relief, immediately dismissing the entire traumatic experience as a late night binge-eating induced nightmare. Though confused as to how she came to be in her mother's new home without recollection, she contemplates the idea that she must have already finished her last two weeks of work and is now on her promised vacation.

She haphazardly tries to remember any details of how she got there—did she drive, take a plane?—but she cannot seem to recall anything. Her mind is groggy. Her flesh feels heavy upon her bones and aches from the surge of wasted adrenaline. Gabrian convinces her internal detective that her brain is in reboot mode—asleep in a haze, and she will remember the specifics when she is fully awake. Lowering her head back down to rest upon her pillow, she closes her eyes, happy to be safe with people she loves and trusts.

With the fear of being kidnapped now dissolved, Gabrian can smell the tantalizing aroma of caffeine that beckons to her from amidst the cup her mother cradles within her hands, and she ponders the thought of getting up.

"I slept fine, but what a nightmare I had! What did we eat last night?" Gabrian inquires, massaging her temples.

For a fraction of a moment, Sarapheane's loving face loses it serenity, but she recovers her smile quickly before Gabrian notices.

"Hey kiddo, when you are ready, get dressed and come down for some breakfast," she suggests softly. "We will catch up then. Okay?"

"Sure, that sounds great, Mom." The smell of bacon cooking in the kitchen has edged its way up the stairs, presenting itself within her room. Her stomach grumbles with approval to its intrusion. "Do you mind if I take a shower first? I feel gross this morning—like I got hit by a train or something." She laughs, forcing herself to sit up again.

"Sure, Gabe." Sarapheane reaches out and pulls at the handle of the ajar door beside her, peeking her head in. "Everything you need should be on the shelf." She starts to leave then stops and looks back at Gabrian. "It is so good to see you, sweetie. Your dad and I are so pleased that you are here." Her eyes glisten, carrying a hint of worry at the edges. The curve of her mouth is upturned, but her lips tremble as her level of happiness wavers.

Gabrian notices the quiver this time and it tugs at her heart. "You too, Mom. I miss you more than you know."

AFTER A HOT shower, Gabrian climbs out of the tub and wraps herself in the fuzzy pink floral robe hanging on the back of the bathroom door. Her mom must have put it there while she was showering. She ties her long dark hair up in a messy knot and heads toward the smell of bacon and coffee.

Pausing on her mission momentarily, she scuffles her feet on the shag throw rug in the hallway just outside her room and inhales the familiar scent of her long-forgotten childhood. She gazes wide-eyed and open-mouthed in childlike admiration of all the beautiful art her parents have filled their home with. Some of it she recognizes from their Manhattan apartment where she spent her adolescent years, but the new paintings that hang tightly to the wall are incredible and abstract—a lot of black and white with minimal colour. Her mother must have started painting again. Pleased with this notion, she smiles.

An unsettling thought crosses her mind—if she did indeed arrive before last night then why does none of this seem familiar? At least one of these paintings should spark a recollection. Shaking her head in confusion, she shrugs and blames it on her fatigued state, continuing her journey toward the kitchen.

She begins her descent down the wooden spiral staircase that is enclosed on each side and it blinds and constricts her line of sight. She doesn't remember this ever bothering her as a child but in a semi-agitated state already, she becomes quickly uncomfortable with this unavoidable restriction and rushes forward with a quickened pace. Bounding and leaping down multiple steps at a time, Gabrian happily reaches the bottom. She looks behind at her temporary entrapment and inhales deeply in reaching its release. She steps forward from the grasp of confinement and halts—standing motionless in a moment of awe.

Opening up before her is a huge, beckoning room—the kitchen. Its splendid lure that she had spent many a day playing in as a young child is made of handcrafted wood and stone. Cuddled next to the wall on her left stands a little nook just for two. In front of her, the large kitchen counter hugs the entire room. Beyond its embrace the sunken living area that is as large as it is open, for its appearance seems entirely made of glass. The sun, still low in the east, easily enters through the windows and warms the entire house, filling it with a welcoming and invigorating glow.

She develops a new understanding of her parents' decision to move back to the country. Their city home was nice and comfortable but its beauty was lost in comparison to the ambience that now envelopes her.

In the center of the vast room, stands a large wooden table nearly the size of a barn door, and it is topped with platters piled with toast, bacon, eggs, and more importantly, yields a spouted portable thermos most likely filled with coffee.

Gabrian hurries across the kitchen floor and slides eagerly into the wooden chair seated at the table across from her mom. She reaches for the thermos. Feeling the warmth of its holdings against her skin, she shivers with delight and tips the top of the container downward, pouring the dark liquid into the cup in front of her. She douses it with cream, a splash of the maple syrup that rests coyly beside the toast and raises it to her mouth—taking a sip. The savory warm liquid is heavenly, and her delight is freely displayed upon her face.

"Some things never change!" her mother teases as she watches Gabrian's moment of rapture with her coffee.

Now aware that her mother is watching her every move, Gabrian gives her a cheeky smile and takes another sip. "Nectar of the Gods!" she purrs with triumph. "Where is Dad this morning?" Gabrian asks, reaching for some bacon and a slice of homemade toast.

"He had some things to take care of in town. He will be back soon to give you a hug." Unhappy about lying to her daughter, she smiles and tries to figure out how she is going to say what she needs to say to Gabrian.

***

AFTER ORRORYN ARRIVED with Gabrian yesterday, Jarrison, Orroryn, Vaeda, and herself discussed briefly about whether or not it would be best if they just came right out and told Gabrian about the Realm and her part in it instead of pretending she was still a child protected by wards and cloaking spells. Since those no longer worked, obviously, keeping her in the dark about who she is could be devastating to her once she figures it out on her own—not to mention how dangerous it would be to everyone around her.

***

AFTER BREAKFAST, GABRIAN falls into step with helping her mother clean up the dishes and tidying up the table. Being close to her mom again and making idle chitchat reminds her of how much she truly misses her parents. After the chores are done, Sarapheane pours herself another coffee, deciding that it is time.

"Go grab yourself another coffee, Gabe, and come sit with me a while." Sarapheane touches Gabrian on the cheek lightly with the back of her fingers and steps down into the sitting room, directly to the side of the wooden table in front of the large stone fireplace.

Gabrian senses something heavy in her mother's voice. She grabs another coffee and goes to sit with her.

"Is everything alright?" she asks, although she is unsure if she really wants to know the answer.

"Gabrian, there are some things that your father and I have been meaning to speak to you about," Sarapheane begins. "But there just never seemed to be a good time or a right time to bring them up. Watching you grow up has been such a wonder and a blessing that we did not want to interrupt any of the incredible things that you were accomplishing with any unnecessary weight."

Confused as to where her mother is going with this, Gabrian's comfort level wanes. She shifts in her chair, coddling her warm cup against her chest, and begins to twist knots in a stray strand of her hair. Is she trying to tell Gabrian that she and her father are getting a divorce? She is at a loss and has no idea what direction this conversation is going to take.

"Just tell me what you need to say, Mom. I am a big girl, and I can handle it. I have even gone to university and earned a diploma that says so," she teases in an attempt to lighten the mood. Unbeknown to Gabrian, the mood was going to get a lot heavier.

Unsure of how she is going to convey the truth without frightening her or making her upset, Sarapheane realizes she just needs to begin. "Your father and I are so proud of you."

"Yes, Mom, I know," Gabrian replies, uneasily taking a sip of her coffee. "You have made that clear many times."

"And you know that we love you."

"Mother!" Gabrian growls, wrinkling her brow and giving her mom the stink-eye in hopes of encouraging her to just get on with it. She never has been one for wading through the mud at low tide in order to get to deeper waters. "Please, just tell me."

If she is going to make Gabrian understand, she must start from the beginning and tell her everything. She takes a deep breath, a sip of her coffee, and looks out the window at the ocean that lies before her as the words find their way to her lips.

"In the beginning of mankind, as the clans evolved and divided, there came to be a group of souls that were much more exceptional than the rest—a gifted people. They lived in peace among the other clans for many years and at first these people were all known as the Aucyen Arguros or in the common tongue, the Ancient Silver ones." Sarapheane watches as Gabrian's brow lifts in disbelief as she listens.

"But as nature would have it, because of their special abilities to do inexplicable things, the other clans began to distrust them. Fear arose amongst those who did not hold such powers. Once rivalry and conflict began to arise within the clans, the others were stripped of their knowledge about the Silvers' abilities. Their minds were swept clean by the Mages with compulsion that was learned by the Elders and thus forward kept in the dark about what they were and the gifts that they possessed since the humans were known to be a cruel race at times, especially about things they could not comprehend."

Unable to take her mother seriously, Gabrian laughs reflexively at her mother's attempts to enlighten her. Wanting to play along, Gabrian bites for information. "Mages...Like 'witches and warlock' stuff?"

"Yes."

"So your big serious talk is just you wanting to tell me a scary bedtime story? Seriously?" She wonders if her mother has somehow fallen off her rocker after she retired and moved out to the ends of the Earth. "About witches? I think it is a bit early in the day for that mother."

"Gabrian, please, just listen," Sarapheane insists, placing her hand gently but firm against the top of her daughter's knee—a straight line drawn across her mouth erases the humor from its edges. As crazy as she knows this must sound to her daughter, she has to know the truth.

Taking another sip of her coffee, Gabrian waves her free hand in surrender to her mother's wishes. "Okay, fine, you win!" she says, unable to wipe the grin from her face, convinced that her mother has lost it. Gabrian based her entire life on logistic conclusions and hopes there will be one at the end of her mother's story. Nothing so far has even come close to resembling anything logical.

"Over time, the Mages and the humans became more integrated, even coupling in marriage at times. Although the Elders frowned upon it, it was not entirely forbidden. If a human proved worthy, then they were permitted to become one of the people of the Realm. Once a member, they were compelled to secrecy and only then were the gifts of the ancient Silvers revealed to them. Only then were their eyes awakened and the silver-coloured auras of the Mages would be visible to them."

As the secrets within her mother's story begin to unravel, hitting a bit closer to home, Gabrian desists her mocking grin as the word 'aura' is mentioned. All the memories of her so-called nightmare come flooding back, it dawns on her that it may not have been a nightmare at all. Suddenly, she is stricken with anxiety and nausea. Eyes that were filled with mockery and jest are now attentive with their plea to be sincere. She gazes with new eyes upon her mother who has stopped talking, patiently waiting for her to mentally catch up. Gabrian clings tighter to her mug of coffee and secures it to her chest like a child hugging its favourite comfort toy in order to feel safe.

With the altering of her daughter's seriousness toward her words, Sarapheane continues.

"A true Silver Mage was blessed with an abundance of gifts. They were able to manipulate Mother Earth's elements; some of them even developed the ability to shift their physical form into the element of their choosing. For example, if the Mage manipulated fire, they could not only summon it, but their aura would change colour from silver into a shade of crimson while their body manifested into actual fire. This ability took many years to master, and many never ascended to this, but those who had were held high in the eyes of their people. It was a sign of a powerful Mage, not to mention a useful skill in times of conflict. This was true with all the elements—Fire, Water, Earth, Air— plus some had the gift to persuade things of a more interesting nature. With some it was the ability to read minds and interpret information in a telepathic manner where others were able to stretch and manipulate the Magik in the shadows, using it to transport themselves within the thin membrane between dimensions to aid in comradery or escape an adversary. And others still that could draw in and relinquish the energy of those around them."

No longer scoffing at her mother's so-called fairytale, Gabrian stares blankly at her mother. Chewing hungrily on the tips of her fingers, she ravages what is left of her nails. Her head swims with these new and overwhelming truths being told to her. Unsure of whether or not she should interrupt her mother with questions, she resolves to remain silent and gather in as much information as possible.

"With the integration of human blood into the Realm, the offspring of the Silver Mages that was once parented by a pure silver bloodline had become diluted with mere human blood. Often the children of these mixed couples would take on different, more prominent characteristics of the Mage's gifts, thus eliminating others, much like that of Charles Darwin's theory of Natural Selection that you studied in school. The creation of different bloodlines had evolved into different, more specific gifts in the Realm, and with it came the need for the classification of different Fellowships."

Studying her daughter's reactions and trying to determine whether or not her truths are sifting through to Gabrian's psychological primal instincts, Sarapheane pauses for a moment and wonders if she is doing nothing more than confusing her.

"Are you all right, Gabrian? Would you like me to stop or shall I continue?"

Now that the reality of her recent 'nightmare' has been somewhat confirmed, she decides the only logical thing to do is to sit and listen to whatever it is that her mother wants to tell her. However demented and deranged this story seems to be, it is the only thing in her present life that appears to have any validity to it—especially now.

"Yes, go on, Mom." Her voice wavers, revealing her internal struggle. She pushes her body from the chair and staggers to the kitchen. Grabbing the coffee pot, she returns to refill their cups. "Tell me about the…Fellowships?" she says in question.

Sitting back down, she pours the remainder of the pot, splitting it evenly between the two cups in front of her. Gabrian reaches behind and pulls on the pink-and-green-checkered blanket sitting on top of the wooden chest beside her. She wraps it around her upper torso then settles back into her chair, hoping it will bring her some comfort.

Pleased that Gabrian is not in total refusal of what she hears—and has not run for the door yet—Sarapheane picks up her cup and sips its contents before she begins again.

"The Fellowships are basically family groups that share the same gifts or traits, if you will. As I mentioned before, due to the human blood intertwined with the Silver Mages' blood, the bloodlines are no longer pure. It had become diluted or infused by whatever strengths or weaknesses each species had to contribute. To my knowledge, there are roughly ten Fellowships in the Realm, each consisting of ten unique forms of gifts."

"Were the people not upset at being classified?" Gabrian sits up a bit, trying to contribute to the story, unsure of whether or not she even wanted the answer.

"At first, maybe, but as time went on and the numbers in each Fellowship grew, it became easier for the people of the Realm to just separate by abilities in order to properly educate and train their children. They were only separated in abilities, not as a people."

Her daughter's attempt to try and involve herself allows Sarapheane a glimmer of hope. If she can manage to gently introduce her into the workings of the Realm, she may be able to make Gabrian's transition into her new world a little less terrifying for her.

"Okay, where to begin?" Sarapheane smiles encouragingly while she contemplates which Fellowship description to start with. Deciding that the primary elemental Fellowships would be best, she begins her clarification of their differences. "Well, let me see...first there is the Fellowship of Zephyr. It is the gift of the Air element. They have the ability to move and bend particles that make up air as we know it. Some of the more powerful Mages are able to create portals which allow them to move from one place to another in mere seconds. While most Zephyr are kind and gentle, they are very dangerous as well. Considering that most living things on this Earth are dependent on oxygen, the Mages' ability to deplete the entirety of air from a space renders almost all hopelessly defenseless."

At the mention of the word Zephyr, Gabrian's mind digs wildly through memories to rest upon the fiasco that transpired at her apartment and the tall crazy lady that stood within the midst of it. She recalls Rachael stating something about her being from there. Her heart flutters at the immediate realization that escaping from that night's events may have been just the beginning of a whole new world of nightmares for her.

With her mind racing—trying to keep this new strange reality straight in her head—she turns to stare blankly at the fireplace, her bluish-grey eyes transfix themselves to the pieces of red burning embers buried within the ashes.

Sarapheane watches Gabrian's movements carefully. With no definite signs threatening her retreat, she continues.

"The Fellowship of Egni, the gifted of the Fire element, can summon the power of fire and manipulate how it will behave. I believe that the legends surrounding that of the Phoenix derived from this Fellowship.

"Then there is Hydor. This is a Water element Fellowship. They, much like the Greek God, Poseidon, that you also studied in school, can control and manipulate water. Even the smallest amount of moisture in the air can be manipulated by them. Most members of this Fellowship stay close to the ocean or some type of body of water as it is in their nature to be more content there."

Thinking of her current surroundings, her eyes jump toward the window of her parent's home. Observing the glimmer of sunlight dancing carelessly on the surface of the ocean barely fifty feet on the other side of her parents' lawn, she begins to wonder if their location and this story have anything to do with one another. Are they from the Realm? Is she and her family water Mages? Even if they are, and she feels incredibly absurd to even fathom the consideration of this, the water traits that her mom describes to her do not match any of the peculiars that she has experienced. Interest in the history of the Fellowships starts to consume her. Leaning in towards her storyteller, Gabrian hugs her knees—resting her mug within her cupped hands just atop her feet, and soundlessly listens with intent.

"The Eorden are the Earth element Fellowship. They are mainly a healing and peaceful Fellowship. The people work as the herbalists and natural healers that we call homeopathic physicians. But they also use the energies within the earth, trees, flowers, and such that allow them to contend with forces that oppose them. Most of the displays of nature, such as earthquakes, landslides, or events equivalent to that are acts of Mother Nature herself—the Eorden can cause them as well. Maybe not to the degree that Mother Earth herself can perform, but they are not to be denied their due. And like any faction, there are some of whom that display the rare ability to communicate with nature's other living creations."

Partly due to the shock that this somehow is true and partly to the image of a certain comedian's face entering her mind, she bursts out laughing. "You mean they are a bunch of Dr. Doo Littles but with Magikal powers."

Her mother giggles with her. "Yes, sort of."

Gabrian chuckles again, running her hands through her hair, pulling it over to one side, and nods in appreciation to the humor that she has miraculously found in all of this. She sips her drink and cathartically traces the bumpy designs of the cup over and over with her fingers. "Of course they are—why wouldn't they be?"

Sarapheane lends a sympathetic ear to Gabrian's reactions. All her life, Gabrian has tried to live in the 'real' world, determined that she would find every answer to every question. But she does not think these are quite the answers that Gabrian had in mind when she went looking.

Getting up from her chair to stretch her legs, Sarapheane drifts toward the large windows in front of them. She gazes out across the horizon at vast and endless sea. She loves the way the morning sun creates the illusion of diamonds upon the water that dance and sparkle just on the surface. She smiles, humbled by the beauty of her favourite time of day.

"The Isa fellowship is a branch from that of the Hydor Fellowship. It is of the water element gift but its Mages manipulate the water in a different way. Not only can they manipulate its mannerisms but can alter its existing form from a liquid into that of ice and snow. It is a spectacular and beautiful gift that can quickly become as equally dangerous. Now we come to the other Fellowships that are…well, less elemental," Sarapheane continues, taking a deep breath.

"What do you mean, 'less elemental?'" Gabrian perks up, curious as to where this topic might lead.

Peeking over her shoulder, her face lightens at the sight of her daughter's inquisitive eyes. Gabrian's interest has increased, and her wanting to jest has almost depleted.

"They are exceptions. Their gifts display more of the interesting attributes to the Silver Mage bloodline."

Gabrian tilts her head, furrowing her brow in reaction to Sarapheane's words. She feels that somehow the Fellowships her mother has already mentioned were more run of the mill than the gifts that she is about to explain.

The embers spark and crackle loudly in the fireplace, giving Gabrian a bit of a start. Normally the noise would not have registered with her, but her mother's early morning, scary bedtime story seems to have her a tad rattled—visions of people made of fire and ice while conversing with earthly beasts that moved with the wind, dance freely within her thoughts—clouding her mind.

"Would you like me to make some more coffee?"

Not fully able to comprehend, nor finding the ability to compartmentalize, her mind is in neutral, spinning but not in gear. Gabrian can hear the tone of her mom's voice, but she is incapable of making out any of the words she says. They echo hollowly at first then cut through the delirium of the free-flowing data overload. Gabrian is caught somewhere within the void. Her head turns in the direction of the noise, and her eyes rest blankly on her mother's. Finally, the lights in her eyes ignite as she registers that she is being spoken to.

"I'm sorry, what did you say?"

"I said, would you –"

"Coffee. More of it, right. Yes, please," she answers. Gabrian's face is long and flat, unanimated as the wheels and cogs turn within her mind. She floats in neutral—feeling the level of mental absorption nearly reaching its maximum point—but she estimates that in all probability there is still a long way to go in this chat with her mom and caffeine may be a necessity in order to keep her brain from completely shutting down on her.

Sarapheane smiles and shakes her head. She adds more grounds to the coffee press then fills it with hot water. Inserting the top of the press and grabbing the cream, she heads back down to the sitting room and places them on the table in front of Gabrian. Gabrian happily concocts her elixir within her cup and awaits her mother's continuation of where she left off.

"Now where was I? Oh yes…the more unique Fellowships." Sarapheane pours herself a new cup now that Gabrian has finished with the press. "First, I shall begin with the Vindere Fellowship, Reincarnates or Mediums—a term that maybe you are more familiar with. They are like the windows between souls in the Realm."

"Okay, this seems a little more believable to me," Gabrian snuffs. "So these Mediums, are they the same kind of loons that are advertised on TV all the time or that have little shops set up in the city? That seems a little Hollywood to me."

"A lot of them are one in the same, but some of them are a little more shameless than others." Sarapheane smiles. "Recognizing that many humans are easily manipulated, they use their ability to read people in order to make a living. More powerful Mediums can sometimes catch glimpses of a person's subconscious and those glimpses makes it seem like they are actually seeing things from their future or the past. But most are more humble and go through life less pronounced, aiding the Mages when need be. They are an important part in keeping the communications within the Realm open and functioning."

Sarapheane takes the opportunity to connect Gabrian's former

108

'human' life to the new world she is being introduced to.

"Have you ever noticed Rachael's extraordinary talent to handle people? Or perhaps you may have noticed from time to time moments where she seems to space out on you?"

Gabrian thinks back over the years since she has known Rachael and recalls some instances where Rachael had seemed like she was not truly there.

"Now that you mention it, yes. She does do that sometimes. And sometimes when she speaks, it seemed as if it was not actually her saying the words." Curious about this revelation, Gabrian furthers her inquiry. "Do these Mages ever use the Mediums to speak through? I mean, use their body and mouths to communicate like those TV advertised Mediums that swear they were possessed by a spirit?"

"Yes, they have the ability to connect with a Mage and allow them to utilize their body as a vehicle in order to communicate to others," Sarapheane confirms. "They also have the ability to block communication as well, like an on-off switch so to speak. Whom they allow access to, and whom they do not is entirely up to them."

Staring off into the distance, Gabrian's focus jumps around the room, her mind racing again. Her mouth droops at the edges as she chews on her bottom lip, grasping the fact that her lifelong and trusted friend is not who she had believed her to be. Understanding Rachael's want to keep her true identity hidden, the bite of betrayal stings bitterly beneath it all as she wonders how many eyes have observed her within the deceptive cloak of friendship. There is a prolonged moment of silence as Sarapheane pauses to let Gabrian process this new understanding of who her friend is. Once her eyes clear, Sarapheane continues.

"The Vindere also have the ability to reincarnate," Sarapheane continues, tucking a lock of her long dark hair behind her ear.

Gabrian retreats from her bout of disheartenment to gather the added information. "How do you mean?"

"Every Vindere folk will walk amongst the people of this world for a set number of years. It can be as little as a single lifetime before their soul is transferred from their particular vessel to another dimension or it can entail a long and adjoined life, being reintroduced to each new vessel by rebirth for hundreds of years. Each Vindere has its own journey and road to travel."

Gabrian swivels her head to gaze upon her mother, her eyes brighten in revelation of this concept and pushes off her momentary sullenness to adhere to her curiosity instead. She has always been fascinated by the possibility of a continued soul but until now has had little to no proof that it was possible.

"You mean that Rachael could be hundreds of years old?"

"That is exactly what I am saying."

"Is she?"

"That is a question that only she can answer. It is not my place to disclose her true age. You must ask her yourself."

"Oh," Gabrian says, not knowing what else to say.

"Another of the more unique Fellowships is the Derkaz. This is the Darkness Fellowship. These Mages have the ability to control, or for a better word, contain all the things that go bump in the night."

"Umm, what do you mean by that exactly?" Gabrian gasps sitting herself upright and clutching at the throw, pulling it closer— building an imaginary impenetrable shield between herself and the 'things.' Growing up, many little children seem to be afraid of the dark—at least she knows she was. If what her mother is telling her to be the truth, then maybe the scary things that she imagined as a child were actually real. "I am definitely going to need you to clarify that a little more for me please or I will never sleep again."

Remembering well her daughter's restless sleeping habits as a child, she is certain that Gabrian will no doubt have a few sleepless nights after today's little life lesson. Sarapheane tries to paint the best picture she can in order to explain what she means.

"There are beings called the 'Keepers of Erebus' or simply Gargons. They are an entity all of their own. As long as there has been life, there have been Gargons.

"For the most part they are harmless and do not interfere with everyday life or bother anyone, but if a being becomes weak or hurt, they will sense it and seek it out. Once they find it, the creatures release a vaporous toxin that is inhaled by the victim. It induces a delirium over the dying and renders them helpless and confused. The Gargons then slither to the surface through the dark shroud beneath and intertwine their own essence to the remaining fragments of life held by its captive. Once attached, they pull and tear away at the essence of a being until it is striped clean and the body is dead, then the soul is carried down into the Darkness."

Gabrian's eyes widen and all signs of colour drain from her flesh at her mother's description. "Into the Darkness...as in the darkness of night, darkness?"

110

Sarapheane smiles at Gabrian's misunderstanding of her words.

"No, no dear. Not the darkness that comes with night. Although, there are more incidences with them becoming more aggressive in the Darkness."

"Not helping," Gabrian hums nervously lifting her eyebrows and gnawing on the ends of her fingers again.

"Anyway, the Darkness is the mist where the Gargons inhabit—the place between Earth and Hades called Erebus—a dimension of sorts that creates a type of bridge between Realms. The dimension is toxic to all beings here on Earth, except for the Gargons."

Sarapheane knows Gabrian was never one for scary stories and is aware of the despairing mental effects that her explanation of the Gargons no doubt has on her daughter, so she tries to comfort her and assure her that fears are unnecessary.

"The Gargons are regularly kept in check by the Black Mages. Hence, the power of the Derkaz. They are able to push the Gargons away if need be and keep them sealed within the Darkness. On a lighter note, the Derkaz can also see in the dark like it was day. And if I were a betting soul, I would say that they have a few other abilities that they have not entirely revealed to the rest of the Covenant of Shadows." Sarapheane chuckles and winks, tapping the side of her nose with her index finger.

Intrigued by the way the words 'Covenant of Shadows' rolls off her mother's tongue, Gabrian interrupts Sarapheane's story to inquire about it. "What is the Covenant of Shadows?"

"Oh! Well…the Covenant of Shadows is a sacred place amongst the people of the Realm. It was a gift of sanctuary, forged together by the Elders of the Fellowships long ago where the Elders of each Fellowship convene to discuss and vote on important matters that concern their people. It is in essence much like that of a modern day government. Though I must admit that the Covenant of Shadows is much more effective than some of the governments I have witnessed over the years."

Gabrian pulls the checkered blanket off her lap and gets up from her chair, stretching her arms up over her head. She ventures forward, toward the fireplace. Grabbing a chunk of wood from the pile, she stirs around flakes of lifeless ash in search of hidden crimson embers to feed.

These things, these odd and ponderous things that are being revealed to her are that of fairytale paraphernalia—a little less twinkly and less periwinkle than the other stories that she grew up with but still she wonders—how did this come to be the world that she is now a part of?

Still picking at the ashes, she stares deep into the speckles of the crimson glow and visualizes a strange imagery of humans wrapped within flame like those described to her earlier. Although all of it sounds completely insane to her, she finds herself oddly pondering what it would be like to possess the power to summon fire. As the thought engulfs her mind, sparks jump as her log becomes consumed by flames. Startled by the sudden ignition, she flounders backward and lets out a high-pitched squeal.

Sarapheane jumps as well at Gabrian's unexpected display. "Are you all right, honey? Did you get burned?"

Gabrian laughs at herself for being so jumpy. "No, I am fine. The fire just took faster than I expected is all." Gabrian turns around and ambles back to the comfort of her chair. Snuggled deep within its embrace, she covers herself up again with the blanket, thinking nothing more of it.

Nearing the end of her list of Fellowships, Sarapheane moves along steadily with her descriptions, leaving the last two Fellowships for the end on purpose.

"We are nearly done," Sarapheane consoles, watching her daughter's eyes glaze over—floating in the deluge of information that she has absorbed. "Now, we come to the Schaeduwe Fellowship or as we are known, the Shadow Walkers. The Schaeduwe are a very unique people. They have the ability to touch and bend shadows in order to manipulate them. This manipulation allows them the ability to enter into the Darkness of the shadows and exit out of another in any location they so choose."

"Enter into them...like a portal?"

"Essentially, yes. But it is much different from that of a portal. Portals only allow you from one place to the other instantaneously. With a shadow, there exists a membrane that the Schaeduwe have managed to learn how to walk within. It is a link or a bridge called the Veil, much like that of the Gargons, to an alternate dimension or world."

Gabrian sits silently. Her jaw is without tension, dangling on its hinges while her eyes stare widely without blinking.

"Before you can ask, no, the Veil is not filled with toxins and harbors the vessel of death like the Gargons, but it does hold its own particular perils. Anyway, I digress..."

Gabrian, no longer listening, strangely sorts through childhood memories. She recalls one instance where she swore her mother was downstairs in the laundry room rummaging through clothes, then in the same instance, she heard the floor creak upstairs as her mother hummed merrily, putting the laundry away. She never really put much into it before as it became the norm, but it always did seem a bit strange to her.

In another oddity, she recalls visitors arriving at their house out of nowhere, like her uncle Tynan. When he did visit them, which was rare because of his work, he never used a vehicle to get there. Now, she may understand the reason why.

Gabrian's mind stumbles back into the present, realizing her mother is still talking but about what seems like another Fellowship. She must have drifted off and missed some of it.

"I am sorry, Mom, what did you say? My mind was somewhere else for a second." Pushing her hair up out of her eyes and letting it drop over on the other side of her face, she focuses on her mom with what means of attention she can muster up.

"Sure, hon, no problem." Sarapheane takes this disruption as an opportunity to have a sip of her cold coffee. Harboring on the most important Fellowship description, she begins again. "I was just starting to describe the last of the Fellowships, the Boragen fellowship, or the Borrowers."

Gabrian's ears perk up once she hears the word 'last.' She pulls her body upright on the chair and hugs her arms around her knees, resting her chin on top of them, feeling relieved that the end of the information blasting session is hopefully nearing its finale.

"This Fellowship has had many trials and tribulations over the years," Sarapheane begins. "They are a powerful people. Don't get me wrong, the other Fellowships are just as powerful in their own way, but the Boragen people possess a similar trait to that of the Gargons." Gabrian's eyes widen with this news, and her head lifts in reflex. "They feed off the energies of other beings. Not only off those from the Realm but particularly from humans."

Feeling an icy cold shiver slice down her spine, Gabrian holds her breath for a second from the terrifying reality that these words bring. Her mind broadcasts the horrifying image of the people she left lying lifeless around her in the park. Tucking her plump lips in under teeth, she bites down, blinking rapidly—her eyes bulge as the shock of horror engages the acids within her stomach as she realizes that this is what happened to her. Her fists clench, and she can feel the warm clammy texture of her palms beneath her fingertips as they start their inherent sizzling. She feels the pressure building behind her temples— the beginnings of a migraine, she is sure of it. She fights the instinct to go lie down and forces her body to remain in place. Although she has heard quite enough, she still needs to hear the rest of the horror story that her mother is about to tell.

Sarapheane's hoarse voice pushes forward to finalize her story, sensing she has Gabrian's complete attention. "Most Boragen, or Borrowers, are cautiously cared for from birth and begin their training at an early age in order to teach them how to care for their gift. Because of their ability to draw in energy, or life essences, they can quickly become a danger to others if they are not in complete control."

"Although highly fatal, there is much beauty in a Borrower's gift," Gabrian hears her mother say, but she is doubtful of its validity. She cannot fathom how sucking the life out of a person could be considered beautiful. "Not only do they have the power to take energy, but they can lend it as well. They are terror to only borrow the unhealthy energies, the dark-coloured ones like anxiety and stress, from their hosts. Then, after they have utilized what they need to survive, they give back the essence they would naturally expel. This in turn causes a positive reaction within the receiver of such energy, much like the chemical reaction of an athlete's endorphin release to their brain. But with good there must also exist the evil."

Sarapheane observes the tensing in Gabrian's jaw as she reacts to this. "If the Borrower decides to not follow his training, and partakes in the absorption of white energy, they can become dangerous. Their minds can become lethargic and confused, causing them to draw in more and more energy until unfortunately they drain the host to its death. Once they do this, they are likely to do it again becoming what the Covenant of Shadows call a Vapir or what modern day Hollywood calls a Vampire."

Gabrian jumps up out of her chair, clasping the sides of her head.

"Sorry, Mom, I have to go lie down."

Almost tripping on the blanket that she had wrapped around her body, she runs haphazardly back into the kitchen and up the stairs to the room she woke up in. As her temples pound violently against her skull, she feels her stomach starting to turn. Unsure if it is the

114

excruciating pain threatening to explode within her head or the unsettling fact that her mother just informed her that she may be a Vampire that causes the churning in her gut, but what she does know is that she is on the verge of vomiting either way. Crashing through the bathroom door and dropping to her knees, she steadies her head over the mouth of the white porcelain God as the contents of her breakfast head in reverse.

Standing outside the bedroom door, Sarapheane hears Gabrian's struggle. Unsure of how to help her or what to do, she succumbs to her compassionate nature and decides to give Gabrian a break from the truth. She wanders down to the kitchen and grabs a glass of water and a few Advil. Upon her return, Sarapheane hears the heavy hum of water running in the shower and sets the glass and Advil on the table beside Gabrian's bed. Hovering just outside the bathroom door, she hesitates for a moment then opens it a crack in order check on Gabrian's well-being.

"Gabrian, honey?" she sings just loud enough to be heard.

Gabrian, now relieved to be done feeding her breakfast to the porcelain God, and feeling a bit better for it, answers, "Yeah, Mom?"

"Everything all right in there?" Knowing full well that it is not, Sarapheane's heart wrenches from her desire to bring even an ounce of comfort to her daughter.

"Yeah, Mom," Gabrian says, lying through her teeth. "Migraine. I will be alright. I just need to go lie down for a bit." Her head hurts, her mind hurts—everything about her hurts. Nothing feels good. All she wants is to go to bed, pass out, and wake up better in the world she knew before the auras started.

"Are you sure?"

"Yes. I am sure." For a moment Gabrian wishes she was a little girl again and that her mom would come tuck her into bed and tell her that everything will be okay.

That there is nothing hiding under her bed in the shadows.

That there is nothing to be afraid of in the Darkness.

And that she is not a monster.

Chapter Fifteen

Fire and Ice

ALL AFTERNOON, GABRIAN tosses and turns from vivid dreams of creatures made of Fire and Ice. She dreams of houses being swallowed up by the Earth, while strangers hide in the shadows, waiting to grab her and take her to the Darkness where the Gargons can turn her into a black zombified corpse that feeds on the living.

Gabrian wakes covered in sweat. Opening her eyes unable to see anything but darkness all around her, fear engulfs her. Still rattled by her dreams, and feeling blinded, Gabrian strains her eyes, trying to focus on something, anything—well, anything that is not scary and going to eat her. She swings her legs over the bed in an attempt to sit up.

"Ouch!" Gabrian yells, hitting her shin on something hard. It is a chair her mother had put there earlier while she sat by Gabrian's side, watching her sleep. Her mother used to do that often when she was a child. She would hold her hand until Gabrian fell back to sleep again from one of her frequenting nightmares.

The door in her room slowly opens and the light from the hallway breaches the darkness. In relief from the blackness, she welcomes it. The silhouette of her mother's figure stands in the doorway. "I heard you yell. Is everything okay?"

Rubbing her sore shin, Gabrian squints her eyes, trying to adjust to the light "I am okay, I just banged my leg on something when I was trying to get up. It is so dark in here, I can't see what I am doing."

Entering the room, and walking directly to the chair, Sarapheane picks it up and moves it out of the way. "Oh, no. Sorry, Gabe, that is my fault," she says. "I forgot to put it back before I left your room."

"You sat by me when I was sleeping? Mom, I think that I am a little old for you to coddle," she teases. Her eyes sparkle as she squints them against the glimmer of light coming from the hall and her mouth curves crookedly to the side into a half-grin.

"How is your head?" Sarapheane asks, rubbing her hand over Gabrian's head before she gently twirls a strand of Gabrian's long dark hair. "Is your migraine all gone?"

Still feeling the remainder of the headache behind her eyes, she rubs her temple and smiles meekly. "Almost. Thank you for the pills. Once my head hit the pillow, I was gone." Struggling with her need for answers, and wondering if she really wants to dive back into the world of the strange, she presses her thumb against her bottom lip, and bites down—chewing on the edge of her nail and decides to takes the plunge. "Mom?"

"Yeah, Gabe?" Sarapheane answers kindly.

"Is all that stuff you said earlier...true?" Feeling unsecure in asking, Gabrian drops her eyes for a moment then looks back up at her mother. "I mean, thinking rationally, it all sounds pretty farfetched."

Knowing her daughter well, she replies the only way she can. "Well, Gabe, what do you think?"

Familiar with her mother's tactics of turning a question back on to her, she hesitates and searches her logical mind for the answer. A few days ago she would have quickly and undisputedly answered no, but now, she can one hundred percent concur that she does not know the answer. "Maybe—I don't know."

Sarapheane gives her a motherly look of understanding and presses her forehead up against Gabrian's briefly then lifts her head up and kisses Gabrian on the brow.

"There is so much that I need to tell you, but I think you have heard enough for one day." She cups her daughter's face in her hands and sighs. "What do you think?"

"Maybe for tonight." Gabrian gently pinches the bridge of her nose to indicate that the remnants of her pain still lingers just beneath her touch. She has had headaches all her life as a child and to her, they have always felt as if they were trying to drill their way out of her head. The one tonight feels like it may have dug a little closer to the surface.

A familiar voice from the kitchen carries up the stairs and into her room. Sarapheane and Gabrian both turn toward the door. "Dad!" Gabrian cheers.

Forgetting all about the question, she hugs her mom quickly then hurries out of bed and bounds down the stairs but stops right before she reaches the bottom as she hears another voice. She listens for a moment unsure but recognizing the other voice to be that of her uncle Tynan, she continues down the stairs. Looking upon her father's handsome, wind-burned face, her whole expression lights up with a smile when he notices her on the stairwell.

"There she is!" he says, getting up from the nook where he and Tynan sit. "I swear you become more beautiful every time I see you."

"Oh, Dad!" Blushing from her father's comment, she runs directly into his open arms to hug him tightly. Even though she is now an adult, she always feels like a child in the presence of her father. Maybe it is because he is such a large man, standing six-foot-four, or maybe it is because whenever she is near him, she feels as if nothing could ever harm her—not even death. Either way she is happy to be in his arms.

"Hey! What am I, chopped liver?" Tynan says playfully to his niece. "Where is my hug?" Gabrian chuckles to herself as she peeks over her father's massive shoulder and grins. Jarrison releases her, and she strolls over to Tynan, giving him a large bear hug as well. Being the same size as her father, and having the same kind temperament, Tynan also gives her the sense of being safe and protected.

"Great to see you too Uncle Ty!" Gabrian says as she steps back away from the hug. "So they stole your house from you?" she says teasingly to Tynan as she walks back to embrace her father again.

"No, nothing like that, kiddo," he says, looking back and forth between Jarrison and Sarapheane. They both shake their heads *no* subtly in unison. Tynan gets the hint that Gabrian is still in the dark about a lot of things. "This house is too big for me, I like the guest house just fine. Less room for me to make a mess of." Gabrian knows that part to be a lie. She has never met anyone in her life more orderly than her uncle Ty, except for maybe her parents. But she can understand him giving up the big house to her parents and him keeping the smaller home. It was only him here as he never married. He always seemed to be on the go, in too much of a hurry to ever think about settling down.

As if sensing something she cannot, Tynan stops talking and tilts his head to the left. His eyes narrow, wrinkling around the edges as a weighted look crosses his face just for a fraction of a second, then he focuses directly on Jarrison. Tipping his cup up and swallowing down whatever is left inside, Tynan gets up from the chair and places the empty cup in the sink. "Well, duty calls," he says with a grin, turning to face everyone.

"It seems awfully late to be going anywhere tonight, Uncle Ty," Gabrian says, wondering where in the world he would be heading at this hour.

"There is a new recruit coming in, and I need to go set up for training," Tynan informs her and winks at her parents. "I hear I have my work cut out for me with this one." He walks over and grabs his coat from the back of the chair he had been sitting in then gently leans over to kiss Gabrian on the top of the head.

"Ah, I am sure you will do just fine," Jarrison assures him. "You turned out all right!" Jarrison gives him a light punch to the shoulder that would have knocked a normal-sized person over, but Tynan barely moves.

"Yeah, but I had a better Mentor than he does," he says.

"Do not sell yourself short," Sarapheane pipes in as Tynan turns to go.

Tynan's face blushes at her words but no one notices since he faces the other way. He stops for a second before he reaches for the handle of the kitchen door. He turns his head slightly to the right then peeks back at Sarapheane and Jarrison with a mischievous smile. Both of their faces go flat as they look at each other then back to Tynan. *He wouldn't!* they both think simultaneously. Tynan slips his fingers into the shadow that hangs to the right of the pantry door and pulls it around his large body, disappearing into the Darkness of the Veil.

Being a logical thinker since the day she was able to speak, Gabrian's brain absolutely refuses to trust what her eyes just witnessed. Her mouth hangs open, and her pupils dilate, watering as she stares at the empty space that her uncle Tynan had just stood in a second ago, searching for some logical explanation as to how he disappeared. She slowly turns and stares at her parents—dewy-eyed and open-jawed—her arms bend upward in front of her, displaying questioning widespread fingers, completely horrified.

Jarrison and Sarapheane glance at each other in disbelief.

Tynan had spoken to them earlier, while Gabrian was resting, and told them that he believes her training should begin immediately. To him, this was the easiest way to kick start her brain into accepting the incomprehensible. His philosophy always was 'Trial by Fire' and they realize that like it or not, he may be right.

Chapter Sixteen

Monsters Under the Bed

FEELING HER LEGS give out underneath her, Gabrian is unable to do anything about it. She falls in slow motion—fully aware of what is happening around her—but her arms and legs will not work. Luckily, she drops straight down, landing on the kitchen mat that her mother kept in the middle of the floor to keep from slipping on the polished stone tile.

Reaching out as quickly as they can, Jarrison and Sarapheane try to catch her but fail to get to her before she hits the floor. Kneeling beside her, hoping she is okay, their hearts weep from the empty, faraway stare that their daughter wears on her face. In a low monotone voice Gabrian speaks. "It was all real wasn't it."

Sarapheane looks at Jarrison quickly. He shrugs his shoulders slightly and shakes his head in a negative way, unable to understand what Gabrian is saying.

"I am sorry, honey, I did not hear you. What did you say?" Sarapheane whispers.

In a louder, more lethargic voice she repeats herself. "It was all real."

Jarrison and Sarapheane struggle to find the right way to tell her and begin speaking at the same time, stumbling with the words. "It is not that..." her father tries to start.

"We did not intend for you..." Sarapheane fumbles.

Gabrian interrupts them, still looking lost. "The monsters I used to hear under my bed at night when I was sick," she says with conviction, not listening to her parents at all. "The things and people I used to see in the shadows when I was alone. All the scary childhood monsters that I hid from under my covers at night, they were all real, were they not?" Gabrian drifts back to childhood, remembering the handsome young man that used to come and talk with her when she would wander out of the house at night to play at the edge of the gate. He had seemed so real to her. Although her parents told her he wasn't. That he was just a figment of her overactive imagination. *Ayden...he was real.*

Understanding that there is no reason to lie to her anymore, they both say, "Yes!" Jarrison and Sarapheane reach for each other and join hands, gently squeezing them—feeling a bit of relief from admitting the small fragment of truth. Knowing that they have a long few days ahead of them in order to help her understand everything she needs to know, they smile compassionately at Gabrian.

Jarrison lets go of Sarapheane and reaches out to Gabrian with his hands and scoops her up into his strong arms. She falls into him like she did when she was a child, desperate for comfort. He carries her to the sitting room and sets her in the chair by the fireplace where she and her mother had sat earlier that day. A sense of dread overtakes her, but Gabrian knows there is no escape from what she is about to learn.

Sarapheane follows behind and sits down in the chair beside Gabrian, handing her a coffee—an indication that this may be a long night. Her father grabs a chair from the corner and sets it beside Sarapheane, directly across from her.

Not able to take any more of the staring, Gabrian speaks, breaking the silence. "Is Uncle Ty some kind of monster?"

Both Jarrison and Sarapheane giggle at the question thinking that her Uncle Tynan would have gotten a kick out of hearing it. "No, dear. Not quite," her mother begins. "Do you remember me telling you about the different Fellowships this morning before you got your headache?"

"Yes, I remember. You said that because the human blood

was mixed with Mage blood, it sometimes caused the children to have qualities unique from their parents," Gabrian reiterated, trying to remember all the different Fellowships her mom had mentioned.

"Exactly," Sarapheane retorts. "Do you remember what I told you about the Schaeduwe Fellowship?" Watching her daughter's face twist from the question, she tries to jog her memory for her. "The Shadow Walkers."

Seeing lights go on inside Gabrian's mind, she knows she must have remembered. "So you are telling me Uncle Ty is a Shadow Walker?" Gabrian asks.

"Yes," her dad answers, nodding his head slowly as he gives her a kind smile.

Remembering that her mother used the word 'we' instead of the word 'they' this morning when describing the Shadow Walkers, she looks at her mom and asks. "And since Uncle Ty is one, does that make you and Dad, Shadow Walkers?" Feeling her whole body tensing up unconsciously from the question, she sits stiffly waiting for the answer.

"Your father and I are from the Schaeduwe Fellowship but from different families," Sarapheane says, dreading the question that is going to be asked next.

"But that does not make sense." Gabrian's face twists again as she tries to put everything together. "Before I came here, I experienced some unusual things but none of them are even close to being attributes of what you described about Shadow Walkers." Jarrison and Sarapheane give each other a glance, and Gabrian swears she heard them say the word 'adopted.'

The reality of adoption was never even a thought to her, ever. She does not resemble her parents identically, no, but what child does? She still had the dark hair like them, she was quite dainty and feminine-looking like her mom, and her skin was only a few shades lighter than her parents. She had no reason to ever consider it but now, she just might.

"You are telling me that I am adopted?" She stares blankly at them, her voice cracking.

"We did not say that out loud, Sarah," Jarrison says. "She must have read one of our minds."

"She is finding herself quickly," Sarapheane utters to

Jarrison.

"Excuse me!" Gabrian yells as large ridges form at the top of her nose, volleying her eyes back and forth between the two. "I am right here, please do not talk about me like I am not in the same room with you. Am I or am I not, adopted?"

A new revelation hits Gabrian like a hammer. "What a minute, did you say read your mind?" Her hands tremble, and she is barely able to hold onto the cup in her grip. She feels like her whole world is crumbling before her. Trying to find a way to deal with the notion of being different from others is one thing but resting on the cusp of realizing that her entire life has been nothing but a lie, she can barely breathe. Feeling drained, she instinctively begins to seek out an energy source to draw from.

"Gabrian, honey, please calm down." Seeing Gabrian's pupils dilate, her aura flares up, finally making its appearance—jetting out in search of sustenance. Finding nothing, she becomes confused and upset. Jarrison quickly jumps up and runs to the kitchen. Sarapheane realizes that Tynan is right. If Gabrian does not learn who she is and how to control her gifts, she could cause a lot of misery for everyone that comes in contact with her.

Returning from the kitchen with a lemon in one hand and a knife in the other, Jarrison slices the lemon into two pieces, holding one piece up to Gabrian's nose and gently rests his hand on her arm, causing her vision to go dim.

The lemon scent is a trick the Boragen instructors use on their younglings in training when they lose their focus and become frustrated like Gabrian has just done. She increases her focus by closing her eyes for her next inhale, but wrinkles crease the bridge of her nose—her nostrils flare as the sharp scent of the sour lemon bites at her senses, jarring her from the hunt, and abruptly brings her back around. Jarrison lets go of her arm once he is convinced that she is calm. As her sight returns to her, the wildness dwelling in her eyes recedes—her pupils their normal size once more. With the rapid fluttering of her lashes, her blinded glare softens into a hazy gaze and the aura that had appeared and threatened to seek out and destroy all in its path, slows its frantic search, floating lazily against her skin.

"Gabe, are you okay now?" Jarrison's soft voice hums through the room, and he hopes that the lemon has done the trick.

126

Gabrian looks around and wonders about the odd look that both of her parents are wearing and what could have happened to make them look that way.

A bit startled of her sudden lapse in memory, she looks to her parents. "Can someone please tell me what just happened here?" Gabrian reaches up and touches the end of her nose with her fingers, feeling the wetness and smelling the distinct scent of citrus. She glances down to the coffee table, noticing a knife and half of a lemon. The other half is in her father's hand. Raising her left brow, and twisting the end of her nose, she bites the edge of her bottom lip—befuddled by the oddity of it, she feels compelled to ask, "Can someome also explain to me why on earth my nose is covered in juice and why dad is holding onto a lemon?"

Chapter Seventeen

Of Love and Pain

SITTING ALONE IN front of the fireplace with the heat from the open flame flush against her skin, Gabrian still feels cold. Her heart is heavy with the magnitude of truths delivered to her today. After her Uncle Tynan had demonstrated a shockingly small glimpse of her new world, and the accidental probe of her parents' minds leading to the revelation of her unknown adoption, Gabrian's heartbeat echoes hollowly within her ribcage—her face, long and drawn out like a ghost irrevocably lost within worlds.

Jarrison and Sarapheane turn to stare at each other with wide eyes, exchanging silent words of sorrow—completely at a loss of how to bring their daughter of twenty-six years into the inevitable need of enlightenment of who she really is. They decide to tell her outright the occurrences of the night they came to be her parents.

Gabrian sits still within a comatose state as they begin to recount the story of her past and how everything came to be.

"It began like most stories do. A story about a boy who meets a girl, and how they fall in love. The boy was one of the Realms' most prominent Borrowers. Though his parents had died when he was young, he was adopted by a couple from the Realm and lived with them, continuing on with his training. As he grew, his gift developed for him with astonishing ease. He had a natural ability to easily lend and draw energy, as well as having the ability to read and persuade thought impressions within the minds of others, and because of this, he held great promise in becoming an Elder for the Boragen Fellowship one day. Though he was kind and thoughtful, he was also assertive and cunning when it came to getting what he wanted. And at that moment, what he wanted was to win over the beautiful Cera. She was the daughter of the last known Ancient Silver Mages—Markim Agryris, Elder of the Auncyen Arguros at the High Table in the Covenant of Shadows."

Recognizing the last name from the mysterious visitor in her office, she whips her head around with eyes no longer in a haze—mouth gaped open and wanting to interrupt, but she doesn't. Something inside her tells her to stop and listen instead.

"Because Cera was a Silver Mage, she had a number of different gifts and attended many classes in order to learn how to use and accentuate her abilities. The classes were insisted on by her father to prepare her to one day take his seat at the High Table. During the day, she went to school like everyone else, but in the afternoon and some evenings, she attended special classes and training at the Arts building that the Fellowships utilized in town. It was where those of the Realm who displayed gifts spent their time honing their talents. One of Cera's gifts was that of the Boragen Fellowship, and since Adrinn was a Borrower too, she attended some of the same classes as the boy.

"Cera could be found on the beach on most mornings when the skies were clear, perched on her favourite rock, waiting for the sun to rise. On one morning, she had an unexpected visitor—the boy. Finding out her weakness for sunrises, he decided to play that card and try to use it to his advantage of getting her attention. It worked. After that morning, they became inseparable. They spent every minute together, not allotted to school or training, which did not go unnoticed. Markim sat Cera down and pointed out her lax of duty toward her responsibilities as a Silver Mage and kindly encouraged her to return to her learning and to leave the Boragen boy alone. So, wanting to appease her beloved father's requests, Cera agreed.

"Cera met with the boy soon after she had spoken with her father and told him of her father's wishes for her to concentrate more on her studies and of his objections to their friendship. Outraged by her father's decision, he confronted Markim. The boy, being young and foolish, lost his temper which led to a brief moment of combat between the two. Being no match for the Silver Elder, and Markim still being that of a gentleman, he allowed the youngling to leave with merely his pride hurt more than anything.

"Cera found him later on at Sand beach, where they had first met, looking defeated and weak. He told her of his confrontation with Markim and what had happened—though he left out the parts not becoming of his own behaviour. Hearing all this, Cera felt that his suffering was somehow partly her fault. Seeing him that way saddened her deeply. Using her Borrower's gift of lending, she pushed a single fractal of her silver-coloured aura through him to the areas that seemed darkened and damaged, leaving him with only light, unknowingly igniting the beginning of their demise. From that point on, their love was to be hidden from her father's eyes.

"Over the next while, the two kept their distance from each other the best they could, but they barely saw each other. In secret, they made their rendezvouses in an old cave they learned about as children they called 'thunder hole.' They continued to meet like this for many months, hiding away from the watchful eye of the Realm—their embraces and exchanging energies became more and more intimate. But with all things, their perfect forbidden romance began to crumble. After one of their usual meetings, though everything started out the same, Cera sensed something changing within the boy. So she decided to follow him after her left her.

"Cera stalked behind him to the Local Café. Not wanting to be seen, she transformed her flesh into a mere bend of air and painfully watched as he began to affectionately embrace another girl. Though she excelled in the knowledge of how to use her gifts, she failed in the world of deceit. While spending most of her time after classes trying to appease her father by training, the boy had grown bored of being alone and began to wander. In one of his journeys, he met a Derkaz youngling named Symone Cole, who was wild and rebelling against her father—the Elder of her Fellowship. They began to spend time together, time that he wanted to share with Cera but was forbidden.

"Distraught from what appeared to her as an intentional deception, Cera left them in their hold inside the café, broken-hearted and confused. Days passed, and unaware that his extracurricular activities had been found out, Adrinn arranged for another meeting with Cera, but this time it was different. She was withdrawn and refused to release any of her essence to him. Confused by her denial, he found the images reeling around in her mind, eventually seeing the vision of him and Symone. He saw the anger and hurt in Cera's eyes and tried to explain to her that this girl meant nothing—that she was only a friend, and that he was in love with Cera.

"Not fully believing his outpouring of devotion, she looked for deceit in his thoughts, but unbeknown to Cera, her simple act of affection of lending him her life essence had caused his mind to become clouded and chaotic. She could not find any coherent thoughts in his mind—his intentions toward the girl were scrambled and unclear.

"Frustrated and hurt, she tried to leave, wanting to be alone. She could not see the madness in his eyes; she could not see that he was suffering from the craving clawing at his insides. He became agitated with her lack of cooperation and grabbed her by the shoulders. He threw her back against the cold damp cave wall and pinned her there, leaning in, to press his forehead up against hers. Without warning, he violently slammed into her aura with his mind, inhaling deeply trying to rip off pieces of her life force.

"Still in shock of his sudden attack, Cera felt her life essence being ripped away and her energy began to drop quickly. Having no other choice, she fought back. With his hands tightly gripped on her, she was forced to let her instincts take over—using whatever Magik that surfaced in order to escape. She finally shifted into her Schaeduwe form before he had a chance to attack her life force again. Pulling herself into the closest shadow she could find, she left him alone with his doings in the cave.

"Cera denied Adrinn's every attempt to apologize. After failing to win back Cera's trust, Adrinn disappeared for a few months; no one knew where he went. His teachers began to ask about his absence, but Cera knew as much as they did about where he was. Then, right before graduation from high school, Adrinn returned.

"She agreed to meet him, sensing that he was more under control and more like his old self again. Cera also noticed that something else had changed within him, but she could not figure out what it was. Cautiously, she began to spend time with him again, keeping him at arm's length. After a few weeks, he told her why he had acted the way he did. He explained to her that he had found a way to control his cravings and promised her that he would never lay a hand on her again.

"As time went on, Adrinn began to make trips to the city. His trips became more and more frequent. Even a few of the other Borrower younglings began to venture into the city with him. He returned to school to finish his studies, but his dedication to his education soon began to slip again, and his attendance at training was almost nonexistent.

"Trying not to focus so much on Adrinn, Cera began to notice changes in her own self as well. Her womanly visitor had stopped arriving—which at first she blamed on stress—but she began being nauseous about things that never bothered her before around the time of the onset of strange dreams that often entailed strange infant-like creatures. Cera realized that her subconscious was trying to tell her something she already knew—she was going to be a mother. Not wanting anyone to know her secret, she veiled herself so that no one could see her changing aura or thoughts. Unable to deal with everything that was going on with her life, Cera confided in her two best friends, Vaeda and myself."

Gabrian's eyes react quickly to Sarapheane's words, becoming glued to her mother's face. She recognizes the name of the other girl, envisioning the tall blonde woman from her apartment.

Sarapheane reaches out to give Gabrian's hand a gentle grasp, but without pausing, she continues with the story. "She did not tell us everything at first. Cera just needed a sounding board, but Vaeda and I figured it out so we were sworn to secrecy."

"Angry with Adrinn for causing Cera so much distress, Vaeda decided to follow him on one of his trips to the city to find out just how he was able to contain his cravings. Having lost sight of him for a moment, Vaeda quickly scoured the city, and once she relocated him, she found him in an alleyway in what would seem a most intimate embrace with a human girl. Vaeda grew angry with his deception, but looking more closely, she realized he was not engaging in a romantic moment at all—he was stealing the girl's life essence.

"He held the girl tightly around the throat with his hand. Once her heart stopped beating, he kissed her sweetly on the lips then let her drop lifelessly to the ground; a sign that he was finished with her. Adrinn then stepped over her body like she was nothing more than trash and strolled away, whistling an eerily happy tune.

"Appalled by what she had just witnessed, Vaeda immediately created a portal and returned to North East Harbor to find Cera. At first Cera refused to believe what Vaeda tried to tell her, but she pushed her memories of Adrinn's monstrous performance toward her friend, making her see what Adrinn was capable of. The images triggered Cera's suppressed memories of Adrinn's not-so-ancient attack on her in the cave, and she knew Vaeda was just trying to protect her—that she only tried to make Cera see what her heart so easily blinded. She thanked her friend and waited apprehensively for his return.

"Unsure of what to do, she mentioned nothing of what she knew when he returned, but informed him she would be unable to see him as much because she needed to attend extended training for her father's upcoming Silver assessment. Clearly upset with not being able to see her, Adrinn stormed off, but things seemed to settle down for a while. He stopped pressing her to meet him so often. She knew that she still loved him, but she was afraid of what she had seen in Vaeda's mind, terrified of what he was becoming.

"On the night of her final training session at the Arts building, she went home and found her father already retired for the evening, claiming he did not feel well. His Guardian, Orroryn, had been called away for the evening. She decided to go to bed early and fell fast asleep. She awoke distraught from a nightmare. Her father had come to her as a spirit, trying to show her something about his last moments. She saw him sipping wine from a goblet before stumbling his way to his room. The vision was blurred and dark, but in it, she saw glimpses of Adrinn standing over her father's bed, grinning and holding him by the neck as he pulled the last fragments of essence from his body before he died.

"Terrified by this vivid dream, she jumped out of bed and

ran to the other side of the house only to find her father's once powerful form completely cold and lifeless. Now entirely alone, the last Silver Mage in the Realm, her life became a whirlwind of responsibilities. With no time to properly mourn for her father, and repulsed by the vision that Adrinn could be responsible for his death, she completely closed herself down. The dream about her father began to eat away at her sanity so she broke down and confided in Orroryn, telling him about it. He revealed to her that before he had left for the Veil, Markim was fine and that his absence from her father had been a false alarm in security. Finding this all too convenient, Orroryn, who was now her Guardian, became extremely protective of her.

"At her next meeting at the Covenant of Shadows, it was brought to her attention that some of the people of the Realm began hearing rumours from the human world that their authorities believed there was a serial killer on the loose in the city of Bangor. They had found at least fifteen bodies left in alleyways around the outskirts of the city, all of which had the same type of marks that linked them—two black bruises around the main artery on their necks.

"Cera immediately envisioned Adrinn's disturbing image from Vaeda's recent share. She quickly shielded the thoughts as to not cause any unnecessary inquiries into her own nightmare. No one in the Covenant suspected anyone from the Realm yet to be the culprit. Once the meeting was over, Orroryn delivered her home safely. He cautioned her to stay inside for the night because he had to leave her temporarily unguarded. She agreed to stay in, but suddenly feeling nauseous, Cera craved the need for cool air against her skin. Contrary to Orroryn's wishes, she left the house and went to the beach.

"Distracted by the thoughts of her father's death and the news from the human world, she did not hear Adrinn as he approached her. Feeling nervous, Cera was ready to shift at any sign of danger from him. Adrinn tried to convince her that everything was fine now, that they could be together, and that the Gargons had enlightened him about the real meaning of the circle of life. He revealed to her that they showed him it was natural to use human life essences to live and that this act was what his true gift was—that he should no longer deny himself this joy. He believed the teachers from the Realm were wrong about using the light and energy of people—they were lying to all of them about its dangers.

"Watching Adrinn going on and on in his crazed tangent prompted the fight-or-flight instincts within her. It finally convinced her that she had to tell the other Elders of Adrinn's mental state. He had become exactly what they warned all Boragen younglings to be cautious of, and what they did not want to become. With the Fever set in, he was beyond help and the taste of death lingered on his tongue. He was a Vampire, convinced it was what he was rightfully intended to be.

"Trying not to arise any suspicion in Adrinn about her true intentions, she promised to meet him later in the meadow by the large amethyst boulder just before nightfall, and they could be together then. He agreed to meet her there. Cera ran as fast as she could to the house after Adrinn left and cast a summoning spell to all the Elders of the Covenant of Shadows. Within moments, she arrived at the Firethorn bush by the end of her gate where Jarrison, who then was Guardian of the Covenant of Shadows, was hailed to guide her through the shadows that led her into the center of the mountain. Inside, all the Elders were in attendance, and she told them everything—well, almost everything.

"She delivered the story of how she had suspected Adrinn was having issues and mentally projected to them the images that Vaeda had shown her from the city. She let them hear his recount of confessions on his theory of stealing life essence, convincing them that his Vampiric Fever was responsible for all the deaths being reported in the human world. They prepared for the meeting that was to take place that evening.

"Saddened by what had to happen, Cera knew as keeper of the house she had to maintain order at all costs, even if the price was her heart."

Chapter Eighteen

Sounds Like a Party

"CERA OPENED THE portal and walked through. On the other side, Adrinn eagerly awaited her. He looked so happy that it broke Cera's heart. She hoped that Ethan, who was hidden nearby, could enter Adrinn's mind and find enough clear thought patterns to determine whether they could somehow save Adrinn from the fever. One by one, the other Elders slid into the vicinity from low energy portals in order to take necessary action if needed. Knowing this, Cera tried to distract Adrinn as best she could so that he might not pick up on their presence until confirmation from Ethan was made.

"Ethan tried his best to secretly press into Adrinn's mind in search of the severity of the fever, and find out the depths of its Darkness, but Adrinn picked up on the intrusion and immediately shot out his senses in all directions, locating the Elders' auras easily. Cera tried to explain to him that they were only trying to help, but he would not listen to her. Feeling trapped, Adrinn found the nearest energy source—Theodon, the Hydor Elder. Without warning, he inhaled deeply and pulled violently at the light surrounding Theodon's body, so hard that he ripped the aura completely from him, leaving the Elder lifeless—prey for the Gargons.

"Charged with Theoden's blue energy, any rationality within Adrinn was gone. It had been agreed upon earlier that if he could not be saved then he must be contained or worse, destroyed. Cera sadly began the incantation. They felt Adrinn pull on their life essence. Having beared witness to the degree of damage that he was capable of, they encouraged Cera to concentrate harder as she began to draw on their individual gifts for the binding spell.

"Suddenly there was a detonation from somewhere, hitting them hard. Adrinn had thrust a ton of mental energy through their minds, knocking them to the ground. Adrinn turned to run, but Orroryn grabbed him and held him down, which allowed Cera to rise up from the ground and begin the binding again, drawing from the Elders.

"Fire, Ice, Air, and Earth, she entered them all into the incantation, pulling fragments of their energies together into a ring that she pushed toward Adrinn—sealing in his ability to draw energy from those around him. Cera was instructed to destroy him, but she could not do it. Feeling her body begin to drain of energy, she became afraid for the life inside her and ordered Kaleb to open the Earth beneath the Orb that encased Adrinn.

"Cera watched as the Earth opened up and yelled to Cimmerian to create the portal to Erebus. Unable to watch his dispelling, she asked Vaeda to make him sleep so he would no longer suffer. Vaeda agreed to Cera's request and within moments, Adrinn stopped fighting. His eyes closed as the air within the orb became stale. Teetering on exhaustion, Cera completed the words of her incantation and pushed the orb into the opening of the black mist. The portal opened, swallowing the orb and dispelled it into the Darkness of the hole, sealing Adrinn inside.

"Cera fell to the ground, clutching her stomach in pain. When she collapsed, Orroryn rushed to her, pulling her into his arms before he stepped into the Darkness of night. After delivering her home, Orroryn begged her to come back into the Veil of the Shadow where she would heal, but she refused in fear that it may harm the baby. Only Shadow Walkers can survive the shadows for any length of time and not knowing if her Magik would be passed onto the baby, she did not want to risk the life of her unborn child.

"Orroryn left Cera's side briefly to return with help—Jarrison and myself. I prepared for the delivery, cleaning the birthing area as best I could before I began swabbing her forehead with a cool, damp cloth. Cera held my hand and kept repeating the same words over and over to me. 'No matter what happens to me, save the baby. Take care of the baby.' She fell into a trance until Jarrison and I promised her that we would. She then closed her eyes and began to chant in an ancient tongue.

"Because Cera had no idea what gifts, if any, the child would possess, she created a spell that would suppress a Boragen gift if it were to be the gift to awaken. She manipulated the spell to hide the child from the Realm. She cloaked the essence around the life inside her to make the aura invisible and seem as though it were of Shadow Walker descent like Jarrison and I. She then placed wards around the borders of her home to keep out anyone that might want to harm the child.

"Once the spell was finally cast, she grew weak. She pleaded with those in the room to tell no one that the child was hers and Adrinn's. She wanted the child to have a chance at a life away from Magik. She told us to tell the Covenant of Shadows and the people of the Realm that the baby was found abandoned after they had dealt with Adrinn. She then gave her home to Jarrison and I for safe keeping until you were of age, asking Orroryn to deliver the papers that she had prepared earlier as a precautionary measure if things had gone badly.

"She took my hand deeper into her own and held it tightly. With one heart-wrenching cry, she pushed with all that was left of her strength and collapsed into unconsciousness. Shrill cries could be heard throughout the house as a beautiful baby girl entered the world."

Sarapheane stops for a moment to take her daughter's hands into her own as Cera had done to her so many years ago. "That baby girl was you, Gabrian."

Knowing all along in the back of her mind that the story of the child had something to do with her, Gabrian is still startled to hear the words. "*I* am the child?" Gabrian's clouded gaze rises timidly to search for truth within Sarapheane's own eyes. Her tongue feels thick as she tries to speak, swallowing hard. "What happened to Cera?"

"After we took care of you and made sure that you were alright, I checked on Cera. She was barely breathing. Her pulse was almost nonexistent. We all knew that she was near death. Orroryn gently scooped her up into his arms then in a low monotone voice told us to take care of the child—to tell no one of what happened there that night, and that he was taking Cera to the Shadows in the hopes of saving her."

"Why would he take her to the Shadows instead of a doctor?" Gabrian growls, straightening her back and sitting upright. She rushes her fingers through her hair, bunching it on top of her head, not understanding the importance of Orroryn's actions. "It does not make any sense."

Sarapheane begins to explain to Gabrian that the Veil of Shadows is a very different and powerful place. Cera held the Shadow Walker gift inside her. She would be able to enter into the shadow dimension and use its Magik to heal her body, hopefully enough to replenish her dwindling life essence.

Gabrian sits quietly for a moment, still dumbfounded about everything she has just been told. She shakes her head and raises her eyebrows as she gets up from the chair and trudges across the living room floor to the window, gazing out into the ocean just beyond the house. She lowers her head then raises it again as if something else has dawned on her. "If she went to all that trouble to save me..." Gabrian's voice breaks. She takes a deep choppy breath as her lips tremble, trying to convince the words to leave her mouth. "How come she has never come back for me?"

Sarapheane gets up and crosses the room to where Gabrian stands. She reaches out her arms and wraps them around Gabrian's waist, trying to offer her daughter some support. Feeling Gabrian tense slightly, Sarapheane becomes saddened at the realization that their bond has now been fractured and may never be the same again.

Putting her feelings aside, she holds onto Gabrian just the same. "It is not what you think, Gabe," Sarapheane begins and hugs her even tighter. "When one enters into the Shadows, time between the two Realms runs differently."

Gabrian's face twists as she turns to look at Sarapheane. "Differently?" Gabrian looks back toward the water. She chuckles sarcastically then with a snide tone she comments, "Let me guess, it is some kind of supernatural event that takes place." She throws and twists her hands in the air in front of her in an over-animated manner.

Giving Gabrian a quick squeeze, Sarapheane returns to her chair and places her right hand on Jarrison's shoulder, giving him the green light.

"When you enter the Shadows, time passes at different rates than if you were to remain in this Realm." Gabrian turns toward him and tilts her head. "If I were to spend an hour inside the Shadows, when I return, it could be more than a day in time passing here—even a day inside, can elapse sometimes up to more than a week in this Realm. It is dependent on how far into the Shadows you go. For those like the Covenant of Shadows Guardians, who spend most of their duty on the fringe of the Veil, time passes somewhat closer to that of Earth's momentum of time. But Cera is resting deeper in the Shadow Veil where she must stay in order to heal. Where she is, the time passes much more quickly for us here on Earth. So what seems like an eternity to some has only been a short amount of time to those inside."

Seeing that this explanation has not erased the hurt from Gabrian's expression, Sarapheane tries to clarify. "She has not come back for you because she is still weak and healing. She is where she needs to be in order to survive—the deepest parts of the Shadow."

Understanding that Cera's absence has only been minimal within the Veil dimension, Gabrian nods her head. Still staring out the window, she imagines the differences in time between the two worlds to be the same as that of a grain of sand compared to the vastness of the ocean. Her mind drifts into nothingness becoming blank and shutting off for a moment in order to deal with her new reality.

"She loves you very much," Sarapheane offers, taking hold of Jarrison's hand, and in a quiet unsure voice she offers a bit more. "And so do we."

Gabrian knows if she lets the emotional side of her brain take over, she is going to break down and lose it. She flinches at the thought of delving into some type of depression that would cause her to want to drown within the waves of slumber, cast her time away, and pretend none of this is real—guarding her sanity within the trickery of denial. Or she can accept her parents' truths, go forward, and try to figure out how to deal with all this in a productive logical way.

After a few minutes of silence, she runs her hands through her hair in her last moment of self-pity. She sighs loudly then turns to stare at her parents. "So...this is it?"

Catching Jarrison and Sarapheane off guard with her unusual question, they look at each other in surprise. "Sorry?" Sarapheane answers.

"This is it. This is my life now? My days going forward, filled with Shadow Walkers who can slip in and out of Shadows at will and Magikal beings who can cast spells. And best yet, people like me who can just suck the life right out of a person without even touching them?"

Not knowing how to take Gabrian's demeanor, Jarrison and Sarapheane stare at each other, searching for words as to how they might address Gabrian's comments.

A slightly hysterical laugh escapes Gabrian's lips as she claps her hands loudly and rubs them together.

"Well then!" She huffs, her mouth turning upward at the corners in an edgy smirk. "Sounds like a whole lot of fun to me. Bring on the party."

Chapter Nineteen

Darkness Within

FINALLY GETTING OVER the shock of learning about her past and who she is, Gabrian realizes she has left her office completely unprepared in case of an extended absence. Sarapheane assures her that all is taken care of, and that right now, she has more important matters to attend to.

After what feels like weeks of being cooped up inside her parent's house, being out and about in her mother's car is refreshing. Gabrian is happy to be in the real world again—even if it meant being on her way to meet a complete stranger that is going to help her learn how to control the monster that lingers inside of her. Or so she thinks.

As they drive along the curved and twisty roads from North East Harbor into Bar Harbor, Gabrian smiles, remembering how beautiful the towns really are. She did not remember everything about living here when she was young, but she did recall faint memories of how they used to spend their summers here.

After her parents had moved them to Manhattan in order to give her a chance at better schooling—so her father said, even though she was quite certain that her education would have been just fine growing up in Maine—they returned every summer to take in all the beauty that the Maine coastline had to offer.

Gabrian finds her mind drifting back to when she was a child playing on the beach. Closing her eyes, she can almost feel the warmth of the summer sun on her face but her jaunt back to childhood is quickly derailed when an icy cold wind blows through the car as her mom opens the door to get out. Gabrian is abruptly pulled back into the present where it is freezing, snowy, and where she is not playing innocent childish games anymore.

She feels her stomach drop when her mother peeks back into the car, giving her a look that tells her she needs to move. They had reached their destination. Completely uncertain of what is about to happen, she can feel the tips of her fingers begin to burn. She sucks in a long comforting breath and flexes her fingers—shaking them out nervously, trying to stay calm. Gabrian closes her eyes and reaches inside herself to find the voice that always tells her to be brave. Finding it, she takes one last deep breath, letting the sound echo in her mind in the hopes it will give her the courage she needs to make herself get out of the car. After all she has heard and seen these past few weeks, this should be a walk in the park. Gabrian shakes her head and thinks, *Never mind, bad idea, Let's skip the park.*

They exit the vehicle and step onto the sidewalk. In front of them is a quaint little shop with the sign De Loon hanging over top of it. To its left is a small purple door that leads to Ethan Borne's office on the second floor. Seeing Gabrian's look of despair, Sarapheane takes her by the hand and gives it a gentle squeeze of encouragement. "Everything will work its way out. You will like Ethan. Don't worry."

Gabrian attempts to deliver a smile but only manages to conjure up a queer toothy grin for her mother. Sarapheane gives her another look and shakes her head accompanied by soft laughter as she starts her ascent of the wooden staircase. Gabrian falls in place and trudges up the stairs behind her.

Moments after being seated in the small waiting room, they hear a raspy voice break the silence with a warm welcome. "Sarah. So good to see you." A very handsome middle-aged man with salt-and-pepper hair appears from around the corner and walks over to greet them. Sarapheane and Ethan exchange a friendly embrace before he turns his attention to Gabrian.

"You must be Gabrian," he says, extending his right hand out to her. Gabrian politely accepts it and smiles.

"Yes," she whispers confidently. "And you must be Mr. Borne."

"Please, call me Ethan. It makes me feel ancient when someone calls me Mr. Borne."

Gabrian nods and lets go of his hand.

"I hope you do not mind, but your parents and Vaeda have both spoken to me about helping you with your training. Normally all instruction is done in the Arts building at the College, but I suggested that because this is such a unique circumstance, that maybe a one-on-one approach might make the transition a bit more bearable." Ethan smiles at both Gabrian and Sarapheane—his eyes sparkle warmly, creasing at the edges.

"Thank you for doing this, Ethan," Sarapheane says then looks at Gabrian. "Do you want me to stay or would you rather do this on your own?"

Gabrian's whole body wants to turn and bolt, but she knows it will not help solve anything so she sighs and softly tells her mother that she will be fine.

"What time should I come get her?"

"Don't worry about it, Sarah. I will bring her home when she has had enough," Ethan replies, looking over at Gabrian with an impish grin.

Unsure of what Ethan means by 'enough', Gabrian gives her mom a hug before being left all alone with a complete stranger who has been given complete control of her life and the challenge of unraveling the beginning of her terrifying future.

Ethan escorts his friend to the door then smiles to himself hearing the unease in Gabrian's mind. He strolls back to where she stands, wide-eyed and alone, chewing on her thumbnail and says, "The terrifying part is only temporary, just to let you know."

Gabrian's eyes sharpen under her squinted brow, and she drops her hand, tucking it around her ribs. Raising her sight to look Ethan directly in the eye, she begins, "How did you...?"

Ethan's mouth twists impishly at the edges then taps the side of his temple with his finger. "The ability to hear thoughts, just one of the special perks of being Boragen."

With Ethan's charismatic smile and easygoing gestures, Gabrian begins to feel like things might not be as scary as what she had imagined the last few days. Deciding to embrace this, she looks upon him with new hope—suddenly becoming more curious about what this man can do to help her take on and excel at this new challenge that now lies before her.

"Can all Boragen read minds like you just did?"

Ethan shakes his head 'no' as he slides around the side of his desk and takes a seat in his swivel-office chair. He waves his hand at Gabrian, signaling her to take a seat wherever she feels comfortable. "All beings have the gift of hearing thought. They just have to know how to listen." Ethan's mouth curls up at the edges again.

"All beings, you mean *everyone*?" Gabrian gasps. "Even humans?"

"Yes. All things, no matter how different they may seem, come from a common beginning," Ethan hums to her knowingly. "When the mind creates a thought, it creates an electrical current through the brain, and it resonates on a specific wavelength. And, if you happen to be one of the few who actually pay attention, you can intercept that wavelength then catch the messages that are being carried through that current."

Ethan watches Gabrian as he explains the process to her. The overwhelmed strain across her lips softens as her somberness passes. Her eyes shift from left to right, playing tag with reason and logic as her interest grows in a more positive direction—one that he hoped to see. "The only way I can really explain how I do it is this—I quiet my mind and let it relax. The thoughts that are the strongest come in broken passages, echoes almost. And sometimes I am able to even visualize what they are picturing in their minds, depending on how vivid their thoughts are."

Gabrian finds all this fascinating. If this is true, then that would explain how many times she was able to diagnose her client's issues so easily while they themselves struggled to find the words to even explain what was going on in their heads.

No wonder it comes so natural.

Ethan observes her as she becomes lost within her own thoughts. "Did you want to begin with this or..."

Thinking quickly about it, Gabrian decides that it might be best to learn how to control herself—a pretty important step to learn if she ever hopes to have some kind of normal life again. She has her practice to go back to. She did not work this hard studying and working her fingers to the bone just to throw it all away.

"No. I was hoping to start with learning control."

"True, that might be the best place to start." Ethan nods his head in agreement, scratching the edge of his goatee with his fingers. "Especially after what happened in the park."

Gabrian freezes, remembering why Ethan looks so familiar to her. He was there that night. He was the one wrapping light fragments around those people—the people she had hurt. Feeling embarrassed and sick about what she had done, her face turns bright red, and her aura appears around her, flickering grey sparks.

Noticing her aura finally making its appearance with a burst of flaming energy, Ethan realizes he may have hit a nerve. Not wanting to disrupt their fragile new relationship, he tries to comfort her by asking her to clear her mind, to try to focus on his energy. Gabrian returns from her dismay and tries to do as he asks—happy to forget that night, she begins to quiet her mind.

She tries to locate the sensations within her mind like before in order to feel Ethan's energy, but she can't find anything in the room. Outside the small office, she feels slight energy vibrations but nothing closer to her. "I can't pick up your energy." She huffs, breaking off her attempt at concentrating and opens her eyes. She notices that Ethan has been watching her confusion all along, smiling—his hands cupped and his thumbnails gently resting on his full lips.

"Right, that is because I am restraining it."

Gabrian's face twists in her confusion.

"I am, in a way, cloaking it from anyone born of the Realm or humanoid with the gift of sight, they are unable to see it or sense it," Ethan explains.

"Is that why I have never seen my parents' auras?" she questions him, eager for answers. "Did they cloak them from me as well?"

"No. It is not the same for them." He laughs softly at her curiosity. "Jarrison and Sarah are Shadow Walkers. A Shadow Walker does not display an aura; therefore, they are not susceptible to the weaknesses that the rest of us deal with when facing a force that might be interested in stealing life essence."

"You mean a Vampire. Right?" Gabrian grumbles quietly.

"Well, now that you have mentioned it, yes, like a Vampire." Ethan sits up in his chair and leans forward, resting his forearms on his desk. "Luckily, we have not had too many issues lately." Not wanting to discuss Vampires right now and discourage her, Ethan tries to get her to continue with her lesson. "We can talk about all that later. Now, I would like for you to try that again and this time, I will release my essence so that you will see the difference."

Feeling nervous about seeking his energy, she hesitates but with a confident nod of approval from Ethan, she closes her eyes once more in order to concentrate. At first there is nothing—like before—but then she begins to pick up subtle vibrations that make her skin tingle a bit. She can feel it now, close by. There is more than one type of vibration though; there are a multitude that vary in strength. Right away she is drawn to the more intense vibrations. Ethan, who is monitoring her thoughts, breaks the silence. "Try to concentrate on the lower vibrations. These are the energies that you will want to seek out. The others that you find so interesting are what we call the life essences and these vibrations are the ones we do not borrow from."

Right away she breaks the connection with Ethan and opens her eyes. Still fearful of harming someone the way she had before, her hands begin to tremble. Her mind relives her recent moments of Darkness, and she wonders if she is like him—like Adrinn; if she is dark and evil just like the monster that he became—if that is the reason why those people in the park got hurt. She feels the panic setting in and decides to find out from the only person who could probably tell her. She lifts her head, gathering her courage and exhales. "Am I dangerous?"

Ethan looks up at her and feels a twinge of sadness sweep through him as he hears the timid words leave her mouth.

"Am I dark inside like those who become swallowed up by the Fever and turn into..." Not wanting any of this to be true, she hesitates and swallows hard as she tries to spit out the words. "...into a Vampire?"

Feeling her fear suddenly fill the room, Ethan becomes aware of the depth of her fright about what she is. He tells her no. "Just because you were born with the gift of Boragen does not necessarily make you a killer. It also does not make you what the

148

world would consider a true Vampire. So you have made a couple of mistakes, every youngling does and you were not entirely at fault. You were left alone to discover the power you possess without proper guidance and counsel—that was our fault."

Looking down at her hands, she wrings them together, feeling vulnerable. She lifts her eyes to see Ethan's kind face staring back at her and takes the next step to finding her answers. "Is it true that you can look deep within the mind and see whether there is Darkness there?"

"Yes, I have done that before. But..." Ethan begins to elaborate but he is cut off.

"Can you do that for me?"

"I really do not think that this is necessary, Gabrian, it is a very personal thing." He drags his fingers through the top of his hair, letting it fall chaotically in place. "Are you sure you want me to do that?"

"Yes, I am sure." Gabrian nods, assuring him. "I need to know."

It is not bad enough that she is dangerous unintentionally; Gabrian needs to know for herself whether or not if she is a monster.

Ethan agrees to search her mind for any signs of Darkness that may lead to her developing the Fever. He warns her that she will feel some slight pressures within her head, and that she might become disoriented for a few moments afterward, but Gabrian insists that it is necessary—to go ahead and do it. She buries any traces of Adrinn and Cera into the deepest parts of her mind before they start. She knows he will probably find out all her secrets eventually, but this one she vows to keep hidden—at least for now.

Ethan takes a deep breath and lets his mind quiet. He listens for Gabrian's wave length and waits for it to cross his. He finds her thoughts, and her mind opens up to him. As he stabilizes the connection within her subconscious, Ethan begins to sift through the colours of her mind for signs of concern. From his many years of working with humans and people of the Realm, Ethan knows that the truth of the matter is that all beings have Darkness in them, even if it is only a small amount.

Ethan continues to search but finds nothing more than what feels like a corridor with normal compartments in it, at first. Then he realizes he has only been allowed access to one of the many rooms that Gabrian holds within the depths of her mind. He observes the illusion of the doors and their similar dimensions. Curious as to what secrets these rooms may hold, Ethan begins to push and probe at them gently, but they are locked, tightly—a fortress impassible from his feeble attempts to breach them. Each time he thinks that he has found a clear passage, Ethan's mind is blinded and pushed back violently by an excruciating bright energy burst. After a couple more attempts to breech the doors, his efforts develop into a headache; an indication that although this girl has the most amazing subconscious he has ever seen, he is painfully wasting his time trying to find out why. Ethan hopes that maybe once he can establish some kind of trust level with her he may have better luck resolving his curiosity at another time.

Finding no sizable measures of Darkness, or signs of the Fever, Ethan recedes from her mind.

He sits back in his chair and rubs his brow in an attempt to appease the now present ache pulsating in his forehead. He lifts his eyes and glances over at her, feeling the weight of her stare as she patiently awaits the verdict. He contemplates his possible choice of wording; cognizant that mentioning anything about the bizarre encounter that he has just had with her subconscious is probably going to be counterproductive in any future attempts to help placate her fears.

Ethan lowers his hand and wedges his fingers underneath the grooved handle attached to the desk drawer in front of him. Pulling gently on the handle, he slides the drawer open and reaches inside, retrieving a much needed bottle of Advil. After opening the bottle and dryly swallowing two of the pills inside, he puts them back away.

"Well..." he announces, chuckling at Gabrian with her crooked lips, drooping at the edges—heavy with torment—and her eyes merely two slits beneath a wrinkled brow. "I can assure you that you are definitely not a monster. So...now that we have determined that you are not destined for Vampirism, at least not today anyways, shall we try again?

Chapter Twenty

Who Wants Coffee

AFTER SPENDING THE last few days working with Ethan, Gabrian has begun to enjoy her time with him. He teaches her how to seek out and draw in the darker energies. These energies are the ones that humans and people from the Realm waste on things like stress or anger. She learns how to use them to replenish her own energy levels. Ethan explains to her that the ability to store and distribute the darker energies throughout their bodies and minds gives them a regenerative upper hand. It allows the Boragen people—or Borrowers as they were more commonly known—to age at a slower rate than some of the others from the Realm. Depending on how well one learns to utilize the energy, they can live for a very long time and appear to some as immortal.

Ethan also explains to Gabrian how the gift of lending works as well. Because the Borrowers take in energy, they also have to expel the excess energy that they do not use. When this energy is released and given back in small doses to the human or beings, it acts like an endorphin in the receiver's brain. It starts a chemical reaction that creates a feel good response much like athletes get after a workout. So in turn, being a Boragen can be a very useful gift at times. Ethan wants Gabrian to understand that the Borrowers were very much a beautiful people with much to share with the world around them.

Gabrian begins to feel better about things, a sense of peace, almost. Her fear of hurting anyone is beginning to subside, but at the end of the day, her fears always seem to creep up on her whenever she has to leave the safety of Ethan's office. Gabrian knows this is something she has to soon overcome as she begins to hear the ticking of the clock becoming louder; her time here in Bar Harbor is quickly coming to an end.

In the middle of her session, while she familiarizes the different energies emanating outside from the people walking on the sidewalk in front of Ethan's office building, Gabrian's mind begins to overload with all her unanswered questions. She hates being in the dark and right now, Ethan is the only one she knows that has any of the answers she needs.

"Ethan?"

"Yes, Gabrian?" Ethan hums as he continues to work on his files.

"Remember when I was at the park that time..." she starts, pulling her focus away from the streets. Her face wheels to the left following the direction of her eyes, continuing to rest her chin on the top of her folded hands.

"Yes, I remember." Feeling her nervousness, he wonders if he is going to have to explain to her again that it was not her fault. "It was not..."

"I know, I know, you already told me that it was not my fault. That was not my question."

Putting down the paperwork he was trying to catch up on while Gabrian 'practiced' on the pedestrians below, he lifts his gaze to meet her eyes. She stares at him with a clear pensive look that Ethan has learned means something important is on her mind. "Okay, I am all ears," he says, sitting back in his chair before putting his hands behind his head. "Fire away."

"When I was in the park, and in my apartment, I remember the energy from the people around me being bright high vibrating energy."

"Yes, those are the life essences that keep our bodies running."

"They felt a lot different to me than the darker, less illuminated energies I have been working on with you," Gabrian explains. "They felt more intoxicating and exciting."

"That is because they are."

"Then, why not learn to use that in moderation?" Gabrian asks. "I mean, I know that it is good to give back, or lend as you call it, to our host but why not use the light?"

"The Boragen, or Borrowers, are very sensitive when it comes to taking in energy. When we use the lower frequency energies, we are able to do so and still be productive. We contribute to the wellbeing of ourselves and to those around us. But when we take or use the life essence of a host, because this essence is so pure and so powerful, it overwhelms us."

Gabrian thinks back and catches glimpses of the elated feelings she had sensed. She recalls how everything became hazy and deluged together in such a state that she could not decipher one thing from another in the experience.

Ethan contemplates the easiest way to explain it to her. He grabs his Advil out of his desk drawer and sets it on his desk. "It is like this. If you were to get a mild everyday kind of headache, would you take one of these?" He picks up the pills and shakes them to make her notice the ordinary bottle. "Or would you go to your doctor and get a prescription for Morphine to use?"

Gabrian looks at him then the bottle. "I would take the Advil, of course."

"Exactly. Effective in relieving the headache without causing any issues," Ethan concurs. "But...what would happen if you chose to take Morphine every time?"

"Well, there is a good chance that I would become addicted to it." Gabrian rubs her temples in a psychosomatic headache, understanding the difference.

"Right, and becoming addicted to it causes people to change who they are in order to get what they want, or what they crave. Many times these cravings lead good people to bad places," Ethan explains. "In the case of a Borrower, on occasion, it triggers something within their brain that causes them to become symptomatic to a condition we call the Fever. Not all who taste the light will get these cravings, but the ones that do...well, it saddens me to say very few resist the thirst."

Keeping her mind locked tightly in case Ethan decides to pry, Gabrian recounts the story that her parents had told her of Adrinn. She begins to worry again about his downfall and her previous lack of control. "What happens to those who get the

Fever?"

"Once the Fever sets in, and the Vampiric instincts take over, it all becomes about them. They no longer think about others as they would have before, at least not usually. They slowly become a slave to the constant craving of energy. As time goes on, the amount of energy they thirst for gets larger and larger. Unfortunately, it will rise to the point that they begin to take all of their host's life essence in order to satisfy their hunger and lull the craving into compliance. And it is because of this that they become a danger to everyone they come into contact with, human and people of the Realm alike. It is not condoned by the Covenant of Shadows to allow such acts of miscreation and therefore is punishable by death. Those who cannot be saved, or most likely do not want to be saved, leave the Realm in order to escape incarceration."

Gabrian turns her head and stares out the window. She watches the mundane civilians go about their business and wonders out loud, "Are there many Vampires out there? I mean, does the Fever occur a lot?"

"It happens more than I would like to admit. But, I also believe that everyone makes their own choices in this world," Ethan offers, giving her a warm smile. His eyes wrinkle at the edges, and his gaze softens, making direct contact with hers, hoping she is not losing faith. "Condemning someone because of what they were born as, is not something I condone—believing in what someone can overcome and achieve is much more important."

Feeling that she might begin to slip backward from all the progress she has made, Ethan decides it is time to step it up a notch in her training. It is time to pull her out of the comfort zone he has allowed her to create in his office. "Enough of this, what do you say we go for a walk?" he says, jumping up out of his chair and grabbing his coat.

"You mean, outside?" Gabrian's eyes widen, and her face becomes absent of all colour like she has just seen a ghost. She feels safe within the walls of his office but now he is taking that away. Gripping the wooden window frame, she feels the tips of her fingers start to tingle and heat up—the same sensation she always gets when she becomes upset.

"Of course outside. Where else do you take a walk?" Ethan laughs, holding out Gabrian's jacket for her as he notices her discontent. "We have been cooped up in here too long. It is time to hit the town."

Tucking her bottom lip in under her teeth, she bites down giving him a wide-eyed pleading look, hoping he will change his mind and let her stay inside. He grins at her and throws the jacket at her playfully. "I need a coffee. The brew here has much to be desired and...from the sour expression that always follows your face after you take a sip of the office blend, you must be craving to have a real one too."

Her apprehension begins to subside at the thought of holding a warm fragrant coffee in her hands.

"I know a great little coffee shop just up the street."

"I guess it would not hurt to step out for a bit." Gabrian pulls her coat on and reaches for the hat in her pocket to ward off the cold that awaits them outside.

"Great!" Ethan cheers and heads for the exit. "To the Coffee Hound it is. They have a great little gingerbread-flavoured Mocha called 'The Enchanted Forest' that you might enjoy."

As they idle down the sidewalk, Ethan asks Gabrian to practice reaching out, to try to feel all the different energies she can find around her. He explains that all energies essentially are the same, but it flows differently from each source. Each individual's aura vibrates at different rates causing the different colours and sizes of fragmentation that occur. Once she allows herself the benefit of the doubt that she will not hurt anyone, Gabrian begins to see the beautiful spectrum of colours that float freely all around her.

From across the street, a Raven catches her eye, bouncing from roof to roof and keeping in exact time with Gabrian and Ethan's stride. At first Gabrian does not think anything of it, but as they continue, she is convinced the darn thing is following them. She knows that they are peculiar kind of birds but even to her this seems a bit odd. It looks at her and stops, noticing her attention. It jumps off the clothing store roof and glides across the street above them, landing on the light post just ahead. It moves its head from side to side as it focuses directly on her then quickly turns its attentions to Ethan and squawks at him loudly. It hops up and down, continuing to caw as to demonstrate its immediate disapproval with Ethan's presence.

"Ah, away with you!" Ethan growls as he waves his hand at the bird.

"Doesn't seem like he cares for you very much," Gabrian pokes at Ethan playfully, laughing at the comical exchange of banter between the two.

"Yeah, something like that," he says, rolling his eyes and continuing on his way past the irate bird. "That is a story for another day."

She laughs again at Ethan's irritation then something else catches her interest. Gabrian watches as a mother and her three young children make their way up the street toward them. The children's auras are bright and vibrant, but she notices the colours around the woman are different. They flicker sporadically with darkened fragments as she struggles to keep her youngest boy from running out into the street.

Feeling sympathy for the woman who has her hands full, Gabrian reaches out, gently pulling at the darken strands that continue to creep out around the woman's body. She inhales like she has rehearsed many times with Ethan, tasting the essences as they enter her body. Letting the subtle waves of electricity soak into her muscles like a warm embrace, Gabrian then exhales, sending out a coloured fringe that encircles the woman as she walks past. She smiles in hopes that her gift will make the journey to wherever they are heading a little more pleasant for the young woman.

Watching the instinctual act of kindness Gabrian has just displayed makes Ethan smile. At that very moment he feels Gabrian is on the right path, and now it is his job to make sure that she stays there.

After they order their lattes from the cashier at the Coffee Hound, they sit at the window and take in their surroundings. Ethan asks Gabrian to continue with the same exercise as she had on their walk there. With more confidence, she begins to gently borrow and lend energies with all those around her—each time finding the people who seem to need it the most. Ethan enjoys watching her help some of the more stressed out or troubled customers that enter the room and how much she seems to delight in it; it is like watching a child with a new toy. All of it comes so naturally to her that it is hard for Ethan to believe that she had only been in training for a couple of weeks.

On the way back to the office—while speaking to Ethan about how he likes having a practice in such a quiet little town—Gabrian notices a very dark aura out of the corner of her eye. Surprised by how dark it is, she instinctively turns her head to get a better look at it; when she does, there is nothing there. She begins to get the distinct feeling that they are being watched.

Noticing her distraction, Ethan inquires if everything is okay.

"Yes, everything is fine." She pulls her touque down and tucks her hair back up underneath of it. She had turned so quickly her hat slipped up on her head. "Ethan?"

"Yes, Gabrian?" He grins, knowing there is an important question that will follow.

"Are all Fellowships Black and White?"

"Black and white, Gabrian?" His face contorts, creasing his brow and twisting his mouth into a crooked grin, not quite sure how to decipher the context of this question.

"Not black and white as in the colour but like the metaphor." She explains in a heavy breath, waving her hands around as if this will help her inability to explain as they reach the office door. Ethan opens the it for her and lets her walk through first. She continues her explanation on their way up the stairs.

"What I mean is, you and my parents have explained to me about the different gifts that the people of the Realm each have or are born with. Then based upon that, they are classified as either Boragen, Shadow Walkers, and so on and so forth."

"Yes, I am listening," he says, trying not to look so perplexed. Sometimes when Gabrian's mind becomes restless, Ethan has a hard time following her. He tries not to pry into her personal images so he often just listens until he can be of help.

"So are they all born with just these specific gifts, you know...Black or White, or are there any of those that take on some of the other Fellowship gifts and fall into the Grey area?"

Reaching the office waiting area, they both take off their coats and hang them up. He smiles to himself at her never-ceasing level of curiosity. "There are always exceptions to the rules in every aspect of life. It is only a natural occurrence that there would be those who would fall in the Grey area, as you like to put it. That, my dear Gabrian, is how we all became to be who we are from the very beginning."

She nods as she crosses the room, understanding the meaning behind Ethan's words—how the humans and the people of the Realm became so different, yet the same. She enters Ethan's office and takes her permanent seat beside the register on the wall. "So if they have different gifts, how do they decide what Fellowship they belong to?"

Walking over to his desk, he picks up the chart he was working on earlier then casually makes his way around to sit in his chair. "Because everything in this world has a more dominant side. A being's most prevailing gift would most likely be the deciding factor as to which Fellowship they would fit into, not always, but more often than not. With people of the Realm and humans alike, we all want to feel that we fit in, to feel like we belong somewhere. That is a trait we all share."

Gabrian sits complacent with her hands folded in her lap, the curve of her mouth curls upward into a smile as she gazes attentively, appreciating how Ethan always manages to explain things in a way that make her feel less like the freak of nature she feels like she has become.

The Holidays are almost upon them and that means she only has a couple more weeks left with Ethan at her disposal. After that, he would no longer be on vacation and had to go back to work—so did she. She has come to understand that time waits for no one, not even her.

Gabrian used to be so confident in who she was and in the world she lived in. Now she feels small, at the bottom of a mountain that she has no idea how to climb.

She must have been lost in her thoughts for a while, letting them roam freely and unprotected. When she eventually drifts back, Ethan stares at her, chin in his hand and the folds in his cheeks showing—pressed into place by his heartfelt chuckle. "Don't worry so much, Gabrian. You are doing great!" he says, trying to instill his confidence in her. "I have no reservations about you going back to Manhattan. Worst case, I am only a phone call away."

She is not completely convinced by Ethan's words of support, but she did kind of miss the hustle and bustle of the city. She has always felt so alive and awake there. Gabrian guesses that with over one point six million people in the Manhattan area, and an abundance of energy in the air there, how could anyone not.

Thinking of the city makes her think of Rachael. She realizes she has not spoken to her in a while and begins to miss her best friend. Gabrian's mom has mentioned that Rachael called a few times to see how she is doing, but Gabrian is not ready to talk to anyone about anything—especially since the last time she saw her, she was ambushed by her in her own apartment. She understands now that Rachael was only trying to help, but she still should not have done it.

You will have to find something else to do tomorrow, kiddo.

Only half listening to what Ethan is saying, she is not sure if he had said it out loud or with his mind. Gabrian turns from the window to face him. "Sorry, did you say something?" she asks, sensing a little tension from Ethan.

Using his voice this time, Ethan repeats the words out loud. "I was just saying that you will have to find something else to do tomorrow."

"Oh," she squeaks, her face dropping its pleasant edges, letting them sag. The nerves beneath her skin prickle as a hint of distress washes through her. "Okay, no problem." Gabrian begins to gently bite her bottom lip with nervousness, worrying about the fact she only has a few days left with him. A wave of panic surges through her from the thought of knowing that now she has even less.

"Don't worry, we will make up the time before you leave somehow," he promises her, hearing her fears. "I have a meeting with the Elders." Her eyes grow large as she hears her name go through his mind. "And yes, it is about you," he softly retorts.

Even though she has only heard the stories her parents and Ethan have told her, she knows nothing about the Elders and who they really are. To Gabrian, they are make-believe people that before two weeks ago, she was oblivious to. Now these phantoms are the deciding factors as to how her future will play out, and she gets the feeling they could make her life a living Hell if she does not fit the bill.

"Gabrian, they only want a progress report. They just want to see how you are coping and adjusting." He tries to console her but realizes until she becomes confident with herself, he will not be able to undo her fear. "Your situation is unique and they were unprepared to find a Borrower amongst us with so much power that does not have the proper knowledge of how to control it."

He gets up out of his chair and walks over to her. He crouches down before her, looking up at her as he reaches out and gently cups her chin. "You are a natural, and you are good; that is all they want to know."

She smiles at him, once again in appreciation of his kindness and patience. If he believes in her as much as he says he does then maybe it is time for her to believe in herself. She nods and takes a deep breath, searching his mind for any signs of doubt. Finding none, she decides to relax a bit.

"Okay?" he says to her.

She shakes her head slightly and shrugs her shoulders in a sign of surrender to him. Then she whispers the words he wants to hear. "Okay."

"Besides..." he says as he gets back up and walks over to his chair. "With me as your teacher, how could you possibly fail?"

Gabrian laughs at his uncharacteristically pompous remark. She knows it is all in an attempt to lighten the mood. He glares at her, raising his left brow, trying to suppress the grin growing on his pursed lips then points his finger at her in a scolding gesture. "Do not answer that!"

She covers her mouth with hand in a playful reaction to his orders. The fact is, whether he knows it or not, he is a great teacher. She just hopes he is right.

Chapter Twenty-One

Giraffes☐ Vampires☐ and Coffee

"SO, ETHAN, WHAT is your verdict?" Cimmerian crosses his arms and glares impatiently at his peer as they all take their seats around the High table. "The Shadwell youngling, has she found a way to control her borrowing, or is the girl going to be a liability?" Ethan barely has a chance to sit down before Cimmerian blasts him with the question.

Taking into consideration of whom the question is coming from, and how he feels about the Boragen Fellowship, Ethan graciously lets the arrogance in Cimmerian's voice slide but meets his glare with a narrow-eyed glance that lingers long enough to let his peer know he will not tolerate any attempt of sub ordinance. "The girl, has a name."

"Yes, yes, so she has. But that is not what we are all here to discuss." Cimmerian leans back in his chair, lowering his eyes and folding one arm across his abdomen while brushing off Ethan's tone with a wave of the other. In the same minute, quickly setting himself upright again, his eyes dance around the table, completely ignoring Ethan in search of some signs of support from the rest of the Elders. "We are here to discuss what this child is, and what she is capable of doing."

Vaeda adds her voice the conversation. "I think what

Cimmerian meant to say is, please tell us how Gabrian is making out with her training?" She glances at Ethan for a moment then rests her attention on Cimmerian as he rolls his eyes at her always pleasant demeanor. Having made Cimmerian aware of her dislike of his unnecessary attitude, she returns to her questioning. "Is she responding well?"

Ethan draws his left hand through his hair, leaving it messy and in disarray. He sits up straight and leans forward, resting his elbows on the marble slab that lies before him. "She is doing very well," he is pleased to announce. "She is not as hesitant as she was in the beginning about doing borrowing exercises with energies. I am in hopes that some level of trust is developing with Gabrian that will allow me to push her training much further than normal before she has to return to her life outside my guidance."

Ethan thinks of all the progress she has made in such a short amount of time—given her circumstances, she is doing better than most even after years of training. He worries that the others will not believe him. Even after all these years of service to the Covenant of Shadows, Ethan still feels like he is an outsider—always having to defend himself and his Fellowship's gifts.

"She is showing amicable qualities that may be of benefit to the Covenant's needs in the future," Ethan offers them. "From what I have observed in my short amount of time with her is that she shows a lot of compassion toward others around her. Gabrian is very intelligent in the way that she makes her decisions, and her skills are growing stronger every day. She only requires time to build up the confidence she needs in order to believe in herself."

From across the table, Caspyous interrupts. "Have you been inside her head and searched her thoughts for possible signs of the Fever?" Normally, Caspyous, the Hydor Elder is the light-hearted and playful one, but today his tone is serious, a bit sullen. Discussions concerning possible Rogue Boragen and the slightest chance of them becoming a Vampire seem to always turn his mood cold and harsh.

The night of Adrinn's capture, the Hydor elder that was killed was Caspyous's father. Since then, Caspyous holds very little sympathy in trying to rehabilitate or give allowances to any Borrower that carries the Darkness within their mind—even if it is dormant. He feels that there have been too many circumstances

162

where the Fever has been awakened and those affected have not been dealt with accordingly.

"Caspyous, I understand your concerns with..." Ethan begins to sympathize with his plea.

"Yes or no, Ethan, it is a simple question," Caspyous spits out at him, lurching forward in his chair and pounding his fist against the cold stone slab in front of him. "She is a Boragen. You being one know the concerns. Have you seen the colour of her mind?"

All eyes turn are on Ethan now, and he feels the weight of their stares as Caspyous finishes speaking. Orroryn gives Ethan a sympathetic look, feeling that the attitude in which Ethan is being addressed is unjust. Ethan takes a deep breath and lengthens his hands straight out in front of him, lying them palms down on the cold stone. His face no longer wears his usual smile.

"I know what I am, and I know who I am. For years I have listened to all of you who are quick to condemn the Boragen Fellowship. Just because our gift makes us vulnerable does not mean we are all born of darkness and evil as all of you would have everyone believe. I know that you all think it because your thoughts often scream out your unspoken biases towards us. Our Fellowship agreed to join the Covenant of Shadows in faith that the Elders might see us in a different light—that they could view us as a people capable of civility and compromise, hoping that you would not categorize us all as the monsters the world has portrayed us to be. We are dangerous. Yes, that is very true, but for that matter, do we not all carry the weight of that mark?"

Heads around the High table turn to observe each other's response to Ethan's candor yet no one makes a sound. "Every one of us here in this room is not above this unfortunate truth but with guided knowledge and understanding of ourselves we have a choice in what we become. So do not sit here and immediately condemn us, the Boragen, for what we are. Condemn yourselves for having thought it."

***

SMELLING BREAKFAST COOKING downstairs, Gabrian quickly jumps up out of bed and pulls on her robe. She makes her way down the stairs and into the kitchen where her mom is just putting the sliced bread into the toaster. Hearing her enter the kitchen, Sarapheane turns around to say good morning and notices Gabrian is still in her pajamas. "As much as I love seeing you in your jammies, I think you might be a little underdressed for your session with Ethan."

"Nope," Gabrian responds. "I have the day off. Now you have the great pleasure of putting up with me for the entire day." Gabrian reaches her arms out and hugs her mom then steals a piece of bacon off of the counter in front of her.

Sarapheane hugs her daughter back, relieved to see Gabrian finally starting to act like her old self again. "The whole day? That is great! You can help me decorate," Sarapheane informs her daughter. She has been so preoccupied worrying about Gabrian that the holiday preparations had temporarily been put on the back burner.

"Sounds like fun to me." Gabrian releases Sarapheane and grabs the coffee from her hand, then grins as she takes a sip from her cup. "A little bit of normality would be nice."

After breakfast, Gabrian and her mom spend most of the morning digging out boxes of lights and decorations to bring up from the basement, trying to figure out where to place them around the cottage. With all the decorations sorted, Sarapheane sends Jarrison out to find a tree.

Gabrian sits beside her mom, stringing cranberries and popcorn for the tree, enjoying the day with her parents. She is pleased to feel like she is finally relaxing and on vacation. But something in the back of her mind tells her that this normal family day is going to be short-lived.

Just as the words run through her mind, her dad bursts through the kitchen door with a giant evergreen tree dragging behind him; bringing in the tail-end of it is Ethan and Orroryn. Gabrian's eyes turn to find the security of her mom immediately, not knowing what to do. The last time she saw Orroryn, he held her in a bear hug in the middle of her apartment while she was trying to annihilate everyone in the room. Sarapheane grabs for her hand and gently gives it a squeeze, telling her that everything is okay. Not sure how she should feel, Gabrian struggles to remain still and continues threading the popcorn.

164

Watching her father's friendly interaction with Orroryn gives Gabrian the impression they have known each other for quite some time. She becomes curious to know more about their friendship and decides to test out one of her new skills. She quiets her mind and gently listens for their thoughts to cross her wavelength.

What she finds is incredible. Thousands of images, memories, and words flood her mind all at once, showing her glimpses of a time well before the markers of her lifespan. Feeling a bit dizzy and overwhelmed with all the information she receives, she stops listening just as she hears someone say her name out loud.

"Gabrian, I would like you to meet a dear friend of mine." Jarrison waves her over to where he stands. She clears her mind and looks over at her mom nervously then gets up and crosses the floor. "I think you two already know each other."

Orroryn's face lights up as he greets her with a familiar smile. "Dr. Shadwell."

If they had been back in her Manhattan office, she would have felt quite confident about their introduction, but in this situation, she is completely at a loss.

She has always tried her best to never make any of her clients feel inferior to her in her office. She imagines now how they must have felt—what it must have been like to be the one sitting in the client chair. She tries to put on her best professional face but images of being constrained by Orroryn before everything went black that day makes it hard to pull off. "Mr. Redmond." Her voice cracks with her reply.

Jarrison grabs Gabrian, giving her a hug just like he has ever since she was a little girl. She stumbles sideways and smiles, a bit embarrassed. "Orroryn and I go way back," Jarrison reveals to her. "He was even there the night your mother and I came to have you."

Remembering the story Sarapheane and Jarrison had told her of the day of her birth, she looks up at her dad with a shocked expression then quickly turns to Orroryn, getting ready to start firing out a barrage of questions about that night.

"I hate to interrupt," Ethan's voice interjects and stalls Gabrian's plan of inquisition. "But that story will have to wait for another day. We are actually here on Covenant business."

"Covenant business?" Sarapheane asks.

"Yes." Ethan turns to make eye contact with Gabrian. "Sorry, kiddo, I guess you do not get the day off after all. The Elders would like to meet with you, and Orroryn was gracious enough to offer to escort us."

Feeling the palms of her hands begin to sweat, and the tips of her fingers start to burn, Gabrian tucks her hands in her sleeves instinctively and pulls herself closer to her dad.

"When do they want to see me?" Gabrian asks, clenching her fists.

"Today." Ethan watches her smile fade as his answer washes all the colour from Gabrian's face.

"Why so soon?" Sarapheane steps into the kitchen to join the conversation and stands beside Gabrian, crossing her arms in front of her. She looks to Orroryn and Ethan for an answer.

"Cimmerian and Caspyous are pushing for it," Orroryn answers. "You know how they get about issues, especially when a Boragen is involved." Ethan's thoughts of ugly times float freely to Gabrian, and he tries to pull them back in before she can see, but it is too late.

She gives him a look of terror at first, but somewhere from within, he sees her push back the fear. She raises her chin just a touch and gently pulls away from Jarrison enough to stand straight on her own. This is her new world, and she has made the decision she is not going to let it get the best of her.

Swallowing hard, trying to clear the lump threatening to stay lodged in her throat, Gabrian glances down at her current attire, trying hard not to panic. She sighs then looks back up at Ethan and Orroryn as she pulls at the sides of her fuzzy animal pajamas.

"So, how does the Covenant of Shadows feel about giraffes?"

Chapter Twenty-Two

Covenant of Shadows

GABRIAN HURRIES UPSTAIRS to change her clothes. On the way back down she hears them all talking about the Shadows, and how they should have prepared her before now.

"She has been through the Shadows, but she was unconscious at the time," Orroryn reminds them all.

"Do not worry, she will be fine!" Ethan says, finishing his last sip of coffee. He walks over and places the empty cup in the sink. Hearing Gabrian tell herself that she can handle this over and over again in her head, he turns and glances over to see her standing in the darkened hallway on the other side of the kitchen's entrance.

"All set?" Ethan asks her, knowing that she probably is not.

"You tell me," she says with wide eyes.

"You have nothing to hide so you have nothing to be nervous about. They just want to meet you." Knowing that there is much more than what Ethan says, Gabrian's apprehensions about the meeting remains.

Gabrian grabs her hat and coat from the hangers by the kitchen door and begins to put them on as Orroryn and Ethan prepare to leave for the Covenant of Shadows. Both Orroryn and Ethan chuckle as they watch her. "You will not be needing your coat, Gabrian," Ethan hums, taking the clothing out of her hands before setting them back down on the bench. "There are some advantages of being escorted to the Covenant of Shadows by a Shadow Walker. You don't have to worry about the weather."

Gabrian looks at them with her head half-cocked to the side, sporting a crooked pout under a twisted brow, and Ethan realizes she has no idea what he is talking about. He walks over to where Orroryn stands and waves for her to join them. She looks at her mom and dad for one last glimpse of encouragement. Seeing them both nod, she then moves toward Ethan.

"Do you remember the night you told me about your Uncle Tynan leaving your house through the Shadows instead of using the door?" Ethan asks, realizing he had taken his vast knowledge of how things in the Realm work for granted.

She nods her head yes. Then with sudden comprehension that this may be the mode of transportation they will use, her eyes widen, and they dart aimlessly around the room as her mind starts to race. Her fingers press lightly against her lips, gnawing their tips on contact—feeling the subtle heat as they begin to burn with the fear building inside of her. She had dealt pretty well with the strange and the weird up until now, but traveling through a Shadow is taking it to a whole new level.

Feeling her energy waver, Ethan enters her thoughts and asks her to calm down. He tries to tell her there is nothing to be worried about—that he travels through the Shadows every time he has a meeting with the Elders. Seeing she is unconvinced, he asks her to search his memories for any signs of discomfort or fear. She closes her eyes for a moment and sifts through Ethan's thoughts, looking for anything that might cause her to worry. Finding none, she drops her hand and tucks it snug against her shoulder as begins to calm down but not completely. All she can find is Darkness.

Better? Ethan's voice enters her mind.

Gabrian hesitantly nods her reply.

"There is one thing I should mention to you before we go," Ethan says out loud.

"What is that?" Gabrian sighs loudly, fidgeting with her sleeves.

"You will lose your sight briefly while inside the Shadows." Ethan scrunches up his nose as he watches for her reaction and hopes it will not freak her out. "And possibly your hearing might become impaired as well."

"Of course," Gabrian retorts with a snide tone in her voice, trying to hide her nervousness in her sarcasm. "Why should anything that happens to me from now on be normal?" Then as usual, her curiosity begins to outweigh her fear. "Wait a minute, why?"

Orroryn cannot help but grin at her sudden wanting to understand. She reminds him of Cera. "It is a safeguard that gets triggered within the minds of those not born with the Schaeduwe gift. Once they enter the Shadows, it buffers brain activity and allows it to continue functioning without becoming overloaded or overwhelmed with the magnitude of information that it would absorb otherwise."

Gabrian is terrified of what she hears and begins to pace nervously, running her hands through her hair. "I'm sorry...can you say that again in English?"

"It stops the mind from going insane," Ethan interprets Orroryn's explanation of how the Veil works.

"That is what I thought he said. Thanks for the clarification." She stops pacing and gives them both a frightful look, her knuckles white from clenching her fists. "Well, great! Sounds like a good time. What are we waiting for?"

They both assure her that it will be fine while Ethan gently probes her mind and asks if she is ready. She sends him a hesitant yes, and he looks at Orroryn then nods for him to go.

"Just breathe, Dr. Shadwell. You will be fine," Orroryn says, giving her one of his disarming smiles. "I promise."

He reaches out and grasps both Ethan and Gabrian by the wrist. Then everything goes dark. Gabrian is unable to see anything. She tries to open her eyes wider in the hopes that it will help, but it only makes things seem darker. Giving up on trying to see anything, she stops straining her eyes, and that is when she sees them—there are shapes moving in the Darkness—outlines of people moving around her, getting closer to her, then standing still like they are watching her. She can hear noises too. At first they are all mixed together like the voices heard while walking down a crowded corridor—only chaos and static noise—but then it begins to unravel into words, not all making sense at first, but there are distinct voices and fragments of sentences being said. From somewhere deep within the Darkness, she hears a woman's voice call out, "Gabrian".

Just as sudden as her sight had been taken from her, it returns. Though the light in the corridor is dim, it still blinds her for a moment at first, but within seconds, she can see clearly again. Ethan and Orroryn immediately focus their attention, studying the reaction of the jump on their inexperienced traveler. Spotting Gabrian's blank, unresponsive, dilated eyes combined with her jagged breath, they both rush at her, shaking her gently with trembling hands and wide-spread, fearful eyes, mumbling urgent words at her, frantic to gain her awareness.

"Are you alright, Dr. Shadwell?" Orroryn pleads as he lets go of her arm.

Not knowing if what she saw and heard is a normal occurrence while traveling through the Veil, she blinks, refocusing her eyes back to where she is with a quick shake of her head and gives him a fake smile. She decides she wants to keep the oddities she encountered in the Shadows to herself until she can figure it out. "Yes, I am fine. Thank you." She quickly buries her thoughts behind the walls in her mind just in case anyone decides they might want to be nosey. "Just a nervous flyer, I guess."

Letting out a deep sigh of relief, Orroryn shakes his head. Rolling his eyes at her playfully, Ethan wraps an arm around Gabrian and pulls her along with him as he begins to walk. "She is fine," Ethan announces to Orroryn, giving him a warm smile while nodding at him with soft knowing eyes as they begin to move forward.

Feeling nervous, she tries to take her mind off of things by practicing reaching out her energy like Ethan has taught her to do in order to get comfortable in her surroundings, but she cannot. She is unable to reach out any farther than a half inch from her own body. Confused by this, she tries again with more force, but still there is no change. Even though she has only been a borrower for a short while, for the first time she feels suffocated and constrained. Ethan notices her sudden discomfort and realizes he had forgotten to tell her about the wards—the Magik that protects the Covenant of Shadows from those who would use their gifts for unethical intentions.

"There is nothing wrong with you." He grins and lowers his

head closer to Gabrian in order to quietly let her in on the matter of her malfunctions. "There are ancient spells that protect all those that enter the Covenant of Shadows. The spells are projected to suppress and hinder all gifts of those present in order to maintain diplomacy at our meetings. Once one enters within the walls of the Covenant, it is intended that you need not fear the Magik of anyone else inside."

"Oh!" Gabrian blushes, feeling a bit embarrassed.

As they move forward, Gabrian's stride begins to slow as the beauty and mystical ambiance steals her attention from her chaperones. She reaches out her hand, letting the tips of her fingers gently slip across the contours of the words and symbols etched into the smooth marble walls they walk within. Gabrian becomes so captivated by the mystery of what meanings may lie behind them that she barely even notices reaching the mouth of the largest room she has ever seen.

She stops walking and stares out into the hall, deluged in awe of this dreamlike place, all of it majestic and strange. Every last detail from the mile-high ceilings that sparkle and shine like diamonds, to the eccentric carvings that encase the walls, seems surreal. She feels as if she is swimming in a dream where everything surrounding her is in an exaggerated state but still remains simplistic in its entirety.

She notices along the edges of the cavernous hall, the folds in the wall are lined with stone cauldrons. Each seems to be specifically placed and lit with a peculiar looking flame—all burning with fire of a different colour. Blue, Red, White, Green, Light Grey, Iridescent, and Violet so dark it looks almost black, but there in the middle of them all, is one that remains empty and unlit.

She stares at it, curious as to why this one is still. Something stirs inside of Gabrian. She becomes strangely drawn to its emptiness and walks over to take a closer look. Once reaching her target, she leans over and looks inside. It is dark, cold, and empty. She runs her hand across the top smooth marbled rim of the cauldron and feels a peculiar twinge of sadness seep into her soul.

Lost in a world she knows so little about, Gabrian sighs and glances over at her companions, remembering what she is here for. They wave and point to the other end of the room, motioning for her to rejoin them. Gabrian turns to leave, letting her hand slide away from the lip of the cauldron as she does. A spark jumps from one of her fingertips and causes a small flare to shoot up from the bottom of the caldron. Then it dies just as quickly as it was born, unnoticed by anyone.

On her trek back to rejoin them, her eyes follow the direction of Ethan's pointing and is stunned by what she sees; she turns toward her destination and strains to keep her eyes open. Sunlight streams in—shining effortlessly through the walls of solid granite rock at the other side of the stone edifice. It seems to be the main contribution of light deep within the mountain surrounding them. Orroryn and Ethan glance at each other briefly with a grin drawn on their faces at her wide-eyed childlike fascination. They explain to her that the wall was manifested as a gift of Magik from many years past from the Fellowship of Zephyr—Vaeda's fellowship—and upon the creation of the Covenant of Shadows, the Zephyr cast a spell of invisibility that harbors only within the walls of rock. It allows the light to pass through from the outside, making the stone walls appear as if they are made of glass. Yet the light is yielded on the inside and cannot pass its secrets of the Covenants' presence to anyone or anything in the outside world. She feels as if she is at the end of the Earth looking out into a place from another time. The only thing ruining her picturesque view is the giant slab of granite. It is a table, shaped and smoothened into a rustic oval centerpiece, surrounded by crude stone chairs. All of it standing out like a sore thumb against its striking backdrop.

The three edge their way toward it. Upon reaching their destination, Orroryn and Ethan stand back and converse amongst themselves, no longer impressed by the table's mammoth size and stature, but Gabrian is very much intrigued by its grandeur and reaches out—laying her hand flat against its cold smooth surface. She begins to wonder how many generations of Elders have sat at this very table. She hums quietly at the thought then raises her blue eyes to reach beyond the slab and becomes entranced by the view. The sun, nearing its retirement for the day, begins its descent into the ocean, casting out colours of fire and flame, igniting every cloud that lies within its reach. Gabrian feels as if the fire has found its way into her very soul.

Gabrian is pulled back into reality when she hears Ethan's voice. He begins to give her some final advice before the meeting starts. "Remember, they just want to talk to you, and see what you are about. There is no need to worry." Gabrian lowers her chin and stares at her shoes. Ethan reaches under her face and cups her chin with his hand to gently force her to look back up. "Okay?" he says, looking her in the eye.

"Okay," she repeats, still not completely convinced that this meeting is going to be as easy as he wants her to believe. Ethan takes her by the arm and guides her to the chair set directly to the right of the High table. It is raised a bit higher than the oval table in order to give all those seated the ability to clearly see the person seated in it.

"Come and sit, Gabrian." Ethan touches the back of the chair in a metaphoric attempt to show her that it is safe. "Orroryn and I have to take our seats at the High table as the other Elders will be joining us shortly."

She nods at Ethan and takes her seat, nervously watching him leave her side. Gabrian folds her hands together and brings then to rest under her chin. She turns her head to the right and watches the remaining fragments of light begin to fade from the sky as the sun slowly slips behind the horizon.

For a moment, her thoughts drift. She wonders about this crazy world she has become a part of. Folding her hands together on top of her lap, Gabrian ponders her new reality. A foreboding sense of fear sweeps over her, sending a shiver down her spine and wiping her face clean of expression except for the dew forming in the edges of her eyes—sadly revealing to her an understanding that she has somehow managed to lose all control of her life. But in that very moment, unlike the sun, she refuses to go down without a fight. Raising her chin to stare at the oncoming loom of darkness, Gabrian decides that some way, somehow, she is going to figure out how to get it back.

Chapter Twenty-Three

Ready or Not

GABRIAN RISES FROM her seated position on the chair and stands—a sign of respect to the Elders. One by one, they enter the room, each emanating with a presence about them that seems larger than life to her, instantly crushing most of her newly found determination to regain her life. She watches as they interact and gather around the table, none of them making eye contact with her. They ignore the fact she is in the same room with them, all except one. Gabrian shivers as she recognizes the tall blond woman who was there the night Gabrian was accosted in her apartment. From the internal conversation of Elders, Vaeda's eyes drift in a sideways glance and rest on the youngling, causing her to gasp in the exchange. Gabrian holds her head as steady as she can and tries to look as fearless as possible, but she knows the charade does not fool the woman.

Gabrian lowers her eyes for a moment then raises them again to observe the others. Their presence so valiant and strong to her—a profound feeling of awe just by looking at them—to the point she cannot even begin to describe it in words. Though she knows there are spells binding the powers of all who enter, to her it feels as if there is not enough room for them to all stand together under this edifice, that the walls may explode any minute under

175

the pressure of a thousand years of knowledge and power being brought together into one space. She sees traces of auras dimly dance around each of them, revealing the different colours of their Fellowships' heritage. As nervous as Gabrian is, she still thinks them to be quite fascinating to look at.

Without warning, the Elders turn their attentions to Gabrian and all eyes are suddenly on her.

Gabrian's cheeks burn from the embarrassment of being caught in her daydream by the Elders. As the angst of their stares bore deep within her veins, she feels the tips of her fingers begin to burn in reflex of not knowing what to do so she pulls her hands inside her sleeves to hide her reaction.

Gabrian's throat has grown dry, and she finds it hard to swallow. It is as if her tongue has swollen up three times its normal size, and she is about to choke.

Gabrian, breathe, Ethan's voice whispers through her thoughts. *They are not going to hurt you, they only want to help you, remember that.* She lifts her eyes to meet his and nods subtly.

"So...this is the human turned Boragen we have all been hearing about." Her brief moment of serenity given to her by Ethan is gone as Cimmerian abruptly begins the inquiry. "Funny how one little girl can cause such a big fuss."

"Leave her alone, Cimmerian," Vaeda calmly reprimands, arching her brow while casting a slight glare down the bridge of her nose at Cimmerian for his snide behaviour towards their guest. "There is no need to be that way. She was invited here, allowing us the opportunity to get to know her."

"Yes, old chap. Lighten up a bit," Arroumis chuckles at his peer. He clasps his massive hands behind his head, tucking his fingers amongst his mess of greying wavy hair. "It is not every day you find a youngling that develops their gifts so late in childhood."

Gabrian huffs and folds her arms across her chest in resentment of the statement.

"So tell us, youngling..." Caspyous hisses at her through gritted teeth while tapping his fingers against the cold smooth surface of the high table, having very little interest in saving her feelings. "How is it that a youngling can go through childhood and not show any signs or indication of being from the Realm? That seems a bit peculiar now, does it not?"

Gabrian's fingers burn and itch even more from being put on the spot. "I don't know," she begins to explain, letting go of the loose strand of her hair she was fidgeting with and tucks her hands beneath her legs—sitting on them in the hopes of easing the heat sizzling within them. "I thought I was just like everyone else up until a few weeks ago." She glances around the table, hoping for a sympathetic ear. "I went to school, had friends, got a degree, and was living a normal life, until..."

"Oh, please, you must have known something." Cimmerian snickers as though he is agitated with her presence. "It is just not heard of. Unless..."

"Unless, what Cimmerian?" Kaleb growls his amber eyes nearly glowing—knowing what Cimmerian is attempting to imply.

"Unless, she was awakened by another." Cimmerian glares at her with his black eyes. Gabrian feels the weight of their hatred burning a hole right through her. "That she harbors the Fever within her."

Not able to give him the answers as to why this is all happening to her—and sworn to keep her true identity a secret from everyone—she is certain that telling them who her father is would cause them to just lock her up and throw away the key. She struggles to find words that she needs to use in order to appease her audience. She tries to bite her tongue, knowing these people are now her Elders—and that she should show them respect—but she is completely horrified that they accost her this way. She is a good person; she did not intentionally try to kill anyone, and she certainly does not deserve to be treated with such hostility.

She raises her head slightly and returns Cimmerian's smug stare. "I am not a monster if that is what you are implying."

Annoyed with Cimmerian's lack of civility, Ethan jumps to Gabrian's defense. "Listen to you all. This is not how we treat our people. She is one of us regardless of how or when she arrived in our world. It is now our duty to ensure that she is treated with equality and at the least with some resemblance of respect."

"Save your speeches, Ethan," Cimmerian barks.

"There is no need to demean the girl or cause her any distress," Ashen says pointedly as she glares at Caspyous and Cimmerian. Her eyes betray her agitation and begin to unfold layers of light blue strands, bleaching out her normal calm royal blue. "Is there, gentlemen?"

"We just want to know if she is one of them." Caspyous flicks his fingers at Gabrian, glancing at her for only a second then looks away in disgust. "And if we need to take special precautions in order to maintain order."

"You mean a Vampire," Gabrian blurts out bravely. "You want to know if I am a killer."

Not wanting to cause any more discomfort to the girl than she has to, Ariah believes that without a little discomfort, this meeting will be nothing more than a frightening witch-hunt for Gabrian—persecuted whether she is guilty or not. It seems that a few of the Elders are looking for someone to burn in order to appease the masses. "Ethan," Ariah hums in a quiet but confident voice.

Normally at these meetings, Ariah says very little but instead, listens to all that is said. Her rarely heard voice surprises everyone and the table hushes as the bickering stops for the moment. "Ariah?" Ethan returns her address. Seeing what she is about to ask does not alarm Ethan, but it does stir the feeling that they will not understand what they see.

"In order to calm the discussion, and to give the Elders of the Covenant of Shadows what they so clearly desire, I suggest that you show them."

"Ariah, what you are asking is very personal," Ethan exclaims with a low restrained voice, running his hands through his hair while staring at the Elder. His focus shifts, landing on Vaeda and then to Orroryn with wide eyes, his hand tightly clasped in front of his face. He seeks their council as they remain the heads of the house and have final say as to what is to be done. "I am not sure this is necessary."

There is chatter amongst all the Elders and the consent seems to be a mutual agreement among them for the display. Confused at what is going on, Gabrian throws a loud thought toward Ethan. *What do they mean, show them what?*

As you can see, one of the only gifts that are not affected by the Shadow of Covenant wards is telepathy, and because of that, they want me to connect to your subconscious and project all that I see into their minds. In short, they are looking for signs of the Fever.

Terrified by what this means, she begins to tremble. All her private thoughts and all the secrets she has to keep are suddenly going to be at risk of being exposed to the scariest people she has ever met in her life. It is one thing to hide it from just one person, but it may be quite another to close them all out. Immediately, she begins to pull down a veil in her mind to push away any thoughts of Cera or Adrinn other than a brief glimpse of a recollection of past history she would have been made aware of.

The room is silent, awaiting the vote. Vaeda and Orroryn nod at each other from across the room. They look at Gabrian who continues to hurriedly close off her mind and announce their verdict. "We believe that this is an acceptable request. One that will end the inquiry without furthering the onset of unnecessary accusations." Vaeda and Orroryn now direct their attention toward Ethan.

"Ethan, are you prepared to do this?" Orroryn makes the official request in a solemn tone, not wanting to.

Ethan knows that Ariah was right in her suggestion, judging by the snickering comments being made in some of the less compassionate Elders' heads. He places his hands together and rests his elbows on the table as he looks up at Gabrian. *I do not want to do this, Gabrian, but please understand that by allowing me to do this, it will end the onslaught*, he whispers to Gabrian's mind. *I have seen your mind. It is clear of Darkness and once they see this for themselves, their judgments will not be as harsh toward you.*

Completely ticked off at how she has been treated so far by the esteemed Covenant of Shadows, Gabrian just wants this nightmare to be over and done with so she agrees to let him in, hoping she has guarded herself well.

Ethan begins his ascent into her subconscious and finds the connection. Like last time, he is in a small section of her mind that is clear and clean with only a small reminisce of Darkness. There is nothing abnormal about the way her mind looks but this time she seems to have more light and colour in her memories which will bode well for her. Feeling secure about his findings, he bends his mind to allow his visions to create pictures and snippets of her life to integrate into the mental wavelengths of the Elders. Staying clear of the corridors that last time caused him to have a migraine, Ethan decides there is no need to open that can of worms today.

Hoping that the Elders got what they asked for, he releases

his connection to Gabrian. Quickly he makes a mental check in on Gabrian to see how she is holding up. Seeing that she is still ticked off and highly irritated, but with only a slight headache, he determines that she will survive.

"We will discuss our findings and then convene with you in two weeks to make our decision on what your future training needs shall entail." Vaeda smiles sweetly as she speaks, trying not to torture Gabrian any longer than she has to. "We are aware that you will be returning to Manhattan shortly, and until then, I suggest that you continue your teachings with Ethan. From what we have observed, Gabrian, you have made great strides in your progress in such a short amount of time, and we hope that you continue to do so."

***

GABRIAN SITS ON a large marble bench just outside the boundaries of the great hall. Having been excused from the Covenant of Shadows meeting early, she patiently waits for Ethan and Orroryn to take her back home. Managing to keep her thoughts private from the mass of people that had snooped around in her head has left her feeling exhausted, and the surge of adrenaline that she has run on has pretty much been depleted. So far, the Covenant of Shadows has been filled with beauty, wonder, and cantankerous old relics of people that she must adhere to. But she also acknowledges the level of profound significance that this world holds for her, and that it is way beyond her immediate comprehension.

Waiting for her escorts becomes a tedious chore, and she decides to wander to the outskirts of the hall, toward the flameless cauldron. She is still oddly curious as to why it is the only one not burning. The closer she gets to it, the more she becomes distracted by the beautifully engraved etchings of what she guesses are words of a language spoken within the Realm as it shows no resemblance to any language she is aware of.

She lets her fingers slide over the lip of the container, feeling its smooth edge. Her fingertips begin to get hot and sparks suddenly ignite against the subtle friction. The peculiar reaction on her skin takes her by surprise, and she lifts her hand in response to

180

it. Gabrian has only experienced this sensation when she feels stress or anxiety, but she is quite certain that this is not the case now. She lowers her hand again, lightly sliding the tips of her fingers across the cauldron's lip. The result is sparks.

Without warning, a strangely coloured flame engulfs the inside of the cauldron. The flame is only brief, but it is enough to scare her. Gabrian hurdles backward and unfortunately, lands on Ethan just as he arrives to escort her home.

Catching her as she falls into him, Ethan looks at her and laughs, wondering if she has tripped over her own shadow again. "Are you okay?"

Pulling herself to her feet, Gabrian quickly glances back at the cauldron. She returns her eyes forward and straightens her clothes then tucks the few strands of hair that came loose back behind her ear. "Yes, I am fine."

"So…that was fun!" Ethan jokes hoping that she is past being upset.

"For a meet and greet, I have to admit that this was possibly the worst one I have ever been to."

"Yes, I have little doubt about that." Ethan raises his hand and scratches the side of his head as he looks back in the direction of the Covenant table. His eyes crinkle at the edges as his mouth turns softly upward at one side. "They mean well. They just sometimes forget that they need to use a little more refinement when dealing with issues that confuse them."

"They made me feel as if I was a criminal on trial!" Gabrian begins to chew on her nails and glances at people moving around in the distance. "Remind me again, why I am doing all this?"

Ethan smiles at her sarcastic question. "Because…you are a part of the Realm now, and like it or not, we are your Elders." He is pleased with how well she held herself together throughout the interrogation and hopes that she continues to fight.

"I understand that part, Ethan. But why can they not be more like you?"

He laughs at her and sighs. "Your gifts, like mine, are the most unstable and vulnerable of all the Realm's gifts. And unfortunately, because of that, they can become very dangerous and hard to detect. This makes the Elders very uncomfortable."

Her lips twist to the side as her eyes narrow. She tilts her head, straining her stare—struggling to gain clarity of his odd choice in words. "Detect? I thought that each Fellowship has its own distinction that is recognized by all those within the Realm."

"Most do," Ethan begins. "But one of the other gifts that the Boragen have is their ability to cloak themselves to resemble everyday humans, making them very hard to assimilate. They can easily disappear and remain hidden if they so desire."

"That is understandable. If this is the kind of reception that they give all the Borrowers out there, I would not want to be found either."

Ethan sympathizes with her and realizes that there is so much about this new world that she does not understand or even know about. He sees an empty sitting area over by the marble wall and gestures for her to go sit with him for a while. She follows and takes a seat beside him.

"The Boragen people are a very complicated one, most of which just want to live their lives to the best of their abilities like everyone else, in peace, but there are some who insist on creating chaos and havoc with every turn they take. This has been the way since the very beginnings of the Boragen. Not all Borrowers want to serve under the Realm or respect its laws."

"Are there many out there that do not follow the Realm's rules?"

"Yes. There are quite a few," Ethan explains. "But there are quite a few that do. As long as they do not cause issues or draw attention to themselves, they are left alone by the Covenant and considered rogues. These rogues sometimes decide to intersect with others of their Fellowship but most of them choose to remain invisible to the Realm—like silent members if you will."

"But the ones that don't?"

Gabrian gives Ethan a pressing look, wanting to know the truth. Ethan frowns, trying to decide how to tell her about what the Fever is capable of—what a true Vampire is capable of. Frightening images begin to play through Ethan's mind of missing persons signs and police activity leading to Borrowers that had gotten the Fever. Her mind links to his thoughts and begins to float in a sea of Darkness and death, catching glimpses of all the innocent faces that have been lost to the Fever's destruction.

Ethan observes her reactions, and his heart wrenches

within his chest. He lowers his chin and closes his eyes briefly, saddened that Gabrian has to know this side of her gift. Watching her face twist in revulsion as she pulls the sordid images through her mind makes Ethan sigh. "As with all governments, there must be laws. These laws are in place to maintain order and functionality within a somewhat peaceful society. All those who do not contribute to their society in a productive manner are considered a hindrance in the eyes of the Covenant of Shadows. Tonight's meeting was to begin the process of doing just that. They wanted to make sure that you were on the right side of the law."

"On the right side?" A bit put off by Ethan's last remark, she fidgets, clenching and unclenching her fists from her annoyance with the Elders' rules. "So what, if they would have found a trace of the Vampiric Fever in me they would have locked me up so that I would not become a problem?" She exhales in a growl, feeling that she just cannot win for losing.

"Gabrian, you must understand that most of their abruptness comes from fear." Ethan reaches out with a tender hand, gently gripping her just beneath her elbow—lowering his gaze to meet hers, needing her to see him and understand the whole truth so that she does not begin to condemn herself again like she had before they started working together. "The Boragen are a strong people. They have the ability to regenerate themselves—quickly if need be—by borrowing the energies of those around them. They can become quite a force to reckon with, especially if they choose the way of the Vampire and use pure life essences."

"I have been meaning to ask you about that," Gabrian spits out, interrupting Ethan's lesson. "When you describe theses Vampires or Borrowers that suffer from the Fever, are you talking Twilight-kind of Vampires? Or Dracula-type Vampires? Or what? Because I have never actually heard anyone mention anything about sucking blood or biting."

Ethan raises his eyes to the ceiling and searches for the words that will clarify it for her. "They are all one in the same but each will draw energy in a way that is most fulfilling for them. For some, just being close to their host is enough satisfaction. They would rather watch their victim while they pull the life sustaining essences from their prey. For others, it becomes something else.

They seek a symbolic form of intimacy and with that comes varying degrees of what they consider intimate.

"I have seen those who draw life while in a lover's embrace, tasting the essence in their mouths while their host helplessly fades away in their arms. But I have also seen those that feel the need to bite, to tear, and pierce the skin, drinking in their blood, convinced that within its warmth holds the purest forms of essence and only through these means are they able to reach their highest levels of desire and subdue their craving for life."

With her eyebrows wrenched upward and her teeth clenched tightly, she again catches glimpses of horror scenes that continue to flip through Ethan's mind as he answers her question. "Hm," is all she can say, shaking her head slowly from side to side in disbelief of all the sadness and pain Ethan has endured throughout his life.

Remembering all the books on Vampires she has read, she snaps her head around recalling something. "But what about the legends about if you are bit by a Vampire, you become a Vampire?"

Ethan raises his left eyebrow in response to her question. "They are just that, legends. All beings, no matter how different they may seem, come from a common beginning. Buried deep within the subconscious mind of every human being and Realmfolk alike, lies the gifts that those of us from the Realm so freely display. The human's gift, by some genetic switch, lies dormant within them, but is yet still very much alive."

Ethan sees the misperception stirring in Gabrian's eyes as he continues to try and clear her confusion. "Once the Fever is awakened and takes over, only then will the Borrower become a Vampire. They will begin to hunt until they find a host to steal from. Instinctively, they will search the minds of those they devour to see if the gift is viable. Those that have the Darkness within them are simultaneously shown the path to the surface as they are being savagely drained of their life. But those that do not are left to the Gargons.

"The Boragen have found great power in using the life energy of others, but it has also led some of them to recklessness, overindulgence, and eminently to the death of many innocents. That is not something that the Covenant of Shadows condones nor wants to be associated with. We, as part of the Realm, have a duty to the Covenant. Those that cannot be contained or controlled must be destroyed for the good of the people and an obligation to all of this Earth, to maintain order."

Gabrian leans forward and squints her eyes, forcing herself to open her mind wide enough to catch some of the thoughts rushing around in Ethan's mind, but they are all intertwined and confusing. "If the Covenant is so afraid of these Vampire Rogues, why do they not set up some type of special task force or something like that to go after them?"

"They have," Ethan answers. Suddenly images of her Uncle Tynan, Orroryn, and many of her parent's friends flash through his thoughts. The white of Gabrian's eyes bulge painfully as her jaw drops, unhinged—her mind instantly thrown into complete shock once she sees them.

"No way!" she gasps at the preposterousness of it.

Ethan nods silently and his light-heartedness slips for a moment. "Yes."

Gabrian shakes her head in disbelief and wonders how her gentle giant of a father and Uncle could possibly be a part of a lethal task force to take down Vampires. *Vampires must be pretty easy to take down then.*

"Killing a Boragen is much harder than you might think."

Gabrian stirs from her daydream and decides to play along with the lesson. "Let me guess, you need a stake through the heart," Gabrian, still in disbelief, jests as she suggests the use of the cliché method.

Ethan just laughs at her and shakes his head no. His dark hair falls into his face as he does. He looks at her and sweeps his hair back away from his hazel brown eyes. "With all the movies and books out there that validate this, you would think that this might be true, but because we have the ability to regenerate by drawing energy, any attempt to wound us would quickly heal. All that you would get from this would be a pissed off Vampire." Ethan chuckles.

Gabrian envisions herself as Wolverine for a moment and chuckles. Seeing the images in her mind, Ethan regains his softness and laughs with her at her interpretation.

"All right, so if you cannot stake them..." She tries to remember all the hunting methods from her books to find another

185

answer.

She thinks, *Bullets?*

Nope, Ethan shoots her down.

Silver?

Nah, not even close.

Fire.

Nope...regeneration, try again.

Finally, she finds the right answer, and it is confirmed as Ethan echoes her thoughts. *Decapitation.*

"Decapitation," Ethan repeats himself. "It is the only way."

"If that is the only way, and they know that you are coming after them, how would you ever get close enough to them to do it?" Gabrian's voice trails off as she ponders the possibilities. "Unless...you blow them up from a distance."

Ethan shakes his head at her in amusement from her vivid imagination. "No, we don't blow them up," he snorts. Tears well up, blurring his vision from the delighted burst of humor of their discussion, and he dabs at them with a folded hand—pressing his knuckles gently into the creases of his eyes. "We have a little more tact than that." The Schaeduwe, or Shadow Walkers, are the only Fellowship that the Boragen have no effect on. Even with our ability to sense energy, we are not able to detect their life essence, and therefore cannot steal it. So because of this blind spot, the Schaeduwe can get as close as they need in order to capture and stop them."

"But you mentioned that the Vampires get strong. How could a Shadow Walker fight a Vampire?"

"Do not let their mild-mannered attitudes fool you. Schaeduwe are exceptionally strong and begin their training in the arts of fighting at a very young age. In our Realm, they are considered to be the Guardians or defenders against the Vampires and other things if need be, " Ethan explains, leaning back against the cold stone wall behind him with a cheeky grin while pulling his ankle up to rest over his knee.

Gabrian's eyes pull away from her Elder and stares blankly out across the gargantuan room before her, envisioning bits of imagery about some of the other gifts of the Fellowships and wonders why they would need the Shadow Walkers to defend them. From what she remembers, most of the Fellowships seemed incredibly powerful. *What need would they have of the Schaeduwe?*

"It is because these Vampires are still Boragen. They can feel the presence of others who may oppose them, thus eliminating the advantage of surprise. Once detected, Vampires can easily draw on their essence without them even knowing about it until it is too late, leaving them weak and defenseless, no longer able to contend with them. As for the Schaeduwe, they do not harbor this flaw, making them the ultimate choice of defense."

Gabrian starts to understand why the Covenant may harbor a hint of contempt toward Ethan and herself. Her heart plummets as she realizes that she is doomed to a life of automatic distrust because of what she is.

"We are not completely without benefit to the Covenant," Ethan interjects, realizing that this revelation is pulling Gabrian back into the shell that he had worked so hard to drag her out of. "Many of us exist throughout a number of respected fields. Most Boragen are naturals in the world of medicine. We work as healers along the side of the Eorden Fellowship for one." Gabrian gives him a look of dismay. "Psychology, for another." He grins at her impishly and bumps his shoulder into hers with a gentle nudge. She smiles back halfheartedly but feels lost again.

Hearing the Elders begin to grumble about his absence, Ethan slowly stands up and looks in the direction of the head table. "I have to get back. The other Elders and I still have a couple of matters to attend to."

From the opening of the corridor behind them emerges Jarrison from the Shadows, still emanating his larger-than-life presence that fills the empty space around him. Ethan and Gabrian both turn to greet him on his arrival. "Your dad is here to take you back."

"Are you ready to go?" Jarrison asks her, wearing a smile that has warmed her heart her entire life. Even though her father is trained to hunt down what she and Ethan are both connected to, Gabrian sees nothing but admiration for Ethan in his mind and nothing but love for her. It saddens her a bit knowing that he is not her true father, but she realizes that blood is only blood—it is powerless against love.

"Listen," Ethan says, halting his leave to stand in front of Gabrian and his friend. "Take tomorrow off and go do something fun," he suggests to Gabrian, patting her on the shoulder. "I promised you a day off and a promise is a promise. I am quite certain that you can find something else to do that is...well, not this." Ethan opens his arms in a wide arc to emphasize the size of the misery of the eventful evening she has just endured.

Recapping tonight's events in her head, she gets up from the ledge and tucks her right hand behind her head, yawning from exhaustion. "I could try Ethan but tonight's fun is going to be pretty hard to top!"

Chapter Twenty-Four

Friends and Kryptonite

GABRIAN WAKES TO the sound of the phone ringing, already knowing who is on the other end of the receiver. Not ready to move yet, she pulls the covers up over her eyes to shut out the light streaming in through her bedroom window. She hears her mother's footsteps lightly tap against each wooden step as she makes her way up the stairs and heads in her direction. Then silence.

From under the blankets, she feels her mother staring at her from the doorway. The scent of coffee wafting from the cup in her mother's hand somehow bores its way through the protective layer of cloth that lies between her and the outside world. "Damn kryptonite!" she whispers. "I can hear you breathing by the door," she mumbles to her mother, still buried under the blankets.

Sarapheane laughs and enters her room, quietly marching to the bed, and sits down on the side of it. Taking a sip of the coffee, she pulls down the blankets that cover Gabrian's head.

Shielding her eyes from the light with her arms, Gabrian grumbles and blinks wildly, trying to adjust to the sudden assault on her retinas. Finally able to see, Gabrian pushes herself up and leans back on her pillows. Sarapheane holds out the coffee in front of her, and she kindly accepts it, sipping it immediately.

"Did you hear the phone ring?" Sarapheane asks.

"Yes, I heard it."

"That was Rachael calling again," her mother informs. "You know you should really call her back."

"I know," Gabrian says quietly, biting the edge of her lip while pulling the covers snug under her arms.

"She is just concerned about you," Sarapheane says, raising her brow and tilting her head to the side.

"I know," she says a little louder, raising her eyes to glare at her mother's guilt invoking stare.

"And she is your best friend." Sarapheane, still giving her daughter doe-eyes, reaches down and taps Gabrian lightly on the nose, catching her attention.

"Okay, I know. I get it," Gabrian blurts out, sitting straight up, grabbing the stray pillow from beside her and wrestling it into a sleeper hold across her chest as she exhales loudly. "I just haven't felt like talking to anyone about anything. I don't even know if I know what is going on yet. How am I supposed to explain it to someone else?"

"It might do you some good to talk to her, even if it is just as a sounding board." Sarapheane raises her hand, letting it softly brush along the side of Gabrian's hair and her eyes pinch at the edges with her smile. She wants Gabrian to understand she does not have to give up the person she is to be the person that she has become. "She is from the Realm, Gabe, she understands."

Gabrian ponders this notion and begins to warm up to the idea. The straight line across her lips relaxes and lifts upward. Her eyes glisten as the torrent of built up emotion breaks its silence, blurring her view—a glimpse of happiness for the first time in weeks—and she realizes that maybe her mother is right. Rachael has always had a way of making things more tolerable.

"Fine, you win. I will call her after I have my coffee," she announces, conceding to her mother's wishes. She quiets as a question enters her thoughts—one of which the Elders had insinuated about her the night before in the Covenant of Shadows. "Did you and Dad know what I was before this?" Gabrian's eyes moisten as she looks to Sarapheane for the answer.

Her mother looks at her, unable to hide the hurt in her eyes, but she understands why Gabrian would ask this. The Covenant has a way of making one feel guilty, even if you are innocent. "No, Gabrian. We only knew that you were born of the last surviving Silver Mage to the Realm and that your birth mother, our friend Cera, had cloaked you with a protection spell. When you grew up without developing any signs of having a gift, we decided not to mention the Realm. There was no need to add more chaos in a world already full of it." Sarapheane looks at Gabrian with soft, dampened green eyes. Her full pink stained lips tremble with sadness. "I am so sorry if you think we have wronged you by keeping the truth from you."

Gabrian searches for any thoughts her mother might have that would suggest otherwise. There were no signs of deception in her mother's mind which gave Gabrian relief. She did not think that she could handle it right now if one of the only people she trusts in this world could not be trusted.

Setting her coffee down on the nightstand beside her, Gabrian reaches out and hugs her mom tightly—sorry, if she has somehow hurt her mother's feelings.

"Forget that I asked. It doesn't matter, Mom." She whimpers, pulling her mother in closer, afraid to let go. "It does not matter," she whispers.

***

PHONE RINGS.

"Hello?"

"Hi."

"Oh, my word! Gabrian!" Rachael screams into the receiver, almost deafening her.

"You can stop yelling now. I am not going to hang up or anything, I promise." She pulls the phone away from her ear and waits for Rachael to calm down.

"Sorry," she squeaks. "I just have not heard your voice in so long and the way things were the last time we talked...I didn't think you were ever going to talk to me again."

Gabrian can hear Rachael pace as she talks. Rachael always has to move around when she is excited or gets worked up over something. Gabrian grins and shakes her head, laughing at her friend's predictability. "Yeah, well...I have been a little busy learning how to use all my super powers for good and not for evil."

Rachael laughs out loud and hopes that Gabrian is really okay. Not wanting to pry too much into the truth, Rachael keeps the conversation vague. "So how are things going? I hear you are working with Ethan."

"How did you know I was working with Ethan?" Gabrian's eyes jar open, and she pulls the phone away briefly, staring at it—pursing her lips in a crooked twist while pinching the bridge of her nose.

"Mr. Redmond...I mean Orroryn was by and told me not to worry about you," Rachael tells her. "He said that you were working with Ethan and making a lot of progress."

"He did, did he?" Gabrian grumbles and immediately sits up on her bed, uncomfortable with the fact that everyone seems to know her business. "Nice to know that the Realm's Grape Vine is in good working order."

"No...it is not quite that bad," Rachael assures her friend. "We are a tight knit community at times and look out for our own—those that have certain importance to us. Other than that, I don't really pay much attention to anything that does not concern me unless it is advised by my Elder."

"That is probably best," Gabrian groans, thinking of all the nonsense she has dealt with.

"Anyway, enough about all that. When are you coming back?"

Eager to get back to her old normal life but frightened by the fact that her life may never be normal again, she sighs. "In about two weeks. Ethan has to get back to his life, and so do I."

"That sounds good. I will have everything ready for you when you get back." Rachael tries to assure Gabrian that everything will be fine. She does not want to give her anymore reasons to stress out; she has enough to deal with on her plate.

"I heard that, you know," Gabrian playfully snaps out. "There is no need to tiptoe around trying not to 'stress me out.' I will be fine once I can get back to what I know."

"Of course you will. But..." Rachael hesitates for a moment.

"But, what?"

"But now I am going to have to find a way to keep my thoughts to myself or else you are gonna think I am crazy."

Gabrian bursts out laughing, feeling a mountain of weight lift from her shoulders. She is so glad that she decided to pick up the phone. "I already know you are crazy. Why else do you think I keep you around?"

"You know being a Borrower does have its advantages," Rachael toys, her words rolling over her tongue sultry and smooth, filled with impish suggestion.

"Oh, really," Gabrian scoffs at her in a slow, high pitched tone, raising her brow and rolling her eyes at her friend on the other end of the phone. "And what would those be?"

"Well, think of it this way," Rachael begins, "you will not have to worry about getting wrinkles or grey hair for a very, very long time."

Gabrian laughs out loud again. "You fool."

They talk for a few more minutes about their families, holiday events, and if they have managed to do any shopping—idle chitchat in an attempt to mend the tear in the fence between them.

Eventually, Gabrian hangs up the phone and it dawns on her that she has the whole day to herself. She sits cross-legged on her bed and wonders if she should spend the day with her mom and dad since she has not had much time with them due to all her training.

In the midst of trying to decide on her plans for the day, a flash of the Elders sitting around the large marble table from the night before creeps into her mind. And with that she jumps up off the bed—quickly resolving the dilemma. She is to get out of the house before someone comes looking for her and drags her back into the Shadows again.

Chapter Twenty-Five

New Dancing Shoes

"I WAS BEGINNING to think that you were avoiding me," Adrinn hisses as he materializes from the dark lifeless ground that resides above Thunder Hole.

Cimmerian turns to face him, fighting back the urge to enclose him within the Darkness that he came from and send him back to Erebus in pieces.

"Ah, ah, ah. That is not very polite now, is it?" Adrinn taunts Cimmerian, tapping his vaporous finger gently against his temple. "And here I thought we were becoming friends. Such a pity." He lowers his hand and rests it under his chin, giving Cimmerian a distraught sulk.

Cimmerian's blood begins to boil. "We will never be friends," Cimmerian fires back at him. "Truth be told, you are only a means to an end."

"Ah, yes. Your precious Symone," Adrinn jeers, stretching a fake frown across his lips before he clasps his hands together, pressing them tightly against his chest. "Trapped in Erebus for all of eternity, and I am the only being that can find her, so really you might want to curb your hostilities toward me for the time being." He snaps, dropping his arms and his pity show. He slowly slithers around and encircles Cimmerian, leaving a haloing trail of dark smoky mist behind him as he does. "It would be a shame if we could not find a way to be civil to each other, now would it not?"

Remembering his reason for dealing with Adrinn, Cimmerian swallows his pride and decides to play along with the game. "Very well, then."

Adrinn stops his orbit around Cimmerian and glides over the large amethyst-speckled stone, pretending to sit on it. He lowers his eyes to the barren Earth below him. "The girl. Tell me about the girl." His eyes shoot upward, now harboring a glare that bores into Cimmerian.

Cimmerian tells him everything that had gone on the night before in the Covenant of Shadows meeting. He reveals to Adrinn how he thinks Gabrian is very naive about what she is, still completely ignorant of any real control. He admits she seems to be intelligent but opinionated and easily stirred. Adrinn grins at this as he remembers her as a child. She is so trusting and easily swayed—hoping that those qualities still remain.

He snaps back to the present and dismisses the memory quickly then focuses on Cimmerian. "Loosen the grips of Darkness on me."

Not believing what he has just heard, Cimmerian gives Adrinn a confused and distrustful look. Any attempt to release Adrinn's body would take a lot of energy that would undoubtedly be noticed by someone. An inquisition would probably follow about the strange disturbance in the Realm—not something he is prepared to deal with. Besides that, he shudders at the thoughts of the destruction that this abomination of nature could unleash upon the Realm if he did. Within the years of Cimmerian's life, he has seen much suffering and pain. All he wants now is to pacify this monster long enough to find his daughter and bring her home.

"I cannot." He lies, hoping his bluff is convincing enough. "This request is not the type of spell that I am capable of. I would need the others to conjure up that kind of Magik."

"I did not say free me. I said loosen the grips." He smirks at Cimmerian like he knows something that he is not saying. "I have watched the Gargons pass through to this Realm under the spell of the moon and cloaked in the Darkness of night. They take form and freely walk about, scavenging for the weak. You know the secrets of the Darkness, and I am certain that the binds that tether me to this infernal damnation can be softened."

Cimmerian hates that this creature of evil sitting in front of him is calling the shots. He can give Adrinn the freedom from Darkness, but he fears that the repercussions of this decision might have a weighty price.

Seeing that Cimmerian struggles with the balance of virtue, Adrinn gives him something to ponder. "If I am to woo the girl and befriend her, I need to become something more than what I am." Adrinn waves his hand before him to gesture his abundance of creepiness and his lack of actual feet. "I am not a threat to anyone if that is what you are worried about. My physical remains lie buried deep within the ground, held captive within Erebus for all eternity. My gift of borrowing is tightly bound, and I am but a mirage, a vapor. Tell me, what harm can I possibly do?"

Cimmerian presses his fingers against his lips, tapping on them, and begins to pace—ignoring his audience as he debates the balance of this request. He decides that if this helps increase the chances of him getting his daughter back then the request is not unreasonable. The Realm is filled with apparitions from multiple dimensions anyway, and like it or not, Adrinn does have a point. What could one more ghost in the mist hurt?

"Very well then," Cimmerian concedes, halting his march and staring coldly at the vaporous menace before him as he keeps his emotions intact.

The mist around Adrinn swirls violently in anticipation of release. Cimmerian raises his hands, and his palms begin to glow its dark purplish hue. Fragments of pure energy begin to crackle and spark from within the mist that encircles Adrinn's form, developing into strings. They begin to unwind and separate, stretching themselves forward and gravitate toward the orbs now levitating above Cimmerian's hands.

Making fists with both hands, Cimmerian quickly grabs the ends of the fragmented strings and pulls back violently, ripping them free from their attachment to Adrinn. A loud snap echoes like a clap of thunder around them and through the walls of Thunder Hole, the cavern below, as the strings fall to the ground and dissipate into the mist.

Adrinn gazes down and grins with delight at the sight of his long-awaited appendages that now display beneath him. "Now that is more like it!" he cheers. Humming a strange eerie melody, he moves his feet around to imitate some sort of dance and grabs the edges of his lapel, tugging on them gently.

"So tell me, old boy...how do I look? Do you think she will dance with me?"

Cimmerian rolls his eyes at Adrinn in annoyance. "Do not make me regret this!"

Chapter Twenty-Six

Come Here Often

IT IS THE day before Christmas Eve, and Gabrian tells her mom she needs to step out and do some shopping. Struggling again with the new complexity of her world, Gabrian explains to Sarapheane that she needs to do something mundane that makes her feel like a human again—even if it is only for a few moments.

Borrowing her mom's car, she heads to Ellsworth for the day. Arriving at the strip mall, Gabrian debates her first store. Having forgotten that she does not have the same shopping venues she would normally have in Manhattan, she manages to pick up a few things in the mall. Jumping back into the driver's seat, she heads a little further down the street and sees an exciting prospect—an L.L. Bean outlet. Loving the new possibilities, she manages to finish the rest of her gift purchasing there.

Now completely shopped out, she glances down at her watch. It is five PM. "No wonder I feel strange," she mumbles to herself, feeling a drain on her system. "I haven't eaten anything today."

Now that she borrows energy, her need for food has waned, but she still craves sustenance, more out of habit than anything. Making her way back up through Ellsworth and heading for home, she sees a coffee express to her right. She puts her signal light on to turn in. Suddenly, the thought of an Enchanted Forest latte overwhelms her taste buds and not able to compromise on this, she switches off the blinker and keeps going—heading for Bar Harbor and to the call of the Coffee Hound.

***

TAKING HER COAT off and settling onto one of the high stools, Gabrian perches herself in front of the large window of the Coffee Hound that overlooks Main Street. Wrapping her hands around the tall cup of latte, she takes a long anticipated sip. "This is definitely what Heaven should feel like," she purrs, savoring its warm euphoria. She stares out into the street and watches the people walk by as she slips into a coffee coma. She is happy to be out and delighted to feel normal, only for a few moments if that is even possible. The word normal just does not seem to fit into her vocabulary like it used to.

Somehow, between watching the sun slowly setting and wondering about the peculiar-looking Raven that has just landed outside the window in front of her, Gabrian's daydreams lead her mind back to the Covenant of Shadows. Still able to feel the weight of them all staring at her from the high table, she stiffens from the recollection in hearing the judgment of their thoughts. She feels lost in a world that seems Hell-bent in chewing her up and spitting her out. If it was not for Ethan, they would probably already have her locked up somewhere, condemned to live out the rest of her life in confinement.

Her plump lips press hard against each other, deflating their delicacy as her contented gaze hardens over into a narrow glare. Her mind filled with the anger that simmers within her veins. Disheartened about how her gifts are seen through their eyes, Gabrian decides to cloak herself. She will no longer allow anyone to see her as a Boragen, thus eliminating the opportunity for anyone to pass judgment on her because of what she is before knowing who she is. She closes her eyes and concentrates on her essence. Finding its familiarity, she isolates all the Grey aura and pulls it back inside her body—hiding all evidence of Boragen essence that normally surrounds her. Gabrian creates a subtle haze of off-white and expels it from her skin, simulating the same hues that humans

200

do. She hears Ethan's voice resonate through her mind and recalls his tellings of others that have hidden from the eye of the Covenant. She might not be a rogue exactly, but she will not let them make her a victim either.

Feeling confident about what she has done, Gabrian returns to sipping her latte in celebration of her minor triumph.

The side door of Coffee Hound opens and a tall larger-than-life young man walks through the café. He reaches the cashier counter and orders a coffee. After training for two weeks straight, he is tired and needs a little pick me up before heading home. He pays for his drink and thanks the cashier before heading for his normal perch. He passes behind Gabrian and takes the seat two spots down from hers. He reaches up and takes his black knitted hat off his head then sets it on the counter in front of him, being careful not to spill his drink. His dark brown curls fall recklessly down around the nape of his neck.

Taking a seat and beginning his normal ritual of people watching, he notices a Raven sitting in front of the window. He watches it for a moment. It seems to be staring back in but not at him. Following the direction of its stare, he looks over to his right to see what the bird is oddly mesmerized with. It is a girl.

He turns his head slightly to catch a glimpse of her, curious as to why the bird seems so interested. Then he understands—the girl before him is bewitching. Though he is consciously aware that he is staring at her, he just cannot seem pull his eyes away. His mind etches the shape of her face, the colour of her lips, and the way her dark hair twists gently around and gathers loosely at the top of her head, held only by a pin. Some type of beautiful phenomenon is taking place before him, and he is afraid that if he looks away now, it will vanish, lost in time forever.

Normally he does not pay much attention to humans, but there is something about this girl that has a hold on him, and it refuses to let go. Even his pulse seems to be responding to her presence. He can feel his heart rate increase—beating wildly under his worn black T-shirt.

Gabrian is pulled out of her daydream by a strange sensation, like she is being watched by someone other than the bird. From the corner of her eye, she sees a large figure sitting beside her—staring at her.

Oh, great! What now? she snarls silently.

Trying to be stealthy, she pretends to take a sip of her beverage as she slowly turns to steal a look at him. She is suddenly frozen, stunned by what she finds. Perched on a similar window stool, only an arms-length away is the most perfect creation of man she has ever seen. The raw natural beauty he exudes makes the breath in her lungs hitch, sending a wave of fire burning through her body.

Both of them are still, caught in a trance. It is as if the universe has slowed around them, however briefly, allowing this one encrypted moment between them to become frozen in time.

Shane's senses tug on him, and his wits return. He shakes his head, trying to clear his thoughts—causing his untamed curls to sway gently. Gabrian watches his every move and inhales slowly, partly to calm herself down and partly to re-enforce her cloak as she tries to remain in her human facade.

"Hi," he says in a low, sanded voice. His mouth curves deliciously upward at the edges, revealing perfectly white teeth encompassed by strong full lips.

Gabrian tries to answer, but her mouth is full of liquid, and she begins to cough as she chokes on her latte.

Watching Gabrian gasp for air and spit coffee all over herself, Shane takes pity on her, feeling partly to blame. "Just hold on. I will be right back." He quickly jumps off of his stool—trying to contain his laughter—and he briskly walks toward the front counter.

Gabrian cannot believe this just happened. The most beautiful man she has ever met in her entire life says hi to her, and what does she do? She spits latte all over herself—nice! Nothing says sexy like coffee flying out of your nose.

He returns with a pile of napkins and sets some of them on the countertop in front of them. The rest are held within the cup framed with fingers the colour of caramel, laced with the trace of intricate blueish painted veins—reaching out toward her. "Here, use these," he suggests softly.

She looks up at him with crimson flaring on latte-splattered cheeks. His heart explodes, sending an irrevocable rush of venom through his blood knowing that until this day, he has never encountered such a soul that he found so beautiful.

From the counter, the cashier waves her hand in their direction. Shane gets up and walks back to the front of the Coffee Hound. In his absence, Gabrian uses the napkins to clean herself up as best she can. She glances up at him as he returns to the seat beside her. He holds out something in his hand.

"Here," he says softly, fighting a grin in an attempt to seem sincere.

"What is that?" she says, narrowing her eyes as she pulls the corner of her mouth into a lopsided grin.

"A latte," he informs her. "It is for you."

"Oh...um...thanks," she stutters politely. "But I already have one."

She holds up her empty latte container and shakes it. *Ah, you idiot, what are you doing?* she thinks to herself. *When a gorgeous guy buys you a latte, just take the damn thing and say thank you.*

"You *had* a latte." He grins impishly at her then points his finger toward her face. "But then you decided to wear it."

Gabrian's faces flushes again. They both grin—engaging in eye contact then burst into laughter.

He holds the latte out to her again. "I thought that you might like a new one."

One side of her mouth curls slightly upward shyly, and she reaches out to accept his gift. "Thank you...wait a minute. How did you know what I was drinking?"

"I asked." He grins and lets his green eyes dance forward, toward the cashier.

"Oh," she says meekly and involuntary scrunches up her nose.

He catches the look and turns to face the window. Not knowing what he is doing, he turns and looks at her again, trying to engage her. "You know, when I say hi to someone, I must admit that this is not the reaction I normally get."

"No. I suppose not," she spits out with disdain, retracting her smile and shifting on her stool to face the window again.

Hearing the condescension in her voice, he realizes how he must have sounded to her.

"No, no. I didn't mean it like that." He sighs and closes his eyes, trying to find the right words. "I normally do not talk to people." Knowing that those were not the right words either, he gives up trying so hard to sound cool. "I just meant that it was not the reaction I was expecting." Seeing that she isn't understanding his meaning, he makes an awkward face—twisting his mouth. "This is not going the way I had played it out in my head."

Gabrian comes the conclusion that this Adonis making an utter fool of himself is just some kind of nerd stuck in a jock's body, and is just as nervous as she is. She is tempted to read his thoughts to see if he is sincere or not but stops herself. She made the decision earlier to appear to be human, so human it is. Taking chances and leaving things up to fate is what humans do so she tells herself she can do this. He is only a boy.

Mustering up some courage, he attempts to introduce himself again. "Can we try this again without all the drama?" He stretches out his hand to her. "Hi, I am Shane."

She smiles and takes a deep breath. Reaching out, taking his hand in hers, she looks up into his emerald eyes and replies, "Hi, Shane, I am Gabrian." Both of their souls become caught once more in an intoxicating embrace as they sit quietly taking in each other.

"So..." Shane breaks the silence, trying to be serious. "Do you come here often?"

Gabrian cannot help but burst out laughing, almost choking on her coffee again. "Now that is original," she swoons, loving the fact that he seems to be so cheesy.

Shane replays the question in his head, finding the humor in it, and begins to chuckle too as he wonders what the Hell is happening to him. "No, I mean I come in here at least once or twice a week, and I have never seen you in here before." His emerald eyes twinkle in the light as he lifts his coffee to take a sip. "Bar Harbor is not that densely populated, especially this time of year."

She lifts her eyebrows and smiles at him. "No, I am only in town visiting for the holidays," she informs him then something dawns on her. He is right. Small towns are notorious for everyone knowing everything about you before you do just by mentioning who you are. She feels a sliver of panic run through her veins, remembering the poisonous dislike the Elders expelled about her kind, about her. Not wanting to continue with that game tonight, and knowing the probability of how this conversation will play out, Gabrian comes up with a plan which stops his inquiry in its tracks.

"Hm. Shane, can I ask you a question?" she inquires, turning her shoulders to mirror with his, and her chin lifts—staring at him with widened eyes that glimmer as her lips taunt him with an impish grin.

"Sure, go for it." He leans in, his stomach fluttering at the closeness.

"How trusting of a soul are you?" The blue in her gaze intensifies as the words cross over her lips.

"That depends on the soul," he retorts cunningly, switching his brow and narrowing his gaze—revealing a flicker of desire building within his sea-green eyes.

"I would like to propose something to you." Catching the spark in his eye, her stomach swirls with an onslaught of butterflies and she inhales slowly—willing herself to continue on, maintaining her brave face.

He tilts his head, and nods slowly—squinting his eyes at her, completely at a loss as to what this girl is doing to him, but she has his attention, and he continues to gaze at her, strangely intrigued. "Okay, shoot."

"How do you feel about experiments?" She blurts out, her eyes deadlocked with his as she throws all caution to the wind.

Now, not knowing where this girl is going with this conversation, Shane sits back in his seat getting a bit of distance.

"Before we pollute this...whatever this is, with small talk about who we know, and where we lived when we grew up, can we try something original?" He gives her a confused look, so Gabrian smiles encouragingly and tries to clarify what she is getting at. "I would like us to be who we are right now in this very moment of time."

He leans back in toward her and rests his head on his hand. He looks into her eyes and becomes entranced by the way they brighten and sparkle as she speaks. "Okay, I am listening."

"No baggage. No predetermined prejudices."

Shane takes a moment to contemplate this concept. He determines that he likes this idea, and that she might be onto something. Not having to navigate around his sordid past is definitely okay with him.

Gabrian moves in closer to him, sliding into the dim light shining above her. He takes in the soft curves of her face and the way the shadows play on her cheekbones, defining them. He swallows, feeling his mouth beginning to moisten as he thinks about kissing her lips.

"Well?" she says, annihilating his daydream.

Realizing that he is staring at her again like a deranged stalker, he gathers his senses. "Fair enough."

"Then who knows..." she chirps, turning back toward the countertop to pick up her full, warm cup of latte. "Maybe one day, if we feel brave enough, we can unlock the closet doors and let the skeletons out to dance."

Chapter Twenty-Seven

I've Got a Feeling

THE RAVEN WATCHING Gabrian from the other side of the window gives up its fascination with her once the daylight fades out completely. Shane and Gabrian, lost in the newness of each other, spend the next couple of hours talking about art, literature, likes, and dislikes. They even come up with a few new exciting things to add to their bucket lists. The more time they spend together, the more they both want the night to linger.

Noticing a group of people walk by the front of the coffee house, Shane has a sneaky suspicion as to where they are all headed. He glances over at the clock on the wall, checking the time, and his pouty lips curl upward into a grin. "Hey, do you want to get out of here?"

"Get out of here?" She chuckles, releasing the grip on her latte and flares out the fingers on her upturned palm, questioning. "And do what?"

"Have some fun," he suggests, standing up and grabbing his hat off the counter. She continues to give him a puzzled look.

"It is seven-thirty on a Friday night," she explains. "In Bar Harbor."

His sly grin continues to grow as he takes Gabrian's coat from her and holds it out to help her put it on. "I know of a little place." He holds his index finger up and presses it softly over his pursed lips, giving her the most desirable look she has ever witnessed. "Shh! It is a secret."

She wrinkles her brow, doubtful then thinks to herself, what does she have to lose? She has lived strictly by the book up until now and look where that has gotten her, thrown into a world filled with Witches, Vampires, Borrowers and Shadow Walkers—that is where. While she is at it, maybe she will get lucky and find a portal that will take her back to a dimension where her old life is waiting for her, and where she is a human again. She stops to think about what she is saying. In her old life there probably isn't a gorgeous guy standing before her, asking her to following him to who knows where. So...never mind!

He picks up the empty coffee cups and tosses them into the garbage then proceeds to gently take her hand. Gabrian fails to resist and trails behind him to the door.

They reach the sidewalk outside, and she points to where she is parked. "We can take my car if you like."

"Nah, no need to drive. The place we are going is just up there." He points up the street, but she does not see anything unusual other than two giant lobster claws sticking out of a store called Geddy's. She is learning that in Bar Harbor, sometimes the unusual is the usual.

"The giant lobster claws?" she asks, narrow-eyed and smirking, her arm outstretched—directed toward the abstract art protruding from their apparent point of destination.

"Yes, ma'am!" he declares proudly.

"Let me get this straight." She places her hand over her forehead as she tries to understand the logistics in his plan. "Your idea of having fun is to go hang out in a giant lobster store?"

He takes a deep breath as he looks up at the stars and begins laughing. "Listen to you, little miss 'experiment.'" Then he bends down, getting closer to her, and takes her hand. "Come on, trust me," he breathes out in a seductive whisper. He tugs at her fingertips gently with his, pulling her closer to him. She feels her heart flutter and does not resist. Slowly she moves forward, involuntarily giving in to his subtle coaxing. He looks deeply into her blue eyes, and she notices that she has stopped breathing. He is so close to her now that she can feel the heat radiating off of his caramel-coloured skin.

He gives her a cheeky grin and slowly leans in closer, his flesh making contact, then quickly turns back around and walks toward the lobster, dragging her flustered body behind him. Gabrian's free arm drops to her side flailing behind, her head arches backward as she glares upward at the polka-dotted night sky and groans—exhaling in agony.

On the short walk there, she makes a quick phone call to her mom to let her know she is okay, and that she will not be too late. Shane teases her about the phone call until they reach their destination. They start up the front steps, and he holds the door open for her to walk through though she is still mystified as to what he is up to.

On the other side of the door, she finds a pleasant surprise—a retro-style pub filled with life of all kinds—Human, Eorden, Hydor and a couple of other Fellowships she cannot seem to recall. All of them are inner mingling without any noticeable concerns, conversing and laughing around high set square tables. The pine-board walls are draped with signage and knick-knacks, all fused together in culture, blending of a thousand styles, filling the room with quirky details of adventure. It is amazing.

Shane holds her hand a little tighter as he pulls her into the bar and heads toward an empty table. He pulls out a chair for Gabrian as she removes her coat. "Thank you." She smiles, admiring the fact that some remnants of chivalry is still alive and well. He slips into the seat directly across from her. Within a few minutes, a spunky waitress with blonde bouncy hair arrives at their table. "What can I get cha's?" she cheerfully inquires as she glances briefly at Gabrian then rests her gaze on Shane.

Shane looks up at her, aware of her staring but takes no interest. "I will have a Sam Adams. Thanks." He returns his attention to Gabrian.

"I'll just have a Perrier, if you have it," Gabrian orders, knowing that she has to drive. Shane twists his brow and frowns with her request. Catching his change in appearance, she purses her lips and grabs the imaginary steering wheel in front of her, weaving her hands. "I have to drive, remember?"

"Ah, yes." He shifts his eyes to the left and wrinkles his brow. Gabrian is certain he is up to something. "I'll tell you what.

Have one drink," he begins his bargaining, giving her a very mischievous smirk. "And if it tastes like more, then I will call you a cab and escort you safely home myself."

She gives him a playfully distrusting look. His sea green eyes cloud her judgment, making her want to say yes to anything and everything he asks her.

"Deal?" he prompts devilishly.

He is incorrigible, she thinks, sighing loudly. "Fine. Deal," she agrees. A look of triumph plays over Shane's face. Gabrian looks up at the waitress whose eyes are still glued upon Shane, almost salivating in an attempt to get his attention. "I will have a Corona with a slice of lime, please."

The waitress turns briefly to acknowledge that Gabrian has said something to her then looks back at Shane. "Great, I will be right back."

The lights above them suddenly dim and a few of the staff members make their way past them to clear a couple of the tables out of the way, making some space at the back of the bar. The elevator music that had been playing in the sound system dies momentarily, then is resurrected, pumping a more upbeat Maroon Five song out of its speakers. *A big improvement,* Gabrian mentally admits.

"So, what do you think?" Shane prods, noticing her curiously scoping out the bar. "Not bad for little old Bar Harbor."

Gabrian shakes her head and rolls her eyes playfully at him. "The jury is still out." She snickers, completely taken with the ambience of the place but decides to toy with him.

The waitress quickly returns with their order and places it on the table. Shane hands her his credit card and asks her to open up a tab for him. "Sure thing, anything you want, hun." She flirts, now hovering very close to Shane. She takes the card from him, touching his hand lightly with her index finger as she does, and in a low voice—barely audible over the music whispers, "If she changes her mind, and does not take the deal, let me know," she hints boldly and gives him a wink, then walks away, looking back over her shoulder with a seductive pout. Shane raises his eyebrows at her gesture and shakes his head, immediately discarding her show of availability.

Gabrian's fingers tingle as she watches the girl walk away,

clearly due to her annoyance with the waitress's candor and the fact Gabrian is sitting right here, quite sure she is not invisible.

Feeling the weight of Shane's eyes on her, she turns back to look at him. Gabrian has never had anyone pay this much attention to her in her life; it is intense, exhilarating, and embarrassing. She can feel the warmth spread through her cheeks, not to mention other areas. Positive that her face is flushed, she looks away and becomes conveniently interested in the people that have congregated on the makeshift dance floor in the back. Gabrian picks up her beer and takes a sip. "It is pretty early to be hitting the dance floor, is it not?" She looks down at her watch. Eight o'clock.

He laughs and takes a big drink of his Sam Adams. "When the only bar in town that plays dance music closes down at eleven, you have to start a little earlier in the evening if you want to have any fun."

Gabrian nods slowly in comprehension.

Shane watches Gabrian closely as she sits quietly analyzing everything around her. *She is too stiff,* he thinks sadly. The music swirling around the bar changes. "I Got a Feeling" by The Black-Eyed Peas bounces out across the room, and Shane sets his beer down in decision. He his mouth curls from ear to ear. "Come on." He waves his hand and looks toward the dance floor.

Her eyes pop and she bites her lip, her head swiveling from side to side on its own as panic sets in. "No way!"

"We need to loosen you up a bit; you are way too uptight."

"I am not!" she snaps at him, even though she knows he is right.

He gently reaches out and takes her hand into his. "Get up. Smile." He makes a smiley face with his free hand over his full lips. "I want to go dance." He grins at her sweetly, his green eyes sparkling.

Her face straightens with pure terror.

"What? Do you not know how to dance?"

"No, I know how to dance, it is just…"

"Well then, take a big drink of your Corona, and come on."

 "Ah!" she grumbles in defeat and hesitantly gets up from her chair. He stops her for a moment and looks at her, tilting his head like he is confused about something, his chin resting in his hand.

"May I try something?" He gestures toward the back of her head. She shrugs, not really understanding what it is he asks, but somehow, he has her under his spell, and she cannot seem to find opposition with whatever it is that he wants to do to her. "We are here to have fun, right?"

She nods at him in response.

"Well, to have fun we must first look the part." He reaches back behind her and gently tugs at the pin holding her hair in place. She catches a trace of his scent as he leans in to her. He smells of summer—of Earth, grass, and of life. She breathes it in slowly, careful not to awaken her gift.

He removes the pin, and her hair falls loosely down around her back in a beautiful chaotic mess. His strong beautiful face is now wiped clean of all expression.

Gabrian's body aches all over—very conscious of how he is staring at her—and instinctively runs her hand nervously through her dark tangles of hair.

He watches her move and it amplifies the magnitude of her pull on him. A wave of exhilaration shoots violently through his whole being, and he inhales raggedly. He thought she was beautiful before but now he is convinced she has to be a descendant of the goddess Aphrodite herself, sent here to wreak havoc on his senses. Everything about her makes him weak, and he knows he is now and forever more irrevocably lost in her. He touches the end of one of the curls that has fallen loosely in front of her and regains some of his composure. He lifts his eyes to meet hers, trying to remember his intentions.

"There," he chokes out, swallowing hard and nodding his head in an erratic motion in an attempt to level out his uncharted emotions, not wanting to reveal to her he is no longer in control. Gabrian's eyes narrow, seeing the oddity in his gaze. "Now, you actually look like you are ready to have fun," he teases playfully and takes her by the hand, leading her through the maze of people and tables onto the dance floor.

Feeling sober and completely out of place, Gabrian looks around at the people surrounding her. Every face she sees is smiling, happy, and living. Flashes of all the stress and fear she has endured over the past month hits her abruptly, and suddenly she feels jealous of all these strangers laughing and having fun in their ease of life.

Seeing her struggle with letting go, Shane gently touches her chin, pulling her face back toward him and traces a smile on his lips with his finger to indicate she is not indeed having fun.

Irritated, that she feels the way she does—and that others can see it—Gabrian remembers the promise she made herself earlier; she will not let herself be a victim. From somewhere deep within, she feels something release—letting go of all the chains she has gotten tangled up in, and begins to unravel, breaking free. Feeling the beat of the song and concentrating on the buzz of the life around her, Gabrian begins to move, to dance—wild and free like this is the last night of her life.

Shane takes notice of the change overcoming her. He observes her transform from the shy wall flower he had met at the coffee shop only hours ago into the wind. He watches her move and becomes fully aware that this girl, this human girl, has managed to captivate every essence of his existence. He knows the course he is on is completely illogical, but right now, he does not care.

Gabrian closes her eyes, feeling the power of the music seep deeply into the cracks within her soul. She raises her hands above her head, jumping up and down rhythmically in a trance encompassed by the influence of her surroundings. Gabrian sways her head back and forth and she pretends that there is no Covenant of Shadows—there is only music and tonight in this moment, she is free.

Chapter Twenty-Eight

A Glimpse of a Memory

GABRIAN WAKES EARLY to the sound of her parents' voices wafting up the stairwell from the kitchen below. Christmas Eve has arrived, and her mom and dad are discussing plans for the day. Since she did not arrive back home until late, she remembers she has presents to wrap.

Instead of jumping out of bed, she remains still and pulls her blanket a little tighter around her. A smile creeps over her face as images of last night's events dance through her mind. She giggles out loud over her embarrassing display of caffeine abuse. Resting her hand lightly over her eyes, her body shivers, remembering how she felt looking into Shane's emerald eyes for the first time and the warmth of his caramel-skin on hers. She softly moans at the thought of the fullness of his lips, the way he smelled as he leaned into her to let her hair down, and the way she had felt so alive on the dance floor.

Touching her lips with the tips of her fingers, she relives the memory of his gentle kiss after he had walked her to her car at the end of the night. She rolls over on her side, snuggling into her blankets and smiles merrily—hoping to drift off to sleep again, wanting to see him in her dreams.

After a short, uneventful nap, Gabrian finally decides to get up and spends the remainder of the day doing holiday festivities with her family. Even her Uncle Tynan took the day off from training to join them for the holidays.

Visitors pop in and out most of the evening. Lady Vaeda and Orroryn take a moment to stop by to check in on them and to wish her family "Season's Greetings." Any talk of the upcoming Covenant of Shadows meeting is avoided out of respect for the present occasion.

Gabrian is beginning to warm up to Vaeda and Orroryn since they seem to be a little more accepting of who she is more than the other Elders. She figures it is probably due to the fact they are her birth mother's friends. She also takes notice of Lady Vaeda's obvious interest in her Uncle Tynan, who seems somehow oblivious to her subtle flirting.

Christmas Eve comes and goes slowly, the hours seem to stretch out, creating a mitosis-type of effect on the minutes—making the day last forever to Gabrian. Shane had asked for her number before they took their leave, and she hoped he would call her once the festivities were done for the day. She becomes bored of all the pleasantries and the 'well wishings' from her parents' friends. Her face grows tired from smiling so she excuses herself and heads up the stairs to her room. She sifts through the assortment of books that her mom has sitting in the small bookshelf that once held her collection of children's books. Finding one of her favourite novels amongst it, she is delighted. Even though she has already read the series twice, it is still one of her favourite stories ever so reading it once more will be fun—like visiting an old friend—and it will busy her mind, making the waiting game a little more bearable.

Gabrian's mind begins devouring the novel, becoming completely immersed after the first few chapters. Her phone jumps to life, ringing loudly beside her head and scaring the crap out of her, filling her heart full of adrenaline. The lamp on her night table lights up like the Fourth of July, crackling, snapping, and nearly exploding. "What the...?"

The continual ringing of the phone soon outweighs the fascination of the buzzing lamp. Gabrian grabs it from the nightstand, and seeing a local number she does not recognize, she begins to grin from ear to ear uncontrollably. She takes a deep breath, trying to calm down, and clears her throat as she prepares to answer the phone.

"Hello?"

"Hi, uh...Gabrian?" She immediately recognizes his voice and is elated. Her heart begins to pound wildly again, but she tries to keep her voice steady—not wanting to sound like she has been waiting all day for his call.

"Yes, this is she," she says calmly, then presses her palm over the mic to let out a squeal, releasing some of the pressure of the adrenaline coursing through her veins.

"Finally," Shane breathes out, sounding exasperated.

"What do you mean, finally?" Wrinkles form across the bridge of her nose as her eyes dart around the room wondering what in the world would make him say that.

"Um, remember last night when I asked you for your number?"

"Yes," she says, listening intently as she slips the end of her thumb to rest lightly upon her bottom lip. Her teeth press down gently against the sides of the nail, keeping it stationary.

'Well, somehow I managed to misplace the napkin you wrote it on last night," he admits, embarrassed.

"So how did you manage to find my number?" The words slip out slowly across her tongue, and her voice wavers as she tries to stifle a building giggle.

"I remembered the numbers that were in it," he says, then there is a slight pause. "Just not in the right order."

She lets her body fall backward onto the pile of pillows behind her and bursts out laughing, wondering how long it actually took him to reach her. "How many times did it take you to get it right?"

"You don't want to know. Trust me," he assures her, laughing at his endeavor. "Listen, I can't talk long, but I need to know something."

"Okay, shoot," she says, pulling her hand through her hair before letting it trail to the ends of her long tangles, twisting them into a spiraled rope that clings daintily around her fingers.

"Are you afraid of water?"

"No," she answers, exhaling the word in a long drug out breath that ends highly pitched. The dreamy gaze that floated merrily around the contours of her room, disappears from her eyes as she pushes her torso to set upright, not able to imagine why he would need to know this.

"Good. Can you meet me at the Northeast harbor tomorrow afternoon around three-thirty?"

Her eyes narrow as she swings her legs to the side of the bed. Her hand reaches to twist at her hair again, completely baffled. "I guess so. Why?"

He gives her a teasing laugh. "So many questions..." he tells her softly. "Just be there. Okay?"

"Okay." She hears voices and commotion in the background. It sounds like someone is struggling or fighting; she can't make it out, but it does not sound like they are having fun.

"Okay, great. See you then," he says then the phone goes silent.

Gabrian wonders about the noises and what sounded like a confrontation to her. *Now what kind of predicament have I managed to get myself into?* She contemplates but soon dismisses it, embracing the new realization she is Boragen—one of the most feared people of the Realm. She does not need to fear anyone or anything anymore. Suddenly elated with this new evolutionary step forward of her mindset, an actual moment of acceptance with who she has become, she is eager to embrace this new adventure she has been haphazardly thrown into feeling ready to face this world head on.

***

ORRORYN ARRIVES AT Shane's unexpectedly. After leaving the Shadwell's, he decides to pay Shane a visit and manages to knock over the woodpile as he does. Shane jumps at the noise, surprised to see his adoptive father so early. He was not expecting him until later. Seeing Shane on the phone, Orroryn waves and makes a face then turns to pick up the couple of pieces of wood that had fallen upon his clumsy arrival.

"I didn't think I would see you until tomorrow morning," Shane says to Orroryn as he hangs up the phone.

"I decided to call it an early night," Orroryn explains. "I was close by so I thought I would come spend some time with you. You seem to be keeping yourself busy these days training to be a Covenant Guardian and all."

Shane's face beams with pride, and he is unable to hide his

grin. "Yeah, I know. Tynan is all business when it comes to training. I am surprised he even took time off for the holidays." Orroryn and Shane both chuckle at this, knowing it is true.

"He is a good man. You should consider yourself lucky to have him as your mentor," Orroryn reminds him, bending his brow and pointing his finger at him. Shane meets his father's serious glance and flashes a meek smile, nodding his head.

"I do," he answers, continuing to hold his eyes steady, but turns his back in order to break the tension and looks away.

"So what is new with you?" Orroryn places his hands on his hips and observes the state of Shane's home, changing the subject. He is not here for a confrontation. He is here to enjoy his time with his son. "The cabin looks great!"

"I cleaned it," Shane jokes then becomes quiet. He takes a seat at the round wooden table set in the middle of the kitchen. Placing his elbows on top of the table and folding his hands together, he rests his chin on the edge of his interlocking digits.

Orroryn takes notice of his apparent troubles as he stews silently, contemplating something. "You look like you have something on your mind."

"Am I that obvious?"

"Yes." He gives Shane a wide smile, rumbling out a chuckle as he pulls out a chair and takes a seat across from him. Shane hesitates to spill his thoughts, biting on his lower lip. "You might as well come out and say what it is you need to say before you chew through that thing."

Shane lifts his head to glance at him briefly with what resembles a hint of fear harboring within his eyes then begins to speak. "I was thinking about something that you had told me a long time ago about the sanctity of Shadow Walkers' relationships—the level of sacredness that they represent."

"They are, Shane, as sacred as their oaths." Orroryn smiles, hoping this talk means Shane's heart has finally started to soften.

"And I know that you chose a human."

"That is true. It was many years ago," Orroryn replies, lowering his voice. His heart lurches within his chest, the ragged edges of the never-mending wound sear as the question pulls it from its slumber—exposing the magnitude of its sting again tonight. As painful as it is to remember, he allows it, pressing forward with the conversation, curious as to where this is going to lead.

"Knowing how we live and exist, why did you..." He hesitates trying to find the right words. "I mean, how did things..."

Orroryn helps his son with his awkwardness in expressing his thoughts. "You want to know why I would choose a human to give my heart to when I know I would lose her so quickly," he states, looking straight into Shane's troubled eyes.

"Yes."

"Ah. Very well." Orroryn's strong lips tremble as memories flood his mind, all of them. He closes his eyes and inhales a ragged breath, taking a moment to push back the pain and the guilt that lives within his heart in every moment of his existence. "It was not a choice of logic, Shane. Knowing that a human's existence sometimes seems like nothing more than a mere glimpse in a Schaeduwe's memory does seem like an illogical match," he reveals while Shane listens intently. "When the heart chooses who it is going to love, there is very little the mind can do to stop it. If you concede to let it win and embrace every moment that you have together, it is in those memories and in those moments that you will find the strength to carry you through even the longest hours of Darkness when nothing else will. It does not matter what kind of love you find as long as you allow yourself the gift of finding it." Orroryn watches his son's expression change. The heavy weight that had been pressing down on his shoulders, lifts as he leans back in his chair. The shadowed doubt lingering in the back of his mind that had washed the light from his eyes quickly fades. Wrinkles deepen at the edge of his gaze as last night's images consume his thoughts.

Shane feels his heart swell, knowing what Orroryn has just said to be true. He smiles at his adoptive father and concretes his decision.

Chapter Twenty-Nine

Come Away with Me

GABRIAN AWAKENS BRIGHT and early, dragging herself down the stairs. At first she just goes through the motions of Christmas morning in a haze. But after a couple cups of coffee, she begins to enjoy her time with her mom and dad as they open their gifts, telling old stories of Christmases past, and eating everything in sight until they cannot move.

After devouring what had been Christmas dinner, she sneaks off to her room and crawls into her bed, hoping for a quick nap—completely exhausted from the morning's festivities. Lying on her bed and patiently awaiting sleep's arrival, her drowsy eyes catch sight of something moving. It is the second hand of the clock that hangs on the wall beside her bathroom door.

It is noon.

It tick-tocks away, and she watches as the hands slowly chase each other around the face of the time keeper. At first, she hopes its rhythmic steadiness will lull her into sleep, but the more she stares at it, the more she feels anxiety begin to stir within her. The ticking continues on and on, but it has become loud, annoying, and is nearly driving her crazy. Not able to hear its madness any longer, she bounds off the side of her bed and heads for the shower. If she is not going to sleep, then she might as well get ready to go.

ARRIVING AT NORTHEAST Harbor dock, Gabrian pulls into the visitor's spots by the edge of the parking lot. She checks herself in the mirror one last time to make sure she does not have anything on her face that is not supposed to be there. Exiting the car and heading toward the ramp leading to the loading dock, she stands at the top and looks out over the harbor. She watches as the voyagers carry their bags down the ramp and load them onto a large boat with the name Sea Queen on its helm. She smiles, admiring its sturdy splendor. A memory of taking day trips around the islands with her folks on this particular mail boat as a child makes her smile. It is one of her most favourite recollections of growing up.

Lost in the moment, she stands in a serene silence, enchanted by the harbor's own mystical beauty, and breathes in the fresh sea air. Then from somewhere down below she hears a low sanded voice calling out her name.

"Gabrian." She looks in the direction of the sound and sees him standing at the bottom of the float—dark, beautiful, and tonight, all hers. He waves at her to join him. "You better hurry up or you are gonna miss the boat," he yells up at her and laughs.

She trudges her way down the ramp as it rises and falls with the wakes of the other boats entering the harbor. She holds onto the rails, trying not to fall. Making it to the bottom without a scene, Shane holds out his hand for her to take and pulls her on board of the Sea Queen. She steps down onto the boat, but it suddenly rocks—tripping her up—and she slips, falling into him as she tries to steady herself. "You are sure you are not afraid of water?" He smiles down at her, trying to clarify any change in plans.

"No, I am good," she coos, assuring him. Being so close, she catches his scent and it makes her want to pull him even closer. But she refrains for now. "I really love it, actually."

"Well, that is good news." Shane smiles and pulls them away from the side of the boat to the back door to allow some space for other folks to board. "Because you are soon going to be surrounded by a lot of it." He winks at her and nudges her playfully.

The engine of the boat roars to life as the Captain turns the key and pulls the throttle down—backing the boat up and pulling away from the dock. It has been quite a few years since she has

222

been on a boat. She reaches out and takes hold of Shane's brown Carhart coat as she tries to stay upright. The Sea Queen gathers momentum, slicing through the harbor's calm waters and heads into the open ocean. Shane cradles her within his strong arms to steady her.

Feeling a little more secure in her footing, Gabrian turns to look behind them. At the dock, she sees people throwing their hands up in the air in frustration at the realization they are stranded, having missed their one and only ride home. She feels bad for them but laughs just the same at their comedic gestures.

Shane glances down at her, still safely tucked within his embrace. "What are you laughing at?"

She raises her hand and points toward the shrinking dramatic scene taking place on the dock.

"Yeah, that happens a lot here," he says, chuckling. "It is a mail boat. It has a schedule to keep. I am still not sure why people can't figure that out."

Once they hit open water, the boat's motion seems to smoothen a bit as it gains speed and plains out. Feeling braver, Gabrian slides out from beneath Shane's protective cover and tries to stand on her own. After a few minutes of awkward stumbling, she finds her sea legs almost as well as the locals who ride the boat daily. She edges herself closer to the side of the stern and stares out into the vastness of the ocean before her. Its untamable fierceness fills her full of energy and engulfs her with the sensation of freedom, like the whole world is being shut out the further into the water they go. Her mind drifts—creating an illusion of where time is slowing down all around them and all the worry she has been carrying around so faithfully has dissipated—left somewhere behind on the dock, too far away to be able to follow her here.

Shane watches as Gabrian stands contented with the wind wiping her hair wildly all around her. A smile creeps over his mouth as he sees the life in her eyes brighten and the wildness of her soul being released as she takes in the beauty of the world before her. She has unknowingly bewitched him.

She glances over at him, and watches his dark curls shifting gently with the wind. The wide smile that had resided on her mouth softens into a grin and from beneath her long dark lashes, icy blue irises freeze him in place—sparkling from the reflections

223

of daylight across the water. For a moment, the few steps between them on the crowded boat seem too far, and he yearns to reach out to her—to embrace her and hold her close. The thought of kissing her lips again warms his body to the core, making his heart ache. Shane slides his hand over his chest briefly in reflex as something dawns on him. From the very first moment he had laid eyes on this girl, he knew that now and forever more, he would only just see her. No other will ever compare.

The boat finally begins to slow as they come in around the dock. She looks up to see a sign that says Cranberry Island. They weave their way to the starboard side of the vessel and prepare to disembark. Shane climbs upward onto the platform and reaches out his hand to help her up off the side of the boat and onto the stairs of the dock. She climbs the wooden, ocean-weathered steps—coated with small white barnacles and bits of sea grass that float beneath the waterline on its lower stages—and waits for him at the top. He helps some of the other travelers up the stairs as the boat rocks to-and-fro with the waves from its wake then jumps back down onto the Sea Queen for a moment to grab his bag from the floor. With a quick leap forward, he lands back onto the stairs and hurries up them to meet his guest.

"So what did you think?" he quizzes, knowing full well what her answer will likely be.

"That was amazing," she says, delighted. Her face beams with a goofy grin through windblown messy tassels of dark hair as her pupils widen while she talks a mile a minute, still filled with emotion from the boat ride. He puts his free arm around her and gives her a gentle hug then reaches down to gather her hand within his own as they walk up the dock leading to the shore. They stop in front of an old beat up truck she is convinced has seen its better days and places his bag onto the empty truck bed. A sharp screeching sound tears through her eardrums as Shane pulls open the battered door and reaches in to start the engine, turning the heater on High.

"Get inside before you freeze," he tells her as he holds the door open. "I will be right back." Gabrian climbs in the truck, and Shane closes the door behind her. He quickly jogs across the haphazard parking lot and up the wide-set steps of the local store, going inside. The sign above the door reads 'Cranberry General.'

Gabrian loves the rural feel of it all. She looks back around and watches as the mail boat reverses and makes its way back out across the water, heading for its next island drop off.

A huge black Raven suddenly lands on the top of the granite stone sitting just in front of Shane's old beater truck. It stretches its beautiful black head and beak toward her. Its feathers fluff quickly, cascading shades of blue and purple in among the black. Something about it looks familiar—which she knows sounds like a strange thing to think since they all seem to resemble each other—but this one *does* seem to be different. She looks closer, watching it observe her every move and notices a flaw in his black ensemble. There is a small fleck of grey just beneath his breast. It has the same kind of marking as the Raven that had told off Ethan the other day on the way to the Coffee Hound. She is certain of it. He is beautiful though, despite his imperfection.

The black bird suddenly looks to its left, and Gabrian turns to see what has grabbed its attention.

Shane bounds back across the parking lot, returning with what looks like a six pack of Corona in his hand and a grin on his face. He opens the door and climbs in, setting the beer in between them on the seat. Gabrian knows she is completely out of her element, and she is delighted.

Putting the truck in drive, they begin their journey up the curvy narrow road. Gabrian tries to study every house they pass, taking in their details and wondering about their stories, taken with the historical feel she gets as they chug their way along the island landscape. Every head turns to wave. Every face has a smile. And coincidentally, almost every person they meet is illuminating with numerous shades of blue hues around them. *Interesting*, Gabrian thinks then remembers that the blue colour is the water aura, the Hydor Fellowship, which would make perfect sense since they are on a remote island—a likely choice for them to congregate here.

Gabrian shudders, remembering all the hostility she had received from Caspyous at the Covenant of Shadows meeting. Shane notices her change in spirit. "Are you okay?"

"Yes, I am fine, why?" she asks, not realizing she had traded her cheery grin for a sullen pout and was now chewing her nails. She pulls her hand down away from her mouth and forces a grin, remembering where she is and tries to shake the mood.

"I just noticed your smile faded all of a sudden." He peeks over at her with a cheeky grin in chopped glances as he tries to watch the road.

"I think I just caught a chill on the boat," she lies, hoping he will believe her. "I will be fine."

He smiles but it is laced with a hint of doubt as his eyes narrow for a moment, giving her a coy stare down look of concern as they come to a stop at the end of a long dirt road. She looks out the window and sees a cedar-shingled building with a glass front at the edge of the road. Shane grabs the beer and jumps out of the truck then runs over to her door, opening it before she can. Once she is out, he closes it behind her then grabs the bag off of the back of the truck. He begins to march across the snow-laced driveway toward the wooden building then stops and turns around.

"Are you coming?" he asks with a playful grin. Gabrian, who is still looking around taking in her scenery, realizes he is talking to her. She comes to her senses and trudges through the shallow snow, following behind him.

Shane waits for her in front of the door of the building then opens it up, stepping inside. Gabrian enters behind him, and he closes the door behind her. Setting the bag on the floor and the beer on the countertop, Shane takes off his winter boots and slips on a pair of ugly rubber-gummed shoes. Smiling sheepishly, he picks up another pair and hands them to her. She looks at him strangely but follows suit and replaces her boots. He grabs two of the beer off the counter, opens them up, and hands her one as he takes a big drink out of the other. Watching the muscles in his throat shift as he swallows down the cold delicious liquid, Gabrian's breath catches in her chest. Her skin prickles as the icy sting of desire washes over her body, and her temperature spikes—reacting to his subtle movements. She pushes her urge to touch his neck quickly aside and eagerly accepts his gift, swallowing down the cool bubbly drink—thankful for its distraction. His mouth curves seductively upward at the edges, making it hard for her to concentrate, but to her relief he soon turns to unlatch a second door in front of them and opens it, walking through in front of her while wearing a grin.

Gabrian is suddenly hit by a wall of heat and an undeniable

scent of summer. So completely captivated by what lies before her, she passes through the door and becomes immediately entranced by where she is. Everywhere she looks there is life, growth, and warmth. She decides that she never wants to leave this place.

Shane watches her silently, delighted with her reaction to his secret little world. Her eyes find him with his hair hanging loosely about his face, the ends curling up just slightly—giving him a boyish look as he picks at the greens tucked neatly in the grow boxes below him and placing them gently in the basket beside his feet. He peeks over at her under his curls, and Gabrian feels her heart flutter and spark with electricity as their eyes meet. Their eyes hold on to each other, not wanting to break the connection— dancing in an embrace of the souls. Gabrian feels the pull between them becoming incredibly intense, and she looks away, filled with fire. She fights the urge to look back at him, but she cannot stop it. Her eyes search to gaze upon him again, and they find him still staring at her. Her face flushes and she feels the blood rush to her cheeks, but she does not care.

Shane's heart races loudly in his ears. He is unable to calm it, helpless to look away. Trying hard to gain control of himself, he forces the words awkwardly out of his mouth. "These are for supper."

She looks down at the greens he has placed in the basket and realizes he is trying to explain to her what he is doing. "I hope you don't mind, I grow them myself."

Swallowing hard and resurfacing from beneath the flood of desire, Gabrian finds her voice. "No, not at all," she chokes out. "I am actually rather impressed."

Shane stands and wipes the dirt from his hands on a cloth he pulls from the table beside him. "It's just something that I like to do," he says, dipping his head low, rubbing his hand across the back of his neck, and looking around the small four-walled haven. "It helps me keep things in balance. It helps me slow down."

"No need to explain. All I have to do is look around to know why you do this," she says, taking a sip from her beer. "Everyone needs a place where they can put the world away for a few minutes."

"Just for a few," he says softly as he walks toward her carrying the basket of greens. He stops in front of her and leans in.

His mouth opens slightly and she feels her body tingle the closer he gets to her. She takes a deep breath, closing her eyes. Then she hears him whisper softly; his warm breath brushes against her ear. "Time to go."

She exhales and opens her eyes. Feeling exasperated, she turns to see him grinning at her then he hands her the basket of greens and opens the door for her. She rolls her eyes and quickly makes her exit while he follows behind, holding the white bag he brought in one hand and the remainder of the six pack of beer in his other.

They leave the warmth of the greenhouse and enter back out into the cold. The sun is fading so any heat the day had held is now fleeting, and the chill of night has begun. She follows him closely as they head up the driveway toward what she assumes is his home. Along the top of the tree line, she notices in her peripheral sight a large black bird hopping along the tree tops, seemingly following them. She smiles and wonders if this is the same bird that found her of interest at the dock.

Gabrian's attention drifts down to her left as they pass by a small white building. It has a similar structure to the greenhouse but it seems to have a different feel to it. "What is that, another oasis?" she inquires out of curiosity.

"No. Not quite," he says as they pass it by, not slowing. "Maybe someday I will let you see it but tonight we dine," he announces with a wide grin, glancing down at her with a quick green-eyed wink.

She looks back at the little building as they make their way forward into the dark. The gears in her mind begin to turn as she wonders what it could be used for but her eyes break from their hold on the little white shack. A glimmer of light catches her attention—breaking through the darkness within the tree branches. They take a few more snow-covered steps along the path and soon before them, awaits the front porch to a quaint log cabin.

A wooden bench sits firm just below the small, aged front window. Beside it, is a pile of split wood with an axe sticking out of one of the pieces. Gabrian loves everything about it already. They climb up the large handcrafted log steps and edge toward the front door.

"It is not much." Shane stops and glances down at her with

small upturned curve to his lips then gazes up at the hand built edifice before them and huffs a breathy laugh. "But it is home." He unlatches the big red wooden door and steps back to allow her to enter first.

Stepping through, Gabrian immediately feels the heat from the fire burning in the wood stove in the corner. It is the kind of heat that warms you right down to the bone, and she feels her muscles relax in appreciation of its subtle strength.

Shane sets the bag and the beer down on the floor. He reaches up, taking the greens from her, and sets them down as well. He turns back around and helps her with her coat. "Come on in. Make yourself at home," he says, hanging her coat up beside the door. Picking up the beer and the bag, he makes his way past her and into the kitchen. Setting his parcels on the far counter, Shane washes the remains of Earth from his hands in the sink then reaches over to turn the stove on to prepare his pans for the feast he is about to cook.

Gabrian peeks through the steps of the staircase on her left. It cascades down from the shallow ceiling above her. Past the stairs, a large wooden table with a candelabra hanging above it welcomes her. She smells the scent of drying herbs hanging from the rafters by the wall behind it. To the left of the room sits a giant oversized chair with a handmade bookshelf placed strategically beside it, in front of the small wood stove.

She inches toward the large table, completely preoccupied by the ease of the room as Shane holds out another beer for her. She looks down her nose at him and twists her lips into a toying pout, hesitating to take it.

"Don't look so worried, it is lite beer," he says, holding it out to her again. "You will have plenty of time to wear it off before you have to drive."

"Is this what they call Beer pressure?" she jokes, giving him a crooked look. He shakes his head, laughing at her, and holds the drink closer to her hand. "Fine, you win. Thanks," she grumbles playfully, taking it from him. He turns back and places the remaining two beer in the fridge, exchanging them for food. She turns to search the staircase that leads to what appears to be a loft.

"It is where I sleep," Shane offers, reading the question on her face. "Um, I am going to start supper now so feel free to scout around." He grins, walking over to the glass door that stands on the other side of the table and opens it. Reaching his arm around the left side of the door casing, he flicks a switch and the space lights up on the other side. Gabrian strolls over to look through, astounded. On the other side of the door, of what she thought to be an otherwise small cabin is a whole other dimension to his home.

The room is large and welcoming; everything is made of wood and stone. The rafters are open, reaching to the sky. At the far side of the room, there is another wood stove, crackling with fire, making the shadows on the walls dance and shift with the burning glow of embers through its glass door. Above her, on each end of the large room, are open lofts with makeshift ladders built on the side of the walls. Sky lights in the ceiling above let in the night sky, making the room's ambience seem even more enchanting.

Everything about the space makes her feel safe and warm. It welcomes her, embracing her with the hum of serenity, and she finds herself letting go of the harshness of the outside world— relaxing just a bit to allow some of this peace inside. She hears soft piano music playing in the background, adding even more sustenance to the already perfect atmosphere. She always thought she needed concrete and steel around her to feel at home. But tonight she learns she was wrong.

Shane yells at her from the kitchen, disrupting her perfect bubble for a moment. "Dinner will be ready soon," he says. "I hope you are hungry."

"I am," she lies, taking a sip of her beer. But she will fake her way through the meal for his benefit.

Once dinner is ready and on the table, Shane calls to her, and she slowly saunters her way back through the glass door into the kitchen. She stops and grins, impressed at what lies before her. Shane had set the table with plates and silverware wrapped in cloth napkins. He even lit the candelabra above the table. She is indeed pleased with his efforts, regardless of how the meal turns out.

During dinner, they talk about their plans for the New Year, about parts of the world they hope to see before they get too old to do it, and Gabrian even compliments Shane on his fine cooking skills without even having to lie about how the food tastes.

The night is a delight. Both find that once they got past the inevitable bout of awkwardness, that their voices became meshed, making it easy to talk and laugh—immersed in the pleasure of each other's company so much that time passes them by more quickly than they had both expected.

Gabrian catches the movement of the clock hands and glances over at the wall, noticing the hour.

"Oh no, the time," she squeaks in a panic. "When does the last boat off the island leave?"

He laughs at her glancing over at the clock as well. "It is long gone," he tells her nonchalantly. She looks at him angrily.

"What?" she exclaims then takes a deep breath, trying to calm her edginess. "Now how am I supposed to get home?" she says out loud, not really directing the question at him. Her eyes find his, and she wrinkles her brow. "This is not part of your plan for the evening, is it? To lure me out here then trap me on this island so I can't get away from you?" she teases. It is not something she would agree to, but it did have an alluring quality to it.

Shane's expression changes, and he stares at her seriously for a second. "Yes, Gabrian. That was exactly my plan." Gabrian looks at him confused and begins to get a bit concerned with his intentions. He sees her trying to figure things out in her head and watches the wheels start to turn. He bursts out laughing, not able to keep a straight face any longer.

"Relax, I am not trying to kidnap you or anything." He snickers, trying to lighten the mood. "My friend has a boat, and he is going to give us a ride back to the mainland."

"Oh," she breathes out, not realizing she had held it. Feeling a bit better, she leans back against her chair, hoping her face does not look as flushed as it feels, embarrassed at her overreaction. Allowing herself to breathe again, she no longer tries to figure out whether she needs to shed her human façade and Vamp out on this guy or not.

"Besides, everyone saw you with me on the boat today," he tells her. "So kidnapping you and getting away with it? Probably not an option anymore." He winks at her as he gets up from the table and begins to clear the dinner plates.

The phone rings, and Shane quickly answers it. While he is on the phone, Gabrian gets up and clears the rest of the table. He waves his hand at her to leave the mess, but she rolls her eyes at him and places the plates in the sink.

"That was Manny," he says, hanging up the phone. "I told him that we were almost ready to go." He watches for her expression, hoping he has not rushed the evening to end too soon. "Is that all right with you? I remember you mentioning before that you had an early start tomorrow."

Her cheery smile fades, but she forces a mock replica of one to appear in its place and looks away quickly—feeling the heaviness of dread creep over her, not wanting to leave. "Yeah, sure. That is fine," she says, trying to hide the disappointment in her voice.

He leaves the room for a moment to turn down the dampers on the fire, slowing their burn. He returns to help her get her coat on then stops as he stands above her, smelling an arousing scent of cinnamon in her hair. He looks down at her and feels his pulse begin to race just from being close to her. She is unlike any girl he has ever met before—she ignites him. She pulls his attention to its knees, making him want to take in everything she does—cling to every word she says. He wants to kiss her so badly it hurts. He can feel his need for her painfully twist in his chest.

He gently touches her hair, letting his hand drop slowly until it reaches her face. She looks up at him, and his heart aches again. His breath quickens as the blue of her eyes cuts through all the doubt like the sharpened edge of ice. Any previous hesitations about her are gone. She has drawn him in like a magnet to steel, and unwilling to fight against it any longer, he will succumb to her mystic spell.

He leans in, lightly touching his lips to hers. Feeling the warmth of her breath intertwine with his, he tastes the sweetness that lingers on her soft lips, not wanting her to leave. But he restrains his desire to devour her. Shane pulls away from her warmth, causing his chest to twist with an excruciating pain.

Gabrian, still in his trance, has her eyes closed, not wanting to open them—longing for this moment to last just a bit longer. She sighs as he pulls his mouth from hers, still feeling the heat from his skin. His hands embrace her face, gently cupping the lower side of her cheek. She has dreamed of being engrossed in a moment like this all her life, and now that it is real, she never wants it to end.

Shane draws away from her, taking with him the warmth of his flesh and leaving only the chill in the air to touch against her skin. She opens her eyes to see him looking at her with just as much intensity as she feels. His mouth edges upward into a grin of wanting, but he sighs heavily as he opens the door for them to leave. The boat is waiting.

They arrive at the dock and waiting for them at the bottom of the float is a more upscale version of the vessel that brought them to the island. It is a beautifully varnished wooden boat with a cabin that looks more like a cocktail lounge than it does a watercraft. A friendly looking fellow awaits them on the starboard side of the vessel. He gives them a wave, and Gabrian notices his brightly-coloured blue hue against the night sky.

"This is a bit of an upgrade," she whispers quietly to Shane as they waddle their way down the ramp to the boat.

"Yeah, just a bit. This beauty belongs to a very wealthy family that summers out here on the island," he says while she stares down at her footing. "We call them blue bloods out here. It means they come from old money that has been recycled down through the generations."

"Oh!" she says, surprised at this.

"And my friend Manny, here, just happens to be the Captain," he says, loud enough for the gentleman at the bottom of the ramp to be able to hear. Shane jumps to the bottom then reaches his hand out to greet his friend. Gabrian waits quietly as they exchange playful male banter. Once they have had their fill of taking jabs at each other, they turn their attentions to her.

"Manny, I would like you to meet Gabrian," Shane says, holding his hand out in her direction.

"Nice to meet you, Miss," he says.

"Likewise, I am sure," Gabrian responds as he holds his hand out to help her aboard his craft. They all cozy into the cabin of the boat where the cool night air is yielded. Gabrian takes in the immaculate-looking room with its brass handles shining and its cushioned seats fluffed and spotless. She notices an opening to a lower portion of the boat and walks over to take a peek, curious as to what is below. It is a fully-operational kitchen and sleeping area. *How incredible it must be to live like this*, Gabrian thinks, no longer paying any attention to Shane or Manny.

She hears the engine roar to life and begin to rumble.

"You might want to hold onto something, Miss, or take a seat," Manny says to her, grinning from ear to ear, his blue aura floating happily around him as he turns off the cabin lights. "Standing can get a little tricky while I pull us away from the dock if you do not have your sea legs yet." With a flick of a switch there are only small dim lights illuminating through the cabin, making it hard for her to see so she grabs onto what she suspects to be a wooden handle protruding out of the front of the boat as she feels the vessel accelerate backward into the darkness.

Shane skillfully slides his way over to where she stands, putting his arm around her back, and standing steadily beside her. They both keep watch over the hull of the boat as they venture out into the open strait that lies between them and the mainland.

"I usually have her tucked away and put to bed this time of year," Manny says, patting the bow of his vessel. "But it has been so mild this year that I just did not have the heart to do so. Maybe in a couple of weeks, I hear we are in for some bad weather this winter."

Shane and Manny engage in conversation as Gabrian rests her chin on her hands, gazing out into the night. She sees the silhouettes of other boats dance against the water from harbor lights coming into view. The tranquility of the darkness surrounds her, and the steady hum of the engine sends her mind into a state of contentment. She replays the evening's events over in her head, and a smile creeps over her face as she sighs in complete and utter delight.

They reach Northeast harbor, and the boat slowly glides into the dimly-lit dock. Shane helps her off the boat, and she waves to Manny as they climb the ramp toward the parking lot. Shane reaches down and takes her hand into his, intertwining his large fingers delicately with hers as they walk silently to her car.

She reaches into her pocket and pushes the unlock button on her keys. "Well, this is me," Gabrian says, placing her free hand on the roof of the car. She looks down for a second then bravely gazes upward into his eyes. They gleam a beautiful emerald green even in the dim lights of the dusk to dawn lamp above where they stood.

Shane remains still with her hand in his, quietly taking in

her beauty.

"Thanks for today," she utters, scratching her forehead, feeling the awkwardness of the silence between them. "And the boat ride and dinner..."

Shane shakes his head and gathers himself back from his absence, trying to figure out how to end the night with her properly. "Yes, of course. You are welcome. I am just glad that you trusted me enough to drag you off into the middle of the ocean."

They both laugh, and Shane looks up at the night sky then glances back down at the boat. "Manny is waiting for me."

"Yes, of course. You should go," she chokes out, turning her eyes away from him and looking down at the exquisite, brown floating taxi rumbling in the water behind them—sad that the night is over for them. She lets go of his hand and awkwardly reaches for the door handle on the car.

"Listen, this is foolish of me to think," Shane spits out roughly and stops her from opening the door. "But...I am leaving again for training tomorrow, and I am not sure if I will get a chance to see you again before you leave to go back to New York."

"Okay..."

"What do you think about the idea of having dinner with me if for some reason I might happen to show up in Manhattan sometime?" he asks her, scuffing his feet in the loose gravel—biting his lower lip as he utters the uncertain words.

Her heart flutters at his evident vulnerability, and her face gives away her immediate approval of his suggestion. "Well, I think maybe, if you just happen to show up in Manhattan then you should give me a call, and we will see if I am available," she says, realizing how corny she must have sounded. He laughs nervously at her and shakes his head.

"Okay, fair enough," he says, softly nodding his head. He glances toward the dock where Manny patiently waits for him. Then with a look of determination, Shane reaches his hand out, softly touching the side of her face. He leans down and presses his lips to hers. He pulls back just for an instant then unable to deny his fire any longer, he kisses her again—hungrily this time, searching for the taste of her mouth.

Gabrian swoons with his every touch, unable to breathe anymore. She does not want to. His mouth is so sweet and inviting and she can hear the thrum of his heart as it beats faster the more intensely they kiss. With every second of their embrace, her body feels as if it is being set on fire, but the heat of his skin sends shivers through her—a sensation she could get used to.

Out of breath and now out of time, Shane restrains his hunger for her, softening his touch and gently biting her bottom lip then moves his mouth to press against her forehead, kissing her on the temple one last time before looking to the skies in torment. He quickly turns, taking his leave and runs down the ramp to catch his ride home. He waves as he jumps on board the boat and slowly disappears with Manny into the water and the shroud of night's darkness. Gabrian finally gets into the car and starts the engine. She dreamily drives home in the dark, staring out into the starry night and searching for her favourite constellation—Orion. Enjoying the remainder of her evening, she drives slowly, not really concerned about how long it takes her to return home.

Hidden in the blackness of the night, an eerie dark mist rises up from the floor. It twists and writhes around in the shadows that cover the backseat of Gabrian's car, cloaking its existence. It stops moving and takes form. Gabrian suddenly gets the strange sensation that someone or something is watching her. She checks all around then glances back behind her but sees nothing but her purse sitting in the middle of the backseat. Shaking her head and furrowing her brow, she quickly dismisses the onset of sudden insecurity and returns her attention back to watching the road, continuing her stargazing.

Noticed but invisible and keeping a close eye on his valuable driver from the comfort of the backseat, Adrinn's hazel eyes flicker with orange sparks around the fringes of his widened and focused pupils. The edges of his mouth coil upward into a deadly grin as he silently watches Gabrian through the rearview mirror.

Chapter Thirty

Master Yoda

THE NEXT FEW days fly by as Gabrian prepares herself to head back to Manhattan. Ethan notices that she seems to have a new attitude toward her training. She has become more focused on controlling her borrowing. He also notices the absence of her aura. He can barely see it and wonders what the sudden change is about. Not wanting to pry into her private thoughts, he decides to ask her.

"So, how is everything going?" Ethan probes from behind the pile of files stacked up neatly on his desk, watching her out of the corner of his eye.

"Great!" she says as she reaches with her mind outside the room and begins to pull in strange fragments of energy from all directions. Ethan watches as they begin to join together, swirling and twisting, faster and faster all around her until they create a blanket of light that covers her entire body, making it barely visible. Then she holds out her hands and one by one the vigorous strands slowly leave their orbit around her, gathering together between her extended fingers before spinning counterclockwise into a spherical orb. The ball of light sparks and flares as it rotates.

Fascinated by what she is doing, Ethan moves closer to her to get a better look. "What exactly are you doing, Gabrian?"

"An experiment," she calmly explains with her eyes still

firmly focused on her manifestation. "The other night something startled me and coincidentally, the lamp that sitting beside me on my table flared up brightly, nearly exploding. Only for an instant, but still, it made me curious."

"Curious about...?"

"Well, if we are made to draw out energy from people, and essentially people are made up of numerous small electrical currents that run continually throughout their bodies, then I began to wonder if I could just tap into the electricity readily available around me?"

Ethan squints his eye, making his brow tilt lopsided across his face and scratches the end of his chin—contemplating the validity in her efforts. "You mean to tell me you are drawing your energy off of the electricity? You are actually absorbing it?"

"No. Not technically," she admits. "I have not actually tried to absorb it. I was just curious to see if I could capture it. It is on my to do list when I am feeling braver or I get bored."

Ethan laughs at her, feeling a wave of relief come over him with her newfound enthusiasm for life. "Are you all set to head back to the city this weekend?"

She glances over at him briefly with a nervous look in her eye as she continues to play with the ball of energy in her hand. "No, not really, but I guess I have to face the real world eventually—not to mention the upcoming visit to the Covenant of Shadows."

"Ah, yes, the meeting with the Elders." He walks over to her, fascinated by her discovery and reaches his hand out to see if he can feel the energy, but when he gets close, it surges—flaring outward in his direction—burning him. He yelps as the wave of pure power sears the ends of his fingertips. Surprised by Ethan's sudden pain, she disengages with the orb and the energy disperses like little white snakes slithering off in all different directions, back into the atmosphere.

"Oh, my word, Ethan. Are you alright?" Gabrian reaches out for his hand to see if he is okay.

Feeling the ends of his fingers sting from the burn, he nods his head. "Yes, I will be fine. I should have known better than to interfere with someone else's experiment."

Gabrian reaches out and touches his hands. She then pulls a

thread of light grey essence from within her hand and wraps it around Ethan's fingers and closes her eyes to concentrate on an image of healing his burns. He feels Gabrian's essence absorb into his skin, healing the scorched flesh.

"Better?" She looks up from his hand with a straight crease in her mouth, her pupils still wide and barely laced in ice blue from her moment within the silent incantation.

"Better. Yes, thanks," he replies, admiring her instinctive need to help and heal others. It would be a quality that would either make her stronger or eminently destroy her. "When did you learn to do that?" he asks, curious. "Another experiment?"

"No," she says, releasing his hand and sliding back down into her perch beside the heater. She turns her eyes away to stare out the window. "I remember seeing you do it in the park to those people I..." Her enthusiasm suddenly leaves her with the memory of what she did, of what she could have done if they had not stopped her.

"That was in the past, Gabrian," he ensures her. "There is no future living in the past."

Her face softens and she releases a soft panted chuckle at his attempt to ease her conscience. "Yes, Master Yoda."

He waves his hand at her, dismissing her playful sarcasm. Ethan decides now is a good time to give Gabrian a word to the wise. "I noticed you were cloaking your aura these last few days."

"Just something I was trying," she answers quickly, fidgeting with the flake of cracked paint on the edge of the windowsill. Keeping her eyes down, she avoids Ethan's prying stare; her skin prickles from his question—feeling a little edgy about the subject.

"You know, Gabrian; you can do whatever you like with your gift when you are back home and in different company. But when we enter the Covenant, I would advise that you release your aura. The Elders will be watching you closely and will notice if your essence is absent. The last thing you want to do is have them thinking that you are becoming a rogue," he says, looking down at her while sitting down in front of her on the edge of his desk, his voice firm and low. "Because if they do, then they will never let you have a moment of peace again."

***

JARRISON AND SARAPHEANE escort Gabrian to the Great Hall of the Covenant of Shadows. She trails behind them as they talk amongst themselves. As dreadful as it is for Gabrian to enter the Magikal edifice, she cannot help but be struck with awe of the power that resonates with these walls.

As she studies the room, it seems that there are more people in attendance today than last time, and she hopes they are not all here to witness her moment in front of the Elders. It is bad enough just sitting before them; she does not relish the thought of having an audience to cheer them on.

They reach the High table and Ethan and Orroryn are already seated while a few of the other Elders edge their way toward their posts. Gabrian takes a deep breath, remembering to allow her colour to show brightly in order to avoid any stirring of lingering insecurities the Covenant may harbor about her. Releasing her aura—although somewhat constrained—she feels a few negative thoughts surface from around the room, but she ignores them the best she can and holds her chin high. She is not going to let them push her down in the dirt this time like a bunch of school yard bullies. She cannot change who she is so she might as well embrace it and thicken her skin in order to deal with those who would condemn her.

She stands back and listens as the Elders finish up with other business of the Covenant that does not concern her. Ethan sends her a cheerful hello through his mind's voice. She looks over at him and smiles graciously. *Are they going to burn me at the stake?* she asks him.

No. You will be fine. Just remember to breathe, he tells her.

Just breathe, she repeats his words. With the heaviness of the wards wrapped around the Covenant of Shadows bearing down on her, Gabrian feels as though it takes most of the energy she has just to do that.

After a few moments, it is her turn to be addressed by the Elders.

Vaeda gives Gabrian a warm smile. "Hello, Gabrian, please come forward," she instructs, raising her hand toward the stone chair Gabrian had sat in the last time she was there. Reluctantly, Gabrian edges her way to the chair and stands erect, head held high. The Elders all turn in their chairs to face her, and her heart races in response. She cannot believe the power these people have over her just by looking at her. Never the less, she does not cower. She remains falsely confident and awaits their verdict about her instructions.

"Take a seat, dear," Vaeda insists. "Gabrian, we have taken into account the fact that you are indeed an innocent, and in conjunction with the positive reinforcement of the absence of Darkness within your mind we have as a whole, the Elders of the Covenant of Shadow, decided it would be in your best interest to continue your studies. We have arranged an opening for you to train at the Legacy School for Gifted Children in our Manhattan division." Vaeda's face remains statuesque, painted with a pleasant upturned curve on her reddened lips. Her eyes smile, pinched at their edges and rest solely on Gabrian as she relays the final decision of the Elders.

Gabrian continues to stare blankly at the table, maintaining her indifferent reaction to their mandate while not really looking at any of them.

"There you will be given an instructor that will, in turn, guide you to the best of his or her abilities in the proper conducts of the Fellowship under the agreed standards of the Covenant."

Gabrian bites her lips slightly, fighting back the urge to say something sarcastic, knowing it will only lead to trouble. "Also, since Manhattan is where Orroryn maintains his living quarters, you will be expected to meet with him on a weekly basis for a probationary period of six months. If your probationary period ends without any issues or setbacks during this timeframe the meetings will be deemed unnecessary and therefore terminated."

As much as Gabrian likes Orroryn, she despises the fact that she is being forced into meeting with him so he can spy on her for them. Gabrian struggles with her façade as she feels her blood beginning to boil.

Just breathe, Gabrian. She can hear Ethan's voice calmly whisper through her thoughts. *It is almost over.*

"We will expect quarterly visits from you to the Covenant of Shadows upon proper notification, escorted by either Tynan, your parents or our own Schaeduwe Elder himself if he so pleases," Vaeda continues politely.

Gabrian hears the snide comments bouncing around the High table between a few of the Elders' minds. She wishes she could summon one of her energy orbs and blast a couple of them with it. Ethan covers his mouth with his hand to hide the grin on his face as he hears her silent commentary of the meeting but is in agreement with her that it would definitely rid them of some unnecessary negativity.

"If you agree to comply with our indisputable decision, state so now," Caspyous demands, leaning forward in his chair—glaring at her while snide comments of his dislike for her kind flare through his mind.

Gabrian swallows down her contempt and drones out her answer loud and clear. She does not want to have to repeat it again. "I will comply."

"Very well, then I see no reason to prolong this meeting." Vaeda announces cheerfully, relieved there are no unnecessary incidents today. "Please, feel free to take your leave."

Vaeda gives her a sympathetic smile knowing her stale coldness is not received well and feels terrible for having to display such indifference toward her. If she had not distanced herself from her affections for Gabrian, the rest of the Elders would have turned the meeting into a circus, crudely attacking Gabrian and trying to cut down her defenses. It would have made tonight's experience seem like a fairytale in comparison. Ethan promises Vaeda he will explain her lack of empathy toward Gabrian once the meeting is adjourned and she is outside the walls of the Covenant.

Gabrian rises, afraid her legs might betray her performance to the Elders. But they hold steady as she finds her way to the other side of the room where her parents await her return. "Can we get the Hell out of here now?" she pleads with them, tucking herself securely between them and gripping onto her mother's arm.

"Of course, dear," Jarrison confirms, gently resting his massive arm around the top of her shoulder. He guides them forward and leads the way back to the exit; a large sculptured archway carved into the marble walls awaits their departure.

Just as they reach the entrance to the passage, Shane and Tynan enter into the Great Hall from an archway, directly adjacent to Gabrian's on the other side of the room. He looks over just in time to see Gabrian and her parents disappear into the shadows.

Shane's heart jumps for a moment at the sight of her but strangely recalls there was to be a meeting today. The Elders were to deliver their decision on a possible rogue Boragen matter. The shock of understanding hits him like a bus—the gears in his mind begin to turn, and he puts two and two together. He suddenly grows visibly tormented, feeling a sharp pain rip across his ribcage like his heart is being brutally torn from his chest.

"What has got you all riled up?" Tynan probes as he notices Shane's sudden change in demeanor.

Pushing his emotions down deep into the Darkest parts of his soul so that Tynan can no longer see—so that he no longer feels—Shane retorts coldly. "Nothing! Absolutely nothing!"

Chapter Thirty-One

A Familiar Nightmare

"GAB...RI...AN," A VOICE calls out in the Darkness. Gabrian slowly sits up and pulls down the covers to free her legs. Swinging her feet to the side of the bed, she slips down to the cool surface below. Feeling a strange texture beneath her feet, she eyes the floor...or what used to be one. Now, all she sees is Earth between her toes— cold, frozen ground. Gabrian turns back around, seeking the warmth and protection of her bed again, but it is gone. She is no longer standing within the safety her room. Her senses convulse, sending painful shivers slicing through her as she looks around. There is nothing in this void but the cold shroud of Darkness to console her.

She sees fragments of light scattered through the trees up ahead and begins to head toward it. But with each step she takes, the Darkness beneath her begins to cling to her bare feet. At first she thinks it is just mud, but it does not feel like Earth; it feels completely different. It is more gas than solid matter. With no other choice, she continues toward the light.

"Gab...ri...an," the voice calls out in broken beats. It sounds familiar, and her mind tells her that it is a voice from the past, from her childhood. It also tells her whoever it is, is getting closer. She strains her eyes trying to see, but all she finds is the dark heavy fog inching closer, surrounding her and thickening with every passing second. An eerie chill runs across her skin, igniting the sensation of looming danger. Confused and frightened, Gabrian starts to run aimlessly, not knowing which direction to go—only knowing she does not want to be here.

Catching her foot on what Gabrian suspects to be a root protruding up out of the cold damp ground beneath her, she trips and falls, cutting her leg on something sharp.

She cries out and reaches downward to grip at the sudden pain in her leg. Catching the subtle copper scent in the air, her eyes drift downward to her bare appendages and the familiarity of the smell is confirmed. Across the top of her knuckles spills a crimson trail of blood—slowly trickling downward from the open wound.

She sits quietly on the cold ground as something catches her attention. She holds her breath for a moment, listening to sounds of things she cannot see shuffling and moving all around her. Whispers of words she cannot understand fill her ears, taunting her fears. The heaviness of the fog begins to pull down on her. She tries to lift herself up onto the tree in front of her, but she cannot wrench herself free from the icy grip that has a hold on her legs. Gabrian gasps as she watches the Darkness continue to grow—clinging to her skin and climbing up her legs, making it impossible for her to stand. Panicking, she yells out for help only to have the fog encase her—entering into her mouth and choking out her sound.

"He is coming!" Squawks echo through her ears from a large black bird that has suddenly appeared above her. It paces back and forth on a branch of the tree beside her. Then it turns sharply, staring behind them and its hops become frantic. Feeling her heart rate respond to the bird's shrieks, the ends of her fingers starting to burn, and she turns to see what looms in the Darkness. A tall foreboding figure slowly slithers its way toward her.

"Gab...ri...an. Come...to...the...gate," the thing chokes out in a distorted voice. The black bird screams at the creature and dives down in an attempt to protect her, but there is little it can do. The creature quickly swipes its ragged limb out at the bird, knocking it to the ground. Seeping up from the cracks in the Earth, the Darkness writhes and swirls with pleasure as it surrounds and cloaks the existence of the bird—smothering it and consuming its entirety.

Gabrian screams involuntarily as fear wells up inside of her and escapes through her anyway it can. She feels the Darkness creeping higher onto her thigh, pulling at her, and draining her.

Gabrian raises her eyes to look upon the nightmarish creature standing before her, still unable to see its face. Strangely, this thing feels familiar to her—not as frightening as it had seemed before. But with the stench of death looming all around it, she still fears for her life.

With the Darkness clinging at her shoulders now, she struggles to stay alert. Claw-like appendages pull and tear at her flesh as the Gargons begin to drain the life out of her. "Learn to fight back, Gabrian," the voice says—the words resonating through her mind. "Or they will destroy you."

She feels weight at her throat as spindly webbed strands shoot out from a hollowed crevice within the mangled Gargon's face hovering over her; it is choking her. Petrified that her demise is marked, her eyes strain to find help. Her lungs burn as she struggles to find the breath to scream out his name, pleading for his assistance. "AYDEN! HELP ME!" Freeing her hand from the Gargon's deathly grasp, she reaches out for him. He lifts what appears to be his arm toward her just before disappearing into the dark mist. The heaviness of the fog overtakes her, crushing her body to the ground as she feels the suffocation of death deliver her into Darkness.

Gabrian sits straight up, gulping for air, and fighting for breath. She swings her arms ferociously at the empty space around her as her mind slowly registers where she is and that she is safe in her room. Her heart beats wildly in her ears as the sweat pours off of her feverish body, drenching her night shirt and the blankets surrounding her.

She jumps, hearing the creek of her bedroom door as it opens. "Are you all right, Gabrian?" Sarapheane asks. "I heard you yelling."

"It was just a dream," she whispers, wiping her forehead with the back of her hand.

"It must have been quite the dream," Sarapheane suggests as she enters the room and makes her way over to sit on the edge of Gabrian's bed.

Gabrian gives her a meek smile then looks away for a moment in thought. She returns her gaze back to her mother's calm green eyes. "Do you remember when I was a child and you used to find me out at the garden's gate late at night sometimes?" she asks, certain her mother remembers all too well.

"Yes. I remember," Sarapheane replies, raising her brow. "It used to scare me half to death when I would go to check on you at night, and you would be missing. For a while it became a nightly ritual for us to go searching for you only to find you down by the gate in your nightclothes."

"I was not asleep," Gabrian confesses dropping her chin and peering at her mother through her long teary lashes.

Sarapheane's soft gaze falters for a moment—her lips no longer carrying a smile. "What do you mean you were not asleep?"

"Late at night, when the house would get quiet, I could hear someone calling my name so I followed it. The voice. It was never inside the house. It was always outside, calling me from within, and it always led me to the gate where I would see him, a boy, waiting for me."

"I see." Sarapheane's eyes dart slowly around the dimly lit room, bouncing off shadows as she begins to recall her memories. "All I remember is when we finally found you, you always told us that your friend Ayden was there with you, and for us not to worry. He would watch over you," Sarapheane recounted, sounding a bit distraught.

"After we moved to the city, I went years and years of not having those dreams. But tonight...they came back. He came back," Gabrian admits, drawing her legs up to her chest—wrapping her arms around them as she rests her cheek upon her knees. "...at least in my dreams."

"Oh," Sarapheane exhales softly.

Gabrian notices the sudden disappearance of Sarapheane's smile. Her eyes no longer glimmer as a soft crease forms on her brow before she turns away—a look Gabrian knows always means worry.

"He told me to learn to fight back," Gabrian reveals, hoping this would help. "Or they would destroy me." Sarapheane quickly turns her eyes back to Gabrian, and she swears what she sees is fear in her mother's eyes.

Sarapheane softens her gaze, and her smile returns. "Ah, Gabe. You just met with the Covenant of Shadows, and they upset

248

you," she says, playing nervously with the fringe on Gabrian's blanket. "And you are leaving today to go back to the city. It is natural to have anxiety, and your dreams are just your mind's way of sorting things out—however deranged the dreams may seem. Don't let it worry you." Sarapheane reaches up and playfully tugs on one of the loose strands of Gabrian's long dark hair.

"Do you think so?" Gabrian runs her hand through the top of her hair, bunching it at the top and grumbles. "Ah, you are probably right."

Sarapheane leans in and kisses Gabrian on the forehead before getting up off the bed. "Now, go get cleaned up, and I will start breakfast. Orroryn will be here at eight sharp to take you back."

The very thought of food causes Gabrian's stomach to churn, but she did not want to offend her mother's kindness. "That sounds great, Mom, thanks." Gabrian's mouth does water at the thought of fresh warm coffee though, with all the strange alterations she has had in her need for sustenance lately, she is pleased to know her craving for caffeine is alive and well.

DONE WITH HER shower and finished with her packing, Gabrian makes her way down the staircase and into the kitchen. Grabbing a coffee from the counter, she heads into the living room and joins her parents. They sit quietly watching the sun steadily climb its way into the sky—chased by the darkening storm clouds that the man on the radio had threatened were on their way. Sarapheane and Jarrison had planned on taking Gabrian back to her apartment in Manhattan but with the return of Gabrian's dreams, they had other things they needed to attend to today.

Without so much as a word between them, they sit and listen to sound of the maple log crackling and snapping as it burns slowly in the stone hearth. The kitchen clock strikes the hour, and the eight o'clock bells begin to chime—echoing loudly throughout the house.

Gabrian stops biting her nails at the sound and all faces in the room suddenly clear of expression. Her eyes seek out theirs and they share a timid smile filled with encouragement. Then, just as the eighth bell finishes its toll, from the wooden kitchen door comes a knock announcing Orroryn's arrival.

Gabrian's vacation is over.

Chapter Thirty-Two

Borrowed Beauty Secrets

BURIED SHOULDER DEEP in paperwork, Gabrian barely hears the knock on her office door before Rachael peeks her head in around the side of it. "Hey, you!"

"Hey," Gabrian replies, setting her files down on the desk. "Come on in."

"When did you get in?" Rachael enters the room, quickly trots over to the chair in front of Gabrian's desk, and takes a seat.

"Early yesterday morning. I couldn't sleep last night so I thought I would get a head start on the day." Gabrian notices Rachael staring at her wide-eyed, then tilting her head—narrowing her eyes. It is almost like she is studying her face, looking for something. "What are you doing?" she quizzes, well-aware that Rachael has always been a bit peculiar at times.

"I am harboring jealousy."

"What?"

"Your face," Rachael replies as she continues to stare at Gabrian.

"What about my face?"

"It looks so different. I mean, it looks the same but you look incredible."

"What are you talking about?" Gabrian clearly has no idea

what Rachael is going on about. After she arrived home, Gabrian had spent all morning cleaning and scouring her apartment from top to bottom from the messy state she had left it in. That night she tossed and turned, her mind racing—sorting through everything that has happened. She worried about being monitored by the Covenant, about meeting the legacy group, about the fact she might Vamp out on her unsuspecting clients—a constant energy source all at her disposal. How could Rachael possibly think she looks incredible when she feels like a ticking time bomb, barely capable of keeping herself together?

"I know that our bodies are young and that aging is not really a pressing issue for us at the moment, but even for our age, your complexion looks flawless. Your eyes gleam a brilliant blue like the colour of water over ice, and your skin looks as smooth as alabaster." Gabrian wrinkles her nose and flutters her lashes in annoyance. "Despite your odd facial expression, I would say that being a Borrower really does become you."

"Rachael, please." Gabrian scoffs at the absurdity of her suggestion. She shakes her head and returns to her papers. "Don't you have something better to do than to torment me?"

Rachael raises her hands in retreat and stands up, turning toward the door. "Hey, I am just stating the obvious here. No need to shoot the messenger."

Gabrian wonders about Rachael's observation and looks up at her. "Do I really look that different?" If Rachael thinks her looks have changed that much, maybe her clients might notice too.

"Relax. If anyone asks about it just tell them you had one of those fancy spa vacations," Rachael advises. "Most people believe those places are like finding the fountain of youth. They will not even blink an eye at it. Although..." she says, raising her finger to her red pouty lips as though she has just realized something.

"Although what?" Gabrian looks up through her lashes and purses a frown—growling at Rachael in frustration with her infamous ability of not finishing her thoughts.

Rachael furrows her brow and grins. "Hm...you might want to make sure to tell them that you went someplace overseas so they will not try to book a spot as soon as they leave their session with you."

"Great, Rach." Gabrian waves her out the door, clearly

agitated by this new dilemma. "Thanks."

Rachael spins on her heels, still wearing a sassy grin. "Glad I could help," she chirps, exiting the room, and closes the door behind her.

Gabrian sighs and leans back in her chair, delightfully amused by her assistant's quirky attempts to welcome her back. She spins around to face the world behind her. Gazing out over the urban landscape from her office window, high above the busy streets below, Gabrian sighs, sensing the subtle hum of life as it begins to stir within the waking city and corners of her mouth curl upward as she takes it all in, glad to be home.

Chapter Thirty-Three

Aged Insight

THE TRIP TO the Legacy School for Gifted Children seemed to take Gabrian less time than she anticipated. She had not looked forward to it all week, knowing she had to go through with it. The meeting with the Headmaster, the tour of the school's facilities, the lectures, and the awkward introductions to her new instructors—she dreaded it all.

When she finally arrives, Gabrian is greeted with sincere humility. There are no false smiles or negative rumblings of the minds' voice coming from any of them. These people are just like her. They welcome her into their establishment with complete acceptance and willingness to support all her endeavors.

As she walks through the hallways of the Legacy building, she feels the age of the walls descend upon her like somehow she is walking back through time. The school itself feels alive, almost like it has eyes watching her as she explores its private innards. Gabrian basks in the fact that this structure of higher learning is old and filled with mystical history.

As well as its age, Gabrian also feels the Magikal energy pulse vibrantly throughout the structure's halls like veins through a body, lending lure and vitality to its character. The walls are decorated with pictures of students long passed, most of them probably still quite able-bodied considering their purpose of attending such an institution.

Being here amongst these people and in these rooms, she becomes hopeful and quite intrigued. The potential of what such esteemed members of the Realm could empower her with and the vastness of the knowledge that they could bestow upon her seems almost limitless. As Gabrian stops to take in the immensity of the universe she enters into, she decides her purpose here will become more about her and less about what the Covenant demands from her.

She allots all the available night courses they provide in order to maintain her work schedule, which she is graciously thankful for.

On her way out, a middle aged man in a charcoal coloured suit—wearing a fringe of grey just around the edges of his ebony coloured hair—insists on walking her to the exit. He—being the Headmaster of the institute, Dean Gideon Blithe—had sensed her hostility when she first arrived but now that the tour is over, he is quite pleased to see it has dissipated and been replaced with her excitement. He looks down at her with pale green eyes and smiles, gazing out over the night sky of the city. Having been there himself some time ago, he understands her frustration about her new world.

"You know, Gabrian, the Realm can be a most beautiful place if filled with the right company."

She stops at the door and glances up at him briefly then turns back to the night. He pauses for a moment to gather his thoughts. "I hope you will not let the mindset of a few overinflated Relics outweigh the importance in understanding a beautiful gift such as yours."

Lines form above the bridge of her nose as her eyes drop— bouncing over each visible flaw in the steps in front of her before lifting them to seek out his moonlit eyes in search of his meaning. "You think my gift is beautiful?"

"Yes I do, very much so," the Headmaster replies, still gazing out over the city.

"Why? Everyone else seems to be afraid of it," she prompts, curious to get a glimpse of insight into how his mind may work.

"You are looking at it the wrong way, my dear."

Gabrian tilts her head as she tries to understand his meaning.

"You are treating your gift as if it were a curse and that is where your trouble lies." He turns, breaking away from his daydream and focuses his attention on her. The reflection of the dusk-to-dawn light hanging overhead casts an eerie glow to fall within his pale green eyes, making his gaze upon her almost haunting and profound—drowning her within his world of knowledge. "I do not believe that anyone would want you to be saddened by it. Instead, I should think that they would want you to celebrate and nurture it. As it is truly that, a gift, handed down to you by the ancients themselves."

Gabrian smiles and nods, grateful for the Headmaster's aged words and for the kindness he has bestowed upon her. She is not sure if it is the meaning of the message itself or if it is the way his voice had wrapped so gently around each spoken word that made their exchange so enchanting, but some of the doors that lay hidden deep within her mind begin to unlock. The physical pressures that harbor within her head—which threatened her with many migraines ever since she was a child—begin to subside.

Gabrian sighs, feeling the instant relief from the strange occurrence. The Headmaster's face twitches for a moment then lightens, seeing her show of content. "Good night, my dear," Gideon says pausing for a moment, pressing his hand against the means of exit. "Before you go, I would like you to remember something."

She nods in accordance to his wishes.

"Tomorrow is a new day, and it is within the bounds of this realization that brings new possibilities."

She glances over at him and wonders just how old he truly must be to have such an ostensible magnitude of unbiased depth to him.

"Good night, sir," she meekly whispers.

Then she turns back around to feel the winter's icy breath on her face as the Headmaster pushes open the school's large wooden door to enable her to take her leave. She stares out over the city that lies before her, and her heart leaps as she envisions the array of endless possibilities that her future holds for her.

Gabrian takes a step forward out into the night, this time with hope, and for once, without shame.

Chapter Thirty-Four

Beauty and Essex

AFTER A WEEK of being back in the city, Gabrian finds herself trying to establish some sort of happy balance between attending night classes and catching up with her clientele. She has been gone for a month so getting back into the swing of things seems a little more trying than usual. The first few days are a bit overwhelming. Her schedule is booked solid with clients and her nights follow with training at the Legacy school. Being busy keeps her mind occupied for a while, but once everything falls into a routine, she finds herself thinking about Shane on her downtime.

Gabrian had hoped to receive a call from him while still in Maine, but he had already told her he was leaving and that the chances were slim. But now it had been a couple of weeks since they spoke, and there is still no call. The silence of the phone begins to eat away at her. Every other second she finds herself staring at it as if that would make it magically ring. *If only I had those kinds of gifts*, she thinks quietly to herself.

Getting up from her desk, she steps toward the window and stares blankly out over the city. She leans forward and rests her head up against the window, hearing the gentle rhythm of rain against the glass. It reminds her of Maine. The soothing sound of Mother Nature's percussion section pulls her back to a time when the steady tip-tapping beat upon the tin roof of her parent's house would hush her to sleep as the sky would open up above them. She felt a twinge of home sickness for it.

Before she had never really taken much notice of the rain, let alone cared to hear the gentle rhythm of its intoxicating lullaby, but now that everything has changed, somehow the little things that seemed so insignificant have taken a more prominent stance to her.

Her mind is all over the place. Whatever she had been before seems to have taken a backseat to the Borrower Magik she has been harboring within her. The focused and dedicated doctor of the mind she had worked so diligently to become reels in her own delusion of what her life is to be.

Gabrian pulls herself back to the present and backs over to her desk, picking up her phone to check the time. It is four thirty. *Thank goodness*, she thinks and sighs deeply. With no more clients booked for the afternoon, her workday is almost over. And since it is Friday, there are no classes at Legacy tonight either so her evening is free.

"Now what to do," she ponders out loud, letting her mind relax and drift for a moment in a hazy state.

Through the cloudy daydream of nothing in particular, her subconscious returns her delightfully back to the night she had met Shane. She stands silently at her desk, sifting through the events and becomes caught somewhere in the daydream, just staring at her phone.

Not hearing Rachael enter the room, Gabrian jumps at the sound of her voice. "You know, if you stare at that thing too long, you are going to get brain damage." Gabrian realizes she had been staring at her phone again, and how strange it must have looked. She shakes her head and slides it across her desk into a pile of files to the left. "Ah!" she grumbles. "Obviously it must be working." She turns to look out the window again and sighs. "What is wrong with me, Rach? I used to be all about helping people and working all hours of the day, but now all I do is think about Maine."

"Is it Maine in general or is there something in particular that has your attention?" Gabrian's aura flashes brightly for a second, revealing a reaction like she has gotten caught with her hand stuck in the cookie jar. Rachael notices the change in her face and realizes she may have hit a nerve. "Or should I say *someone*."

Feeling her face flush, and knowing she is unable to hide it, she turns to meet Rachael's stare. "I met this guy."

"I knew it," Rachael squeals as she practically jumps across the room to where Gabrian stands. "I knew it had to be something like that. Well, something else besides all the crazy Magik stuff, I mean, but I knew it."

"Really," Gabrian sarcastically retorts while she rolls her eyes at her friend.

"Listen, hold that thought." Rachael reaches out and grabs Gabrian by the hands and squeezes gently in excitement. "We should go out to supper tonight. I promise that I will feed you this time. It has been forever since I have seen you, and you look like you could use a little distraction."

With Gabrian agreeing to give Rachael's favourite restaurant another try, Rachael hurriedly makes another reservation at Beauty & Essex then double checks their standing again before leaving to go.

THEY ARRIVE AT 146 Essex St. and walk through the pawn shop, headed for the big wooden door at the back. Once on the other side of the bouncer and through the door, they are quickly seated at the bar and the maître d' sweetly promises them there will only be a short wait. Excusing herself and heading for the front, Gabrian is quite certain Rachael is checking on the reservation again.

Taking her coat off and settling into her seat, Gabrian notices a familiar orange hue coming from the end of the bar. She sees the profile of the same incredibly handsome bartender that had been working the last time she and Rachael were there. He finishes up with his current customer and begins to wipe down the top of the bar, then noticing her out of the corner of his eye. He turns and starts toward her with a wide smile—his ocean blue green eyes gleam. It is indeed, Thomas.

"Hey, there! I remember you," he says, cozying up in front of her on the other side of the bar. He furrows his brow for a second, revealing rows of laugh lines around his eyes. "Gabrian," he says in a confident tone. "You were in here about a month or so ago."

"You remember me?"

"How could I not?"

She bites down on her bottom lip as her eyes flare open—feeling a jolt of recount rip through her—as she hopes it is not because she had passed out and caused a scene. He grins at her impishly. "You stole my heart."

Gabrian laughs out loud at his cheesy attempt at flirting with her, feeling the tightness around her heart loosen just a bit and enabling her to actually breathe without having to try so hard. She feels the warm kiss of crimson on her cheeks, but she does not care. The easy playfulness of the encounter makes her feel better about things and so she decides to try something new. She raises the edges of her mouth seductively and widens her eyes, reciprocating his warm flirty smile.

Rachael returns from her wanderings and joins them at the bar. She sits down and begins to recite the accounts of her walkabout to her friend when she notices the strange look Gabrian has on her face. She turns her attention toward her friend's muse and understands what it is that causes her to grin from ear to ear.

"Hm, hm. Are you going to introduce me to your friend?" Rachael says, remembering the handsome bartender—interrupting their silent exchange.

"Oh, of course." Gabrian apologizes, not realizing Rachael had actually returned.

"Rachael this is Thomas. Thomas, Rachael." Thomas turns to look at Rachael. She gives him her best 'I am available' smile which normally, with her pouty lips, stunning red hair, and perhaps a little drop of hocus pocus, would capture any man's attentions, but tonight it only catches a mere glance as Thomas nods briefly at her then returns his undivided attention back to Gabrian.

"Huh!" Rachael mumbles to herself quietly, her brow lifts crookedly—widening her dumbfounded caught-in-the-headlights look from his lack of interest in her and stumbles into the seat next to her rival.

"Soooo...what can I get you lovely ladies to drink tonight?" Thomas asks them, never taking his eyes off of Gabrian. "If I can remember correctly, it was just before the holiday and you two were drinking...Grinches."

The name breaks Gabrian from her daze. Both Rachael and Gabrian look at each other simultaneously, spitting out the same answer in unison. "No Grinches!"

Not understanding their apparent dislike to his suggestion but not challenging it either, he puts his hands up in surrender. "Okay. Okay. You win, no Grinches."

Gabrian and Rachael both exhale and playfully chuckle. "I will just have a Corona," Gabrian offers then looks over at her friend. "Rachael?"

"Me too," she says, remembering the last time they ordered drinks from there with the hope there would not be a repeat tonight.

"Not very adventurous, but you're the boss," he utters playfully—drawing in close for a moment—shaking his head and letting his focus swim over Gabrian's. He inhales slowly then slips back to stand upright again, his orange hue blazing against his honey-brown skin like a summer sunset as he walks away, still grinning. He opens the upright cooler at the end of the bar and grabs two beer out of it, stuffing them with lime. Before he returns to deliver their drinks, the maître d' greets the girls and announces to them that their table is ready.

Unlike last time, Gabrian is not really worried about being seated, to be honest. She is quite enjoying her current placement. Frowning a bit as she gets up to grab her things from the back of her bar stool, she pulls her wallet from her purse and places it down on top of the bar, opening it to get money for the drinks. Thomas places his large warm hand gently on top of hers.

"Put that away. They are on me. If...you promise to come back sometime soon."

Gabrian looks up into his eyes, and she feels a subtle wave of electricity wash over her body, causing her face to flush again. She looks down at her feet for a moment. Finding a new source of inner strength bubbling inside of her, she meets his gaze again. This time without bashfulness, she raises her chin. Her pupils widen, creating an electric icy-blue halo to swirl around them as she holds his gaze, the debut of her own confidence in whom she has become. "I promise."

His orange hue flares as he hears her soft words of agreement, removing his hand from hers. "I am here every weeknight from five to eleven," he reveals with a grin. Across his cheeks, a rose hue surfaces beneath his warm skin. He glances over at Rachael, who stands with her arms crossed, watching this ongoing production patiently. "It was nice to have met you..."

"Rachael," she reminds him, forcing her mouth to curve upward into an ugly smile that refuses to reach her eyes in her fake pleasantry, completely put off and confused with his lack of interest in her.

He points at her in acknowledgement. "Rachael. Right, sorry."

"Yeah, you too," she huffs flatly then quickly turns and wrinkles her nose at Gabrian as she walks by her toward the dining area.

Gabrian places her wallet back into her purse then reaches for her beer. "Thanks again." She raises her beer slightly to cheers him and turns to follow her friend. She begins to wonder about what she has just started but then giggles lightheartedly in delight of it all.

The maître d' ushers them through the center of the restaurant, surrounded by tables topped with crystal glasses and a bountiful assortment of strange foods. The walls alluringly wrap around them, dressed with what appears to be hundreds of antique time pieces. The ceiling dances above them, laced with drapes of pearls that sway gently causing the illusion of an ever-changing sky.

The lively chatter of voices resonates all around them from the diverse collection of patrons out and about tonight, enjoying themselves in the company of one another. Gabrian studies them and their colours. She remembers seeing all the different hues here before, but tonight their colours take on new meaning for her.

It is like an underground haven for all those wishing to escape from their human facades and to be completely free, uninhibited by what they are. Gabrian is entirely absorbed in her delight of the sanctity of this place, but her moment is interrupted briefly by the Maître d's announcement. They have reached their table. It is a cozy leather-padded, half-moon-shaped booth with a bucket of ice sitting in front of the table, already filled with Champagne.

Intrigued and wholly consumed by the magnificence of this place, Gabrian slides into her seat. The Maître d' waits for Rachael to follow suit then hands them both a swanky black menu. He pleasantly opens the champagne and pours them each a glass then reassures them that someone will be along shortly to take their order before insisting they enjoy their meal.

Gabrian opens her menu and takes a few moments to look it over. Finding that the only thing on it that even looks remotely enticing to her is the alcohol and the coffee portions of it, she quickly closes it and sighs. Protein in its rarest form seems to be the only real means of sustenance she can stomach since her transformation. Though she does not condone it, she understands why Vampires who drink blood while taking essence would actually enjoy it.

She considers her present company and wonders if the kitchen has ever had a special request to see if they had any waiters on hand not opposed to donating a cup or two of O positive for a nice fat tip in return. She chuckles to herself at the thought of it then realizes how deranged the image actually is and shakes her head, deciding to just stick with drinking the champagne sitting idly on the corner of the table.

Laying the menu down, Gabrian scans the layout of the restaurant—taking in its intriguing ambience, thankful for all its possibilities of distraction, but Rachael notices her friend's slight dismay. "What is wrong?"

"I don't even know why I bother to go to restaurants." Gabrian continues to people surf as she slips the edge of her Corona across the plumpness of her bottom lip in subtle hypnotic rhythm, not taking a drink. "Nothing looks good to me anymore."

"Hm, that is funny," Rachael says, looking back at her menu with a quirky grin.

Gabrian's eyes return from their scouting and rest on her friend, who seems to have found something peculiar. "What is funny?"

"I noticed that the bartender seemed to look pretty good to you a few minutes ago," she spits out at her playfully, but her eyes narrow into nothing more than a set of small lines filled with fluttery dark lashes and just a hint of disdain.

Gabrian rolls her eyes and laughs at her friend's all too obvious stabs at her. She cannot help but feel a bit embarrassed by the fact Rachael witnessed her interaction with Thomas. She has always been one to keep her personal life very private, but she is not the same person anymore. Her little bout of flirting today is nothing to be ashamed of so she quickly brushes off Rachael's comment. Besides, this is her best friend in the whole world and of all people, she should be the one Gabrian can let her guard down with.

Gabrian glances over in the direction of the bar but turns back quickly and raises her chin reflexively. "Just a bit of harmless flirting is all that was." Truth be known, Gabrian is just as surprised as Rachael about the whole thing.

The waiter arrives and asks them if they are ready to order. Rachael asks for the pasta in red sauce, and Gabrian opts out for the bone marrow appetizer—in order to appease her companion and to not arise any concern over her lack of interest to consume real food. She does not remember Ethan ever mentioning anything about the probability of her diet changing, but then again, she never asked him either—this may have been an important topic to cover.

"So," Rachael interrupts her train of thought. "Tell me about this guy that has the wise and powerful Gabrian all tangled up in knots."

Gabrian's cheery grin disappears from her face—erasing the spark from her eyes, and flares the edges of her grey aura that had been no more than that of a ghost floating around her form. A heavy weight pulls down on the corners of her mouth as she feels her heart deflate and sink deep within her chest as soon as the words come out of Rachael's mouth. She was content thinking about Thomas and worrying about her lack of food, and now wishes Rachael had not mentioned it at all.

The brief moment of freedom she had from her torment is gone, and she longs to have it back. She reaches for her Corona and tips it up to take a large drink. The smell of the beer sends her mind flailing helplessly backward, reliving the few tender moments she had shared with Shane.

So much for a distraction, she thinks as her anxiety over his absence returns.

Rachael sees pain seep into Gabrian's eyes and decides that teasing her about it may not be the best move. Deciding to forfeit the playful banter about this mystery guy that she had planned on, Rachael realizes maybe now would be a good time for her to soften up for a moment and be the friend she is.

Gabrian's cheeks flush with a light rose hue that spreads gingerly across her porcelain skin—feeling ridiculous about losing her composure like this, especially in a public place—but she cannot seem to get a handle on it. She feels the moisture as it wells up in her eyes. She quickly reaches for her napkin, unfolds it, and removes any evidence of weakness.

"What is wrong with me, Rach?" Gabrian knows her friend has a lot more knowledge in the department of the heart and hopes she has some answers. "What is going on with me?"

Rachael puts down her drink and softens her expression, giving Gabrian a motherly look. "Well, you have either caught some kind of East Coast Fever that has temporarily altered your neurons or I would dare say that you have fallen for this guy."

What Rachael has so clearly pointed out, Gabrian's emotional side has known all along. But hearing the words out loud somehow reaches and breaks through all the barriers her logical side had set up to deny its actual possibility.

"Why does it have to feel like this?" she questions, almost pleading with her friend to give her the words she so desperately wants in order to end this torment. "Why does falling in love have to be so hard?"

Rachael reaches across the table and cradles Gabrian's hand gently within her own. "Because if it were not, it would be that much easier to throw away when things do not go the way we want them to. It would not hold as much meaning to us or have as much power over us that enables us to keep pushing through the bad times we all endure. It has to be that way in order to survive."

She always thought Rachael to be wise beyond her years in her own way and today, Gabrian knows why—thankful for its presence.

"Have you heard from him?"

"No," she whispers, embarrassed to say it out loud.

"Do you have his number?"

"Yes."

"Well, then pick up your phone, be a modern woman, and give him a call," Rachael says, waving her fingers around at Gabrian. Then she tucks them inward, creating a cradled imaginary phone, she presses them lightly against her face to imply she is on a call and winks, grinning triumphantly as she picks up her beer and takes a drink. "Problem solved." Knowing that one way or another this will give Gabrian the closure to her issue, she can put her mind back in order. Whichever order that may be, she is not sure; all she knows is that it will be done.

"Really?" Gabrian's eyes open wide with the thought of calling him. "I am not so sure about that. This is not really my expertise."

"And what is your expertise, Gabrian—sitting around, driving yourself crazy, overanalyzing every last little detail to death...yeah, that is much better."

Rachael reaches into Gabrian's purse hanging on the side of the vacant chair to her right and takes out Gabrian's phone, placing it on the table in front of her. "Pick up the phone and call him already! You are a Boragen. A powerful Borrower. There is no reason for you to be afraid of anything, let alone talking to some human boy."

Gabrian knows Rachael is right. But it is not talking to the boy she is afraid of—it is hearing what the boy has to say that scares her.

Chapter Thirty-Five

Oath of Honour

EVER SINCE GABRIAN left for Manhattan, Jarrison and Sarapheane have had strange premonitions—something bad is lingering around the edges of the Shadows. Unsure of what kind of disturbance it is, they become concerned for their safety and the safety of Gabrian.

The secrecy around Gabrian's family tree has only ever been divulged to the Shadow Walkers and a selective few others. Knowing their duty as Schaeduwe, and being realistic about possible events of their demise, they address their concerns with their people.

Since Orroryn has already served his two consecutive oaths with Markim and briefly with Cera, the internal workings of the Schaeduwe people have agreed that Shane, being of Orroryn's house, should be the next in line to act as the Shadow Guardian to the Silver bloodline.

Sarapheane and Jarrison took on their promise happily, but are bound to the girl out of love more than duty. There had been no need to pass this ritual down—until now.

***

"WHAT DO YOU mean I have to be her Guardian? Why can't Tynan do it?" Shane screams at Orroryn, wrenching the dishtowel within his hands—turning his knuckles white—then throws it at the kitchen counter, furious with what is being asked of him. He begins to pace, tormented by the absurdity of the decision. It is just too much for him to swallow.

"Because Tynan has other obligations to the Realm," Orroryn tries to reason with Shane, but he is worried that the importance in this request will be lost on him in his rage. "She is the offspring of the Silver Mage. Only those who serve the Ancients can this oath be bestowed on. And you as my adoptive son must take on this honour as I have and my father before. This is our liege to carry on. From the day you became part of my family this responsibility fell on your shoulders, and like it or not, to refuse this would bring much shame onto yourself and your house."

Orroryn can see the wheels turning within Shane's mind, hoping he has reached the logical side of it. "And, it would mean a great deal to them and to me as well."

Shane stops moving for a moment, only to glare at Orroryn. "But she is a Boragen—a bloody Vampire," he yells. "I have trained all my life, from the time I could wield a weapon, to destroy these things and now you are asking me to put my life on the line for it?"

"Yes. That is exactly what I am asking." Without missing a beat, he continues speaking before Shane can interrupt. "Oh and It, is a she. And she is the direct blood of a Silver," his voice softens, not rising to Shane's challenge. He realizes that if he gives Shane an ounce of fuel, he will just continue on with his fury. "So you might want to try and remember that when we meet with Jarrison and Sarapheane tomorrow to swear your oath of Shadow Guardianship."

"Besides the fact that this is ludicrous, you know how I feel about Vampires." Shane's face turns bright red, exasperated by this defeat. "What do you want me to do...save her from herself?"

"Shane, not every Boragen is a bloodthirsty Vampire. You cannot keep judging every single Borrower you come across as vicious rogues with no respect for the law like the ones that killed your Parents."

"Oh no?" he spits at Orroryn. "Watch me." Shane grabs his coat from the back of the chair and walks away before he says something he will regret.

Orroryn knows Shane. He has been the boy's caretaker for a nearly a century, and he knows that when it comes right down to it that Shane will do the right thing. He will take on this request for he is through and through a Shadow Walker.

Throughout the Realm, Shadow Walkers are known as the most honourable of all the Fellowships—held in the highest of regards. This bestowment is seen as a great honour and for this reason only, Shane will take the oath.

Chapter Thirty-Six

After Midnight

CIMMERIAN SITS STRAIGHT up in his bed, feeling the presence of an unwanted guest. He looks at the clock; it is three in the morning. Twisting his hand in the air, a dark purple ball of energy appears from his palm and hovers over his bed like a disco ball. It creates a shimmering black light effect and illuminates the room just enough for him to see who is sitting in the corner chair—although he did not really need the light to know who it is.

"What do you want, Adrinn?" Rubbing his eyes with the back of his hand, Cimmerian tries to focus on his company.

"Oh. You are awake. Great! I did not want to wake you." Adrinn taps his fingers together in rhythm with Cimmerian's clock's second hand, and his mouth turns awkwardly upward into a demented smile that would disturb even the darkest of souls. "I was enjoying watching you sleep though. Did you have a nice dream?"

Cimmerian's mind jumps back to the last memory of his dream and finds his daughter's face as the only image he can recall.

"She was such a lovely girl," Adrinn taunts, drawing out each word in a slow dramatic speech as he glares at Cimmerian with unblinking, cold eyes.

Realizing Adrinn played with his subconscious, and it had

been he that made Cimmerian dream of her. The orb hovering above them flickers and sparks in response to Cimmerian's sudden flood of anger.

"Enough of your games, Adrinn," Cimmerian snaps, closing his eyes. His knuckles whiten as he clenches his fists in an attempt to soothe the itch of the fire that dwells within them—burning just beneath the surface, and aching to be released with his silent wish of ridding himself of this irritating pest. "Tell me why you are here disturbing what few precious moments I have to myself."

"Tsk, tsk, tsk," Adrinn jeers, shaking his head primly at Cimmerian. "Really now, is that any way to treat your company?"

"Adrinn! I swear I will escort you back to Erebus myself if you do not get on with it!"

"Fine! Since you are going to be like that." He turns away, pretending that Cimmerian's shortness with him has hurt his feelings somehow. "I need you to do something for me."

Cimmerian can already feel the dread creeping inside him for even thinking about giving this deranged monster any kind of help. "What is it that you want now?"

He grins at Cimmerian, sickening him—knowing whatever it is that Adrinn wants will not lead to anything good. "I want you to disable Jarrison and Sarapheane's Shadow."

"What?" Cimmerian shouts at him, pinching the bridge of his nose and glares at him through squinted eyes—shaking his head in disbelief of the absurd request. "You are out of your mind. No!"

"It is only temporary." Adrinn stares down at his outstretched hand, admiring the shape of his nails then pulls his gaze away to glance at his host. "Just for an hour or so."

"What in the Realm for?" Cimmerian opens his eyes and stares at the lunatic infesting his peace and quiet, hoping for some kind of an out.

Adrinn softens his face, masking it with sincerity in order to assure Cimmerian that his intentions are completely on level. "I just need them out of the way for a bit. It would seem that the girl fancies the company of Shadow Walkers, and I would like to have the opportunity to spend some time with her without one of them stepping out of a shadow and interrupting us," he explains. "It is really no big deal, Cimmerian. I just need some privacy with her.

Then after that, they can pop in and out of the shadows to their heart's content." Adrinn's explanation becomes animated as he waves his hands around as if he is performing a child's puppet show. "Oh and by the way..." he adds once he stops moving. "I need this to happen exactly at noon tomorrow, okay? No sooner, no later. Do you think you can handle that?" Adrinn demands snidely, infuriating Cimmerian whose patience wears thin at the condescension in his tone. Adrinn has him hanging by a thread, and he knows that, trying not to break the delicate ties.

Every nerve in Cimmerians body screams at him to throw this lunatic back into the Darkness where he belongs, but his mind cannot let go of the possibility of seeing Symone again.

"Fine," Cimmerian concedes. "But only for an hour. After that, you will have to find some other way of entertaining your demented mind."

"Excellent decision, old boy." Adrinn claps his hands together and jumps up out of the chair, straightening the imaginary wrinkles on his suit--preparing to take his leave. "You are such a lovely friend. I am so glad that we get to spend these precious moments together."

"Get out!" Cimmerian yells, waving his hand in dismissal of the annoyance in front of him, causing the flaring disco ball to launch straight toward Adrinn's head. The orb's mission is a direct hit but passes completely through its target without damage. Adrinn simply snickers at Cimmerian's reflexive act of frustration.

"You really must work on your people skills," he taunts, tugging on his lapel and fading into the Darkness.

Chapter Thirty-Seven

Fallen Shadows

RICHARD GRAY RUBS his eyes, weary from the long twelve-hour night shift he has just put in at the Brightside Boat Company in Northeast Harbor. In celebration of finishing their last boat order for the day, he opens a beer and drinks it down quickly before heading home. Pulling the keys out of the pocket of his brown Carhart jacket, he slowly walks to the parking lot and climbs into his Ford Escape.

After starting the engine and heading out of the parking lot, he turns right on Main Street, heading for Seal harbor where his bed awaits his return. From out of the murky depths of Erebus, Adrinn takes his place in the passenger's side of the truck beside the unsuspecting driver. Richard jumps and pulls instinctually at the wheel, startled by the sudden appearance of the ominous creature siting no more than two feet from him. The truck swerves to the right as he jolts, almost landing in the ditch.

"What the..." Richard gasps as Adrinn's pupils widen and pulse, pushing through the driver's consciousness to seize control of his mind.

"Now be a good lad and turn this hunk of junk around. We have a date with destiny to keep," Adrinn says in a sickeningly sweet voice.

Richard nods his head robotically and slows down the truck to a full stop at the side of the road before making an unauthorized U-turn back toward town, headed for the Somes Sound passage. Adrinn rubs his hands together briskly in anticipation of the trip as Richard continues on his course, driving faster and faster along the narrow road with Adrinn in full control of the out-of-control driver.

***

JARRISON HOLDS HIS hand out to help Sarapheane as she gets up away from the table at the Sea-Wich—their usual brunch spot. As dependable as clockwork, they have spent every Monday here for as long as they can remember.

Like the true gentleman he is, Jarrison never fails to get Sarapheane's jacket first and have it open, waiting for her. She turns to face him. Her eyes gleam with admiration and love for him while he gently pulls at the lapels of her coat, drawing her nearer to him. He lets his fingers slowly brush against her long dark hair, tucking back the loosened locks behind her ear.

Jarrison leans down to rest his warm gentle mouth against her temple and kisses her softly. Turning, he takes his place by Sarapheane's side and waits for her to take his arm as they depart.

From the Sea-Wich, they take a left turn and begin their usual scenic drive down Somes Sound, heading for Northeast Harbor. Jarrison scouts out across the water that fills the fiord of Somes Sound and watches as an osprey dives down from the cliffs—quickly snatching up its dinner from the waters below.

He sees Sarapheane smiling at him from the corner of his eye and gives her hand a tender squeeze, bringing it to his mouth. "I will never get tired of this."

"Tired of what, Jare?

"Of holding your hand...of being near you."

Sarapheane grins girlishly. "You are such a smoothie, Jarrison Shadwell."

"No, I mean it." He kisses her hand again. "I would be lost without your smile to wake up to every morning."

"Well, Mister Shadwell. It is pretty easy to smile when everything you will ever need is sitting right beside you, holding your hand." She winks at him, and Jarrison gives her hand another gentle squeeze as she turns back toward the window to gaze out across the sound.

"Do you think Gabrian is doing okay?" Sarapheane probes, her eyes still turned away as she studies the ledges of the wall of rock on the other side of the fiord, looking for wildlife.

"She is fine. You worry too much," Jarrison comforts, glancing briefly in her direction with a one-sided grin while gripping her hand. "She is way too stubborn to admit defeat."

"I guess. She never was one to give up." Sarapheane smiles at the recollection of the daunting trials and tribulations of Gabrian's determination as a child. "Cera would be so proud."

"Stop worrying so much. Gabrian knows we are here for her if she needs us. I'll tell you what. If it will make you feel better, we can drop by later after she is done working and check in on her. Okay?" Sarapheane's face lights up with delight, pinching the edges of her eyes with a smile that grows across her mouth in anticipation of seeing her daughter again so soon.

Jarrison smiles, knowing Sarapheane is fighting the urge to leave for Manhattan this very instant. "Anything for my girls." He raises her hand to his mouth again and kisses it once more.

He peeks over at her and his heart begins to ache wildly. Looking back at the road, he notices a vehicle heading toward them, and it is coming fast.

"Sarah..." Jarrison tightens his grip on her hand, just enough to get her attention.

"Yes, Jarrison?" she answers, pulling her attention from her daydream of visiting Manhattan soon to rest her gaze on her husband.

"Something does not feel right." He gives her a quick glance. His sea green eyes, now serious, flare as a flag of caution.

"What do you mean?" Sarapheane questions, seeing the warning in his eyes. Her own eyes, now on high alert, dart purposely around at the world encompassing her.

"I don't know. It is just a feeling." He stares unblinking straight ahead, though his voice remains soft, it wavers, unable to hide his fear. "Be ready."

Both of their eyes locate the nearest Shadow within the truck. Sarapheane turns to Jarrison and sees the glistening of real concern haunting his eyes, hardening his expression as his lips fold under his teeth—pressing tightly together in to a grim line across his mouth. She slowly faces front and watches the road, noticing the truck heading toward them.

She feels the rift in the energies too.

***

ADRINN SNEERS AS he sees exactly what he has been hoping to see up ahead. "Floor it!" he commands in a hiss. Richard's foot increases its pressure on the accelerator until the pedal lies flat on the floor of the truck, sending it on a dangerous course forward.

***

JARRISON STEERS THE truck as close as he can to his side of the road—careful not to get too close or they risk the possibility of weakening the edge and going over the cliff. Sarapheane holds Jarrison's hand tighter and tighter as the truck speeds closer.

"He is crossing the line, he is...Jarrison!"

"Into the Veil, Sarah! Jump!"

Sarapheane tries to grasp the edge of the Shadow below her, but the fringe is not there. Her efforts are in vain. "It is no use...it's gone!"

***

WITH ONLY SECONDS to go before impact, Adrinn sits upright, tugging the edges of his lapel. His eyes gleam seeing his target only feet away and smears his face with a smug, repulsive grin.

"All right, then...time for me to go. I would love to stick around to watch the ending of the show, but you know how fickle survivors can get if in fact they do survive. Let us just say, someone might snitch on me, and we cannot have that now, can we?"

He looks over at his driver and pretends to pat him on the shoulder.

"Best of luck to you."

Adrinn releases his hold on Richard's mind—hoping he has gotten what he asked for—and vanishes, leaving Richard still dazed and confused from his mind compulsion to face the eminent onslaught of disaster.

***

SARAPHEANE AND JARRISON look at each other one last time, knowing this may be goodbye. Jarrison unbuckles his seatbelt and leaps across the dash of the truck, using his body as a shield to protect Sarapheane from the oncoming vehicle. The white Ford Explorer heads straight toward them and barrels full throttle into the front corner of the Shadwell's vehicle, causing the pickup truck to flip violently into the air and crash headfirst into the cliffs below, consumed in a fiery rage.

Chapter Thirty-Eight

Paradise Lost

GABRIAN LOOKS UP from her file when she hears a knock on the door. Rachael enters her office, clouded by a heavy aura. Something is wrong; she can feel it and see the seriousness of it on Rachael's face, but she does not breach Rachael's mind to find out why. She promised Rachael before that she would leave her friend to her own thoughts.

Ororoyn appears from the dark corner of the room to her right, his eyes shadowed by the storm brewing within them-making his face flat and void of readable expression. His focus darts from Gabrian, then across the room, immediately finding Rachael, and she blankly stares back at him. No one says anything, and it irritates Gabrian to no end. Promise or no promise, she cannot stand the silence any longer and pries into both their minds.

She does not understand what it is she sees at first. Then the images and thoughts come together—all the unfathomable news broadcasts loudly in her head.

Gabrian's heart begins to pound so hard she is unable to hear anything Rachael and Ororoyn say. Everything around her decelerates, and she feels herself being pulled downward by an invisible unstoppable force. Unable to do anything about it, her

283

legs give out from beneath her as she descends.

Orroryn bolts across the room, noticing her falter. His arms stretch out in front of him, quickly trying to catch her before she hits the floor.

From that moment on, everything fades in and out for Gabrian. She sees Rachael trying to say something to her, but her words sound slurred and incomprehensible, like she is speaking to her through a long tunnel. Gabrian is completely lethargic and just nods in response, lost in her own world.

"You take her home," Rachael instructs Orroryn, who still cradles Gabrian within his arms. "I will take care of things here. She needs to be in Maine."

Orroryn tries to smile, but his lips quiver, and the attempt is lost. "I will make sure she is settled. If you need me to, I will come back to escort you to the Shadwell's home." Rachael's heart jumps at his kind gesture, but a cloud of guilt pours down on her for thinking about herself at a time like this.

"Thank you, Orroryn. Please meet me at her apartment tomorrow morning. I will gather some of her things she will need for the..." Rachael fights back her grief, trying not to cry. "I will go stay with her as long as she needs me."

Orroryn stands up, holding onto Gabrian a little tighter as he crosses the room. He glances back at Rachael for a brief moment then steps forward, slipping into the Shadow's Veil with Gabrian in tow.

FOR THE NEXT few days, only flashes of people coming and going in and out of her parents' house registers with Gabrian. Their words of support and efforts to try and console her in this time of hardship fall of deaf ears. All she can do is smile and nod, not able to find the strength to speak.

Rachael arrived the next day after Gabrian with the help of Orroryn. She set up her things in one of the small rooms downstairs and vowed to stay until she feels Gabrian does not need her any longer.

The service is to take place at the local funeral home in Northeast Harbor, but her parents' bodies had been already carried back into the Shadow's Veil before the caskets were sealed. It was the way of the Schaeduwe Fellowship, and Gabrian let Tynan honour that.

Tynan makes it a point to check in more the last couple of days and somewhere between her bouts of silence, she finds the strength to talk to him.

"How could they die?" she whispers to him as they quietly sit on the couch. Tynan holds her securely within his arms and gently strokes her hair. "I don't understand. You are Shadow Walkers. I thought that meant that you are supposed to be almost immortal?" She looks up at him with moisture-ridden eyes, grasping for closure.

The heavy weight of sorrow that pulls on Tynan's face lightens, and he forces a smile, tightening his embrace just for a moment—she misses them as much as he does. "No, it is complicated, Gabe. We are not immortals. None of us are. We all must die someday."

She looks away, fighting the tears. "Then why would they not just jump into the Shadows?"

"I am not sure, Gabe," Tynan admits. He is still trying to wrap his head around the confusion as well. "I know things like this have happened before, but it is a rare thing for a Shadow Walker to be caught off guard like that. It does not make any sense to me either. The authorities said that the driver of the other vehicle does not remember anything about the accident—only that he had left the bar after one drink—and the next thing he knew, he was in the hospital, barely alive. They tested his blood for alcohol levels. He was not intoxicated."

Tynan feels Gabrian's small frame shake lightly under the weight of his arm as she begins to sob. Feeling overwhelmed as well by the loss of his brother, and Sarapheane, he awkwardly tries to comfort her by changing the conversation.

"That is enough talk of doom and gloom for today." He kisses the top of Gabrian's head as he gets up from the couch and heads toward the kitchen. "I am going to make us some lunch before I go take care of some things, what do you feel like having?"

"I am good, Uncle Ty," she forces out in a mumble, not able to think about food. "Make whatever you want. I will get something to eat later." She crumples into the cushions of the couch, gathering the blanket beneath her into a ball and hugs it. Somehow, by just responding to Tynan, it has exhausted any energy she had left.

Tynan finishes up with his lunch quickly. He has unfinished business with a certain Shadow Walker, and he insists on giving him a friendly reminder about his responsibilities as oath taker before Tynan leaves in a few days to return to his post at the edge of the Veil.

Chapter Thirty-Nine

Survival of the Fittest

THE NEWS OF the Shadwell's death spreads throughout the Realm like wildfire. "It has been almost a century since such a travesty has occurred," a young man in the back of the class whispers to his friend.

Cimmerian hears the buzz of voices chattering behind him and turns around to inquire about what all the commotion is for. "What is so important that you need to disrupt my class?"

"You mean you have not heard, Sir?" a young blond-haired boy asks him in surprise.

"Have not heard what?"

"About the tragedy in the Veil."

Cimmerian swallows down the vomit that wants to surface in his throat, hoping he is wrong about whom he suspects is involved.

"Jarrison and Sarapheane Shadwell were in a car accident."

"Are they all right?" Cimmerian asks, quickly wishing for a miracle.

"They died," the boy divulged to his Headmaster. "The Schaeduwe community are completely distraught over it. Nothing quite like this has happened before."

A wave of excruciating guilt rushes through Cimmerian. He

turns to face the board as the words strike the breath from his lungs, and his hands tremble—struggling to hold the chalk still within them. Willing himself to regain control over his senses, he turns back toward the room full of Derkaz Younglings and quickly dismisses the class for the day. After the last student has made their exit and the room is cleared, he heads toward the door and locks it from the inside.

Once he is sure that he is alone, he moves his arm in a circular motion over his head. The air around him shifts and twists, quickly cloaking his body in Darkness, enveloping him completely. Then he is gone—vanished from the school—and arriving instantly above the last known address of the monster he has come to see.

Cimmerian summons two large dark purple orbs of energy to emerge, one in each of his hands. He throws one of them directly at the black, barren Earth. The ground shakes and rumbles from the impact of pure magic.

"Where are you?" Cimmerian bellows, turning in circles as he searches for any signs of movement amongst the trees. Waiting a moment for a response but receiving no reply, he fires another orb directly at the blackened Earth.

"I know that you are in there somewhere. Come out or I swear I will seal you in there for good." Cimmerian flicks his hands slightly and two more orbs appear within his palms, reloading for his next round of fire. Raising his right hand again to strike, he hears the voice he is searching for.

"Hold your fire there, Tex. There is no need for that," Adrinn says, appearing just behind Cimmerian. He slowly turns to face Adrinn, trembling with rage.

"What did you do?" Cimmerian spits out at him through gritted teeth.

"I, did nothing. As for young Mr. Gray..." Adrinn continues, looking away from his guest, pulling his hand up nonchalantly, as if to inspect his vaporous nails for any traces of blame. "well, I cannot speak for him, but..."

"Enough! You made me an accomplice to murder," Cimmerian shouts, his dark violet aura bursting violently around him, rippling the energy outward in a wave from his fury.

"I did nothing of the sort," Adrinn snaps, pulling his hand back in. His eyes jump to Cimmerian, glaring at him with his chin up and wearing a straight face. His dark smoky aura swirls carefree, flickering momentarily only once due to his minor annoyance of Cimmerian accusation. "It was merely an inconvenient coincidence...for them. That is all."

"You used me," Cimmerian bellows, looking away while starting to pace; his hands tremble as sporadic stray sparks flare from his palms. "You have turned my love and my desperation to help my daughter into something ugly and cruel." He stops and points his finger at the fiend, resisting the searing temptation within to end him. "And now you have managed to entangle me in this deadly game you are playing."

"Well, if you say it like that, of course it is going to sound bad." Adrinn looks at Cimmerian and grins slyly at him. "Really, Cimmerian, do not be so dramatic."

"Dramatic!" Cimmerian screams at him, furious that he would drag him into his sick game. "I will show you *dramatic*!" The ground underneath Adrinn's feet begins to rumble and shake as Cimmerian raises his hands slowly up toward the sky.

Adrinn's eyes dart around nervously, realizing he may have gone a little too far in toying with Cimmerian. Getting sealed back into Erebus would put a damper on his plans.

"You know, I am just going to go now. It would seem that you are not thinking rationally at the moment, but I would like to remind you we are working together toward a common goal. Or have you forgotten that part? Besides, you know how things work. Sometimes death is necessary to preserve those who would live."

Cimmerian's eyes turn completely black, and the orbs in his hands spark, sending out fragments of magic into the air around them. Adrinn feels Cimmerian's irritation soar then lessens a bit in his comprehension as the words of the monster sink in.

"It was lovely to see you again, Cimmerian," Adrinn says smugly as his bodily image starts to vaporize then adds a jab just before he completely disappears. "But you might want to work on that temper of yours."

Cimmerian claps his hands together quickly, sending the orbs racing forward on a collision course with Adrinn's fading presence, only to slip into the void with him—resolving nothing, and leaving him to stand alone to face the guilt of his own doing.

Chapter Forty

A Lover's Hate

GABRIAN STANDS MOTIONLESS in front of the large sitting room window overlooking the ocean. The rain taps incessantly against the panes of glass and threatens to follow her wherever she goes, drowning her in a world full of sadness where she is unable to move in any direction—stuck within this catatonic state.

She turns away to venture back to her dark room just as she sees a familiar figure across from her. It is Shane. He stands in the doorway, larger than life. Though hesitant about it, he makes his appearance at the house after the procession is over and Tynan had found him to deliver his reminder. He manages to keep a low profile by lurking in the corners of the less populated rooms of the house, avoiding people as much as possible.

The weight around Gabrian's heart lifts at the sight of him. But only for a brief moment—something is not right. He glances at her, and his mouth almost curves into a smile then his face grows cold and blank as he looks away from her, turning to leave.

Gabrian almost pushes her way through the living room, weaving in and out of the grips of the sympathetic well-wishers.

"Hey!" she calls out to him and reaches out to grab the edge of his shirt sleeve. He stops but exhales loudly like he is irritated and glares down to where her hand holds the cloth. Gabrian feels the ice in his stare and lets go of his shirt.

Perplexed by his unanticipated reaction, she bites her lip. "You did not call me." Her voice cracks as the words surface.

He tilts his head to the side, just enough to look her in the eye. "No. I didn't."

Her eyes withdraw from his glare and dart around the room. She tries hard to contain her emotions, but Gabrian feels the wetness in her eyes already and swallows down the lump building in her throat. She gathers her strength and once more turns her eyes to face the ice in his.

"I am confused. The last time I saw you, you could barely let me go. Now you act as if you can't stand to be near me."

He breaks his stare and looks away, fidgeting a bit in his stance as he shuffles his feet. "You're not confused. You are right," he drones out—his tone flat lines as he returns his arctic glare.

She gapes at him in horror from the poisonous words delivered. Gabrian tries to respond, but the words will not come. She opens her mouth to try again, but Shane's expression changes. The emotionless stare shifts and his eyes narrow—draining them of any kindness—slicing through her tendered soul like a dulled dagger being dragged through her chest, slowly amplifying her pain and choking the life out of any attempt to speak.

"Listen, just save your breath. I am only here out of obligation to my father's house and yours."

"*Obligation?*" Completely dumbfounded by his frigid attitude toward her, Gabrian grasps for any recollection of clues that will reinforce Shane's sudden change.

"Or didn't anyone tell you?" He scoffs at her in disgust. "Against my better judgement, I took the Guardian oath, and now I am sworn to protect and defend the Silver bloodline. And since that is you...well, you're a smart girl. I think you can figure out the rest of the story."

All Gabrian can do is stand and stare.

"Don't bother looking into this too much, Gabrian. Even though I am now your Guardian, believe me when I say I am not happy about this. We are sworn enemies by birthright but refusing would have brought shame upon my house. And that is not an option."

Gabrian feels her limbs and her core begin to tremble from

292

within, paralyzing her, and stands helplessly statuesque as she witnesses the remaining pieces of her heart being painfully torn out of her chest and ripped to shreds in front of her with every word spoken. Leave it to her to fall in love with the only person who was born to destroy her.

"There is no more. There is no less." Shane looks down at her with dead eyes, the warm sea green sheen she fell in love with is now a dull dark green, exuding his lack of empathy toward her as he delivers his message, robotic and without emotion. "Now that this little misunderstanding you had about us is cleared up, I need to go find Orroryn before he leaves for the city," he announces as he walks away.

His departing footsteps thunder like gunshots through her ears. She feels herself beginning to shut down, overloaded with grief. Not wanting to feel the suffrage in her circumstances any longer, Gabrian gives in to her brain's desire to stop registering anything at all.

She does not remember climbing the stairs or crawling into bed. To Gabrian, the last few days have been nothing more than a distorted nightmare. Rachael comes in and out of her room periodically, checking on her to ask if she needs anything, but other than that, her mind is barren.

AFTER A COUPLE weeks of her self-induced coma, Gabrian finally decides to get out of bed. Walking over to the window in her room, she gazes out into the night and notices that the snow has melted, revealing bare ground. With all the rain they had gotten, she is not surprised. She opens the window to release the staleness from her room and let in some fresh air. The mist clinging to the night's warm breeze quickly covers her face with moisture. She does not care. After lying in bed for what seems like an eternity, she happily invites it in.

"Okay, Gabrian. Enough is enough," she demands out loud—loathing in self-pity never was her thing. She closes the window then turns back to face her room. Scouting through her things, she finds her running shoes and an old pair of sweatpants. After a moment of hesitation, she heads downstairs toward the kitchen door.

Rachael looks up from her book—one she found in

Gabrian's bookshelf upstairs. "Hey, you, feeling better?"

"I guess."

Rachael notices the running shoes dangling from Gabrian's hand. "Where are you going? It's dark and raining out there."

"Yup, it is," Gabrian continues to tie up her shoes then pulls on her mother's reflective windbreaker still hanging on the wall. "I need to run," she mumbles on her way out the door.

At the end of her parent's driveway, she takes a right on Route Three, leading her out of town. The road is bare and the night strangely warm for this time of year. The air feels clean from the rain, so a nice long run might just be what the doctor ordered.

Hearing the gentle repetitive beat of her footsteps tap against the wet surface of the asphalt sends her into a meditative trance. All the noise in her head begins to quiet as her endorphins kick in and take over. She breathes in its splendor and just runs.

Before too long, she sees the sign for Somes Sound up ahead on her left, meaning she is about four miles out of town. Figuring this is far enough for tonight, she takes the road to the left that heads back to town. The run back is a bit more picturesque, even in the dark. The thickness of the forest begins to disperse, and through the thinning trees, the vastness of the Sound comes into view. The echo of water lapping against the cliff mixes in with the sound of the raindrops and the rhythm of her steps.

Yellow caution tape flapping in the wind up ahead brings Gabrian to a dead stop. Blocking everything out worked a little too well. She completely overlooked the fact that the Sound was the place where her parents' truck had gone over the ledge. Unable to look away, she continues closer to the tattered remains of the barricade. The black skid marks are still clearly visible where the collision occurred. The energy surrounding the embankment does not feel right to her. It is dark and tainted. Still uncertain of how all the different energies feel, she assumes that maybe this is how death feels.

She rips through the tape in front of her and steps to the edge of the road, overlooking the Sound. The dusk to dawn light above her flickers dimly, but it still allows her enough light to vaguely see the disturbance in the rocks below. Her heart starts to pound wildly. Envisioning her parents' demise causes anger and frustration to consume her like fire, and she screams out into the night with all her fury.

"You promised me that you would always be here for me! Now what am I supposed to do?"

Every ounce of energy she has left shoots out against the darkness, sending a massive surge of energy tearing through the power grid above her. The abundance of power overloads its maximum capacity and it explodes, lighting the night sky for a brief moment then leaves her alone in the darkness. Only crimson embers chewing their way through the innards of the transformer remain, and the shadows move in a menacing dance around her.

No longer having the strength to hold her own body upright, Gabrian slumps to the ground and begins to cry.

***

SHANE, WHO HAS been absent more than he has been present, finally shows himself just outside Gabrian's room. He takes off his coat and lays it on the bench beside him in the hallway. Figuring he should check in on her, he knocks on the wall outside her bedroom door—no response. He reaches down and twists the door latch quietly in case she is still asleep, and opens the door to look inside, but her bed is empty. He begins to search for her.

Rachael hears Shane's heavy footstep coming through the floor from upstairs and shakes her head in disgust at his blatant attempt to shirk his duties. Not finding any sign of her, he takes his search elsewhere. Reaching the bottom of the stairs, he sees Rachael who sits at the kitchen nook. "Where is she?"

An evil grin begins to grow across Rachael's face as she toys with the idea of just keeping quiet and letting Shane search for Gabrian until the moons shift course, but for some strange reason, she changes her mind. "She is out for a run."

"In this weather?" He shakes his head but knows he should probably go look for her since he has been gone for a while. If something were to happen to her, the blame would rest upon his shoulders. "Great!" He stomps back upstairs to put his coat on.

Shane edges his fingers onto the shadow lingering in Gabrian's room. Once inside the Veil, he stills himself, searching for her vibration, and he finds it in mass. Not sure as to why her energy trace is so abundant, he quickly pulls himself to it and appears in the trees, just on the other side of the road where Gabrian is hunched over on the ground.

She looks up, sensing his familiar presence, and their eyes lock for a moment, sending chills through them both. She notices that his glare is not as loathing as it has been. Gabrian knows he is there to take her home. She gladly drags herself up from the ground and takes a step toward him.

The winter frost has wreaked havoc on the Earth, causing it to crack and split. Now with all of the rain they have received lately, any trace of stability the edge of the road had held has been devoured. With her weight, the edge breaks free from the road, and Gabrian loses her footing and slips backward—falling into the ravine. In seconds of falling, Gabrian's head makes hard contact with a protruding boulder sticking out from the ledge, knocking her unconscious. She continues to fall further down, helpless to save herself.

Shane throws himself into the Shadows and drags the Veil around him. He emerges out of the Darkness just below Gabrian. Wrapping his arms around her like a shield, he catches her. Freeing his left hand, he grabs for the edge of the shadow beneath them, pulling its Magik quickly around them and vanish back into the Veil just before they hit the water.

Into the darkness of her room, Shane emerges with Gabrian wrapped securely within his arms—wet, dirty, and unconscious. He crosses the room and places her on the bed, pulling the quilted blankets over her to cover her small body. He ventures quickly to the bathroom and retrieves a wash cloth from the cabinet, dampening it with water before he heads back to sit on the bed beside Gabrian.

Looking down upon her with soft eyes, he gently tries to remove the hair covering her face, but her hair and cheeks are caked in mud. His strong agile fingers diligently dab at the dirt, struggling to erase its blemish from her skin. He stops for a moment, gazing down at her. She looks so helpless and fragile. He exhales deeply as his heart wrenches painfully in angst.

What have they become?

Hearing Rachael scurrying up the stairs and toward the darkened room, Shane quickly moves away from the bed and turns on the light. She rushes into the room and hurries past him to the

296

bed where Gabrian lies, unmoving.

"What happened to her?" Rachael demands, twisting her head to unleash an icy glare at Shane, then returns to analyze any apparent damage—noticing the side of Gabrian's head is dark with bruises and caked mud.

Shane steps forward, hovering over the two girls then takes a step back, brushing his fingers through his wet tangles of hair and huffs out a reply. "She slipped and fell, hitting her head on a rock where her parents' car went over the cliff."

"What!" Rachael exclaims, nearly breaking her neck to glare at him again, wanting to cross the room to throttle him for letting this happen to her.

"I got there just as she slipped," he adds as he turns to leave.

Gabrian begins to stir. Her head aches; it feels as if there is a jackhammer thrashing around inside of it, trying to break through her skull. Hearing familiar voices, she keeps her eyes closed and lies as still as she can to listen.

Shane stops just as he reaches the doorway and looks back at Gabrian then raises his eyes to meet Rachael's.

"You know, when I said I would protect her from herself, I did not actually think I would have to do it." He looks up at the ceiling, shaking his head in disbelief. "Stupid girl," he grumbles under his breath as he walks out the door.

The words that fell from his lips are loud and clear in Gabrian's ears, and the hatred that burns within them sear painfully through her already shattered heart.

Chapter Forty-One

Just After Dark

GABRIAN SIGHS, STARING up at the ceiling in her silent room. She listens to the constant thrum of her heartbeat, wondering if she could actually die from the pain she feels inside. Images of her parents flash through her mind. Their smiling faces haunt her dreams at night. She awakens hoping it is all just a nightmare, yearning to hear their voices in the hall. She tries to push the sadness away, but it never leaves.

Dragging herself out of bed, she idles over to the window and watches the light slowly fade from the sky as night approaches. The last remaining moments of the sun as it dips further below the horizon turn the sky the colour of blood. She closes her eyes, trying to capture the image, but when she opens them, the light is gone. The only thing that remains is darkness.

Something inside her stirs, and her thoughts rush to the memory of the bottle left on the counter by someone after the funeral. Quickly making her way to the kitchen, she searches the countertop for the bottle. Finding it, she quietly heads back up the stairs, careful not to disturb Rachael.

She turns the light on in her bathroom and notices the water glass sitting on the side of the sink. Gabrian opens the bottle and fills it almost to the top. She tips the glass, dumping the liquid down her throat, not caring what it is. She just wants it to wash through her and take her someplace else. She turns the knob on the shower to start the water. The room starts to fill with warm hazy mist. Gabrian grabs the bottle and fills the glass again, swallowing it down, feeling the warmth of the venom inside beginning to work as she de-robes and enters the shower.

She wipes the mirror with her towel and looks at the reflection. The girl she sees before her is a stranger—a ghost of the person she used to be. Her eyes that once held light and passion now seem to be filled with nothing but Darkness and anger. Gabrian welcomes its bitter delusion because right now that is the only thing that helps suffocate her misery.

She inhales deeply, picking up hints of Rachael's essence from downstairs, and it becomes dangerously obvious she is suffering from starvation. "I need to get out of here."

Riffling through the bag of clothes that Rachael had thrown together for her in Manhattan, she finds the black dress she wore at the funeral and holds it up to the light. She rips the hem at the bottom of the dress, shortening it about six inches, then tears off the sleeves, leaving it with only the main straps to hold it on. "It is a little morbid, but it is going to have to do for tonight."

Not usually one for makeup, Gabrian pulls out her blackest mascara and defines the darkness in her long full eyelashes, making her ice-blue eyes unavoidable to look at. She paints her lips in crimson red, almost resembling the colour of the sunset earlier. A strange grin creeps across her painted lips—her wild look oddly invokes a wave of pleasure to wash through her. Gabrian idles at the mirror, studying her reflection—strangely enjoying her new look, and figures since she is technically a branch of the Vampire family tree, she might as well play along and look the part.

She pours herself another glass of the minty liquid she has been consuming, closes her eyes and tips it back—emptying it. Gabrian's mind swims with images of her parents, the caution tape on the cliff, and the hatred in Shane's icy eyes. Folding her arms securely around her torso, she howls as the agony slices through her soul. Her eyes open to the stranger staring back at her, and she slams the empty glass straight into the mirror, striking her down.

Feeling the room shift around her, Gabrian suddenly loses

her balance and grabs for the sink, hoping it will stabilize her. Stronger than she realizes, she falters sideways and rips it partially out of the wall, sending all of the contents on it crashing to the floor.

In moments, the bathroom door flies open and Rachael rushes in, concerned for her friend. She looks at the sink, half-destroyed, and the mess of broken glass and makeup covering the floor. "Are you okay?" she gasps, looking at Gabrian in the center of it all who appears to have stepped out of some overpriced fashion magazine. "I heard a loud noise, and I got worried."

"I am fine," Gabrian huffs, looking up at her with an icy stare. Gathering her legs beneath her, she pushes herself up on her knees—straightening out her makeshift dress and brushes off the traces of unwanted makeup debris collected from her fall.

"I was just concerned..."

"I am fine, I said," Gabrian snarls, cutting her off.

Gabrian's heart begins to quicken, and her mouth starts to water as she becomes painfully aware of Rachael's bright iridescent aura flooding the room. Gabrian slides her way closer to Rachael, inch by inch, drawn to her essence by instinct.

A wave of panic strikes Gabrian as she realizes what she is about to do. Gabrian jumps up and quickly pushes past Rachael, trying to get away from her before she does something she will regret. She has not taken any energy in weeks, and she can feel her energy lust burning wildly inside, causing tremors of pain to shoot through her body just from the closeness of Rachael's light. Her lust for life is at war with her strength of will. "I am going out," she yells to Rachael, running out the bedroom and down the stairs.

Rachael leaves the mess and hurries behind. "Do you want me to come with you?"

"NO!" she snaps. "I mean, no. I just need to get out of this house. I need to breathe." Trying to pull on her black knee boots, she fumbles with the zipper. Her hands tremble as she strains to contain her thirst for Rachael's light.

"But it would only take me a minute to get dressed."

"I just need to be by myself," she forces out calmly between gritted teeth. Her eyes focus in the direction of the door to hide the hunger within her widened pupils. Turning the latch to open the kitchen door, she glances back at Rachael for a moment and feels nervous about what she might do tonight but then decides she does not care.

Chapter Forty-Two

Share and Share Alike

GABRIAN SITS IN the darkness of her mother's car, watching people stumble and dance about in the street in front of the bar. She grits her teeth at the thought that one of these mere powerless humans somehow managed to steal the life of her near immortal parents.

Her hands clench, forming into fists as she feels the anger grow inside from watching them enjoy their pathetic lives when all she can do is suffer. Between the pangs of starvation and the torture of grief, she truly cannot decide which hurts the most.

Gabrian never condoned violence, but tonight, her mind is clouded. All she wants to do is inflict pain and suffering on someone, to share the agony of sorrow and rage that has been building up inside of her, burning like fire against her flesh. Her teeth begin to grind as the temptation of stealing essence from those who flounder obliviously before her becomes magnetic. They taunt her hunger and her mouth salivates with yearning. The lust for energy wildly awakens, so close to the surface that she can almost taste it.

Flashes of images she has seen in Ethan's thoughts, the ones of true Vampirism, flood her mind—creating intrigue within her. Gabrian starts to envision herself within the chaos of it and wonders what it would be like to devour a soul or two.

"I would not do that if I were you."

Gabrian shrieks and jumps back in her seat, startled by the voice. She swings her arm out to defend herself but her hit does not find contact with the intruder. Instead, it slams hard into the back of the seat behind him, leaving her passenger unscathed.

Unable to defend herself physically, she tries to blast this thing with an energy flare from her hands, but she is so weak from hunger that it nearly knocks her out as a mild wave shoots forward, passing completely through him. Terror enters her heart, taking over where the pain had left off. Jolts of adrenaline sear through her heart and eat away at her muscles—taut and ready to fight though they remain idle and motionless, useless to protect her.

She looks at this apparition, or whatever it is, and studies his face.

"Do not be afraid," he murmurs to her, giving her a kind smile. "I will not harm you."

Squinting her eyes, she tries to figure out why this thing feels so familiar to her. Then it hits her. This thing has the same face as the young man who used to call to her in her sleep and ask her to meet him down by the garden gate where they would talk all night until the sun came up or until her parents would find her sitting in her night dress in the freezing cold.

"I know who you are." She stops squinting and looks at his face more confidently.

A little apprehensive of her statement, Adrinn searches her mind but relaxes again.

"I remember you from when I was a child. I called you Ayden."

His mouth curves upward in a grin of pleasure as he senses her comfort with him beginning to grow. Unsure how much the Realm has told her about Borrowers and Vampires, he keeps his true identity to himself—not wanting to lose faith with the girl prematurely.

"You are a hard girl to find, you know," he teases. "I have been searching for you ever since you left me so many years ago."

"You have been looking for me?" She contorts her face in confusion to his statement. "Why?"

"Because you and I are different," he says, playing on the

304

insecurities he has stumbled on within her subconscious. "And everyone needs a friend."

For whatever reason, those last few words manage to strike a painful chord within her. Her body slumps back into the seat, no longer poised for danger. Too tired to defend herself, and now feeling the repercussions of depleting her last few ounces of strength trying to blast this thing into oblivion, she turns her head sideways against the seat to look at him. "What are you, anyway?"

"I am the result of what happens when love and hate become conflicted within one's soul," he announces with a tone resembling remorse—looking down at his hands with a furrowed brow—hiding the miniscule trace of compassion still left to roam within his soul.

She shakes her head. "I don't understand."

"Hm, let me see. How can I explain this a little better?" He taps his index finger on the front of his bottom lip, looking straight ahead at the wayward drunks dancing in front of the bar. "I am like a genie trapped within a bottle, stuck for all eternity, awaiting the day when someone comes along and lets me out."

"You mean to tell me that someone did this to you?" She slides her hand over and waves it through his fleshless form freely. Adrinn rolls his eyes at her, a bit annoyed with her taken liberties. Gabrian notices his discontent and stops, immediately dropping her arm but continues to stare through him.

"In a word, yes." Not wanting to get into all the sordid details of his predicament and needing to engage her dislike for the rules of the Covenant, he decides to enlighten her with some truths. "With being a part of the Realm, staying within the rules of the Covenant is a must if you want to stay in their good graces, but if you actually want to live, rules are meant to be bent and sometimes necessarily broken."

Gabrian remains passive, listening intently as Adrinn continues with his lesson.

"The way it works is like this—the Covenant only tells its faithful followers what they want them to know. They feed them only enough of the truth of what is going on to keep them loyal and threaten to destroy all those who would disturb its delicate balance of peace, instilling fear to keep them from straying."

He rubs the end of his chin in thought. "How does the saying go again? Oh, yes. Those who cannot be contained must be destroyed."

Gabrian's eyes light up at this familiar bit of information.

"It is their motto so to speak. And, because the Elders sit within the great walls of the Covenant of Shadows, unscathed and unchallenged, they tuck their heads in the sand when it comes to understanding how the real world works—throwing fear into those who are shallow-minded enough to believe them."

"And with beings like us, whom they do not truly understand, containing us is a bit of a challenge. To them, we are a danger which causes them to fear us and well...let us just say that beings like us sometimes do not exist very long in this dimension."

Gabrian remembers all too well about what the Elders thought from her time inside the Covenant of Shadows. "So are you now a ghost? Did they kill you?"

"No, they did not kill me," Adrinn admits, crossing his legs and folding his hands around the top of his knee, turning to gaze upon her over his vaporous shoulder with gilded eyes. "But they did banish me, and I am bound to the Darkness. I cannot die nor can I live either."

"Like the Genie in the bottle thing you said before..." she chirps in, flicking her hand at him, facing the front and returning some of her focus on the crowd.

"Essentially." Gathering all his niceties upon his face and forcing them into a peculiar grin, he turns his body toward his driver and leans on his arm now resting on the top of the seat, and gazes at her impishly. "And I am your little secret."

"My secret?" she squawks, jerking her head around to question him.

"Yes. They do not know about me." His hazel eyes gleam in the shadows as he reveals his secret to her, making the hairs on her flesh stand on end in warning, but she is too tired to care and listens intently as he continues to ramble on. "The Realm, the Covenant, all of them are oblivious to my existence."

"Really?" She wrinkles her nose in a half-hearted inquiry, wondering if this childish delusion is for real or whether it is just another lie.

"If they knew that I existed they would surely do away with me for good, sealing me into the Darkness simply out of fear," he assures her, willing his lip to waver as he delivers her his saddened outpouring of his possible demise if found out.

Gabrian's mind spins with Adrinn's story, having witnessed their cruelty, she accepts the validity of his tale, adding fuel to her growing hatred of the Covenant's cruelty.

"Now if you want to become like me, go ahead and carry on with your plan to tear these oblivious humans to pieces in order to feed. But, I would not advise it. I assure you there is a better way, a more civilized way. Drawing attention and bringing the Covenant of Shadows down on yourself is probably not something you want to do."

"I don't care anymore what the Covenant thinks." At the mention of the Covenant, Gabrian's hands begin to clench again. She withdraws from the conversation and becomes quiet as the sadness finds her once more. "I just want the pain to stop. I don't want to feel like I am dying inside anymore." She slams her hands against the steering wheel in front of her and buries her face in her fists, trying to fight the whirlwind inside—desperately grasping for something to keep her still.

"I can help you, you know." His voice is gentle, becoming earnest.

She sits up, revealing her tear-stained cheeks. She drops her hands to her side, wanting to believe he has the answer.

"I can show you how to make the pain go away."

"But..."

Adrinn smiles at her assumption. "But all I ask in return, when you are strong enough, is that you lend me some of your reapings."

No longer angry, all she feels is the emptiness of loss, and it cuts through her like a dull blade. She knows there may be a good chance that this deal maker is probably just as crazy as she feels, but Gabrian decides to take the offer—anything is better than this.

***

ADRINN ENTERS THE bar with Gabrian at his side. Although he is completely invisible to everyone else but her, she can see him and walks by his side—feeling strange about his ability to walk right through people. They sit down at the bar, and she orders a Cape Cod.

"Enjoy it for the both of us, will you?" Adrinn says, licking his lips. His stare never leaves the sight of the crimson drink, clearly missing the taste of alcohol.

A dark mood swallows Gabrian up, and her placid blank look is replaced with widened pupils and a wrinkled brow as her eyes dance over the crowd—watching the light show of floating auras before her. Her innards begin to burn, making her testy from hunger.

"No worries there. I will." She tips the glass up and swallows it down, hoping it will take the edge off, but it barely scratches the surface. "You said you would teach me how to feed and end my suffering." She reminds her invisible friend, getting antsy to start feeling the after effects of his promise.

"I did indeed," he purrs as a menacing grin creeps across his mouth, narrowing his eyes—making the gold flecks of his irises shine from behind his dark lashes.

"So...teach," she growls, tipping the rest of the drink down her throat before turning to meet his stare with icy eyes, no longer caring what he is as long as he keeps his word.

"I want you to look out into the crowd of people," he says, drawing near to her—stretching out his transparent arm and waving it over the unsuspecting masses. "I want you to watch them, observe how their essence flows around them. Find the one that appeals to you the most and concentrate on it." He turns to her and presses his fingers to rest on the center of his temples, closing his eyes. "Focus only on it."

"Okay," she drones, looking through him, and searches the room with her mind.

"Once you find your muse, use your mind's voice to get their attention." His eyes open, and he taps the side of his temple before curling his lips into a grin. "Make them believe that they want to be near you, and that they need to be close to you. When they come to you, let them." He releases his stare and returns his gaze to scour the bodies piled together on the dance floor like fish in a barrel, waiting to be taken. "Let the fractals of light dance around and encase you in their splendor. But be careful to pull gently at them and take only what you need. Then release them, still intact."

Gabrian turns to look at him abruptly, and he smiles at her knowingly.

"It is very important that you to stick to this rule." He twists again in front of her and points his finger in her face, ensuring that he is stating his words and making them perfectly clear in her mind. "That way there is no harm, there is no foul."

"What if I cannot stop?" Gabrian stops her aura surfing and searches his eyes for an answer—biting her lip, flooded with guilt as she recalls her few moments of indiscretion at the park.

"You must learn to stop," he says calmly, his face drains of the little colour it holds, and he stares at her with golden eyes that have seen too much. "If you drain them, or take too much, the watchers will know."

"Watchers?" Tilting her head and glancing over across her bare shoulder, she glares at the vaporous form beside her, searching for understanding.

"Yes, Gabrian." He meets her naïve stare, his eyes filled with answers that teeter somewhere between truth and deception then lets them drifts back into the crowd. "Do you really think the Covenant is just going to let you walk around freely?"

She does not know what to say and her face goes blank, lost in thought. She knew they were keeping an eye on her after training and gave her a probation period when she left for Manhattan, but after the funeral, she never truly thought too much about it.

"Do not let them fool you, Gabrian." Getting close to her so she can see his face, Adrinn locks his focus on her, making her a little uncomfortable. "You are under their thumb now. And because you are Boragen, of the Vampire bloodline, they are never going to leave you alone. They are ready to pounce—eager to squash you like a bug."

Angry from Adrinn's words, but knowing there is truth in what he says, she hesitates with going forward with her friend's plan to renew her energy and settle her suffering.

Hearing her concern filter through her mind, Adrinn quickly acts and attempts to pull her back on board. "What are we doing, sitting around talking about this nonsense? We have the whole night ahead of us. Let us find someone for you to dance with."

"I am not sure about this anymore. What if I get caught?"

Adrinn knows she is faltering on her decision and pulls out another cruel truth that may hit the nail in the coffin. "What would be worse, Gabrian, my dear, getting caught and being punished by the Elders of the Covenant of Shadows or living out the rest of your life tortured by pain? Either way you look at it, you are in Hell."

Chapter Forty-Three

Running with the Devil

NIGHT AFTER NIGHT, Gabrian tells Rachael that she needs to go out, not returning to the house until the early hours of the morning. Tonight will be no different. Again, she slips out, leaving her friend standing alone at the kitchen door, helpless to comfort her and knowing she needs her space.

Eager to learn from her new teacher, and yearning for a taste of tonight's forbidden fruit, she smiles wickedly as she hurries out the door, sliding into the driver's seat of her parent's car. Flying down the driveway, she sees Ayden standing by the gate, waiting for her. She does not bother to slow down as she reaches him. Ayden materializes in the passenger's seat beside her once the gate is crossed.

"So, what is on the agenda for tonight?"

"Well, the last few nights, you have done very well, my dear." Adrinn grins, hiding a little something up his sleeve. "So tonight, I thought we might go on a bit of a journey to somewhere special."

She does not care where they go. All she knows is that these last few days since she started following Adrinn around—and obeying his rules of conduct—she can actually say she feels good. Her mind is clear, her energy is up, and her nightmares have left her alone, at least for now. If he asked her to go to the moon at this point, she would not even question it.

"I think it is time we step your training up a notch." She raises her eyebrow at his suggestion and glances over her shoulder at him briefly—trying to keep her eyes on the road, curious as to what he has in mind. "I do not want to draw too much attention to you. A girl that looks like you in the small town of Bar Harbor, attention is all that you are going to get." His eyes drift across her body, studying her attire while wagging a finger pointedly at the shortened hem of her dress then looks away, tapping his finger on his bottom lip. "No room for mistakes here. So what I propose is a jaunt to Bangor for the evening."

"We are going all the way to Bangor?" Her eyes leave the road once more to peek at her peculiar passenger, seeing a wide grin spread across his face.

"Indeed, my dear girl," he concurs, turning to meet her infrequent glances with a mischievous glint in his eyes. The rings of golden flecks that orbit his widened pupils brighten against the silhouettes of night's shroud "It is bigger; it is louder—" he continues with vigor, rubbing his vaporous hands together, causing his smoky aura to haze the edges of his form. "—and I know just the place where you can go to let us say...spread your wings a bit."

Her eyes jot over quickly once more, hearing the enthusiasm in his words. Ayden has not done anything but help her since the night he showed up in her car and stopped her from killing someone, so for Gabrian, trusting him is not an issue. So seeing the exit sign up ahead with 'Bangor' shimmering against the glare of her headlights, she turns the blinker on and grins at him, following his counsel willingly. "Sure, why not."

Within the hour, they hit downtown Bangor, and she already hears the music slamming against her eardrums from outside the night club. Now that she feeds on pure essence, her own senses are becoming more acute to stimuli, sometimes causing her the need to shut things out once in a while to be able to concentrate on normal everyday activities.

She sits in her car, sensing the abundance of life thriving from within the walls of the bar, pressing up against the stone entryway and seeping out every time the door opens to let someone in.

Not able to resist her curiosity of why she is here any longer, she steps out of the car, onto the asphalt, and slowly glides across the parking lot in her short, black tightknit dress that she had purchased earlier that day. It hugged and accentuated every curve of her body but offered little constriction to her movements in case of unforeseen difficulties. Her long black hair hung loosely down her back, gently swaying with the rhythm of her purposeful movements—each step eloquent and precise, like a hunter on the prowl. Every head that stands waiting in line to enter the bar turns her direction and watches as she heads for the entrance.

The front door opens and two people stagger down the stone steps, out into the night. She catches the eye of the bouncer. After many years of working the door, he knows what makes for good bar business, and he yells out into the crowd, but it is only meant for her.

"I can take one more." He waves his hand for her to come up the steps and enter the bar. The crowd grumbles at his decision to trump her to the head of the line but still continue to wait their turn, not wanting to lose their place.

Gabrian's mouth curves upward provocatively as she glances briefly at Adrinn, who keeps pace with her advancement. "Shall we?" she purrs.

He returns her smile with an evil grin. "After you, my dear."

She carefully ascends the stone steps and enters the bar with Adrinn slithering behind her, unnoticed by all.

Inside the doors, the bouncer displays a special interest in her and roams up and down her sleek body with his hungry eyes. He gives her a wanting look and licks his lips, implying to her she might look like something he would like to taste.

Gabrian is revolted by his presence and by the disgusting fantasies generating within his half-witted brain. *Yuck!* she screams in her head but smiles seductively at him anyway, keeping up her facade.

His breath quickens at her engagement, and he bites his thumb unconsciously. "No charge for you tonight," he insists, getting uncomfortably close to her.

"Thanks." She runs her long delicate-looking fingers across his sweaty knock-off designer shirt, letting them linger over his stomach as she slowly walks away and disappears into the crowd.

"Disgusting pig," she utters under her breath once she is through. She wipes her hand on her dress, trying to remove his scent from her skin. Gabrian wonders if maybe this guy is the sort of prey she should test out her new skills on. She is quite sure that if she messed up and lost control with him, it would not be much of a setback for her or any other girl.

Catching a waft of familiar cologne, her subconscious conjures up thoughts of Ethan. She hears his gentle voice in the back of her head telling her that she should not punish herself for making mistakes. A twinge of guilt flutters through her as Gabrian recalls all of Ethan's kindness toward her.

Feeling Gabrian slipping back to her old self, Adrinn moves in to kill any conscience that may ruin this for him. He slides in close to her, and whispers in her ear, "Come along now, Gabrian. Everyone is waiting for you to come out and play."

She shakes her head, pushing Ethan out of her thoughts, and follows Adrinn's lead. With the crowd swarming all around her, and the colours meshing in amongst each other, she quickly forgets about Ethan's lessons and becomes elated with all the possibilities that lie before her.

Adrinn stands quietly beside her with his hand holding his chin, grinning from ear to ear as he watches her become excited with her new surroundings. She takes a moment to survey the large open dance floor stuffed with people then quickly looks over at Adrinn, like a child waiting for permission to go play on the playground—only this playground is for hunting. He releases his hand and waves it out over the crowd, inviting her to join in on the fun.

She immediately falls into her new routine, scouting for the most vibrant essence there. On this hunt, it happens to be a young dark-haired girl about Gabrian's age, with skin the colour of toffee. She quiets her mind to listen for the girl's thoughts, preparing to allure her, but to her pleasure, the girl is already quite aware of her presence. *This is going to be easier than I thought.*

Gabrian catches the girl watching her and smiles back at her with a devious grin, sending her amorist images to help bait the trap. Listening to her muse's response to her suggestive gestures, Gabrian becomes certain that she now has the female's full attention and steps down into the crowd, heading for her dinner.

Chapter Forty-Four

Missing in Action

AFTER A COUPLE of weeks of being absent again, Shane returns to check in on Gabrian. Stepping out of the Veil and into the hallway upstairs in Gabrian's house, he quietly walks over to her bedroom door and looks in. Not finding her there, he begins to check the rest of the house.

Rachael hears his footsteps on the ceiling above her as he marches from room to room, knowing exactly what he is looking for. He stomps his way down the stairs and enters the kitchen.

"She is not here," Rachael says, refusing to look up from her book.

He stops and glares at her. "Well, where is she?"

"Out."

"What do you mean out?" Shane's stomach turns in an uneasy flutter, remembering the last time Gabrian had left the house alone.

"She is out. Gone. Not here," Rachael growls at him through tightened lips, spitting out each word heavily laced with disdain just for him.

Growing impatient with Rachael's intentional cattiness, Shane's voice grows louder, and he reaches over to slide her book down, away from her face. "I can see that. Where did she go?"

"I have no idea. I didn't ask her where she was going," she offers, setting down her book and inhales a deep breath—glaring at him all the while.

"Why did you not go with her?" Shane rubs his hand through his dark chaos of curls, looking around the room to avoid her icy stare.

"I offered to go, but she didn't want me to," Rachael says, shrugging her shoulders while picking her book back up and plants her eyes into its tale, much more interested in what it has to say than listening to him. "She wants to be alone."

"You should have gone with her." He rushes to the nook and grabs the sides, leaning in to bare down on her with an attempted intimidating look. "The last time she left the house alone, she nearly killed herself."

"Umm, the last time I checked, I was not her keeper!" Rachael spits out, slamming her book down on the table and returns his glare, unscathed by his efforts. "That would be your job, if I recall correctly."

Shane rubs his hand through his dark curls and begins to pace the kitchen floor, frustrated with the conversation. "She has been lying in bed for days. She hasn't moved. I can only watch her sleep for so long before it drives me crazy." Not sure if Rachael buys his alibi or not, he continues to pace and tries to turn the blame. "I have only been gone a short while, and the minute I leave, she takes off."

"The minute you leave? Are you kidding me?" Rachael fumes at his attempt to deflect his neglect. "Ah!" she grumbles in agitation, taking a deep breath as she tries to calm down. "Whatever!" She huffs, waving his lame excuses away with her hand. She narrows her eyes at him, hoping they will bore a hole through his senses and his ego. "The fact is, you were gone."

Shane stomps around the kitchen, trying to think of where she might have gone. "What a nightmare this girl is."

"Listen, you overinflated idiot." Shane stops moving immediately and turns to glare at Rachael. "She is suffering and in pain. And if you had been doing your job and fulfilling your obligations properly, you would have noticed that."

Shane attacks her verbally, feeling the sting of guilt setting in. "Do not talk to me about pain. I know far more about pain than you, little youngling."

"Really? Huh." Rachael shakes her head with disgust. Folding her arms across her small frame, she sits back in her chair and tilts her head then twists her pouty lips into a smirk, not feeling any concern for his well-being. Becoming bored with his act of self-pity, she decides to try to get to the bottom of his problem with Gabrian. "So what is the deal with you anyway?"

"What?" He jerks his head sideways to scowl at her—his eyes flare in reaction to her statement—confused, and his messy curls bounce from the quickness of his movements.

"First you like her, then you hate her?" Rachael asks, fluttering her doe eyes at him condescendingly, and flips her hand pointedly back and forth between the imaginary choices. "What kind of game are you playing?"

"There is no game here," he barks at her, ceasing his march, and places his hands on the edge of the counter, leaning into them, head down while pressing his eyes close to dull the taste of hatred upon his tongue as he continues. "She is Boragen. A Borrower."

"So?" Rachael's face contorts, twisting unnaturally into an ugly pose. She raises her hand, fingers reaching upward, accentuating her probe into his prejudice. "Just because she bares the gift of Boragen does not make her evil!"

Shane crosses the room and hovers over Rachael, his chest rising visibly from his quest to contain the fury within. His eyes wrench within their sockets and bore down on her like a dark, cold forest encompassed in crimson-laced skin, inflamed by the fiery rage just beneath the surface. "It was the Boragen who killed my parents. She is one of them."

"Yes, she may be of Boragen descent, but she did not take their life. It was a group of rogue Vampires that ambushed your parents on a hunt. Your parents were outnumbered and deceived into believing they could contain the situation. And besides, that was a long time ago—long before Gabrian. She had nothing to do with it. You cannot continue to condemn her for what someone else did or for what fate gave her. Up until a couple of months ago, she thought she was a human. She was dragged into this world as what she is, it's not like she had a choice."

Shane laughs in her face.

Rachael clenches her fists, wanting desperately to smack

him so hard it would knock the smug look off his face.

"If you could just get past your Shadow Walker I-am-above-anyone-else self-righteous attitude for just a second, you might realize that she is trying really hard just to fit in and do right by the Covenant. The only thing she had holding her together was just ripped from her arms, leaving her alone to fend for herself from all the monsters and now, the one who is supposed to be protecting her from them cannot be bothered!"

Shane stands in front of her, silent, unable to find the words to defend his actions.

"It doesn't matter what she is. What matters is that you took an oath to protect her as a Shadow Walker. Maybe it is time that you started acting like one."

Angry at Rachael for calling him out, he growls at her but knows her words are the truth, and he does not argue. He glares at her as he grabs his coat off the counter and heads for the Veil to find Gabrian.

Chapter Forty-Five

I Love the Nightlife

GABRIAN WEAVES HER way across the dance floor and steps in front of the source of attention. She lets the vibration of the music move her body, mirroring the girl's own actions. Sensing the girl's desire, Gabrian pulls her in close, caressing her on the small of her back. Delighted with this wanted attention, the girl does not resist.

From behind, a tall muscular man slinks up to Gabrian's back—too close for her liking. Put off with his forwardness, and not wanting to be disturbed while dining, she turns to face him. His blurry eyes wash over her body slowly, and he gives her a wink—licking his thin-lipped mouth as he does. Gabrian tilts her head as she meets his intoxicated gaze and grins at him. She raises her arm and stretches it out, gently resting her hand just under his jaw to cup his chin, coaxing him to give her his full attention. Her eyes widen. The center of her pupils flicker and spark, bleeding into her irises to make them appear entirely black.

The Shadow in her eyes bends inward in a subtle pulse as her mind begins its Magik. "Be a good lad now and bugger off," she says sweetly to her new would-be admirer then turns her back to him to refocus on her girl. The interaction is seamless. Confused but completely obedient, the stranger wanders off into the darkness.

Now, with her male suitor out of the way, she is able to concentrate on what she is there to do. Gabrian sways to the music, feeling its rhythm stir through the crowd, and hungers for the girl in front of her. Relaxed and totally naïve about what Gabrian really wants, the girl swoons in close to touch Gabrian's waist with no desire to leave.

Gabrian twists the girl around. Her back is pressed up against Gabrian's chest, and she holds her firm with her right arm, swaying still with the music in a hypnotic dance. She begins to pull at the girl's luminous aura, watching it move and sway around her.

Eager to sample the essence and see how it tastes, Gabrian commences the extraction and inhales. She gently lures the fragments to break away from the girl. Twisting and swirling around, heading straight for her, she opens her mouth and lets it touch upon her tongue to taste the light, savoring the distinct sweetness of pure untainted energy.

Remembering to only take a small amount at a time as to not draw attention, she releases it, setting it free to flow easily around the girl again.

Shane manages to locate Gabrian's energy trace and arrives at the Club. Resting just within the Veil, he searches the crowd for her. In the mix of people, he notices that there are a lot of members from very distinct Fellowships out tonight—particularly, Borrowers, with their Grey auras openly on display.

Curious about the actual ongoing interactions of the members in the establishment, he begins to study the crowd more closely. Seeing nothing out of the ordinary, he relaxes a bit and watches the different Realmfolk as they intertwine on the overcrowded dance floor, resuming his search for Gabrian.

The DJ changes the song and the tempo of the music switches to a faster beat, causing the crowd to go into a wild rhythmic frenzy. Finding Gabrian now seems like an impossible chore for Shane, but from the middle of the dance floor, he sees her.

Her arms sway about in time with the music, her eyes hiding behind closed lids, and her body rocks slowly at half-tempo with the song. Her alluring presence has entranced him, and his eyes are glued to her every move on the dance floor. She is careless and free—like the first night he saw her in Bar Harbor and made her dance with him at Geddy's. He has been so caught up in being miserable with her that he has forgotten how beautiful she actually is.

Lost in his reflections, his heart lightens for an instant, and he allows himself to smile.

Gabrian opens her eyes and gazes upon the dancing girl before her and licks her lips. Hungry for more of her essence, she pulls her in close—tightly, and up against her stomach, careful not to hurt her.

They sway to the music in unison, and Gabrian inhales once more. The light fragments break away more quickly this time. She opens her mouth to taste the light and her eyes close once more, allowing her to enhance her senses and truly savor her prize.

Her mouth begins to salivate, and she clenches her teeth in efforts to maintain control of herself. But as her tongue touches the edges of her teeth, she gets an intense sensation of wanting to bite. The soft sweet-scented flesh of the girl's neck beckons to her, driving her closer to madness. Gabrian opens her mouth, no longer wanting to resist. She coaxes the girl to lay her head to the side and runs her tongue along the length of her neck.

Gabrian feels her own pulse quickening, trying to convince her conscience that she needs this. All she has to do is give in. She runs on desire now. Gabrian leans her head back. Her instincts scream at her, telling her to bite, to tear, to taste.

Suddenly realizing what Gabrian is about to do, Shane emerges from the Darkness of the Veil beside the main bar—no longer smiling and no longer reminiscing about their first encounter. He marches straight forward—barreling into the crowd on a mission.

Her eyes flare open wide as she feels a familiar presence— an angry familiar presence, plowing its way through the dancers like they are weightless and invisible. Gabrian looks at the girl who is still caught up in the euphoria of their exchange, oblivious of what is happening between them, then she looks back at Shane. His eyes are wild and piercing with anger.

What Gabrian was just about to do hits her like a lightning bolt.

"What the Hell do you think you are doing?"

Gabrian looks around the bar in panic, searching for her

accomplice, but Ayden is gone. He dissolved himself as soon as he caught sight of Shane.

Shane follows her stare, trying to find what she is looking for, but he does not see anything. What he does notice though is that all the Grey auras of the Boragen, which had been so freely out on display a few moments ago, are now no longer anywhere to be found. All traces of their heritage have been cloaked and camouflaged as humans.

Feeling betrayed and alone, by both Ayden and Shane, Gabrian surges with anger. The budding warmth at the tips of her fingers intensifies quickly. The delicate edge of her jaw bulges as she stands alone to face Shane's wrath, gritting her teeth to hold in her contempt. She drowns any guilt she had about her own actions to the side.

"Go away!" she snarls and tries to walk away from him, dismissing the girl.

"You need to come with me." He reaches out for her wrist to gently coax her to come with him, but she whips her arm around and away from him before he can grasp it.

"Leave me alone."

"Come on, Gabrian, the party is over. I think it is time to go." He tries to reach for her again. This time it is with more force, but she moves too quickly for him and catches his arm, deflecting it. She pushes him backward, hard. Not prepared for her retaliation, Shane has to take a couple steps backward in order to keep himself from falling.

"I said, leave me alone," she growls, staring him down. Her eyes show no fear, only anger. "It is what you are good at, right? Leaving me alone."

Gabrian's eyes bore a burning hole through Shane as she glares at him then rips her eyes away from the sea-green reflection, and her focus darts haphazardly around the bar. She drags her hands through her tangled hair and clasps them behind her head, wound in a messy knot while her emotions run amuck all over the place. She cannot decide which she is more—angry with him for showing up and trying to boss her around or hurt that Ayden just up and abandoned her. She calls it a draw.

"Just go. Leave me alone," she says, walking away from him again with more fire in her step, quicker this time in an attempt to lose him in the crowd.

Shane had hoped to quietly convince her to come back to the house with him, but he gets the feeling that is not going to happen. Now he has to be a little more creative in his attempts to retrieve her. He rubs his hands through his loose curls of brown in frustration and growls.

"I was hoping that I would not have to resort to this but..." He follows behind and stops her, turning her around to face him. "Just remember, I tried to do this diplomatically, but you would not have it. So you only have yourself to blame for what I am about to do. You left me no choice."

"What are you...?"

Shane bends down and picks her up at the waist, heaving her over his left shoulder. Gabrian twist and pulls at him, trying to get away, but he tightens his grip on her just enough to keep her from escaping.

Everyone on the dance floor stops what they are doing to stare at them, but no one bothers to come to Gabrian's rescue. Mostly due to the fact that the majority of the people there tonight are from the Realm, and they know exactly what he is. Not wanting to be the one involved with interfering in Shadow Walker business, they turn a blind eye.

Gabrian screams at him to release her. She continues to pound on his back with both her fists, but he keeps walking straight ahead, heading for the exit. The vulgar bouncer that had welcomed her in only moments ago quickly gets to his feet from the stool he is perched on seeing his damsel in distress being carried out.

"Hey, buddy, what do you think you are doing? I don't think that the lady wants to go with you!" he states, stepping out in front of Shane.

Shane continues on route, changing his direction a step to the left without missing a beat. He extends his right arm out with lightning speed, giving the bouncer a swift push in the chest that sends him flying through the air into the wall behind him. Without slowing, Shane walks past the other bouncer who does not want to end up like his friend and keeps true of his mission moving forward toward the exit.

Gabrian looks down at her knight in sweaty clothing, who is

now out cold, crumpled into a big heap of disgusting flesh on the floor and smiles, thinking to herself that at least the night was not a complete loss.

Chapter Forty-Six

Meet in the Middle

"WHY DID YOU follow me to the bar tonight?" Gabrian asks, crossing her arms across her chest and scowls at him through the faint glow of the dashboard lights—still perturbed that Shane had pulled such a barbaric move on her and carried her out of the bar over his shoulder. *I will never be able to show my face there again.*

He reaches over and turns down the music on the car stereo so that he can hear her better. He glances at her briefly then shifts his eyes back in front of him to watch the road—one near accident is enough for him.

"I came there tonight to try and keep you out of trouble, and it is a good thing I did from the looks of it."

She contorts her face at him and turns to the passenger window, pretending to look out at the night. "What do you care anyway?"

"Because I am your Guardian."

"Ha!" She scoffs sarcastically at his words. "Since when? You have been gone for days, or should I say weeks. Is that how Guardianship works? You just come and go as you please, checking in whenever it is convenient for you?"

Shane rolls his eyes and sighs, knowing he deserves the backlash she serves him. "I know, I know," he says softly. He turns to look at her. "And I am sorry I have not been around much."

Gabrian's eyes shoot toward him, but her face screws up into a scowl. His display of compassion throws her off guard.

"I had a few issues that I needed to work out in my head about all this."

Her face remains twisted, deepening the lines around her eyes as she continues to stare at him in distrust.

He notices that she is not showing him any amount of sympathy toward his confession so he tries to think of something to bargain with her.

From somewhere deep inside of her, a curtain lifts revealing her logical, more calm side, and she lets go of some of the anger raging around inside of her head.

"I went to a bar in Bar Harbor the first time because I wanted to find someone to hurt, like I was hurting inside."

Shane turns to her briefly, not expecting her confession. He engages sincerely as she begins to talk. "And did you?"

"No," she says softly, biting gently on her thumb while staring out into the darkness. "I did use them though. I took some of their essence." She looks over at him, meekly. "I stole it."

Without saying anything to her, he nods his head in acknowledgement.

"It was just a small amount, but it silenced all the voices screaming in my head, and it numbed the pain. It let me take all the suffering to a place that was tolerable. At first, I felt guilty about it and told myself that I would not do it again," she admits, knowing that with this confession to a Shadow Walker, he can turn her in to the Elders where she would be sent to trial for breaking the Covenant's rules. She gives up the fight and continues to tell him anyway.

"But then the pain returned. Once the rapture of the light was gone, it came back and seemed crueler than before. It was the only thing that seemed to stop the pain." Her voice cracks.

Shane glances over at her and sees a tear roll down the curve of her cheek as she confesses.

"And in those few precious moments while I was drowning within the euphoria of distraction, I was able to forget."

Shane's left hand unwraps from his grip on the steering wheel and rushes to clutch the cloth above his chest as the flood of guilt rushes through his conscience, thrusting a jagged dagger through his heart. Because of his selfish choice of absence, and lax of duty, he is partly responsible for her acts of treason to the Realm.

He pulls the car over to the side of the road and kills the engine. Somewhere in the middle of nowhere and Northeast Harbor, they sit quietly in the dark. With both hands now on the wheel, Shane stares out into the night. He turns to face her. His eyes gleam in the darkness, looming over her and boring dauntingly into her soul. Her heartrate accelerates, worrying that he is about to ditch the car, pull her into the Veil, and head straight for the Covenant of Shadows to turn her in.

"How about we make a deal? Let us call a truce."

Exhaling in a loud huff, she sits still, quietly pondering his words—not expecting this kind of response—and wonders if he actually means it or if this is just another game of his.

"How about this...I promise to watch out for you like I should have been doing all along, and you pull it together."

She pumps her hands to flex in and out of fists while she tries to take in what he is saying.

"You go back to training with Ethan or enroll at the academy in Bar Harbor until you decide what your next move is going to be, and I will not mention anything about your few moments of indiscretion." Still staring her down, he extends his large strong hand out to her, as an offering of collaboration of sorts, and patiently waits for her decision. "How about it? We can go see Ethan tomorrow and figure things out. Alright?"

Searching his mind for some clue to as why he has suddenly had a change of heart toward her, she finds traces of shame littering his thoughts, betraying his facade of being nauseatingly righteous. She comes to the logical conclusion that this accord is good for the both of them.

She places her small slender hand in his. A wave of heat blazes through her on contact with his skin. Gabrian ignores her reaction to his touch and shakes his hand in agreement to the terms of truce. Awkward silence swallows them up. Gabrian's reaction to their touch is not isolated to her alone. Shane's veins burn like fire as he forces himself to let her hand go.

Shane exhales and reaches for the keys to turn the ignition

then pulls the car back onto the highway, heading for home. Shane's eyes keep finding their way over to Gabrian. She looks so small and fragile, but he knows that without guidance—if she were to turn into a hunter—this small and fragile girl with her beauty and her brain would become lethal.

Shane's thoughts drift as he drives through the darkness, reflections of all the Realmfolk at the bar keeps entering his mind. He wonders how it is that she came to find that particular place. He has heard the bar's name mentioned before in conversations involving minor issues with rogues in the Veil, and after finding her there, he begins to question a few things.

"Gabrian."

"Yeah?" she says quietly.

"Why did you pick that particular club to go to anyway? Bangor has plenty of places that are more mainstream, less obscure and easier to get to than that one."

Feeling strange about answering the question, and knowing that she promised not to tell anyone about Ayden, she lies. "It looked loud and dark. I just wanted to get lost for a while." She turns her stare back to the window, hoping that was a good enough explanation.

Shane recalls Rachael mentioning that Gabrian had been going out every night for a couple of weeks. After watching her on the dance floor, about to commit to the next step, he has a sneaky suspicion that somewhere along the way she met a rogue Vampire at one of the clubs and was grooming her, enticing her into turning completely. Not able to push this idea out of his head, he decides that as of this moment on, he would become her shadow for real.

"Hey..."

She turns to look at him.

"The pain will not hurt this bad forever." His eyes meet hers. Knowing the consumption of her struggle, his face softens as he gives her a hopeful smile then directs his attention back to the dark road ahead of them.

All Gabrian can do is stare. His voice held the same kindness it had before they knew who each other were—back when things were still an experiment. Not able to speak, she nods and turns back to the window. Tears silently escape from her tired eyes, blurring her vision, and she tries desperately to fade back into the

328

night.

Chapter Forty-Seven

Bar Harbor's Best

HESITANTLY, GABRIAN AGREES to meet with Ethan in front of the Bar Arts Building. As Shane promised, he says nothing to anyone about her involvement with using light energy, but she confesses everything to Ethan anyway. She tells him as way to find freedom from the guilt of her sins, but she is terrified of what he is going to think of her once he has heard what she has done.

Without even blinking an eye, he smiles at her with his kind, hazel brown eyes, warming her heart and melting the ice that has encased it.

"Everyone falters, Gabrian." Wrapping a strong arm around her shoulder, Ethan gives her a quick encouraging hug—giving her a bit of physical incentive when he noticed her hesitation. "Even I have had my moments of weakness."

She looks up at him as they walk the path toward the academy. "I can't believe that for a second, Ethan." She continues along with him, shaking her head, not able to conceive his open confession. "You are always so in control. Everything is composed and eloquent in your decisions. You are an exception to the rule."

"Ah, if that were only true, Gabrian. I am no exception; I am just like every other rogue that the Elders ever feared," he admits, glancing down at her. His eyes see her, but his vision is far away—

clouded by memories of a darker time. "The only difference between them and me is that I just try a little harder than they do, and...I have hope." He looks over at her with his noble face and smiles knowingly. "Believe me, it is a constant struggle that I fight every day."

She stops moving forward for a moment, processing the message he has just sent her. Shane nearly trips over her from behind and gives her a look of confusion. She just shakes her head at him, waving her hand to tell him it is nothing, then hurries to catch up with Ethan before they reach the school.

"There he is," Ethan tells her as he points to a tall dark-haired man that just opened the front doors and stands waiting for them on the steps, his grey aura flaring brilliantly around him. Gabrian feels her energy level rising just from his presence.

"This is Matthias," Ethan says out loud to Gabrian and reaches his hand to greet the man. "Thank you for meeting with us."

"For you, anything," Matthias replies. Lowering his head, he dips his chin to his chest ever-so-slightly as a show of respect for his Elder, and accepts Ethan's hand in comradery. "When your highly respected mentor asks for a favour, it is not something you say no to." They both laugh and the two men share a warm embrace then return their attention to the true matter of their reunion.

"Matthias, I would like you to meet a good friend of mine."

Gabrian looks up at Ethan, surprised at his introduction of her but pleased that he sees her as such.

"This is Gabrian Shadwell."

"Yes, so I have heard. The human-turned Borrower," he announces playfully. "I was wondering if we would ever meet."

Normally, whenever she heard someone refer to her that way, she always got agitated with them, but for some reason, it did not seem to bother her when Matthias said it.

Shane hears the flirtatious tone in Matthias's voice, and suddenly, he feels very protective of Gabrian, deciding immediately that he does not like this guy.

"Matthias is our head instructor here at the college. You will be in good hands."

Matthias smiles, acting a bit embarrassed about Ethan's high praise.

"Hm, hm." Feeling left out of the conversation and purposely being ignored, Shane becomes irritated with his apparent invisibility. He pulls back his shoulders and folds his arms across his chest—raising his chin in defiance, he announces his presence.

Ethan realizes he has overlooked Shane and introduces him. "Sorry about that, forgive me. Matthias, I would also like you to meet Shane Kage." Shane glares at Matthias but reaches out his hand anyway to exchange polite greetings.

"What, no hug?" Matthias jests, not bothering to return his gesture.

Shane's brow furrows, giving the Borrower in front of him an icy glare. Biting down hard on his tongue—trying to remain silent—he grinds his teeth as he retrieves his hand quickly and steps back, not impressed with his joke.

"I know who he is," Matthias reports to everyone. "He was to be in the next generation of Shadow Guardians deployed for the Covenant of Shadows. First in his class, from what I was told, and quite a fearless warrior, so rumour has it."

Shane's face flushes a bit, still upset about having to put his commitment to the Guard on hold due to his oath to Gabrian's parents. "Such a pity. What happened with that anyway?" Matthias says, baiting his new acquaintance in order to see what kind of a rise he can get out of him. "Change your mind?"

Hearing the condescension in Matthias's voice, Shane clenches his fists, refraining from his longing to squeeze the life out of Gabrian's new instructor. "No. I did not change my mind. My oath to Gabrian's parents took precedence over my own wants. I am still training... would you like a demonstration of my skills?" Shane steps forward as he finishes his question.

"No, that will not be necessary. But thanks," Matthias taunts. He puts his index finger flush with his firm pouted lips and looks at Shane as if he is confused about something. "Funny though...?

"What?" Shane grunts, eager to lay him out.

"The thought of a Shadow Walker actually protecting a Borrower," Matthias says smirking at Shane. Chuckling in a breathy way, he cups his chin and shakes his head—taunting him with unkind eyes. "I guess if you live long enough, you will see everything."

Realizing Shane is about ready to tear Matthias's head off,

Ethan decides that now might be a good time to move inside with Gabrian's introductions.

"Anyway, I am sure Gabrian would like to get settled in and become familiar with her new surroundings," Ethan interjects, placing his hand on Gabrian's shoulder. He gives her a slight nudge to get her started toward the door. "Shall we?"

Shane begins to follow them into the school when Matthias steps in front of him and stops him dead at the door, holding out his arm to block his entrance.

"No need for Shadow Walkers inside these walls. We are quite capable of making sure she is well taken care of."

Matthias's condescending tone shreds at Shane's nerves, but he stops at the doorway, watching Gabrian and Ethan continue on without him down the corridor.

"Run along now, Schaeduwe," Matthias hisses. His eyes focused and severe, he waves her Guardian away like a bothersome pest that needs to be done away with. "She will be fine."

Instinctually, Shane growls in frustration and steps into Matthias' space, towering over him; his body casts a shadow that consumes the instructor's form as he exhales his words of warning. "Have her at the door by four."

Matthias gives him a sickeningly sweet smile then replaces it with an undaunted and mirrored stare, his eyes unblinking and still. He turns his back to Shane and darts into the building, letting the large wooden academy door swing shut and slam in Shane's face. Matthias smiles in triumph and hurries to catch up with his guests.

"What was that about?" Gabrian asks him, squinting her eyes and brushing her hand through the loose tangles of ebony hanging around her face, twisting the ends around her fingers as she wonders if this is the kind of behaviour she can expect from him.

"A little harmless fun is all," Matthias assures, glancing across his shoulder in her direction and shrugs, still wearing a cheery mischievous grin. "No need to worry."

They walk a few more steps forward through the warm pine-coloured walls that line the hallway of the academy. The pictures that hang on the wall are like those of the New York Legacy School, but the life that roams so freely within these walls feels different—unsettling yet familiar—like an old friend that has been estranged by harsh words.

"Here we are." Matthias points at a sign on the solid dark brown door to their right.

ENERGY CONSERVATORY. It says in big bold letters.

The entrance looks different than all the other doors they had passed. The closer they get to it, the more Gabrian's fingers begin to burn. She reaches out to touch it and pulls her hands away quickly, feeling something odd about it.

"Why does this door look so different from the rest?" she asks, guessing that the answer must have something to do with Magik.

"The door looks different because it is," Matthias explains. "It is enchanted. Come inside and see."

She gives him a wide-eyed glance. Cold prickles skate across her skin causing her to looks away and study the peculiarity of the door once again, reserving her trust until it is earned.

"Come on, it is fine." With a subtle pull at the edges of his firm strong lips, his mouth curves upward, reaching the corners of his eyes, and enhances the gilded shimmer of hazel within them. He reaches down and opens the door in front of them to reveal a large chamber filled with strange objects Gabrian has never seen before. The room is partitioned off into what seems to be very particular patterns.

There is something off-putting about the room that makes her feel leery of entering it. She awakens the energy within her and walks through the archway. In the middle of the doorway, something surrounding the entrance causes her senses to go wild for a moment. A feeling of being constrained encompasses her like that of the wards inside the Covenant of Shadows. But once she steps through the entry, the pressure is gone. She looks back and sees Ethan still standing on the other side of the door.

"You are not coming?" she asks, watching him examine the doorway.

"No. I have to get back to work. Matthias has offered to help you while I am working. I have no worries about his ability, and neither should you. You are in good hands, and besides, I was his mentor. How bad could it be?" He chuckles and gives her a big toothy grin. "You will do fine. I will check in with you later to see how things went. Okay?"

She looks at him, unsure about his decision to leave her there, but decides that if Ethan believes Matthias is capable of her instruction, then she should as well. "Okay."

"Have fun," he says, giving her a slight wave as he walks away, back toward the entrance of the academy.

She stands in the doorway, watching him go. Out of instinct, she searches for the hum of energy inside herself and pushes it out against her surroundings, getting a feel for the room like Ethan had taught her. She tries to expand her reach but feels it stop short at the strangely curved metal walls and then at the doorway.

"Not the trusting kind I see." Matthias' voice finds her from the back of the room, and his words invade her concentration.

"It is not that. I was just curious about the room."

"Curious is good," he says, his voice much kinder than it had been earlier—no longer pompous like it had been when he spoke with Shane.

"I know I asked you already, but why did you taunt Shane like you did?"

He swaggers over to where she is with tender humor whispering on his lips. She sees a more attractive side of him now that he is not being a pretentious jerk.

"I am not particularly fond of Shadow Walkers. Especially ones with over exaggerated self-worth complexes."

She lets out a burst of involuntary laughter at his candor then quickly covers her mouth with her hand to smother the sound. Although she has never said it herself, she completely understands the meaning in his words, and laughs again, feeling the binds loosening from the stranglehold that her life has had on her for months.

The tension that Gabrian had felt about this strange new arrangement between Matthias and herself resolves to some degree at Shane's expense. She starts to think that maybe this new acquaintance has something to teach her after all.

Chapter Forty-Eight

Jealousy or Duty

MATTHIAS BEGINS GABRIAN'S training where Ethan had left off. After a few weeks with Matthias, Gabrian finds her confidence again, no longer doubting herself. Matthias, much like Ethan, has a way of making her feel appreciated, and helps her to find the beauty in her gift again.

Now that the weather is turning, and the cold stretch of winter is about to be over, they start venturing out and about the village. Matthias explains about usage of energy more in detail. He helps her understand that they are not limited to the essence of humans but that of animals as well.

They take daily trips to visit the nearby hospitals, hospices, and even a few animal shelters—any place he thinks might lend some help. She is learning that her special abilities really are a gift—making life a bit more bearable for everyone she touches is like being witness to small miracles every day—and the fact she is the one responsible for them slowly fills the empty void she has carried around since her parent's death.

Though Shane is not welcome inside the academy, Matthias holds no jurisdiction over the outside world. Shane follows them from a distance everywhere they go but lets them have their space. He watches as Gabrian's kindness invokes her ability of control and it flourishes with each gift of light she offers the sick and suffering. He cannot help but feel happy for her, seeing the radiance of her beauty begin to show in her aura.

He also begins to notice that Gabrian and Matthias are spending more and more time together. On occasion, he has also noticed that Matthias takes the liberty of touching her face while removing a strand of hair that has fallen and has begun to put his arm subtly around her while explaining a lesson. The bond between them becomes much more familiar than Shane is comfortable with. He convinces himself that it is strictly out of duty that he cares enough to be upset about it.

While mental training is one thing, Gabrian's need for physical training is a bit of a surprise to her. Ethan had encouraged her to start running again to help with her concentration, but Matthias insists she take on some combat skills as well.

She struggles at first with it, but Gabrian learns to listen to Matthias' thoughts while he spars with her. She takes note that he does not guard his intentions very closely and begins to anticipate his moves before he makes them—using this flaw to her advantage. Lately, her black feathery friend has been making it a habit to join in on the fun as well by squawking loudly at exactly the right moment to distract and irritate him. Gabrian is pleased with this added bonus.

In mid-spar, Gabrian's face loosens its grasp on her feral mask, the one she shrouds herself within when engulfed in combat with Matthias, and steps out of her stance, dropping her hands. "I have been thinking," she says.

Matthias keeps his guard up, not trusting her to keep her hands to herself. "Oh, you have, have you?"

"Why do I need to learn to fight?"

Matthias lowers his hands, and his face softens—slipping his pressed lips into a lop-sided grin, surprised by her unexpected inquiry. "Well, like the Shadow Walkers, the Covenant also recruits Borrowers to uphold certain aspects of the law. If there ever is a need to track down someone that causes the Covenant of Shadows to become concerned then we, as the peacekeepers, need to be prepared to do so. We need to be strong enough to contain and on occasion, destroy them."

Gabrian recollects the flashes of bloodied bodies from

Ethan's mind that he had allowed her to see when she first inquired about Vampires.

"From my experience in peacekeeping, the desire to stay alive normally outweighs the need to serve the law, making the hunted that much more dangerous than those who hunt for them."

She rubs away the sweat beading on her forehead with the back of her hand then nods in understanding, but the confusion of why she needs to be trained has not been explained to her. Matthias sees the conflict in her mind.

"And from what I have witnessed so far, with your mental capabilities, and an unexpected but intriguing ability to outfight even me, I think that you would make an excellent candidate for a peacekeeping tour."

Gabrian laughs at his preposterous suggestion, and suddenly springs upward. She twists herself around in mid-air; landing behind him, she slides her arm around his neck, committing to a chokehold.

"Now, that would be ludicrous," she jeers playfully.

Shane arrives at the Arts Center to take Gabrian home. Though he normally waits for Gabrian at the front door, he finds himself being drawn to the back of the building. He cuts to the side of the rugged stone structure and continues to edge his way to the back of the building until he reaches the courtyard. Once he sees what waits for him, he understands the lure.

Gabrian and Matthias are engaged in a sparring match. They are surrounded by a wall of solid granite blocks assembled meticulously halfway up the trunks of ancient willow trees, keeping watch with lonesome solemnness over all those who would walk among them.

Watching quietly from the corner wall, not wanting to disrupt their practice, Shane observes closely while Gabrian delivers three quick punches to Matthias' face and torso, then blocks a left hook powered forcefully by Matthias in order to gauge her speed. She grabs his arm, pulling him forward into a chokehold to the throat, and sweeps her left leg under his right, clearing its weight from beneath to land him flat on his back on the ground.

Shane smiles, impressed with her speed and the fierce agility in her attack. He finds himself enthralled by the amount of power she wields and how incredibly beautiful she looks doing it.

Gabrian smirks at Matthias as she reaches down to help him up, and he grabs her by the arm, pulling her down hard. He flips himself to hover over her with his hand in a position to rip her throat out. "Never let your guard down."

She looks at him and frowns, realizing she got too confident, and it can mean her life in real combat.

Seeing her disheartened, he softens. "Don't be discouraged. Every person, no matter how strong they may seem, all have their moment of weakness." Then with his finger, he gently brushes away a strand of hair that has fallen across her face. "Even I have my weaknesses."

Matthias grins at Gabrian, keeping his hazel brown eyes locked on her ice blue irises. Gabrian's pulse quickens at this touch. She looks away from him and gasps. Her eyes flare in a spur of wildness that stirs within them—biting her lip—confused by this strange feeling now whirling in the center of her stomach. Guilt floods her as she immediately thinks of Shane. She pushes herself out from underneath him and gets up, smiling uncomfortably.

Matthias looks down at the ground for a moment then raises his head to look at her. "I am sorry, I should not have been so forward. I have made you feel uncomfortable. I don't know what came over me."

She blushes but grumbles at herself for feeling bad. Shane despises her and ignores her most of the time, so why should she feel guilty when another man—a very handsome man at that—shows her attention? He is Boragen, a Borrower just like her. There is no judgement in his intentions.

"No. Please, don't apologize. I just was not expecting that."

"I think you have managed to wrap yourself up in so many layers of invisibility and defense, you have lost yourself under it all," he says, quickly getting to his feet. He glances down at the grass on his clothes and brushes it off.

"I have become accustomed to putting up walls because of what I am, of what I have become." She kneels down to pick at the grass, deflecting his eye contact. "I am consumed by trying to learn how to control this thing that I am."

Matthias walks over to her and squats down beside her so that he is face to face with her. "Your gift does not get to determine what you are or who you become, Gabrian. You do," Matthias says

340

as he takes her hand in his own.

Gabrian knows deep down he is right. She is strong, intelligent...

"And beautiful," Matthias says, reading her thoughts. "Something tells me that you have been so caught up in self-loathing the last little while that you may have overlooked that part."

She blushes as he touches the side of her cheek with his fingers then moves in closer, and it dawns on her that he is about to kiss her. Her heart races, and her fingers begin to burn. Matthias's intentions radiate off him like fire, and Gabrian feels the heat from his lips as they briefly touch up against hers.

"Hm! Hm!"

She pulls back from Matthias, hearing an agitated voice behind her and recognizes it immediately. Her porcelain skin begins to brighten with a rose hue as she feels the heat of embarrassment flood her face, but she meets Shane's fierce glower and stares back at him, straight in the eye, not faltering.

"Impeccable timing." Matthias huffs and rolls his eyes at Shane's interruption. He rises from the ground, making himself as large as he can in Shane's presence.

Gabrian rises with Matthias. "I will see you tomorrow," she says to him softly then kisses him quickly on the cheek as she walks away toward Shane, heading for the front of the school.

Shane's blood boils with rage as he watches the exchange between Gabrian and Matthias. Matthias grins at him with a triumphant sneer.

Gabrian walks past Shane who is ready to launch himself at her instructor. "Leave him alone," she threatens him calmly, shooting him a deadly glare with her narrowed eyes—warning him to heed her words. "This does not concern you! Let it go!"

Shane feels a slight twinge of hurt as she dismisses his feelings. "I don't think that he is a good choice for you," he says, following behind her.

"Oh really, and why is that now?"

"Because I don't like him."

"You don't like anyone. Besides, you do not get to choose who I include in my life anymore. That is an option that you reneged on a long time ago. So drop it and take me home. This conversation is over."

Chapter Forty-Nine

Dinner is Served

GABRIAN JUMPS INTO the shower as soon as she returns home, trying to wash the sweat and dirt off of her body from combat training with Matthias. She smiles at the thought of what it would be like if she and Matthias were to become close. Before today, she had never really thought about it, but now that he has made it clear that he wants to be more than just her instructor, she has to admit she is intrigued with this new direction of her training.

There is a knock on her bedroom door, and she is jarred from her daydream.

"It is open," she says as she brushes her long black hair, trying to remove the tangles.

The door opens, and Shane peeks his head in only far enough to lean against the door casing. "Hey."

"Hey," she says in return, continuing to brush her hair without looking over at him.

"Do you want to get out of here tonight?"

"What?" Gabrian stops brushing. She looks over at him through the mirror—her face flat and her mouth ajar—struggling to find an emotion that fits. She sets the brush down and turns to lean on the back of her chair to stare at him, caught off guard by his suggestion.

"I was thinking that maybe we could take a jaunt over to my place tonight. I have been neglecting it pretty bad lately, and to be honest, I am starting to get a little 'cabin fever.'"

She finds herself grinning at his meager attempt at humor, shaking her head at his pun. "But Rachael is already making supper."

"Yeah, I saw that. But between you and me, I swear that girl has definitely got something against cooking meat. All she eats is rabbit food, and right now, I could really go for a steak." He grins in hope that his pleading will tip the scales a bit in favour of some meat.

"You do know that she is a vegan, right?" She raises her brow and looks down her nose at him mockingly, then lets her mouth curl up into a toying smirk.

"Well, now I do." Shane lets his eyes jump over his shoulder to look in the direction of the vinegary-smell wafting up from the kitchen, then scratches the back of his head, messing the already chaotic curls. "That might explain the no meat thing."

Gabrian smiles. Rachael has been wonderful to stay with her and take care of her, but she understands that her vegan meal plans are not exactly a hit with the present company. "Yeah, I could go for a steak."

"Great!" he exclaims, clapping his hands together before wringing them excitedly—his mouth watering at the thought of charred steaks on an open flame. "Get dressed, we are out of here."

"What about Rachael?" Her lips bunch together in a heartfelt pout, looking at the floor for a moment then returns her gaze to the man standing at her door. "I feel bad about her going to all the trouble of cooking."

Already turned and heading for the stairs, Shane stops and gives a wide grin—shrugging his shoulders, his eyes gleam in the overhead lights. "So invite her."

Gabrian is surprised by his thoughtfulness but laughs, getting the feeling that he really just wants to go home. They ask Rachael to join them, but she sees the way Shane has been watching Gabrian lately and declines their invitation.

"Thanks, but I think I will just stay in tonight.

"Are you sure?" Gabrian asks. "You do so much around here, come and relax. I promise his cooking is way better than his

344

manners."

Rachael rolls her eyes and laughs. "I will take your word for it. Maybe next time."

Shane reaches up and grabs the keys from the hook by the kitchen door. Gabrian looks at him in surprise. "Not taking the shortcut tonight?"

"Nope, not tonight." He remembers how much she seemed to love taking the boat the last time she visited the island so he decides he could at least do that for her—however insignificant the gesture is. Shane and Gabrian jump into her mom's car and start toward Northeast harbor, headed for the island.

SHANE PREPARES TWO thick steaks for them he had picked up at the General store after they disembarked the Sea Queen and left the dock. In a few moments, he manages to whip up what seems like a full course meal. She only picks at the sides but devours her steak that Shane slapped on the barbeque just long enough to say it was on there. It is perfect.

"Is that all you are going to eat?" Shane says, noticing Gabrian's lack of interest in anything other than the meat.

"That is all I need," she explains to him. "Now that I am maintaining my energy intake with more consistency, my body only craves a bit of protein now and then to keep it happy and functioning."

"Huh," Shane says, hesitating briefly before he loads another heap of potatoes onto his plate. "Fine, suit yourself."

She watches him eat in silence, not knowing what to say or what she should talk about. They have not exactly been close since their accord—civil, yes, friendly, not so much.

Her eyes jaunt around the cabin, still completely in love with it, but her heart begins to ache as her mind plays back how different things were between them the last time she was here. Though she will never admit it, somewhere tucked deep inside her heart, she will not let go of the hope that Shane might once again see her the same way Matthias does now.

She has not tried to read his mind since the night he saved her from the fall off the cliff. The poison he displayed toward her then was enough. She did not care to know what he thought of her now.

They finish the remainder of their meal in partial silence, only making idle chitchat, and both of them feel awkward that they are all alone without distraction. Gabrian gets up to help him clear the dishes from the table and take them to the sink.

Shane sets down the plates and rests his hands on the top of the cupboard, staring out the front window into his yard then sighs loudly.

"Look, this is stupid." He exhales and gathers his courage to continue. "I am bound to you until your last dying breath, and that means we are going to be stuck together for a very, very long time. So maybe we should go out on a limb here and try to make the best of this. We could at least try to be more civil toward each other."

Gabrian turns the tap off before the soapy water reaches the top of the plates. She reaches in and fills her hand with the thick mound of bubbles. She rests for a moment and gazes out the window, thinking about his words, and debates the outcome of her own thoughts. Her face lightens and her mouth grows into a peculiar impish twist. Quickly raising her hands up to her left, she smashes him gently in the face with her handful of suds.

"I...am perfectly civil. Maybe you should give it a try." She covers her mouth with her wet hand, trying to stifle her laughter from his Santa-like resemblance.

Shocked by her actions, Shane immediately scoops up a handful of soapy warm water and throws it in her direction, splashing her. She jumps back. Her face dripping with warm water, she calmly reaches for the tea towel on the cupboard and wipes her face. After she is done drying off, she grabs a salad bowl from the counter in front of her and fills it with warm water. Sliding over the cupboard curtain below her, she pulls out a small wooden stepping stool and drags it out in front of her. Grabbing the bowl with her hands, she turns and steps up on the stool then proceeds to raise her arms over her head, still holding the bowl.

"You would not dare."

Gabrian tilts her head and the grin widens. "Wouldn't I?" She quickly flips the bowl over Shane, dumping the full contents of it on his head.

His eyes observe the state of his clothes as he looks down, completely drenched.

"Now you are in for it," Shane warns her playfully, grabbing the bowl out of her hands and rushes to the sink to fill it with the warm soapy water. Gabrian squeals as she darts toward the middle of the room, headed for the stairs to try to escape the onslaught of her doings, but Shane flies across the room, quickly catching her halfway up the stairs and drenches the back of her body with the bowl full of water.

Tossing the bowl to the side, he reaches up and cups the back of her leg, holding her firm so she is unable to go any farther. They look at each other and both begin to laugh hysterically at the drenched messes they are.

The laughter is filled with hurt and relief all in the same. Gabrian slides herself down a couple steps, barely inches from his face and looks at him as her laughter subsides. A strange impulse comes over her, and she leans in, kissing him softly on the mouth.

Shane's laughter stops, and his eyes widen with this unexpected gesture, but instead of pulling away, he leans forward and kisses her back, passionately and longing for her—hungry to taste the sweetness that lingers on her lips once again. His whole body feels like it is on fire and rekindles every emotion he has ever felt for her. They kiss feverishly, touching and pulling each other closer and closer until there is nothing left but damp cloth between them.

Without warning, Shane pulls away from her as his consciousness becomes aware of what is happening between them. He longs to hold on and embrace her with all his might, but anger washes out his desire for her. He is ashamed of his weakness for her and with himself for letting this happen.

"We can't do this." He winces, pushing himself away from her before stepping back down the stairs into the kitchen.

Gabrian remains still on the stairs with her hands over her face, feeling confused, hurt, and stupid for letting herself feel again. She raises her head and speaks in a monotone voice, devastated by his rejection. "Why not?" she drones out from beneath her hands then drops them lifelessly in her lap, staring at the wood stove in front of her—feeling as cold and empty as it looks. "Why is it so wrong to you?"

Returning to his stance at the kitchen sink, he stares out into the night, conflicted and in pain beyond all measures. "We are mortal enemies, Gabrian. It is already a conflict of interest with me being your Guardian. I really do not think me leading you on is going to help the situation."

"Leading me on?" She edges herself down the stairs and starts to pace back and forth across the floor. Swimming in a fusion of emotion, she clutches her fists tightly at her sides. She swings them up hard and presses them to her temples briefly then lets them drop again—teetering somewhere between being furious and being crushed. "Is that what you were doing?"

He glances her way briefly but remains quiet, not knowing what to say.

"So your jealous performance that you had earlier today, was that just an act too?" She raises both her hands and runs them through her hair, feeling confused and frustrated. "So let me guess how it works for you. You don't want me, but you don't want anyone else to have me either, is that it?" she snarls as her voice grows louder. She stops pacing and glares at him coldly. "I think you should take me home."

"Gabrian..." he stutters, trying to explain but it only infuriates her more.

"Now!"

He nods in defeat then gently wraps his large fingers around her small slender forearm. In the few moments they are cloaked and drift within the Shadow's Veil, Gabrian feels something strange. It is pain, but it is not coming from inside of her. It radiates from within Shane, and it feels heavy and draining—much like the suffering she has endured but different somehow.

She closes her eyes for a moment, and when she opens them, she is standing in the middle of her room. There is no light other than the dim glimmer coming from the small lamp she must have forgotten to turn off on her dresser. She wrenches her arm free and hurriedly steps away from Shane, wanting him to be gone and this night over.

"Gabrian, I..." He steps toward her, his eyes pleading and glassy as he reaches his hand out to touch her arm.

"Leave me alone," she says softly, her lip trembling as the words slip out, and she moves back just enough to avoid his touch.

He looks up at the ceiling and grabs his brown messy hair in both of his hands. His body stiffens as he fights against himself to say something. He turns to look at her.

"Just leave," she whispers.

He slowly walks to the corner of her room that harbors the darkest shadow and stops. He glances back at her, but she stands with her back to him. His heart sinks as he faces the shadow once more and slips into the Veil. Not drifting too far in, Shane stands close to the Shadow's edge and waits to keep watch over her. Suddenly, he hears her cry out.

"I didn't ask for this! I didn't ask for any of this!" she screams, dropping to the floor on her knees as the sadness consumes her. Gabrian tucks her arms tightly around her torso and rocks gently back and forth, sobbing. "This is not how my life was supposed to be," she whispers with a ragged breath.

Shane's legs deny him any support, and he slinks down to the floor within the Veil. He places his head in his hands and feels his heart rip and tear at his soul as it tries to convince him to go back out there to her. He is torn between the love he feels for her and the hatred that simmers inside of him because of what she is. His heart screams at him to go to her, but he stands firm— confused and tormented with his own inner demons. Alone in the Darkness, he sits in his silent torment, watching her suffer as a tear escapes its confinement and slips down his cheek.

Gabrian pulls herself up off the floor and crawls into bed, not bothering to change her clothes. Quietly remaining on the cusp of the Veil, Shane continues his guard. Every time he has left her before, trouble always managed to find her so tonight he will wait until he is sure she is asleep before taking his leave.

She finally drifts off to sleep, exhausted from crying, and Shane steps out of the Darkness. He quietly crosses the room to where she is, looks down at her, and sighs. Reaching over and grabbing a quilt from the bench by the window, he spreads it out, pulling it up around her shoulders to protect her from the chill in the air.

Sitting down gently on the edge of the bed beside her, he watches her breathe, finally peaceful. He slips his nimble fingers in under the strand of hair that covers the side of her face and pushes it to the side to tuck it behind her ear. He gently runs his finger down the shadow of her jaw, feeling the warmth from her skin but is careful not to wake her. His eyes begin to water, distorting his sight—his emotions beginning to betray his control.

Convinced that she is asleep, he gets up and turns off the lamp. He walks over to the window and looks out into the night. With one last glance at Gabrian, he exhales, feeling the twists of pain in his chest rip through his innards. In that moment, Shane refuses to believe that this is how he is destined to live out the rest of their eternity together and steps into the Veil—on his way to seek council.

Chapter Fifty

Just the Two of Us

"GAB...RI...AN." FROM SOMEWHERE deep inside her mind, she hears someone calling her name. "Gab...ri...an. Please help me."

Gabrian sits up in bed and swings her legs over the side. She raises herself up off the mattress and walks slowly across the floor to her bedroom door. She carefully edges her way down the stairs, listening to her instructions.

"Quietly now, you do not want to wake them. They would not understand, and they will try to stop you."

Gabrian just nods and continues on her course. She reaches the bottom of the stairs and enters into the kitchen, heading for the door.

"Quickly now, my dear. You must not dally," the voice insists.

Unlatching the lock on the door, she steps out into the night—leaving it ajar behind her. Entangled deeply within sleep's web, Gabrian helplessly follows the voice of the spider within her dream.

Chapter Fifty-One

To the Heart of the Matter

"I WAS WONDERING when I was going to see you," Orroryn says, smiling at his unexpected late night guest, and takes a sip of his earl grey tea.

"I am sorry it is so late, but I needed to talk to you," Shane declares, stepping out of the Veil and into Orroryn's living room.

"Still having trouble being around Gabrian?" he asks with a raised brow, fighting the urge to grin knowing that it may do more harm than good. He is genuinely concerned for the both of them, especially having firsthand knowledge of how stubborn Shane can be when he chooses.

"You could say that. But it has gotten complicated," Shane reports as he starts to pace back and forth between the wall and the couch in front of where Orroryn sits. "Much more complicated."

"All right, I will bite, what did you do now?"

Shane stops pacing and takes a seat in the brown suede chair beside Orroryn's. He looks at his adoptive father with tortured green eyes. Orroryn sees the distress and leans in to listen more intently.

With his elbows resting on his knees, Shane leans forward and rubs his hands through his hair in angst, then sits up to look upon Orroryn. "Do you remember the girl I had told you about a few months ago, the one I asked you advice about?"

"The human girl?" He tilts his head and peers into his son's troubled eyes, feeling at a loss with the hope he will be able to help him.

"Yeah, the human girl," Shane says in a breathy tone, looking away and biting his lip.

"Yes, I remember." Orroyn sits back and nods his head, wading through the details of the conversation.

"Well, it turns out that she was not so human after all." He puts his head in his hands and rubs them through his hair quickly then looks up at his adopted father.

"Oh? She is from the Realm then. Well, that is good, right?"

"Not really."

"Okay, now you have lost me." Orroryn furrows his brow and takes another drink from his cup of tea.

"It turns out that the girl is Boragen. A Borrower." The lights turn on in Orroryn's mind as he understands what Shane's issue is. "The girl was Gabrian."

Orroryn sits back into his chair and sips his tea again. "I see."

"'I see.' That is it? That is all the wisdom you have to offer?" Shane gets up and begins his repetitive course again. "I was expecting a little more than, 'I see.'"

"Well, if you would stop that irksome pacing and sit back down then maybe I might have something more to say."

Shane stops immediately and takes his seat. His leg begins a subtle jitter until Orroryn shoots him an irritated look—a look much like the one he used to get as a child when he would fidget during a lesson.

"You know the war you have with that girl is none of her doing."

"I know but..." Orroryn puts his finger up to signify that he is not done talking and Shane goes silent.

"It is okay to be angry, but what happened to your parents is in the past. Staying angry at the whole world will not bring them back." Shane gives Orroryn a quick glance, his eyes narrow and his pouty lips pulled tight across his face, but Orroryn continues. "How long are you going to punish her for the pain that someone else is responsible for? If you do not let it go, you will one day regret it. It is only going to eat away at you, leaving you empty and alone. Trust me."

Shane bores down at the floor, mulling over the words, and tries to find an ounce of retribution to stand on, but deep down he knows Orroryn is right. This is not her fight. This battle between them has been going on long enough, and it was he that drew the sword, not her.

Orroryn observes his son's expression and watches as the creases around his eyes soften and the muscles in his jaw unclench as his Darkness passes.

"The thing about love is that it shares no prejudice. It does not see what the eye sees or heed what the mind harbors. It just knows what it wants and when the heart leaps, it holds little concern as to where it lands." Orroryn slides forward in his chair and sets his tea cup down on the coffee table beside him. He reaches out and gently rests his hand upon Shane's wrist, looking him straight in the eye. "From what I have witnessed about love, the heart has always been much braver than the mind."

Shane's eyes meet his father's, and his face lightens in a smile, replacing the scowl that had been there.

"The universe has its own plans that do not always go along with what we have envisioned for ourselves. Sometimes, worlds collide in order to create something new, something better, something stronger. It is how we all came to be as we are today. It does not make it right or wrong, it just makes it real."

For the first time in months, Shane's heart feels light. Free from the grip of pain he had plagued upon it, a true sense of peace begins to peel away at the layers of hatred he has held onto for so long. He reaches for his father's hand and squeezes it.

"Thank you," he offers softly. The shadows of the dark cloud that had been hovering within his eyes is gone and a glimmer of hope emerges in its place as he gets up of the couch.

"Now, go and straighten out this mess you have made. Plead your case to her, and try not to bugger it up again if she forgives you," Orroryn teases as Shane heads for the Shadows he had stepped out of. "If that is possible." Orroryn throws in jest.

Shane shoots Orroryn a disapproving frown just as he enters the Veil.

Chapter Fifty-Two

Not Present and Unaccounted For

AFTER KNOCKING ON her door for a few moments without any reply, Shane turns the knob and opens it to look in.

"Gabrian," he says, but there is still no answer. He enters into the dark room and inches toward her bed. Seeing it empty, he eyes the bathroom door to his right, but the light is not on. Not sensing her energy in the room, he quickly makes his way to the hallway and heads down the stairs as the feeling of dread consumes his thoughts and surrounds his body.

"What is all the racket about?" Rachael grumbles as she staggers out of her room beneath the stairs, snug in her flannel jammies.

"Where is Gabrian?"

"She is in bed." She points up the stairs and wanders to the kitchen nook, half asleep. "I checked on her after you too had your spat. She was sound asleep. Oh and by the way, what did you do to..."

"She is gone," he interjects, thinking this is getting to be a common theme in this house. He pinches the bridge of his nose and starts to pace.

"What?" Rachael awakens from her foggy state of mind and runs up the stairs to check.

"I just came from there," he yells after her as she rushes up the stairs to Gabrian's room. "She is not in there, and I really need to talk to her."

Rachael hurries down the stairs, one hand pressing her weight against the wall as she steps while rubbing the sleep out of her eyes with the other, still stuck in an awakening state of confusion. "That does not make any sense. She was there no more than an hour ago."

The kitchen door bangs as it slips open and hits the side of the house as a small gust of wind catches it from outside. Rachael and Shane both look in the direction of the noise.

"Why is the door open?" He rushes over and looks around outside at the darkness covering the yard then pulls the door closed and then open again, examining the locking mechanism.

"I have no idea." Rachael scratches her head and strains her squinting eyes as they dart around the kitchen in a slow spiraled circle, searching for anything out of the norm—a hint of some kind as to what happened. "I am sure I locked it when I went to bed."

Shane's heart starts to pound, and his mind begins to imagine the worst possible outcomes especially considering Gabrian's track record for disappearing.

"Her shoes are still here and her coat. Where would she have gone this time of night?" Rachael wonders out loud and looks at Shane with wide eyes.

"I don't know." He grabs a coat from the hook by the door then turns to Rachael and tosses it to her. "Here, put this on. You are coming with me."

"What?"

"I am not sure where she is, but I have a feeling that when I find her, I am going to need some backup, and right now, that would be you." He reaches out and wraps his large fingers around her forearm gently but securely, and looks down at her in her flannels and slippers. "You ready?"

Rachael glances down at her attire and shrugs her shoulders. "Ready as I will ever be."

Chapter Fifty-Three

Tangled Webs We Weave

DRIFTING INSIDE THE Veil, Shane finds Gabrian's life source and immediately steps out of the Shadows with Rachael in tow. Sensing a dark energy as well, Shane and Rachael take cover behind the great amethyst stone, a few feet from where Gabrian stands in order to monitor the situation.

He quickly places his hand over Rachael's mouth and puts his finger in front of his full lips to signal her to be silent. They slowly move toward the side of the stone to get a better view of Gabrian. Horrified by what they see, Rachael gasps and Shane gives her a stern look for her involuntary noise.

Standing in the middle of a circle of people on their knees with their heads down is Gabrian. In front of her is a young man dressed in a grey suit. His lips move like he is saying something to her, but Rachael and Shane cannot hear his words.

Gabrian nods her head slowly in agreement to whatever this guy has just told her. She closes her eyes and begins to shimmer in grey light. Her arms raise from her sides as she concentrates on the auras of the circle of humans that surround her. She inhales and exhales slowly. The essences dance and sway with every breath she takes. The fragments of light twist and split apart from their host and hurry their way to Gabrian's mouth, eager to meet with her demand.

The suited man begins to smile widely and grips his hands together in a monogamous handshake with himself, obviously pleased with her performance. He releases his hands and sways them around from side to side, speaking again in a tone far below hearing range.

They watch as the Earth around Gabrian starts to darken and shift. Its takes on a different form that is not solid at all then they realize it is not Earth they see—it is the Gargons emerging from the Darkness, surrounding her from beneath.

Shane slowly creeps back behind the rock again, dragging Rachael with him.

"I am not sure about what is going on here, but I do know that stuff out there surrounding Gabrian is the Darkness of Erebus—lethal to anyone and everyone under the right circumstances."

"What do you need me to do?" Rachael asks him, looking up at the Shadow Walker through blurred damp eyes that volley back and forth between him and quick peeks of her best friend—understanding this is getting real, fast.

"From the looks of those Gargons, it might be a good idea to have a Black Mage nearby to contain them if things somehow get out of control." His mouth pulls tight across his face, deflating his plump lips as he stares down at Rachael—his only line of defense right now—and reveals to her the magnitude of his fears that harbor within his eyes. "So what I need is for you to find one."

"Okay," she confirms, lowering her chin and closing her eyes to begin her search but whips her head back up, eyes flared as an unsettling thought hits her. "Wait...what are you going to do?"

"Get her back," he reveals, not dropping his eyes from their focus and rubs his knuckles across the bottom of his jaw, feeling the soft resistance of the stubble against his fingers.

Rachael's eyes narrow. She peers up at him and presses the vagueness of his answer. "And...how are you proposing to do that?

"Like I always do," he says in a low soothing tone—lowering his eyes to meet her skeptical glare. "I'll wing it!"

Rachael shakes her head and hides her eyes in her hand. "Ugh, that is what I was afraid of."

"Stay out of sight!" he insists. Shane steps out from behind

360

the rock and walks clearly into sight.

"Ah, as I expected," Adrinn cheers, acknowledging Shane's sudden presence, but he does not bother to look at him. He only smirks in his preconceived notion that sooner or later the Shadow Walker would arrive. "You are the Schaeduwe youngling that interfered the last time Gabrian and I were trying to have some quality time together at the bar, pity that was. Oh well, let me assure you that I will not allow you that liberty this time."

"So you are the reason she began to turn. I knew it had to be something like that," Shane accuses him.

His smile widens, and he turns his head to stare at Shane. "My dear boy, she has the dark gift for being a Vampire within her. All she needs is some nurturing, and I intend on making sure she gets it. Maybe not in the civilized way like I had hoped, but none the less, once I am through this last lesson, it will be done, and you can have whatever is left of her."

Shane's instincts flare into overdrive. He is certain Gabrian is in immediate danger, and that time is of the essence. "Gabrian! Gabrian!" he yells to her, but she does not respond. She only flinches a bit at the sound of his voice.

"Go ahead, yell all you like," Adrinn encourages, waving his hand around loosely atop his folded arm nestled snuggly against his vaporous form. "She cannot understand what you are saying anyway. She is dreaming," Adrinn reveals to Shane in a pleasant upbeat tone, his lips painted in a sickeningly sweet smear.

"What do you mean she is dreaming?" Shane's face contorts, twisting the corners of his face into painful ridges to show the depth of his stress. "You are telling me that she is asleep?"

"You can call it that if you like, but I prefer the word 'inaccessible.' She is in a trance—a delusion, if you would. And since I have such a soft heart I thought it would be kinder to allow her the belief that her demise was for a noble gesture."

"What are you talking about?" Shane feels the pain come alive within his chest at the thought of her coming to any harm.

"Right now, as she dreams, she is harvesting energy from all around her, from any and all sources she can find. She believes this to be a necessary measure—that she is doing something honourable. She is creating as much energy as she is able in order to give it to me so that I have the strength to protect myself against the Elders of the Covenant of Shadows and the Shadow Walkers."

Shane's eyes wash over Gabrian's idle body, keeping the mad man in his peripheral while he watches her drain the life essence from all around her. Remembering that Rachael is hiding nearby, he hopes that by some small miracle, Gabrian's search for energy overlooks the iridescent light of her best friend.

"You see, her hatred for the Elder's unspoken prejudices against her and that of her kind, fuels her desire to help me and to save me from their need to destroy all those who do not bend at the knee to their wishes and their rules."

"Gabrian, wake up!" Shane's yells become frantic. He clenches the muscles in his hands so tight the colour is drained from his flesh, turning his fists white. He paces the small perimeter between them wearing a thin path in the dirt beneath his feet and feels helpless to advance, knowing he is stepping on live wires.

"Please, do continue," Adrinn encourages, laughing as he chimes out his cruel words at Shane's persistence. "Your voice only adds to her delusion." Shane turns to glare at Adrinn, fighting to keep his anger under wraps with the hopes that help arrives soon.

"You said she cannot hear me." Shane's eyes burn as he stares down the evil soul that taunts his control on his emotions, confused by his insufferable riddle. "How does that add to anything?"

"Forgive me." Adrinn stops his entranced admiration of his creation before them and turns to smirk at the young Schaeduwe. "What I meant to say was that she cannot hear your true words," he jeers, watching Shane's frustration grow by the second. "I am the only one that can touch her mind. What she hears from your voice are the words that I choose for her to hear," he says, tapping the center of his own chest. Then raising his hand, he swirls his pointed finger around the edges of his temple and finally lets it come to rest on the fleshy part of his earlobe, executing a cheery, widespread mouth. "So, right now as you bellow out your heartfelt pleas," he continues folding his fluttering hand just beneath his chin and returns to stare gleefully at his muse. "All she understands is that you are here to kill me. And Gabrian, being the benevolent fool that she is..." His daring eyes glance over to engage Shane, taunting him, taking pleasure in his suffering. "...will sacrifice every ounce of her life essence thinking that she has saved me from the evil Shadow Walker—you. With her generous contribution to my cause, I will be able to live for a thousand years or as long as it takes in order to find my key."

"Key?" Shane's eyes pinch tight, wrinkling around the edges in distress. He twists his torso, and his eyes flash a brilliant green as he yells at him, horrified that Gabrian's worth is being compared to that of an inanimate object. "You are going to kill her for some key?"

"Essentially." He shrugs, taunting his guest with a quick and unconcerned glance. "You are brighter than you look, Schaeduwe." Adrinn face loses its pleasantry, and he wipes an imaginary piece of lint from his jacket. "I hate to be rude, but I grow tired of our trifling conversation..."

Knowing that his time is dwindling, Shane launches himself through the air toward the man but passes through him and falls to the ground, rolling to his feet on the other side of his target empty-handed and helpless to stop Gabrian's captor.

A sharp pain slices through the middle of Adrinn's abdomen where Shane tore through his fleshless body. He looks down in shock of this unexpected sensation.

"Interesting," he mutters, wondering about the viability of the Shadow Walker ruining his evening. "It is a good thing I do not travel alone." Adrinn waves his hands through the air, and Gargons begin to rise and swirl around Gabrian in a counterclockwise motion. "I have had enough of you for one night!" he says as he steps inside the darkened mist of Erebus, not wanting to deal any longer with this unpleasant circumstance.

Shane charges after Adrinn, and attempts to grab hold of his arm before he can escape, but his hand makes contact with the mist. A blinding sear of pain jolts through his hand like it is caught in a hot waffle iron, and he wrenches it free from the Darkness.

Orroryn, Ethan, Cimmerian, and Matthias step out from behind the rock where Rachael hides, crouched down between the Earth and the stone. She points to the other side of the rock, toward the sound of sizzling flesh that fills the air between them. They all rush toward the sound and find Shane standing breathless while holding his hand as he observes the scene of zombie-like humans kneeling on the ground at the base of a wall of blackened mist before them.

"What kind of nightmare is this?" Orroryn questions, sliding toward his son.

"Some crazed apparition thing has all these humans in a trance and has Gabrian trapped behind this wall of Gargons. He is planning on draining the life out of her if we don't stop him."

Cimmerian's brow furrows, and he regrets his attendance at the party already, knowing exactly who it is that they have to deal with.

"Hm, I see you have brought your friends," Adrinn's voice blares out in an ear-splitting hiss from within his impenetrable wall. "Well, that just will not do."

Without warning, a blast of energy tides out from within the toxic shroud and sends them all flying backward into the air in different directions and slams them onto the Earth.

"What was that?" Shane shouts, shaking his head and staggering to his feet.

"I think he is using her as a weapon," Ethan replies, wiggling his fingers in reflex as he recalls Gabrian's experimental parlor trick of abstracting energy and propelling it. "She must be drawing in electricity from some nearby source in order to push out with that much force."

Ethan's memory is jogged back to another instance of when he had experienced a similar occurrence. He contemplates the possibility of a connection between these two interactions and out of curiosity, he listens for thought patterns within the black toxic orb in front of them, finding not only one but two familiar minds.

"Ethan, can you help her or at least, do something to wake her up?" Shane pleads loudly, jarring Ethan from his enquiry.

"I don't know, Shane. I will try." Ethan runs through Shane's mind and grabs the details of the events that took place previous to his arrival. "I am going to try to connect with her mind. Maybe I will be able to reach through the compulsion and make her see what is going on."

Ethan pushes through the Darkness that clings heavily to Gabrian's consciousness and searches for a link. He finds her, but her thoughts are confusing and distorted—nothing more than a delusional smear of colours and emotions at war with each other. Her face remains clear of expression as her mind remains lost within her reality. She does not recognize his friendship and

364

strikes out at him violently with a blinding light, burning through his mind which sends him to his knees, reeling in pain.

"It is no use; she is under some kind of mind compulsion. She does not even know who I am and somehow sees me as a threat. I can't help her," he chokes out, holding his head. "I am sorry, Shane."

Shane's attention lands on Cimmerian, who tries to fade into the background of it all. "This is your department, is it not? He is an apparition—summon up some of that black Magik stuff of yours and take him out with an energy wave or something. There must be a way to push this monster back into the Darkness."

Cimmerian stands up straight and steps out from behind Orroryn's shadow. His eyes wash over the people on the ground, helpless within their trance before him. He studies the swirling sphere of death that holds the root to all this evil.

"I could, yes, but if I do that it would take everything encased within it down into Erebus. Gabrian would be consumed by it as well."

Through the layers of Gargon vapor, they see the silhouettes of the inhabitants and the motion of Adrinn moving his lips. A bright greyish light leaves Gabrian's body and begins to saturate Adrinn. His head rises in exhilaration, and he glares over at the group of onlookers standing outside the wall. His hands begin to glow, revealing to them the orbs of energy he has created.

Ethan, knowing who it is they deal with, bellows out a warning to them in remembrance of what comes next.

"Get down!"

But it is too late.

A massive surge of energy blasts toward them, knocking them with the force of a hurricane, flinging them helplessly into the trees behind which knocks Matthias out cold. Shane's ears ring from the harshness of the impact but through the ringing, he hears Adrinn's evil cackle as he focuses back on Gabrian.

She cries out in pain as the light between herself and Adrinn burns brighter.

"We have almost won, my little Vampire."

Her upright stance begins to waver as she begins to drain of energy. The Gargons fester around her, moving in quick erratic jolts like that of a shark that has gotten the scent of blood. She screams again from somewhere in the Darkness.

Shane forces himself to his feet and reaches down, grabbing Cimmerian by the collar of his coat. "Do something! He is killing her!"

Cimmerian understands his fear and focuses his eyes back toward the frenzy. An image of Symone rushes to the forefront of his mind, tormenting his judgement, but he is being watched. If he does not do the right thing, he knows suspicion will follow him, and things will get ugly.

He crawls up onto his feet and raises his hands. Deep violet light glows within the palms of his hands. Cimmerian closes his eyes to concentrate on the task at hand. The crusaders watch without a sound as he applies his efforts but nothing happens. The walls of the sphere stand firm, not wavering in the least.

"I don't understand it." Cimmerian's head rocks backward, only for a moment then slips ahead to gather a closer examination as he gazes at the ball of unrelenting beasts from the underworld, refusing to obey.

"What?" Ethan asks with wide eyes, not understanding his falter.

"The Gargons, they are not responding at all to my requests," Cimmerian reveals in confusion, his hand still out-turned and flaring with the dark Magik that stirs within, awaiting their next command. "It is like he is controlling them from within."

"There has got to be something you can do," Shane yells, leaping the distance between them to stand next to him, his soul wearing an intense shroud of flesh that towers over the Black Mage, desperate for action. "If you can just find me a way in, I will get her out!"

Cimmerian's eyes flinch, and the corners sting with the dew of sadness as he registers the pain surfacing within Shane words.

"Please," Shane's voice cracks as he forces out the word, his last plea—his only chance for saving her.

"I will try to make an opening." Cimmerian pulls himself together, looking away from the boy and readies his hands. He shakes them in quick snaps and dark violet sparks explode from their centers, alight with new vigor and reason. He glances over his shoulder beneath his damp lashes then returns his focus to the task before him. "Get ready to move, because I am not sure how long I will be able to hold them."

"I am ready. Just do it." Shane nods. His body flexes and vibrates in anticipation of even the slightest breach within the wall, desperate to get to Gabrian before it is too late.

Cimmerian's palms crackle and spark dark violet fire as he extends his hands out and reaches inward toward the Gargons, pulling at the intricate web of Darkness. Sweat appears at the top of Cimmerian's brow from the pressure of the feat. Suddenly he sees it—a crack in the wall. Shane strikes like lightning and disappears, injecting himself into the sphere.

Gabrian, barely alive, is curled into a ball on the ground, having succumb to her debt of sacrifice. Shane slides his arms around her waist and secures them then pulls her free from her entrapment before Adrinn even knows what has happened. They slip back through the fissure in the sphere and disappear into the night's shadow, heading for safety.

Cimmerian releases his grip on the wall, falling backward for a moment, but continues his grip on the Darkness. He knows he has to send Adrinn and the Gargons back into the Darkness, but his heart is torn. He does not want to lose Symone again. He cries out in frustration but does what he must. His Magik crackles again within his hands as he thrusts a circular motion at the Darkness, creating a force field around the sphere. He seals Adrinn inside his Gargon's tomb, heading back to Erebus.

Adrinn scream as he begins his descent back into the Darkness. Pieces of his body pull into fragments of space. He glares at Cimmerian and mouths a heart-wrenching sentence that is meant for only one.

"I will remember this."

And with that, Adrinn disappears. The swirling mist of Darkness sinks into the Earth, taking the Gargons home.

Cimmerian, looking defeated, slumps to the ground on his knees.

Orroryn cocks his head to the side as he recognizes who it was that Cimmerian sent away. "Was that...?" He stumbles with the words.

Cimmerian stares blankly out into the center of the circle of unconscious humans that lay motionless on the ground before them then turns his head to the side, looking up at Orroryn beside him.

"Yeah, it was him."

"But how did he get out?"

"I don't know, you tell me," he says, pushing himself up off the ground using his left arm for leverage. Cimmerian brushes his hands across his body and dusts off the dirt from his clothes. "But there is something I do know."

Ethan walks over to stand beside Cimmerian. "Yeah, and what is that?"

Cimmerian turns to Ethan then turns to stare blankly at the spot where his last hope to save his daughter had stood only moments ago. "I think I just pissed him off."

Chapter Fifty-Four

From the Dream Awake

SHANE LOOKS DOWN at her small fragile body covered in bruises. Her clothing is tattered and torn from her ordeal. He watches helplessly as Gabrian continues to fight violently against the war inside her head. Tethered and bound by her arms in order to keep her from harm, she lets out a loud cry filled with suffering.

Ethan hurries into the room, hearing her struggle.

"She is still unconscious," Shane whispers to him. "She has been like this for days. When is she going to wake up?"

"Be patient. She is still in there, fighting her way through whatever kind of compulsion Adrinn had her under." Ethan closes his eyes for a moment and searches for her thoughts. He finds her spark. It is weak, but it is definitely hers.

"What if she does not recover?" Shane's voice falters, revealing his fear.

Ethan opens his eyes and places his hand on Shane's shoulder. "She is strong. She will find her way back," he says and cracks a smile. "Besides, she is too stubborn to give up."

Kaleb Dimiri enters the room, holding a large wooden bowl filled with herbs, flowers, and a few small vials filled with a number of different coloured liquids. He sets the arrangement down on the nightstand beside Gabrian's bed.

Taking out one of the vials, the colour of mud, he opens it and lets it hover above the opening of her mouth. Gently, he pulls at her bottom lip with his index finger and opens it just enough to create a small crevice. He tips the vial upward, allowing a small amount of the liquid to escape and drip onto her full lips—down onto her tongue.

"This will help her sleep more peacefully. I will come back later to apply some of the other herbs. She has been depleted and since her body insists on pushing out the IV in her arm, I have to administer an alternative means of giving her sustenance to help her heal."

"Thank you, Kaleb, for all your help," Ethan says, grabbing a damp cloth from the dresser and hands it to Kaleb to wipe off the excess medicine from Gabrian's mouth.

Kaleb takes the cloth and nods. "It is no trouble. From what you have told me, the poor thing seems to be destined for hardship," he says, cleaning Gabrian's bottom lip. "I will do all that I can to help."

Shane glances over quickly at Kaleb. Hearing his words stings Shane's conscience with the bitter reality of knowing he is partially to blame for her struggles, and it tears him up inside. He thanks Kaleb as well for all he has done to comfort Gabrian then watches in silence as Ethan walks Kaleb to the door. Shane reaches out, gathering Gabrian's small slender hand and cups it between his own, hoping his warmth will find her. He lowers his head and rests it lightly on top of their entwined fingers.

Gabrian twitches as she struggles to open her eyes. Everything is blurry and bright, making it hard for her eyes to focus. She feels heat coming from her right hand and looks over at the dark figure hovering over it. The pounding in her head thuds against her skull like booming canons as she strains, trying harder to see who or what, is touching her.

Realizing it is Shane, Gabrian quickly rips her hand back to get it away from him. She teeters between realities. In a frightened state, she turns her head from side to side, desperately seeking someone.

"Where is she?" Gabrian demands. "Where is she?"

Shane looks up. She is completely awake, panicked, and staring at him. He yells loudly for Ethan.

Gabrian retracts her body to put as much room between herself and Shane as she can, but when she does, pain shoots through her everywhere. Every inch of her body screams at her to stop moving.

"Where is she? I have to find her, she is weakening."

Ethan rushes into the room, immediately pushing his thoughts out to find her mind to try to send her into a calm state before she can hurt herself more.

"I can't leave her there. I need to save her!" She pulls and rips at the tethers, trying to squirm her way free.

Ethan firmly places his hands on her, holding her down by the shoulders. He feels her fear taking over her, disorientating her logical senses which makes it hard for her to coherently grasp what is happening.

Prying harder, he finds the familiar connection he is looking for and bombards her mind with euphoric-like emotions, setting off a chemical reaction that floods her with endorphins and releases some of the hold the compulsion has on her. She stops fighting and lies completely still. She blinks, her eyes widening— still filled with caution—as she tries to understand what is going on and where she is. Her eyes drift around the edges of her surroundings and for the first time quiets herself. She recognizes her room in her parent's house, and her world slows down enough for her to focus. A soft familiar voice wafts its way in through the tangled web that now is her mind and settles the last remains of her nerves' jagged ends as it whispers to her. *Just breathe.*

"Welcome back, kiddo," Ethan says with a smile of relief.

She lowers her lids in response of his answer. A sliver of pain gnaws at her temples from the sound of his voice—even though it is low and soft, it booms through her ears just the same. She forces her lids to open under a pressed brow, and grimaces at him, her eyes merely two slits of a broken line, and wonders why she is tethered to her own bed, covered in bruises and in tattered pajamas. "What is going on?" she inquires, raising her hands to indicate her bindings. "And why do I feel like I just survived a train wreck?"

"That is because you did," he says to her as he unties her left wrist. "Well, sort of."

She half-glances over in Shane's direction as he loosens the

371

other binding around her right wrist. She pulls it away quickly and rubs her skin, giving him an icy glare—warning him to keep his distance.

"What?" She looks back at Ethan. "I am confused. I survived an actual train wreck? What was I doing on a train?"

"No, no. You were not on a train." Ethan gives her a coy grin and tries to explain it to her. "It was just a figure of speech..." He stops for a moment and looks at her seriously. "You were kidnapped and compelled by a very dark and devious Vampire that long ago was bound into the Darkness of Erebus."

Gabrian's face twists as she bites on her lower lip, her head shaking involuntarily as she struggles to comprehend the words coming out of Ethan's mouth as he tries to explain all of the sordid details of her capture. She tries to remember, but she cannot recall anything. She struggles to believe any of the things Ethan tells her to be true. She can only gather fragments of thoughts and creates a compilation of chaotic visions of her struggling to help her friend find freedom from the Covenant's grasp.

She catches Ethan's eye. Leery to talk about her secret friend, she decides it is all right since they have all seen him. "He was a Vampire turned apparition? How could a Vampire become a living apparition? None of this makes any sense. And why would he want to hurt me? He was my friend."

"I don't understand it either, Gabrian. All I know is that somehow he managed to return to this dimension. Then he decided to use you as his personal power supply. He was using your ability to harness energy to strike out at us as a defense while he drained you of your life essence."

Gabrian quickly jumps to her friend's defense. "He would not do that," she snaps at him with wide-eyes—her mouth ajar as she openly grows upset—refusing to believe that the only one that took her side when she needed it most, would turn on her.

"Here, sift through my memories, and you will see it is true."

Trusting Ethan, she relaxes and tries to tune into his mind frequency to find his projections, but every time she touches on an image about that night or her friend, a piercing light rips through her head and blinds her mind from seeing any of them.

She releases her connection with Ethan and rubs her temples. "I can't, it hurts when I try."

"It is no doubt a compulsion he implanted in your subconscious as a defense mechanism," Ethan concludes. He edges toward her window and stares off into the distance in thought. Then he turns back to her and crosses the small distance between them to sit down beside her on the bed. "It does not matter now. All that matters is that you are safe, and that he is gone."

"It was the woman who led me out," she says softly, looking down at her hand.

"What?" Ethan says.

"Cera," she says, still looking down. Ethan lifts her chin with his fingers, making her meet his gaze. Gabrian looks up at him, her eyes glassy from the tears threatening to surface, but she holds his gaze, unleashing her words slowly while remaining calm. "I was surrounded by the Gargons. She grabbed my hand and told me to run toward the garden gate. Once we made it, she pushed me through. I tried to reach out for her, but the Darkness grabbed her before I could help her."

Ethan pats her hand gently to try and calm her. He glances over at Shane who is sitting quietly and observing it all with attentive eyes. He hides the tremble of his lips beneath his folded hands, pressing tight just below his nose. "Try to get some rest, okay?" He jumps up off the bed and clears the used vial from the bowl. He rests his hand on the top of her shoulder and turns to leave the room. "We will talk later."

Gabrian follows him with her eyes as he disappears out the door, becoming brutally aware that Shane is still there with her. The anger and the hurt that has been building inside her bubbles to the surface and she snaps. "Why are you here?"

His emerald green eyes show the hurt from her tone, but Shane understands that he deserves it. "Because I was worried about you."

Gabrian swings her head to the left and crosses her arms in front of her chest as she stares out the window, not wanting him to see she is still hurt by his rejection. "What do you care anyway? I thought you hated me."

He lowers his head and gapes down at the floor, building up the courage to come clean. "I cannot hate you, Gabrian," he whispers.

She turns quickly at his reply and snaps at him again. "Oh,

and why is that?"

He raises his eyes to meet her glare and swallows down his pride. "Because my heart will not let me hate you."

Gabrian's angry glare fades, and her eyes soften under her wrinkled brow as her heated emotion is suddenly replaced with confusion. "What?" she barks at him taken aback. "What are you talking about? Last night you made is painfully clear that you and I were a conflict of interest!"

He looks at the ceiling and runs his rugged fingers recklessly through his hair then exhales. "I am an idiot! Okay?" Shane's bottom lip quivers subtly as he faces her, eye to eye, completely defenseless and at her mercy.

She pulls herself upright on the bed into a sitting position, wincing in pain, and rests her shoulders on the pillows behind her. "But, you..."

Shane stands up out of his chair and quickly moves to sit on the side of her bed. He reaches out with his left hand and touches the side of her cheek softly. With the other hand, he presses his finger against her lips, barely touching them. He exhales in a low seductive hiss then carefully lowers his forehead to touch his skin against hers, slowly meeting her lips with his own. Wanting to push him away, and yell at him—still angry from their last encounter—she feels the angst subside and everything around her starts to spin and the heat between them begin to rise. Shane pulls back just far enough to see her face. "How do you feel about experiments?"

The simple words melt away any remains of ice in her veins as a smile curls at the edges of Gabrian's mouth, sending Shane's desire for her into overdrive. "Experiments are good," she whispers.

He leans forward and kisses her again, softly at first then pulls her in close, longing for the sweet taste of her mouth. Gabrian raises her left arm and fights through the pain ripping through her muscles, ignoring their plea to remain still, and places her hand behind his head to entangle her fingers in his loose curls. Holding him close, she pulls him in tighter to her as she relishes the fire that has begun to burn within her.

At this moment, Gabrian does not care if this is real or not. All she knows is that the pain in her heart that has tortured her for so long has stopped.

"Looks like someone is feeling better," Ethan teases as he enters her room.

Gabrian and Shane slowly pull themselves away from each other, their eyes still locked in deep desire. Gabrian breaks the connection with Shane's eyes but lowers her hand to lock her fingers in his. She looks across the room, meeting Ethan's eyes with confidence, and he returns her acknowledgement with a grin of delight, waiting a moment to approach her. She smiles back, welcoming him in.

Ethan checks her vitals over and notices that her bruising seems to be healing already. The herbs that Kaleb gave her to boost the regenerative abilities within her veins must have started working. He does a quick mind sweep to see if he can assess what kind of damage Adrinn has caused, but he cannot get a good connection in order to say how bad it is.

"How are you feeling?"

"Tired, but good, I guess," Gabrian says, trying not to complain. "I have a headache, though."

"You are lucky, that is all you have." Ethan reaches out with his hands and places them on each side of her head. He closes his eyes and finds the source of the pain. He pulls at its colour, loosening its grip, and releases it from it nestled spot. Ethan then presses a small wave of light into the space where the Darkness was embedded within her mind. His eyes open, and he looks at her.

"Better?"

Her face relaxes in gratitude. "Better."

"Listen, I have been thinking."

"Oh, about what?"

"I am not sure what your plans are, but when you are feeling better, I was thinking that maybe we can have a chat, and I can talk you into sticking around Northeast Harbor."

She cocks her head to the side and gives him an old fashioned stink-eye, trying to decipher his roundabout intentions.

"...and coming to work with me." He glances at her with a sly grin as he tidies up the table beside her. He grabs the empty glass and turns to her. "I have heard a lot of good things about your practice in Manhattan, and Bar Harbor could use another gifted psychologist. Especially in a small town overrun with, well, let us say...unusual clients."

Gabrian returns Ethan's grin then looks over at Shane who still has a hold of her tiny hand. "I will think about it."

Already knowing what she has decided, Ethan nods and starts for the kitchen with the empty glass in his hand. "Okay, kiddo. You do that."

Chapter Fifty-Five

Greetings from Erebus

THE HEADLIGHTS FLASH, reflecting off of the front window as Gabrian pulls into her new parking spot outside of Ethan's office. She exits her car and steps up on the sidewalk in front of her. She takes a moment and listens as the distant chatter of the other early morning risers make their way to the smell of coffee as well. Judging from the emerging lineup, she is glad she decided to grab her caffeine from the Coffee Hound first before heading to work, and takes a much anticipated sip of her Acadian Turtle Mocha. Breathing in the delightful aroma of coffee mixed with a hint of salt wafting in the air from the ocean nearby, she looks down the sleepy street lit only by dusk-til-dawn lamps and the first fragments from the light of dawn and smiles, grateful to be alive and welcoming the morning.

A movement in her peripheral vision catches her attention, and she turns to see the familiar feathered stalker watching her from the street sign above marked Main Street. He dances back and forth across the top of the sign with his head bobbing up and down, a low cooing sound rumbling from his throat.

She smiles at his persistence and decides that since he has decided to become a constant, he should have a name.

"Good morning to you, Theo."

The raven rumbles an uneven call to her to signify his approval then fluffs its feathers.

Gabrian laughs at her new friend and crosses the concrete sidewalk block to unlock the purple office door. Pushing it open, she begins the trek to the top of the stairs that leads to her new office. Reaching the top, she flicks the switch on the side of the wall to her left and the soft glow of the overhead lights illuminate the main waiting room. The office is empty because she is in an hour earlier than she needs to be. She wants to get a jump on the paperwork that awaits her.

Gabrian makes a mental note to send a quick email to Thomas to let him know her new contact information since she did not have it with her when she went back to Manhattan to gather her things and make good on her promise to visit him at the bar. Though their encounter was less than what Thomas had hoped for, he was still happy to see her and something told Gabrian that her new acquaintance was going to become a good friend she would be able to count on if need be in the future.

She wanders across the small waiting area to the filing cabinet that sits behind Rachael's new desk and takes out a couple of the client files that Ethan has distributed to her. She opens them, hoping to familiarize herself with her new clients before they meet later. Hearing a noise coming from her office door, she turns and notices that it is slightly ajar. She does not remember leaving the door open when she went home yesterday afternoon.

Strange.

She idles over and presses her right hand against the door, then pushes it open. She edges her head forward and peeks into the darkened room. Something does not feel right. Stepping just inside the doorframe, she slides her hand up the wall on the left side, and flicks the switch to the small pot lights at the back of her office above her desk. She freezes, noticing movement in the swivel chair behind her desk.

Instinctively, her energy flares out searching for signs of whom or what sits in her chair. Seeing the back of a head above the backrest, she is quite certain that it is a male and there is familiarity about this intruder—a familiarity that tells her he is not a stranger.

Her heart races wildly, filling her veins with unhealthy

doses of adrenaline as her mind spins noisily with chaotic thoughts, torn between her fear of what he may have tried to do to her and the longing to see her friend again. Ethan's horrifying accounts of their last encounter echoes through her mind, continually conflicting with the memories of her selfless attempts to save his life.

She feels her body readying itself for anything as the chair begins to turn; her muscles tense—trembling and poised. She stops breathing and her assumptions become confirmed once the chair comes to rest.

Leaning his head against the back of her leather chair with his fingers erect and taping against each other rhythmically, his mouth begins to rise upward in the corners, displaying to Gabrian the most terrifying grin she has ever seen.

"Hello, little Vampire. Want to come out and play?"

His cynical laughter fills the room, echoing loudly through her head and tearing at her eardrums. She raises her hands to cover her ears, trying desperately to drown out the excruciating noise. Her fingers become hot, igniting with fear. Gabrian feels the coldness of death reaching out for her, suffocating her, and cutting off her air. She struggles to breathe, trying find enough air to call out for help, but finding very little, she falls to the floor—choking on the lifeless vapors.

Gabrian refuses to give in to the Darkness. Its toxins threaten to engulf her, but she fights to stay awake and wills her eyes to open. Feeling a presence close by, she presses her body from the cold floor beneath her and looks up to see Ayden standing above her.

Gasping for air, Gabrian gathers the last remains of her strength and reaches out to him in despair, but he laughs at her in her final attempt to save herself. Closing his brown hazel eyes, he opens his mouth and inhales, drinking in her last ounce of life.

The feeling of falling sends a strange helpless sensation through her. Her arms instinctively extend before trying to prepare for the point of impact, but it never comes. Twisting aimlessly in the Darkness, Gabrian struggles against the thought of death and the void that consumes her.

Anxiety stirring deep within her subconscious mind eats its way violently to the surface, sending her understanding of reality into shock as her flailing arms fetch up with something solid and she is propelled forward. With her arms extended and her torso erect, she sits straight up in bed.

Her hands clutch at the damp cloth tangled around her body, drenched in her feverish sweat. She searches frantically in the dimly lit room for any signs of Ayden then realizes it was only a nightmare that she has survived.

She exhales in relief, but her body still trembles from the vividness of her dream. She is alive but within the welcomed embrace of safety also harbors with it the reality of knowing what this message truly means. A foreboding chill runs down her spine as she whispers the words softly to herself in the darkness of her room.

"He is back."

FELLOWSHIP HIERARCHY

ZEPHYR – *AIR*: ELDER VAEDA KARRIN
EGNI – *FIRE*: ELDER ARRAMUS URIE
HYDOR – *WATER*: ELDER CASPYOUS WILEY
EORDEN – *EARTH*: ELDER KALEB DIMIRI
ISA – *ICE*: ELDER ASHEN GRACIE
DERKAZ – *DARK MAGIK*: ELDER CIMMERIAN COLE
BORAGEN – *BORROWERS*: ELDER ETHAN BORNE
SCHAEDUWE – *SHADOW WALKERS*: ELDER ORRORYN REDMOND
VINDERE – *REINCARNATE/MEDIUMS*: ELDER ARIAH FELLOWS
ARGUROS AUCYEN – *SILVER MAGE*: ELDER CERA ARGRYIS

GLOSSARY: ZEPHYR TONGUE TRANSLATION

WENDAS – AIR IN MOTION (TO THE WIND)
BOTAH – BODY
MOMENTOMUS – MOMENTUM/ENERGY
TERMINATO – TERMINATE/STOP
ENCORPUS VEILUS – VEIL THE BODY/CREATE A VEIL AROUND THE BODY
DECENTE – DECEND/COME DOWN
VAPIR – DEVOURER OF ENERGY/VAMPIRE
AWAE CENAN – AWAY/CLEAR HER MIND
EODE – BE GONE
WEALL – WALL
SOLIDUS – SOLID
PULSUS – PUSH
CLAUSTRA – WALL
SILOZAN – SHUT
DVARAH – DOOR
EAREM – AIR
SILPNAS – SLEEP
RETRAHERE – TO RETRACT/WITHDRAW
TORAN - PORTAL

About the Author

Kade Cook

Kade Cook is a mom of five and a semi-retired IT Professional turned author with her fantasy book series, The Covenant of Shadows. Book one of the series, GREY, was Shortlisted for the 2017 Emerging Writer's Prize on June 27th for Canada's best new books in Speculative Fiction.

Born and raised as a 'Maritimer' through and through, Kade will always be at home around good times and kind hearts, proud to be a daydreamer with a story to tell.

You can visit her at http://www.goodreads.com/Kade_cook or come hang out on her website:
https://kadecook.wordpress.com/ or Facebook page for more information on her works in progress:
https://www.facebook.com/kadecook.author/

Theo & Quinn Creative Works
Shediac River, New Brunswick E4R 6A7, Canada

Join the newsletter to get all the latest events
At kadecook.author@gmail.com
https://kadecookbooks.wordpress.com/
twitter.com/CovOfShadows

Also by KADE COOK
Book Two
In
The Covenant of Shadows

CALICO

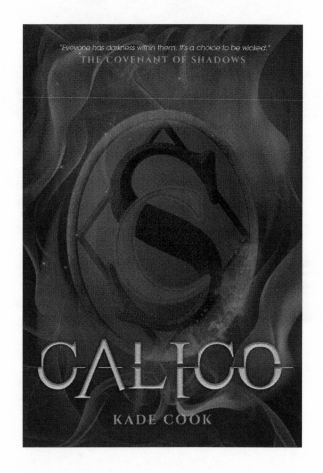

Made in the USA
Middletown, DE
01 August 2020

14105541R00236